C000157617

The Alchemist's Daughter

"Set during the twilight years of Henry VIII with vibrant characters, a compelling plot and accurate historical depictions, *The Alchemist's Daughter* brings the darkness and danger of Tudor London vividly to life as it weaves its suspenseful tale. This beautifully written addition to the medieval mystery genre is sure to delight all fans of the period."
—Sandra Worth, author of *Pale Rose of England*

"A smart, scientific sleuth . . . Lawrence uses her enthusiasm for Tudor England to create an historical novel within a mystery."
—*Portland Monthly*

"The writing is terrific, with great period details. There are lots of red herrings and a surprising amount of action that will keep readers engaged until the very last page."
—*San Francisco Book Review*

"I absolutely loved *The Alchemist's Daughter*—the characters, the authentic feel of the period, and of course the richly drawn story."
—Dorothy Cannell, author of *Murder at Mullings*

"Lawrence proves herself to be an excellent storyteller with this grim tale of murder, mayhem and medicine."
—*CentralMaine.com*

Death of an Alchemist

"Lawrence excels at exploring themes—parent-child conflict, dreams of eternal life, and the limitations of medicine—that have period and present-day resonance."
—*Publishers Weekly*

"Another exciting adventure on the back streets of sixteenth-century London."
—*RT Book Reviews*

"…is quick, consuming, and wholeheartedly driven by its insatiable heroine."
—*Portland Press Herald*

The Alchemist of Lost Souls

"If Tudor London is a place you want to go, Lawrence is an author who will take you there, with the intrepid Bianca as your guide."
—*Criminal Element*

"Atmospheric and enjoyable. The author strikes the perfect balance between Tudor language and history and accessibility."
—*Tulsa Book Review*

"The plot moves swiftly . . . A satisfying and engrossing read."
—*Historical Novel Reviews*

The Lost Boys of London

Books by Mary Lawrence

THE ALCHEMIST'S DAUGHTER

DEATH OF AN ALCHEMIST

DEATH AT ST. VEDAST

THE ALCHEMIST OF LOST SOULS

THE LOST BOYS OF LONDON

The Lost Boys of London

MARY LAWRENCE

Red Puddle Print

RED PUDDLE PRINT
www.marylawrencebooks.com

Red Puddle titles are available through Ingram and Amazon.

ISBN-13: 978-1-7347-3610-6

First Red Puddle Trade Paperback Printing: May 2020

10 9 8 7 6 5 4 3 2 1

Printed in the United States of America

For Calvin and David

What should I say,
Since faith is dead,
And truth away
From you is fled?

—Sir Thomas Wyeth (1503-1542)

CHAPTER 1

The twists and turns of an inconstant king are as serpentine as the lanes and alleys of London's Castle Baynard ward. At one end squatted massive St. Paul's Cathedral. Licking the ward's toes at the other ebbed the greasy, gray Thames. In between were four parishes and enough bread shops to adequately keep the inhabitants' heads filled with guilt and their stomachs filled with gluten.

This warren of tightly packed residences, ordinaries, mercers, stationers, chandlers, and cordwainers sat in unremitting penitence near the ominous cathedral, and never was their compunction more intensely felt than during the bleak days of this midwinter. The incremental gain of daylight was not enough to cheer the citizens. They didn't notice they did not have to light their tallows quite so early, nor did the lengthening days remind them that spring would soon ... spring. Nay, the winter felt interminable, as did its dark, shivering days.

For England was at war.

Harry had lightened his coffers by hiring German and Spanish mercenaries to aid his British soldiers in subjugating the Scots to the north and the French across the sea. He'd spent his money on fortifications along his southern coast and on growing his fleet of warships. Such is the price of hubris.

Though King Harry grew in girth and petulance, he ignored signs of his diminishing health. His leg wound ulcerated, emitting a foul odor while his physicians scurried about trying different poultice wrappings, even cauterization, in an effort to offer the king some relief. Short of amputation (for who would dare mention, much less attempt it?) little could be done.

So, Harry continued to plant apple trees in his orchard in Kent and busied himself with the politics of war. And the citizens of London, indeed of the entire realm, continued to labor and abide by the whims of their peevish king.

To a boy with two younger siblings and a mother struggling to feed them, a king's impulsive policies didn't matter a spit. All he knew was that his father had gone away to fight, and he was the eldest son, and as such he understood he should tend to the welfare of his family.

While his mother embroidered a stomacher for a lady of wealth's fine dress and fended off a two-year-old's attempt to pull the thread, Fisk edged out the door of their tenement off Ivy Lane. He scampered down the dreary side street, threw a stick for a dog in the opposite direction, leapt over a steaming turd almost before it was too late, and headed toward Westcheap Market.

Although he had learned the lesson of stealth, he did not notice his younger sister Anna trailing behind at a safe distance. Anna had always been a keen observer of her older brother, and she studied his methods. She knew how to fold into a crowd and when to freeze to evade notice by not being obvious. He'd caught her before when she was less experienced, and had made her swear on their mother's grave that she would never follow him again. But, reasoned Anna, their mother wasn't dead.

Fisk hurried down Paternoster Row, pulling his cap down over ears turning pink in the wind that blew raw against his cheek. His hands were nearly white with cold, and he jammed them under his armpits and tucked his chin so that he looked up beneath his brow, like a goat butting his way through town. When he passed the church of St. Michael le Querne, he glimpsed Eleanor's Cross ahead and the myriad of sellers with their awnings stretched taut over their goods.

Fisk approached, carefully slinking along the perimeter, and blended into the crowd. His chances of filching some meat for his mother's pottage depended on finding a vendor who could be easily distracted or who was too busy to notice a small boy stuffing it under his jerkin. After a thorough tour of the market, he found a butcher displaying bacon at one end of his cart, exposed, an easy nab provided someone showed an interest in the pork bellies on the opposite side.

Fisk studied the fellow. He noted how the butcher became completely focused on an interested buyer to the exclusion of everyone else. But something gave Fisk pause. At first, he thought it was that little spurt of conscience he'd feel whenever he contemplated stealing. He took off his hat and scratched his scalp. Nay, it wasn't that. Puzzled, he put his cap back on. Looking to the left he saw no one watching or even walking toward the stand. To the right was a row of buyers, mostly women vying for the butcher's attention. Now would be the opportune moment—yet …

Something was behind him.

He could feel it.

Fisk spun on his heel and immediately spied his little sister falling in behind a woman selling mittens.

"Anna!" He stomped over and pulled her aside. "You swore you'd never follow me again."

Anna shrugged and looked down. Her blue eyes focused on the mud caking her worn shoes. There would be no passing these poor leathers on to her younger sibling.

Fisk lifted Anna's chin so that she had to look at him. "You should be home helping Mother with Janeth."

"I want to help you." The wind caught hold of her coif and blew it to the ground, exposing her fair hair. Anna went after it and plopped it back on her head.

Exasperated, Fisk watched her tie the strings under her chin.

"Do you want to help?" he asked when she had finished.

Anna nodded enthusiastically.

"Then go home!"

Her bright face clouded. "I followed ye all the way here and ye didn't know it till now," she said indignantly.

"If I'd known you would go back on your word, I would have been watching for you. Just because you think you can trail me without me noticing, doesn't mean that you should. I've got important matters to tend to."

"Like what?"

"Like making sure you get home and stay there. I'm not spending the day keeping you out of trouble."

"I'll watch myself. You won't even know I'm here."

"If you don't turn around now and walk home, I'm going to tell Mother you're a nuisance at market, then she'll switch the back of your legs until you can't walk."

Anna twisted her mouth, thinking twice about arguing. She looked past his shoulder at the vendor he'd been watching.

"What're ye going to do?"

"Nothing I'd tell you about."

"Ye was going to snatch something, wasn't ye?"

Fisk's patience had run out. He seized Anna's elbow and pulled her through the market all the way to Old Change Street before he let go.

"There," he said, pointing to Paternoster Row. "I'm going to stand here and watch until you turn the corner for home." He gave her a little push in the right direction. "Go on."

Anna took a couple of reluctant steps, then looked dejectedly over her shoulder.

Fisk waved her on.

With a sigh of resignation, Anna put one foot ahead of the other and plodded down the street. She stopped for one last look over her shoulder. There he was, her older brother, watching just as he said he would; his arms folded over his chest and his dark eyes boring into her even from that distance.

Fisk waited an extra minute to be sure that Anna didn't reappear, then walked back to Westcheap and took up where he'd left off. He was glad to see the butcher still busy with customers, and gladder still to see the flitch of bacon still displayed.

Again, he studied the vendor and eyed the sellers on either side of him. One did a brisk business selling nuts and the other stared off into Scotland with only an occasional bypasser showing interest in his woven cords. So long as the fellow remained in dazed inattention, Fisk believed he could pilfer the defenseless meat and be speedily gone.

The little thief sidled up to the cart, giving himself enough room to break into a run if needed. He insinuated himself beside a vocal woman of some age who did her best to flag the vendor's attention. A more perfect foil would have been difficult to find.

Fisk stood quietly, unobtrusively, biding his time until the moment was right.

This wasn't the first time he'd stolen to help feed his family. At first, he'd had to explain to his mother how he'd come about getting a loaf of bread and a stray head of cabbage. Every story became more fantastic until finally she stopped asking altogether.

When one has several mouths to feed, he guessed necessity mattered more than a clear conscience.

The snaggle-toothed butcher finished with his customer and as the woman leaned forward, waving her arm at the harried seller, Fisk snatched the flitch of bacon and slid it under his jerkin.

Just as he started to leave, the woman rocked back on her heels and with a look of dismay pointed to the empty space where the handsome slab of meat had been. At first, the butcher looked bewildered, then his face flushed red. Fisk took one look at the two of them, and turned tail.

He took off in a wild sprint. Amid the commotion of shouts and yelling, he dodged shoppers, barrels of produce, and stray dogs. But Fisk was fleet of foot and, with some distance, the shouts soon faded. He slowed, then glimpsed over his shoulder, expecting he had outpaced his pursuers. Indeed, it appeared he had escaped them all.

With a smug grin, Fisk stooped over to catch his breath. He could almost taste his mother's pottage that night. He rubbed his stomach to silence its hungry growling. Maybe she would make it especially thick since there was plenty of meat.

Once his breathing steadied, he began walking as if nothing had ever happened. No one knew the wiser what was under his coat. His steps took on the carefree lope of a typical ten-year-old boy—but just to be sure, he cast a furtive glance over his shoulder.

To his utter horror, the cord vendor, that dozy-eyed mound of muscle rounded the corner, huffing for breath and looking for him. It was as if no one else was around, for the vendor spotted him straightaway.

Fisk ran like his shoes were on fire. With no thought about the muddy conditions, he slipped so badly that the vendor made a swipe for him, but Fisk outmaneuvered the lumbering adult and changed direction.

Fisk pressed his hand against the bacon trying to slide out from under his coat—all of this effort only to lose the meal would be a sad thing. He dipped and sidestepped obstacles, remembering an alley close by with an egress between two buildings. Only a child could navigate such a narrow space. And, if his timing was right, it would look as if he had vanished in thin air.

When he got to St. Michael le Querne he turned down Old Change, where only moments before he'd left his sister. Surely he could outrun a fat old goat. How could the fellow fare any better than he? Even with his shoe pulled off by the sucking mud, Fisk knew he could outrun the galumphing oaf.

Why did the fellow care so much? wondered Fisk. Most grown-ups tired quickly, especially if it wasn't a matter that directly concerned them. They would have given over to the painful stitch in their side. Of course he would have to keep a wary eye out for them because if he were ever caught…well…at the very least he'd get a thrashing he wouldn't soon forget.

The alley was on the cathedral's side and, without slowing, Fisk rounded the corner next to a draper and plunged into the shadowy ginnel. His feet slapped the mud, his steps echoed off the stone buildings. A slender shaft of light revealed the opening.

He had only used the gap once before and that had been a year ago. He didn't suppose he had grown all that much since then, but it had been a snug fit, especially in the middle. He'd had to turn his feet heel-to-heel to inch through the passage. Once he got halfway through, he could come out the other end and get away before his pursuer had time to backtrack and catch him.

Fisk paused to glance around. Was this the gap that he had used before? It looked different. Perhaps he had been mistaken. He took a few more steps and peered down the opening toward the bright sliver of St. Paul's courtyard at the opposite end. The passage looked impossibly tight. He would have to turn his head to one side and keep it that way for the entire length.

Fisk had turned sideways to start down the passage when the cord vendor slid around the corner in a display of cursing and grunting and windmilling arms. From the look on his face, his determination had not waned. Fisk squeezed himself into the gap, turning his head to keep an eye on his pursuer.

Crabbing his way between the damp stone walls, Fisk made enough progress to keep out of the man's reach. The space was painfully narrow and void of light. He had no sense how far he must go to reach the other end. Fisk tried not to think of getting stuck, but the fear kept whispering in his ear, telling him he would surely never get out. Panicked, Fisk kept moving. He pushed and wormed … until he couldn't.

The cord vendor's face appeared at the gap.

"Ha, ye little knave. Ye looks to be frightfully wedged." He guffawed rudely. "A fine fix ye is in, I'd say. But then, I did say it."

Instead of construing where Fisk might emerge, the vendor delighted in Fisk's predicament. For a terrifying moment, Fisk thought he might be permanently stuck. But a boy's ribs are more malleable than a man's. He took a deep breath of musty air, enough to change his shape and he wiggled forward. He even felt a breeze on the back of his neck. He was making progress.

"I sees ye fleerin' at me. It is not me ye should hold so carelessly, little thief, but the honest man whose goods ye stole. I only means to make ye pays for what ye took, but then I'd say ye is, of a sorts, paying for whats ye did. As ye did it to yeself, getting wedged that is, I'd say. And I did say it."

There was no avoiding his tormentor. Fisk wished he could turn his head or clap his hands over his ears to muffle the man's taunts. Instead, he did the only thing he was able—he worked his feet as fast as he could.

"Where is ye?" asked the cord vendor, his head bobbing,

trying to see. "Ye is in the dark, now." He stepped away from the passage and looked toward the entrance of the alley as if someone was coming. He turned back and leered at Fisk. "Ot, I see yer outline, lad. Ye won't make it to the other side that fast." Then, just as abruptly as he had appeared, the cord vendor left.

A stream of water trickled down the back of Fisk's neck, adding to the chill he already felt, pressed against the stone wall. Perhaps he should scream for help. Where had the vendor gone? Had *he* gone for help? Mayhap the vendor was sussing out where the other end of the gap was. Fisk whimpered. If he was rescued, he'd surely be in a heap of trouble. One thing was for certain, he needed to get out of there and quickly.

He reached his arm to the side, hoping to feel the corner of the building—but alas, he only felt the stone wall beneath his touch. He inched and squirmed, concentrating on making himself as thin as possible. No one appeared in the alley. Fisk closed his eyes, imagining himself free.

Somehow, he felt he was inching forward. If he could only reach the courtyard before the vendor did. And if he ever got out of this miserable fix, he would change his wicked ways. He knew he took a chance by stealing. He might end with one less hand, or, if the magistrate was merciful, one less finger. But how else could he feed his family? There were no options for a family such as his.

As he edged closer to the courtyard, he heard a priest's vitriolic sermon echoing in his ears. For as loud as the preacher at Paul's Cross was, and for as guilty as Fisk felt, the priest might as well have been standing at the end of the gap, admonishing and damning him. Most of the time, priests mumbled the convoluted word of God that no one else understood. What was the use in that? Fisk sighed. He was cold and miserable and God didn't care.

For all of the inches he managed to gain, Fisk lost heart when stymied by yet another tight space. The meat under his jerkin had now become a hindrance. He completely regretted having nabbed the smoky comestible. All this to no avail. He couldn't even kick a stone in frustration.

Fisk's eyes welled with tears. He cried out in despair. No one knew where he was except the cord vendor, and for all he knew, the fellow had abandoned him there to starve. He should have let Anna follow him. She could have gone for help. He'd be in trouble, but at least he wouldn't die lost and forgotten between two buildings. Tears spilled over and froze on his cheeks.

He reached out his arm, his fingertips raking the stone. Still, he had not reached the end of the gap. His view of the alley swam in a blur. Panicked and scared, Fisk screamed.

"Fisk, stop your mouth! Give me your hand!"

"Anna? Anna, is that you?"

"Ye silly goose. I can almost reach ye. Give me your hand and I'll pull you out."

"Is anyone coming?"

"Nay, but if you keep squawking there will be."

Fisk dutifully raised his arm and his little sister grabbed onto his wrist. Being just a twig of a girl, Fisk doubted what use she could be, but still, he was glad she was there and thankful for her human touch. He had no choice but to put his faith in her.

Anna leaned back and Fisk felt his shoulder being tugged. He let out a yowl, then stopped his mouth. If she pulled his arm off, so be it.

"Pull harder!" he cried, trying to lean toward her. He felt her sustained weight like she must be bracing her feet on either side of the gap. He sucked in his breath. Slowly, his body began scraping the walls. His optimism returned. Just a little more and he'd be free. "Anna, you can follow me wherever you want," he said with tears of joy streaming down his face. "If you want to play bladder ball, I'll make sure you don't get tackled."

"I don't like bladder ball."

Fisk felt Anna's grip start to slip. He snatched for her hand, but she fell away.

There was a shrill yelp, then a dull whump.

"Anna, speak to me!"

Fisk strained his ears to hear her move. Even a moan would have been reassuring.

"I fell," she said at last. Her feet squished in the mud. "Mother just washed my kirtle. She'll beat me."

"She won't. I won't let her. I'm almost out of here! Hurry, take my hand!"

"Shh! Someone's coming!"

"Who? Who's coming?" Worried it might be the cord vendor, Fisk described the man. "Is it him? Is he looking at you?"

But Anna didn't answer.

CHAPTER 2

"The king's policy is foolish," said Mackney, the portly curber, as he finished off his ale at the Dim Dragon Inn. He tugged on the skirt of a passing serving wench to order another.

"Fie! The walls have ears, and do ye want to end in Newgate for disparaging the king?" Smythe, his partner in pilfering, looked over his shoulder and slunk down, making himself small.

"Did I say the king is foolish, or his politics?"

"One is the same as the other."

"I think not." Mackney shoved a fist under his cheek and dug a fingernail of the other hand into the trestle, following the grain of wood. "You should be grateful you avoided conscription. A soldier never returns the same as he left."

Bianca exchanged looks with Cammy Dawney, her friend and tavern wench sitting opposite, slurping porridge before returning to her work serving customers. The two had been commiserating over their paramours being gone, now nearly ten months.

While Cammy's beloved Roger had showed exemplary archery skill, Bianca's husband, John, had made a muddle of his chance to impress the officers. His View of Arms had ended badly, with him being made a pikeman—arguably the most dangerous assignment in the king's army. They were the first into battle, with the explicit task of protecting the bowmen.

The two young women often met at the tavern and shared their thoughts over a meal and ale. Neither of them knew if their men would return home from the borderland or whether they had found their final rest in a field beyond the River Tweed, but the two found consolation and a source of strength in their camaraderie.

Word about the campaign on the northern border was as coveted as news from across the sea in France. It seemed to the four of them sitting there in the Dim Dragon Inn that each conflict was fraught with miscalculations that had resulted in dubious gains at best. But any news making it as far as this seamy tavern in Southwark, had, no doubt, been misconstrued by miles of weary couriers and newsmongers, so that God's honest truth was neither God's, nor honest.

Bianca had listened to the incoming tales of war and had tried not to ruminate too long on matters that she could do nothing about. Still, it gave her pause when men talked of a "union" with Scotland. If King Henry desired to bring a rogue country into England's fold, then why did he order his men to burn and pillage their villages?

Last spring, not long after the men had left, stories of towering flames over a castle on a hill filtered down to London. The burning of Edinburgh was horrific and almost impossible to imagine or listen to, and they both hoped that John and Roger had not been involved in the debacle. Henry meant to punish the Scots for rejecting the Treaty of Greenwich. The Scots refused a marriage between infant princess Mary, and Henry's six-year-old son, Edward. Of course, there must be more to sending an army north than just a failed marriage plan, thought Bianca.

Mackney grinned. "The king stands on the roof of Hampton

Court Palace and sees the Papists in Scotland and France waggling their crucifixes back at him."

"The Scots do love the pope," said Cammy.

"Because the pope doesn't rape and ruin them," said Mackney. "The French are wise to help Scotland. A river of English money keeps being diverted north instead of to France. The French mean to distract Henry from Boulogne."

"But Boulogne is his," said Bianca.

"True that. However, it is late winter and the season for war is nigh upon us. The French will retaliate. How could they abandon their land to a king from across the sea?" Mackney smiled at the wench delivering his refill. He took a long quaff and wiped his mouth on his threadbare sleeve.

"Henry fears a French invasion on the coast," said Smythe.

"As well he should," commented Mackney.

Bianca often wondered how Smythe had successfully avoided conscription for so long. Perhaps officers noted his scrawny build, his skinny calves, and bony arms. They must have concluded that he would be dead two days out and not worth the time to train.

"My meal is done," said Cammy, rising from the board. "Alice is giving me the eye." She put a hand on the small of her back and stretched. Several locks of ginger hair had worked loose from her headrail and she took a moment to tuck them in. The former farm girl took up her bowl. She had just wished Bianca and the two crooks a good day when the door opened, letting in a burst of weather and a bedraggled-looking fellow.

His cheeks were ruddy from the wind and a rough beard rimmed his face. His hands were wrapped in wool and the overcoat he wore was dingy from hard use. He made much of his entrance— that moment when customers turn to gape at whoever just arrived. Poised as if he was lord of all, he cast a world-weary eye about the room. Bianca had never seen him before, and Cammy showed no sign of recognition. They watched as he wended between the tables and found a place at a trestle next to theirs.

"You look as if you've had some travel, sir," said Cammy. "A tankard for your weary person?"

"Aye," he said in a gravelly voice.

Mackney's eyes slid askance, studying him. He watched the fellow unwind the wool from his hands.

"From whence did you come, traveler?" he asked once the man had pushed the pile of rags aside.

"The borderland."

Cammy placed a hand on the table, leaning forward toward the man. "Sir, pray tell what news do you bring?"

"You have come from the border to Southwark?" asked Bianca. "It is a long journey."

"If by sea, it is not so long," said the stranger.

"Say not another word, sir, until I return with your drink." Cammy scurried off to the kitchen and the others eyed their guest with curiosity, finding it difficult to keep from asking questions while waiting for her return.

Cammy reappeared carefully toting a pottle pot filled to the brim. She set it before him and slid onto the bench next to Bianca, ignoring the perturbed stare of Alice, who wished for some help serving the clientele.

"What was your business so far north?" asked Bianca.

"I brought supplies to the Earl of Hertford and his men."

"Earl of Hertford?" Bianca glanced at Cammy. "Is he not responsible for the burning of Edinburgh?"

Smythe answered for the fellow. "Aye, he is. Henry tasked him to 'put every man, woman, and child to fire and sword.'"

The thought of it made Bianca wince. Neither she nor Cammy had ever known how many men were dispatched to the border or how they had been organized. The less she knew the easier it was to imagine Roger and John had not been involved in the rumored brutality. While she was curious to know all that the stranger had to say, she braced herself for the worst.

Apparently, Cammy thought the same. "Roger and John may not be under his direct charge," she said. "We do not know for cert."

Bianca fidgeted in her seat. "Does the earl have other commanders under him?" she asked.

"He does. But they follow the earl's orders." He took another drink of ale, closing his eyes to savor the taste, scrunching his face in judgment before setting it down. "And the earl follows the king's bidding."

Mackney entered into the discussion. "We only hear dribs and drabs, stranger. Mostly hearsay. Your witnessed account would please us well."

"But wait. By what name should we call you?" asked Cammy. "Forgive us not asking."

"I take no offense," said the stranger. "I see by your worried brow that the border conflict concerns you." He paused, meeting her eyes. "Call me Baldwin. I am returning home to Croydon."

"Was this your first trip to the border?" asked Bianca.

"Nay. I have been once before. But I have not been so far north as to see the destruction of Edinburgh. Though if it should be similar to what I saw in Kelso and Roxburgh, then I believe there is not much of it left." He looked into his tankard as if a scene of destruction floated in the amber liquid beneath his nose.

"We heard that Edinburgh burned for four days," said Bianca.

The man gave a slight nod. "So it has been said. And, after what I saw in Kelso, I have no cause to doubt Edinburgh's complete ruin. There is nothing left of Kelso but the graves of the slaughtered."

"It was our victory," recalled Mackney.

"Victory," huffed Baldwin in disgust. "Tell me, sir, what victory is there in massacre?"

Smythe thought the answer obvious. "The fear of retaliation is slim because there be no one left to take up arms and resist. It is the way of war."

Baldwin's brow furrowed as he studied Smythe. Bianca could almost hear the man wondering why a young fellow—a young, tart-tongued fellow—was not contributing to his king's efforts. If indeed, those were his thoughts, he kept his opinion to himself. "It is an unjust means of suppression. There is no lasting benefit in harsh exercise."

Bianca agreed. She did not say so aloud, such sympathies being more common with women and less widely voiced among men. Still, she appreciated Baldwin's sentiment and wished the king felt similarly.

"Resentment festers and only breeds more hatred," said Cammy.

"Still, sir," said Smythe. "You benefit from this war."

The man's eyes flashed. "I do what is asked of me. It earns me coin, but I should not be sorry if I never went again." He stared hard at Smythe. "What one must understand is that the people living on the border have no allegiance. They care not for our king, but neither do they think of themselves as Scots. They favor whoever gives them money or whoever leaves a village vulnerable to their plunder. The wind is more predictable than their loyalty."

"A lawless land," said Cammy.

"A dangerous one," added Bianca.

"The earl knows how to sway the Borderers to his side. Whether by threat or by bribe, he plays the clans to work in his interest. The grievances between these border families run long and deep. Feuds last for generations. They are a vindictive people."

The table fell silent as they considered Baldwin's opinion of the Scots. Bianca wondered if their enemy shared the same opinion about the English. But for all of Baldwin's information, he only had a cursory knowledge of the campaign in Scotland. He did not know the whereabouts of John or Roger, or who their commander was, or where the forces were exactly. Still, his words were of some use. They gave her a better understanding of the predicament in which John found himself.

"Have you heard, sir, about the army in France?" Bianca had heard enough about the horrors on the border and wished to learn more about the conflict across the sea. There was always the possibility that John and Roger might end up there.

"The king continues to hold Boulogne despite leaving a relatively small contingent of men to defend it. Henry worries that the French will invade our southern coast. He spends heavily to fortify the area from Gravesend to Portland. And it is thought he will extend his armies to Lincolnshire and Suffolk and more."

"But tell us more about the borderland," interrupted Cammy. She held up a finger to Alice, whose hand had gone to her hip in annoyance. "Are there enough men in England to do everything the king wants? How can he have armies in all these places?"

"He hires men from Spain and Germany to do his bidding," said Baldwin.

"If his immediate fear is a French invasion on the coast, should he not bring home his own men to defend it?" asked Bianca.

The stranger tilted his head and shrugged. "If he brings men home from Scotland, the border will return to lawlessness. He will need to leave some men behind to keep order. They will have a difficult task."

Cammy and Bianca studied the traveler, wondering what the future held for Roger and John. Their expressions must have mirrored their concern, for the man's rough manner softened.

"Kind maids, you suffer needlessly. Unless you learn word

that your men have succumbed, worrying serves no useful purpose. Besides," he added, "I helped replenish stores for an army of five thousand. Unless the Earl of Angus can rouse enough volunteers to stop them, our men shall continue their triumph."

Mackney seized the optimism in Baldwin's message. "With numbers so large, how can the effort fail? John and Roger might soon be coming home."

Bianca and Cammy's eyebrows lifted and they both smiled tentatively, both wishing to believe it might be possible, but keenly aware of its slim likelihood.

"One can always hope," said Cammy, and she squeezed Bianca's shoulder before collecting the empty tankards and plates from the table.

CHAPTER 3

Fearing for his sister's safety, Fisk rose on his toes and found a smidge more room farther up the wall. He squirmed and leaned, braced his hands against the stones and leveraged himself higher. It worked. He inhaled, expanding his chest more than he'd been able, and his fingers found the corner of the wall.

Then he heard a scream.

"Anna!" Fisk struggled with the last bit of passage and landed in the open courtyard of St. Paul's Cross.

His worst fear was realized.

The vendor held Anna about her waist. She fought valiantly against him, repeatedly stomping his shoes and trying to bite his arms. He lifted her and she started kicking his shin.

"Let her go!" shouted Fisk, scrambling to his feet.

The vendor ignored this request until Anna jabbed an elbow where a leather codpiece would have been helpful. He doubled over, dropping Anna, and she ran to Fisk.

"Is that yer little sister, boy?" asked the man, once he could straighten. He eyed Anna peeping from behind her brother. "I see troublemaking runs in yer family." He spat on the ground and tipped his head toward a crowd gathered to hear the latest sermon. "It wouldn't take much for me to summon yon beadle and tell him about your mischief-making."

"If you come near her, I'll scream," warned Fisk.

The corner of the cord vendor's mouth rose in an indulgent smile. "But then, if ye give up what ye stole from the butcher, I'll return it to its rightful owner. I'll tell him ye dropped it, I will. No one is the wiser. Ye get on your way, and no one loses a finger."

"You'll keep the bacon for yourself," challenged Fisk. Far be it from him to give up his hard-earned booty. He wanted to run, but he worried whether Anna could keep up. True, she'd gotten some speed on her of late, surprising him a couple of weeks ago by outrunning him and his mate when she'd taken the spike they were using to play quoits. Still, if the vendor caught up to either one of them it could end nastily.

"Naw, no," assured the vendor, easing forward. "The butcher and me looks out for one another. There be lots of rascals like ye. Little thieves, boys needing to be nipped. If ye don't stop now, ye'll end in a bad way. Ye might look on me as doin' ye a favor."

Fisk gave Anna a slight nudge with his elbow and their eyes locked.

"Ye'll not get far," said the vendor, reading their intent. "Give it over and avoid a frightful consequence. Because, have no doubts—I *will* catch ye."

If Fisk had given it any more thought, he would have frozen with inaction. After what he had gone through for this bacon, why would he just hand it over? This was his. This was for his family. With nary a hint, Fisk took off running.

Anna sensed her brother move before his feet even twitched. Completely in step with her brother, she was at his side, keeping pace.

They ran for the door of the cathedral. "Meet me on

Knightrider," shouted Fisk. "You take the first lane and I'll take Do Little."

The two entered St. Paul's Walk, the long corridor inside the cathedral, haven to news mongers, thieves, and strumpets. They ran abreast, knocking into men of station taking their noonday walks, intent to learn the latest news and court gossip. Paul's Walk was not exclusive. There were plenty of beggars and those with mad thoughts with nowhere else to go, taking shelter from the weather. All manner of humanity gave audience as the young pair ran willy-nilly through the nave.

The buzz of conversation continued in spite of the ruckus. Words rose to the buttresses overhead and bounced off the limestone arches, then fell to the floor below, replaced by new. The commotion made by two wild children was of no more consequence than the strange myriad of other disruptions upsetting the peace in this house of God.

Alas, so it is on earth as it is in St. Paul's Cathedral.

No amount of hollering by the cord vendor made any difference in the loud confusion. People stepped aside and watched the boy and girl avoid collision while their red-faced nemesis charged after them.

At the main entrance, Fisk and Anna pounded down the front steps, free of the church, and cut between two buildings nearby to Carter's Lane. Once there, Anna veered toward Knightrider. Fisk kept on running, then turned down Do Little Lane. When he emerged on Knightrider he expected to see Anna ahead of him. If the vendor was following, he hoped the man was chasing him and not his sister. But there was no sign of her. He checked behind him in case he'd gone too far. He did not see her. But neither did he see the vendor. Puzzled, he stood a second to rethink. He cut over to Sermon Lane. Carts and pedestrians moved along the narrow street, but no Anna.

Fisk turned around and looked up and down Knightrider. Could she have reached the road before he did? Had she waited, then decided to run home? Again, he felt the demon of panic slithering down his spine.

"Anna!" He spun about, frantic, but there was no answer.

Despite a sense of impending danger, he started down Sermon Lane to search for her.

He slowed at every alcove and stooped to peer under every shop stand. She had disappeared, gone. Mystified, he returned to Knightrider and stood in the middle of the lane, making himself obvious. If his pursuer was still after him, it wouldn't take him long to find him.

Fisk had effectively baited the vendor to come after him, but as he stood there, vulnerable and confused, the thought that kept working its way into his conscious loomed suddenly large. What if the vendor had caught his little sister?

He could think of nothing else but to return to the cathedral. He raced up the steps and turned around for one last look at the busy lane in front of the cathedral. There was no sign of Anna, so he went back inside.

The nave was just as noisy and congested as before. Fisk wended his way to the opposite end and stood, all the while keeping an eye out for Anna. Finally, he went back outside. The wind spat at his face, its cold breath mocking him. He took shelter beneath an arch and watched the street for his little sister. Perhaps she had just gone home. But how could she have gotten away from him so quick?

The slab of bacon under his jacket was a sorry reminder of his misadventure, but not knowing what else to do, he began walking home. Perhaps Anna had had the good sense to get away from the area and not try to find him. But nearing Old Change Road, he felt the need to retrace his steps one last time.

He was beyond the church of St. Mary Magdalen when he heard quickening steps from behind. He spun about and to his astonishment, the cord vendor was back in pursuit and bearing down on him. The fellow was determined, if not a bit witless, decided Fisk. But he took off running again, running as fast as his legs could carry him.

At Friday Street he rounded the corner, colliding with a young maid and spilling her basket of walnuts in the muddy road. He had now entered an unfamiliar area. Some of the residences bordered on plots of garden, and as there was not much distance between him and the vendor, a web of intersecting thoroughfares and footpaths offered the only means of escape.

He chose a curving path that divided into three offshoots. Without a thought, he took the one on the right, which soon divided, offering another two possibilities. Both were dark and winding, but he took the one more poorly lit. Halfway down the narrow space he flattened himself against a wall.

His lungs heaved and his legs shook. He concentrated on softening the sound of his heavy breathing. All of this for a silly flitch of bacon! If the cord vendor found him now, he would just hand it over. He wanted to go home. He was tired and scared and the thought of his mother's thin gruel seemed not so terrible now.

One thing was for cert, Anna must have gotten away. Otherwise, why would the man still be chasing him? Unless, of course, the vendor had caught Anna and was holding her captive.

Fisk imagined his little sister in a gibbet suspended over a boiling kettle of water. Mayhap the ogre wanted to throw the bacon in the pot along with Anna and eat her for dinner. He thought of his poor sister and worried how he'd tell his mother, when he heard the slapping sound of steps in mud.

The vendor ran past, completely unaware of him plastered against the building. Fisk waited for the man's steps to fade, then blew out his breath. He had escaped for now, but it wouldn't be long before the vendor doubled back.

Fisk pushed himself off the wall and retraced his route, then turned down a different fork. Surely it would eventually lead him to a road he recognized. He had turned himself around so much that he didn't know which direction he was headed. Where was St. Paul's? He couldn't smell the river and he couldn't see above the leaning upper stories of the buildings.

The sooner he got free of this warren, the better. It was all he could do to keep from crying out in frustration.

Soon he was running full out, turning corners and slipping in putrid, untraveled spaces. His ears filled with the sound of his pounding heart beating like a funeral drum leading him to his grave. The tangle of lanes branched, taking him nowhere, tricking and confusing him. He wondered if he would ever get out.

Surely this labyrinth of lanes would eventually intersect with something he knew. He focused on this crumb of common sense, believing and praying that this was not some sinister maze leading him to hell, when he turned onto a path that looked as if it opened onto a brighter lane. Ahead he saw the comforting sight of people walking by. Fisk almost laughed out loud as he stopped running, relieved that his ordeal was over. Wherever he was he'd be able to find his way home now.

Regrettably though, his respite was short-lived. As he started for the busy street, a shadow fell across his path and a man blocked his way.

"Hello, boy," said an unwelcome voice.

CHAPTER 4

Restored to his placid ward north of the river, Constable Patch had grown bored these past several months, answering occasional domestic disputes and petty thievery complaints he could do nothing about. This ward of chandlers and broderers were a peaceful bunch, content to sell candles and embellish silk and linen for nobility and wealthy merchants. At first the constable had enjoyed the position, but one could only indulge in so many naps before needing some sort of stimulation—at least every once in a while.

Today it came in the form of a murder.

While keeping an eye out for suspicious activity (as was his nature), and going for his daily bread, Patch took Do Little Lane, a different route than usual. He was puzzling over why any street would be given such a demoralizing name, a name christening a neighborhood to modest expectation and low achievement, when he was met by a group of citizens next to St. Mary Magdalen's church.

All chins were tipped upward, their necks craning for a better look. At first, he did not see what they were gaping at. He thought if nothing else, he would break up the gathering, for they clogged the narrow lane and would soon be a nuisance to those wishing passage into and out of his ward. But as he neared the broad side of the building with words of reproach perched on his tongue, he soon spied the object of their fixation.

Halfway up the exterior, a body swung from the grotesque decorating the dripstone over a window. A strong gust blew through the narrow lane, and from his spot on the street below Constable Patch could see the limp feet bump the glass.

"Who is it?" he asked.

No one could offer a suggestion. No one could see the victim well enough to say much about it except that it was probably a male and not very well dressed. One shoe was missing and the bare foot, even in this poor light, looked blue.

Though Castle Baynard ward was not his jurisdiction, Patch felt it his duty to take matters in his own hand until the ward constable arrived and could take over.

"Who found the body?" he asked. "Is he here?"

"I saw it when I left me rent," said an older woman, stepping forward. Her raspy voice made it difficult for Patch to understand her. "At first, I thought it strange. I couldn't tell what it was so I stopped to take a look. My eyes, I have never seen such a sight." She shook her head. "There be no saying how long he could have been hanging there before anyone thought to look up. The birds could have picked 'im clean before anyone noticed."

"How long ago was this?"

"Only just now," she said. "When I realized it be a body—I screamed." She crossed herself quickly. "People came running to see what was wrong."

Patch looked round at the onlookers and realized that news of the spectacle would soon blaze through the parish. All of Knightrider and its side streets would soon be congested with bug-eyed dawdlers milling about, scratching their heads, offering dubious explanations, getting underfoot.

"Cut him down," Patch ordered, as if this plebeian group of gawkers would do his bidding.

No one volunteered.

Patch pointed to the woman. "At the very least, we needs the sexton. Go tell 'im he's got a yank-neck he needs to remove."

The woman protested. "Why do I have to do it?"

"Because it is yer civic duty!" said Patch, pointing her in the right direction. "And gets the priest and constable!" he called after.

As Patch had predicted, the lane began filling with curious pedestrians and residents. Patrons from the Boar's Head Tavern left their morning porridge to file into the lane, their napkins still draped over their shoulders. Speculation ran the gamut from name-guessing that it was a fellow caught foining Maggie Wait— that slatternly widow bent on trying every pizzle on Milk Street— to someone suggesting it might be a street urchin who'd gotten his what-for after stealing one too many times.

Patch listened to every suggestion; the more preposterous ones he stashed in his pea brain to be trotted out later because that was just how he was. In due time, the woman returned with the sexton, who bore a mistrustful scowl. The fellow stood back and peered up at the eaves searching for the body. His grimace turned to disbelief spotting it.

"God's nails, how does a man hang 'imself from such a height?" He looked round at Patch and the others. "One can get the same result from a roof rafter." Then, realizing he would be entrusted with getting the body down, his astonishment turned to stubborn refusal. "I'll not take on the likes of that," he said. "I don't like ladders."

"How do ye manage yer duties if ye don't like ladders?" asked Patch, thoroughly annoyed. "They be a necessity to yer office."

"I am not the only one who maintains the building. I'll find Phinn. He is nimble of joint and he likes the view from the bell tower."

"Then get him!" said Patch. "We are wasting the day."

"Sirrah, if I may," said the sexton, scrutinizing Patch, and recognizing that he was not the constable of Castle Baynard. "Should we not summon *this* ward's constable?"

Patch's upper lip twitched. "He has been summoned. An' until he arrives, I am in charge. My ward borders this one and if a street gets blocked here, it will clog the road in mine." He resented being questioned and committed the sexton to his list of disliked humans.

With a snide smile on his face, the sexton went off to find Phinn, his surefooted cohort.

Patch surveyed the crowd, then returned his gaze to the unfortunate victim. He wondered if this might be self-murder as the sexton suggested. He agreed that hanging oneself from a dragon grotesque seemed a bit drastic when there were plenty of other venues easier to scale. Self-murder or not, the height alone was an unnecessary undertaking.

"Are you the constable?"

Patch turned to answer a man dressed in a cassock with a fur-lined gown over it. "Are you the priest?" he responded.

"I am," said the man. "Though I am not the priest of St. Mary Magdelen's, if that is what you mean. I am Father Foxcroft of St. Andrew's."

Patch looked the man up and down. "St. Andrew's is a few blocks away near the Wardrobe. Word travels fast in Castle Baynard ward."

"I came as soon as I heard."

To Patch's mind, not that much time had passed. "And how dids ye hear?"

"Well," said the priest, taken aback. "A parishioner told me a

29

crowd was gathering at St. Mary Magdalen's." A hesitant smile quivered at the corners of his mouth. "Priests take care of one another. I've come to offer my support to Father Rhys."

"He isn't here," said Patch.

Foxcroft looked at the body overhead and crossed himself as silence stretched between them. Patch kept searching the crowd for the sexton's return and Foxcroft stood next to him, subdued and praying his paternoster.

"Such an unfortunate incident," said the priest, attempting to make conversation.

"Aye," said Patch.

As they waited, Constable Patch's thoughts turned to Bianca Goddard across the river in Southwark. He wondered if the constable of Baynard Castle had anyone as knowledgeable as she to advise him. Patch would never admit that he had come to depend on her skills of observation and reasoning to solve questionable deaths such as this one. He preferred to bask in the assumed glory that he, alone, had brought several murderers to justice. His success had landed him this current plum of a position. His irascible wife appreciated his advancement, and his needy ego readily allowed his taking credit. Patch could never go so far as to show appreciation to the dubious daughter of that wily alchemist, Albern Goddard. A man who, Patch was certain, was up to no good; the rumors swirling about him were grounds enough for an investigation, should he ever get the chance to do so. But alas, Albern Goddard did not reside in his ward.

Patch supposed that everyone had questionable associations of one sort or another. Some were familial, some were actively cultivated. And, he had to admit, they often served a purpose.

Patch blew in his hands to warm them and watched with agitation as the crowd of spectators grew. The sexton was taking interminably long to find this Phinn fellow. He would like to leave to send for Bianca but didn't dare miss the chance that the body would be cut down and removed before he could find her. It came as a welcome surprise when one of his minions happened onto the scene.

"Cyndric," he said, hailing his slouch-shouldered associate.

At the sound of his name, Cyndric hunched even more in an attempt to shrink into the crowd. Patch worked his way over and clapped his hand on the man's protruding clavicle.

"What handsome luck. I needs ye to fetch Bianca Goddards in Gull Hole. Bring her straight away. If she isn't in her room of Medicinals and Psychics, then seek her at the Dim Dragon Inn."

"What's happened, sir?" asked Cyndric, finally looking up.

"A dangler. Now get on!"

With Cammy returned to work, Bianca gazed out the tavern window and saw that the sun still had not broken through the gray mantle that had settled over London for nearly two straight weeks. She began to wonder if the jolly orb had gone elsewhere, preferring instead to shine on the blue waves of ocean, or perhaps the fields in France. This sullen gloom had seeped into her marrow, and she found it increasingly difficult with every passing day to pry herself away from the friendships she'd cultivated at the Dim Dragon Inn and attend to her work in the cold, dreary interior of her room of Medicinals and Physickes in Gull Hole.

Only the gentle burps of a simmering concoction kept her company these days—the sounds of her industry creating medicines from plants. Sometimes she heard the neighbor's chickens clucking, or a horse clop by, and certainly Hob's vocalizations provided some discourse with another living being— but he was a cat, she reminded herself. And while she cherished the peace of creating her balms and salves in her inconspicuous little hovel, she did miss her married life with John.

They had married two years ago in the spring of 1543, when the fields beyond Paris Garden Manor were vivid green and white with clover, and the sun had chased every cloud from the sky. John had found a biscuit-colored doublet from a fripperer, and his tail of wheaten-colored hair shone beneath a scarlet flatcap he'd borrowed from his master, the French silversmith Boisvert. John struck a handsome figure, standing taller and more svelte than most. She smiled, remembering the subtle curves of his muscles, the beguiling arms that had held her close.

Meddybemps had performed their handfast, and the streetseller was of good cheer that day—but then, she thought wistfully, he was of sunny disposition most days. His silly dance and nonsensical patters had kept them laughing despite the sanctity of their marriage rite. She still had the embroidered apron he'd given her, and on occasion she would take it out of her chest and lightly run her finger over the colorful flowers, appreciating its simple beauty and being glad for their friendship. The truth was that she relied on him not only for his unwavering loyalty, but because he helped her survive by selling her tinctures at market.

However, their friendship had been tested of late as his duplicity had come to light over a matter involving her mother as well as her father's discovery of a dangerous element some ten months before. But with time she had learned to accept that often the right choice of action was not always a moral one. Be that as it may, she considered Meddybemps her family, more so than even her own parents. Bianca took another sip of ale, its taste bitter on her tongue, and returned her thoughts to a love more true.

She'd known John since they were children running about the streets. For a girl with no siblings, he seemed at the time to fill a missing familial bond. John and his older brother had been abandoned by their mother and had learned to survive on the streets with only their wits to keep them alive. Bianca and John had in common the bold cunning that came with self-reliance—and never having enough to eat. Their friendship began when John saved her from an angry butcher and constable whose intent was to make Bianca an example of what could happen if one were caught stealing. Something had passed between the two rascals, perhaps an understanding born from similar circumstance. Bianca had trusted him implicitly, and when John had suddenly kicked the constable in the shin, they had started running and she reached for his hand. She had never let go of it.

Though John would have preferred that she dedicate more time to cooking savory meals instead of medicines, he was not so selfish as to demand that she give up her fascination with chemistries and herbs. He knew that her desire to experiment with different combinations of plants was a skill learned in part from her mother, who was a neighborhood white witch, and that adding unconventional ingredients such as salt of tartar, then setting fire to the concoctions, may have been influenced by the long hours she had spent assisting her father in his room of alchemy. John was not about to discourage her from this "dabbling." Even though the king had made it treasonous to practice conjuration and sorcery, as long as she didn't flaunt her discoveries or draw attention to her work she was safe from people misconstruing her efforts to help the sick. Besides, it was a means of making money. And with John gone, there was no more stipend from his apprenticeship.

Bianca rose from the table and bid Mackney and Smythe a good day. She collected her scarf and was winding it around her neck when the tavern door swung open and constable Patch's deputy appeared. He was the kind of man who shied from scrutiny and as he stood discreetly surveilling the room, his conspicuous Adam's apple traveled up and down his skinny throat. His eyes came to rest on Bianca, steadily watching him. The flash of recognition relaxed his face and he swiftly wove through the grid of trestles to get to her.

"Bianca Goddard," he said, with a slight nod. "Constable Patch requests that you accompany me to Castle Baynard ward."

"In regards to what?"

"He thinks there has been a murder."

CHAPTER 5

Borderlands of Scotland

Almost a country away, John Grunt, Bianca's husband, leaned against a rock and ate his rations of mutton, biscuit, and a pint of ale. It had been nearly a year since he had sailed for the Firth of Forth and stepped foot in this rugged yet majestic land. Sailing had been the first of many new experiences that had left him awestruck and even terrified at times. This terror, this gnawing, insidious fear—a constant of war—he struggled to hide.

Until then, he had never laid eyes on the sea stretching before him, sometimes blue, but most often gray. If the sea had been smooth with following winds he might have taken to a sailor's life. But a vicious wind blew from the northeast, a sharp cold that lashed at his face and chilled him to the bone. For days the rain slanted sideways and he stayed below as much as he could, enduring the stagnant air and collective stink of men. Spring brought the change of seasons, when the wind turned over the ice in the lochs and brought men in galleons to wage war.

They arrived just after Edinburgh burned, the smoke still

hanging over the town like a malevolent veil. The air smelled of destruction and decay, the rotting stench of death. A smell that would become so familiar as to lose its salience. Not a single house stood. Nearly every building had burned, the ash and smoldering timbers the only remains of what life once was. In the end, only the castle stood; it had been decided not to waste any munition trying to destroy it, for the fortress sat high above in a position of strength and its cannons warded off siege by pummeling High Street, its only access.

While Henry's men continued to lay waste to every village within seven miles of Edinburgh, Sir Nicholas Pointz, by order of the Earl of Hertford, crossed the river and won the town of Kinghorn. It was John's first battle and, with the smell of ruined Edinburgh still fresh in his nostrils, he rose to the occasion. It was kill or be killed. The time for introspection had passed.

He took no satisfaction in burning Kinghorn to the ground. He hung back when a rushlight was passed to him and he shook as he lowered it to light straw placed against a house. He watched the seed of his treachery grow; saw the flame run like a wild rabbit, hop sideways, and double, then triple again in its breadth and ferocity.

The screams of the dying, of women and children, cut through the roar of fire. His head filled with their agony, and his. He stepped back, shrinking from the heat of the flames, unable to stop what he had done, and disbelieving it.

Perhaps disbelief is the sustaining mindset of men at war. It is not I, but *they*. It is not you, but *them*.

And as his fellow soldiers set fire and slaughtered those who dared try to escape, John lacked the jangly intoxication of subduing his enemy. His veins did not run with the fever of power—they ran with the gravity of murder.

John thought back to that first week, where there was no rest between raids upon villages along the coast. He recalled his commander repeating the Lord Lieutenant's words in a rallying cry to justify their cause—

"Whereas the Scots had so many ways falsed their faiths; and broken their promises confirmed by oaths and seals and certified by their whole parliament, as is evidently known unto all the world … our Lord Lieutenant, the Earl of Hertford, was sent thither by the King's Highness to take vengeance of the Scot's detestable falsehood … that unless they would yield up their town unto him frankly … he would put them to the sword, and their town to the fire."

And after these exploits had been done to Edinburgh and the immediate countryside, the Earl of Hertford determined the Scots had not been punished enough. The men could not rest until every ship or boat belonging to any village or haven on either side of the Firth was burned or brought away. Some fifty miles of humanity and its accoutrements were razed and destroyed.

This endless campaign on every village in southern Scotland had taken its toll on John. While his comrades had resigned themselves to the destruction and followed their orders with as little thought as pulling on their shoes, John still struggled with the taking of innocent lives. After Kelso and Roxburgh, he became more withdrawn, grateful for any time to rest or do anything other than plunder and pillage. He watched his fellow soldiers grow more confident and cruel. They believed wholeheartedly that their cause was just. They hated the Scots with as much vehemence as their king.

John finished his ale and rested his head against the boulder.

He thought of Bianca and counted out the months since last he'd laid eyes on her. Ten. Nearly a year had gone by. She would have had the baby by now. He wondered if his little boy was strong—for he was certain their child was a boy. The certainty came only from a feeling, but it had become unshakeable. A thrill of pride swelled inside of him and he smiled at the thought of seeing his family when he was at last sent home.

"Methinks we have a monkey in our midst. Look on his mad bliss."

John didn't answer for a moment. He had no desire to release the happy scene floating in his head. Besides, he recognized the voice. It belonged to the persistent burr in his side; Roger the archer, blowfart—and, sadly, Cammy's lover.

He felt a kick to his thigh.

John opened his eyes to glare at the offender.

"Ha, there is no time for idle pleasures," said Roger. He was joined by two other archers who stood on either side, sneering down at John. The disagreeable trio were never content to while away their free time mending their quivers or resting before battle. Instead, they made the rounds antagonizing the very men tasked with protecting them. That they had lived so long unnicked by combat spoke better of their billmen than of any special talent with their bows and arrows.

For as much as John would have enjoyed punching Roger's sarky face, he commendably refrained from doing so. There were plenty who would have cheered him on and who would have merrily contributed a few punches, but the trouble he would have heaped upon himself was not quite worth it. Because in Henry's army, the archers were the favored mavens, the men who were to be protected at all costs.

"You would do well to give me leave," said John. He resisted reminding Roger of a billman's duty, for Roger was the kind of man whose belief in this imposed hierarchy of ascendant archers, meant that he could disrespect those beneath him and think them expendable.

"Pray tell me why ... thou sapless foot-licker?"

It was enough to stir the most phlegmatic of men, which John was not. But John had survived too many years on the streets of London to risk himself more misery by lashing out. If there was one thing that he had learned in the past ten months, it was that no one escaped being affected by war. Let the churl plant his seeds of discord, for he would eventually reap the reward of his false conduct. Of that John was certain. For John was not the only underling to suffer Roger's tongue.

John spoke. "Because soon we march for Melrose. And while you trouble yourself with me, I see a monkey yonder, with more malicious intent, inspecting your quiver and bows." John tipped his chin toward the direction from which Roger and his lunkheads came. Plenty of men were milling about, but it did appear that someone was looking over their abandoned weapons. "Methinks he supposes they would serve him better."

The surly expression on Roger's face fell like a rock in water. A second later, he abandoned John, and his hapless cohorts trotted after.

"*Droch áird chúgat lá gaoithe*," said Glann McDonogh, an Irish pikeman, one of the many foreigners Henry had hired to fortify his army. He gave John a hand up.

"Smooth out your briary tongue. Its sounds are strange."

McDonogh's eyes narrowed, looking after Roger. "May he be badly positioned some windy day."

John smiled. "Aye. Mary make it so."

The Irishman slapped John on the back. "Would I sit with six Scots to one of those," he said, and John agreed.

"Take care when you say that," said John. "Though we men of sticks oft think it." The two walked across the field, away from the immediate camp. They looked out over the gently rolling hills in the direction of Melrose, their next conquest. "We are nearly five thousand strong and we have not known a defeat since I've been here. There is hardly a village that has not been touched. Surely the

Scots have had enough."

Glann McDonogh picked up a pebble and threw it as far as he could.

"These Scots have seen everything they've worked for destroyed in a matter of minutes," said Glann. "If it was by God's hand, then they would accept it. But it wasn't God's hand that did this to them—it was ours. We've ruined a people and a land. And if we stay here long enough, they will find a way to avenge their dead."

"For a lowly billman, you are wise, my friend."

McDonogh found another stone and aimed it at a raven picking apart a field mouse. The stone landed short and the bird flapped its wings before settling back to its meal. "We're like that bird. It's going to take more than a rock to move us on."

CHAPTER 6

Bianca sat opposite Constable Patch's minion as the boatman steered their skiff toward the stairs at Baynard's Castle. Cyndric informed her that a body had been found hanging from St. Mary Magdalen's church and that it would take some time to get it down.

It had been nearly a year since she'd done any criminal inquiry. With John gone, she had settled in to a predictable and innocuous routine—that of making medicines, collecting herbs and various ingredients, and experimenting to her heart's content. John had always argued against her pursuing any sort of skullduggery; he worried for her safety. If she had to keep her inquisitive mind busy then he preferred that she occupy herself with herbal remedies instead. (Though, truth be told, there was plenty of danger in brewing some of her medicines; a recent mishap had caused a percussive boom that brought her neighbor running to investigate. The fire was easily dashed with a bucket of water, but it took Bianca a good day to recover her hearing.) But, in a sense, John would be glad to know that for several months she had concentrated on her medicines, and when she hadn't, there had been a good reason why. She sighed, feeling a twinge of regret as she smoothed down her kirtle over her now flat stomach.

When they landed, she followed Cyndric up to the church on Milk Street. They arrived just as the body was cut loose from the window's dripstone. The sexton was of stocky build but agile enough to drape the lifeless body over his shoulder while sawing at its tether. Beneath him, the ladder bowed and bounced precariously as two men held fast to the bottom, wearing anxious looks on their faces. All the crowd had fallen silent, held spellbound and breathless watching him balance on the bendy ladder halfway up the exterior of the church.

"Bianca Goddards," said Constable Patch, seeing her approach.

"Constable Patch." Bianca's eyes flicked up to the sight overhead. After a moment she said, "Mayhap you might consider clearing the crowd if he or the body should fall."

"I have assurance that this fellow knows what he is about. Besides, the crowd would break his fall."

Bianca gave Patch a weighty look, and without another word he began shouting for people to move back.

"I hope I am wrong," she said when he returned to her side.

Patch informed her of what he knew, and while he was talking to her Bianca noticed a priest standing within earshot, watching them. She met his gaze and tucked her chin in acknowledgment. "Is that the priest?"

Patch glanced over his shoulder. "It is *a* priest," he answered, rolling his eyes. "Father Foxcroft," said Patch loudly, while turning toward the man. "This is Bianca Goddard. She often assists me. She is of keen eye."

Father Foxcroft obviously noticed Patch's irreverence, for his expression showed mild annoyance at his handling. The priest was a tall man, somewhat thin, but like Bianca's husband possessed the complexion of a healthy man. For a priest, his attire looked new, or perhaps he was a meticulous dresser. Guessing from his marten-lined gown and cuffs, he was a man pushing the limits of sumptuary law.

"Do you know the priest of St. Mary Magdalen?" asked Bianca.

"I do," replied Foxcroft. "I am sorry he must deal with such a troublesome incident."

With a final flourish, Phinn succeeded in cutting through the rope and a piece of it fell into the crowd below, causing some excitement. He then began climbing down, struggling under the weight of the lifeless body.

"Do we know who the victim is?" asked Bianca, keeping her eyes trained on the sexton.

"Nay," said Patch. "No one seems to recognize 'im. Then, toos, all we could see was the bottoms of his feet."

Just then a loud crack issued overhead. One of the rungs broke and Phinn rode the ladder down, to the gasps of the spectators, until his feet caught a foothold several rungs below. His hands raked the weathered sides, and he must have gotten them riddled with splinters for he cursed loudly and shook out one hand, then the other. After a few Hail Marys he eventually calmed himself enough to continue his descent.

The closer Phinn got it became obvious that the victim was not a man.

"He looks familiar," said Patch. "I feel as if I have seen this lad before."

Bianca's heart dropped. The victim was a child.

She was used to examining and thinking about adult fatalities, but a young boy robbed of life tore at her heart. The familiarity of a mother's loss struck painfully close. Bianca prepared herself to look upon the child, hoping at the very least that she did not know him.

The child wore threadbare, ill-fitting clothes, too short for his growing limbs, exposing his wrists and ankles to the elements. One shoe was missing, and the other seemed of little use with a gaping hole and two gray toes poking through.

Cyndric moved forward to help Phinn with his burden and they laid the body on the cobbles next to the ladder. Immediately, the crowd surged forward for a better look. Constable Patch and Bianca had to squeeze through the tightly packed throng in order to get close.

"Stand away, give us leave!" shouted Patch. He and Cyndric managed the crowd enough so Bianca could crouch beside the body. It took several more minutes and the help of a few additional men to back away the mob before Bianca finally got enough light for a good look at the victim.

Father Foxcroft wormed his way next to her. The toes of his fine leather shoes peeked from under his cassock—a gentle reminder of his presence. Bianca ignored his imposition and focused on the poor victim lying before her.

The first thing she noticed was a rosary wound around the victim's neck. Two loops ended in a carved wooden cross. Bianca lifted the crucifix off his shoulder and saw that it was made of boxwood. She slid the wooden beads along a cord made of hemp.

Bianca studied the boy's dirt-grimed face and pushed back the lips of his slightly open mouth. He had his adult front teeth, but from the size of the others and with some missing, Bianca approximated his age.

"He must be around nine or ten years," she told Patch, who had just returned to her side.

Instead of acknowledging this, Patch issued a warning to onlookers that they were encroaching. His irritation extended to Father Foxcroft.

"Unless ye is planning to bless the poor boy, there be nothing ye can do, Father. In facts, we needs some privacy to fully disgust the findings."

Bianca heard a quick exchange between the priest and Patch, then saw the man's fine leather shoes step away.

Relieved of his intrusive presence, Bianca rocked back on her heels for a general look. The boy's unevenly shorn dark hair clung to his head and he wore no cap. Besides the overall grime on his face, dried mucus crusted his nostrils like he had been sick or perhaps crying.

However, as she considered his overall appearance, she was struck by how peaceful he looked. If she didn't know better, he could have been mistaken for a sleeping child. She pulled back his eyelids and saw no swelling or broken vessels. A victim of strangulation would have looked markedly different. Bianca loosened the paternoster, revealing a telltale furrow from the noose where it had dug into the skin, angling up to the jaw. She then ran her fingertips down his spine. A break indicated the boy had been dropped a sufficient distance to have caused a fairly quick death. Given the length of the rope and height from which he was hanged, it was lucky he had not been decapitated.

Each wrist showed bruising—evidence, she believed, that he had been bound. However, she found no fibers or remnants of cloth, and his hands now hung free.

Patch crouched beside Bianca.

"Have you gone through his clothing?"

"I have not gotten that far."

He opened the boy's outer coat and searched an inner pocket.

"Nothing," he announced, removing a lump of lint and flicking it off his finger.

"The boy doesn't look as if he suffered," said Bianca. "He looks quite peaceful."

"He wasn't strangled with the paternoster first?"

"I think not." Bianca lifted the boy's head and ran her hands over his scalp. "I don't feel a gash or any blood. He wasn't bludgeoned." Bianca pulled up his smock and rolled him to one side and then the other. "His torso is smooth, he wasn't stabbed." She looked over at Constable Patch.

"Could he have been poisoned and then hanged?" Patch tugged his scraggly chin hairs in thought.

"If he was poisoned, there would be some redness around his mouth, and his clothes are dry, there is no vomit." Bianca thought a moment. "I'm certain the noose ended his life." She arranged the smock and jacket to cover the child. "But the boy's peaceful expression is certainly strange."

"Could it have been self-murder?"

"That is a height to climb for a boy toting a rope. Even if it was self-murder, the will to live would have prevailed and we would see signs of struggle in his expression."

"It woulds be odd for a child to be so content," commented Patch.

"I am puzzled," said Bianca. "The only way this boy could look so peaceful is if he was already dead and then hanged." Bianca looked at Patch. "Mayhap the coroner might be able to explain this." The two of them got to their feet. Bianca pulled her cape over her shoulders and straightened her bodice, lost in thought. "But why would someone go to such lengths?" she said. "Why hang the victim from a grotesque above a church window? If the boy was still alive, I would think it would have been an impossible task."

Patch squinted in distaste. "And what is the purpose of twining the paternoster around the lad's neck?"

"It must be meaningful in some way." Bianca wondered whether it was put there as a talisman by the murderer, perhaps a conscious effort to wish no more harm on the child's soul than had already been perpetrated. Or, thought Bianca, perhaps the killer was using it to make a point. "Possibly it is a message."

Patch offered no suggestions. He stared at Bianca with one side of his face scrunched in dismay. "Maybe stringing him up from the side of the church is a way to gloat."

"Gloat?"

"Wells, the murderer has a certain ease in scaling churches toting a body. We don't knows whether the boy was alive or dead, but either way it takes some skills to manage such a feat." Patch continued to tug his billy-goat chin hair.

"But a church," said Bianca. "Why not the bridge, or the cranes by the river?"

"Mayhap the murderer does not like this church."

"Or churches in general," said Bianca. "And the paternoster around the neck ... giving the impression of having choked the boy ..."

"Mayhap the killer dislikes Papists," suggested Patch.

"But people still have their paternosters whether they prefer the old religion or follow the king's."

"Aye," agreed Patch. "But ye see less of them these days. No one wants to be accused of being a Papist."

Bianca considered this. "The paternoster was meant to be seen. Leaving it on the body was done on purpose. And maybe it is significant that this particular church was chosen."

Just then, a loud voice drowned their conversation. "God's tooth!" came the cry. "What is this about?" The voice cursed and insulted spectators who failed to move out of the way.

A belligerent fellow broke free of the bystanders and stood a moment, hands on hips, taking measure of Patch and the body on the ground, ignoring Bianca. He strode over with an unsteady swagger. Even though the air was bracing, the man wore his doublet only partially buttoned, exposing a grungy smock underneath, untied at the neck. His flatcap sat at a rakish angle, brash for a man of law.

Constable Patch stood a full head shorter. He puffed out his chest and lifted his chin to compensate for his inferior height. "This is a body, sirrah. I woulds think that obvious."

The fellow's eyes narrowed and his body swayed slightly. "Ye think me a half-wit?" He drew near enough so that his thigh touched Patch's overstuffed codpiece. "By whose authority do you act?"

Patch retreated a step. "I am a constable. I have some responsibility in keeping the lanes of commerce open."

"A constable?" said the man, incredulous. "You are not Castle Baynard's appointed constable."

"Nay, I am not."

"Nay ye are not," said the fellow, mocking Patch with a simpering voice. "Ye are not," said he, again drawing close, "because I am." The fellow glowered at the tittering crowd, then smiled churlishly at Patch. "And the name by which you go ... Constable?" He emphasized the first consonant so harshly that it practically cracked against the stone walls.

"Patch."

"P...at...ch?" came the response. He snorted, then belched without embarrassment.

"And I presume people have a name fer ye?" inquired Patch in return.

"Berwick, sirrah." He hooked a long fingernail between two teeth and spat out some gristle. "Suppose ye tell me the ward from which you hail?"

"Bread Street."

"Ha! Bread Street. Ye lord over bakers and candlemakers! Such a dull neighborhood. Nothing happens there except the occasional theft of standard loaves. Is this the reason why you jump to duty in a ward matter that does not concern you?" He tilted his head one way and then the other. A cynical smile appeared.

"Discovering bodies is exciting, is it not? But I assure you, Pat... ch," he said, again emphasizing the name. "I no longer need your assistance."

Bianca had heard enough. "Sir, the officials of St. Mary Magdalen's need to be informed," she said. "If you would make the introductions it would speed this forthwith."

For the first time Berwick took notice of Bianca. He seemed momentarily intrigued, and his boorish attitude warmed. "Tell me what has been learned, then I shall consider whether to make introductions."

Bianca explained what had happened, omitting telling him that Patch had summoned her for an opinion. She claimed to be helping Patch keep his facts sorted, alluding to Berwick that the constable needed some assistance in that matter. (Patch took offense at this, but realized it was a safer explanation than telling the truth. He would save his response for later when they were alone.)

When she had finished, Berwick, despite his inebriated condition, ordered the body carried inside to await examination by the coroner. He then led the way into the church with Bianca in step beside him. Patch followed petulantly behind, and, close on his heels, Father Foxcroft.

Unfortunately, the priest of St. Mary Magdalen's had still not yet arrived. In his stead was a church official and the sexton with whom they had first dealt, who informed them that Father Rhys had been notified and would arrive soon.

They stood in the narthex, and halfway down the nave a woman knelt in prayer with a young man beside her. The woman's susurrations were stippled with exclamations of "Hail Mary, full of graces," that were loud enough to draw everyone's notice. The son remained silent beside his mother, listening to her feverish pace, without looking around. Unfortunately, the cavernous space amplified her voice to the extent that Bianca could not ignore the distraction. She asked the men if they might find an area away from the penitents.

Not about to be inconvenienced, Constable Berwick didn't mind bothering someone else. He marched up to the pair and told them in no uncertain terms that they must leave. "There's been a death here!" he said in his booming voice. "You must go elsewhere."

"We shall not!" sputtered the woman. "We will stay until Father Rhys hears Huet's confession."

"When Father Rhys arrives he will have more important matters to attend."

Mortified at the constable's poor handling, the vestry official hurried over to intervene. "Goodwife Jane," he implored, "Father Rhys is on his way, but we do not know when, exactly, he will arrive. There is, however, another priest who could hear your pleas." He opened his arm generously toward Father Foxcroft.

Jane looked over her shoulder and scrutinized each of them from across the way, especially Father Foxcroft. "I want Father Rhys. This is my parish and Father Rhys is my priest."

The vestry official attempted to reason with her. "Of course," said the vestry official, "I am not so insensitive, but there is a matter here that is of the utmost concern."

"What is of more concern than a parishioner's soul?"

The official leaned forward, folding his hands against his chest as if in prayer. "Mayhap, then, goodwife," he said in a voice straining to remain cordial, "might you lower your voice?"

Out of patience with niceties, Constable Berwick's face screwed up. "Out!" he blurted. "I am the constable here, and I say you must leave!" He then addressed the toady vestry official. "If you do not want St. Mary Magdalen's parish ruined from untoward rumor, then follow my advice. Clear the church and only allow entry for those of office and position. Once we have conferred, then do as you please. But this woman must go."

Bianca cringed hearing Constable Berwick's coarse words.

The woman's jaw dropped as she considered the two men and her mistreatment. Her companion, a large-boned adolescent, rose from kneeling. Slowly drawing up to his full height, he stood even taller than Berwick. He looked down at the men berating them, his face showing a mix of confusion and distress.

"Huet," said the woman, patting him gently on the chest. "They mean us no harm."

She turned to the men and her voice became sharp. "We shall leave as you wish. But Father Rhys shall hear of this." She took hold of Huet's elbow and steered him past everyone, her eyes fierce with anger.

"What is her name?" asked Bianca of the official when he returned.

"Jane Clewes. She has been coming to our church of late. A widow, methinks. The young man is in her charge. Though I wonder who would have tasked her with such a burden. They are private in nature."

With a layman posted at the entrance, the group moved into the nave and resumed their discussion. They were in the middle of debating where to bury the body when they heard the door open. Moments later, Father Rhys met their stare, and before greeting them strode to the baptismal font. Bianca watched him conduct his ritual with an enviable calm given the circumstances, but she presumed serenity came effortlessly for a devout man who put his faith in his Creator and not in his earthly counterparts.

Introductions were barely finished before their attention was drawn a second time to the front door. Jane Clewes had regained entrance and was berating the poor layman standing guard. Her voice so grated, that Father Rhys excused himself to take matters in hand. He spoke in hushed tones, to which Jane Clewes favorably responded by lowering her own voice. After laying a reassuring hand on the woman's arm, Rhys announced to the rest of them that he would first hear Huet's confession. "I shall not be long," he assured them.

Constable Berwick mumbled under his breath as the three walked past, headed to the confessional.

"Let us hope the good father has the sense to dispense with a few paternosters and get on with it," he said. "I have no patience for idle chin-wagging." Berwick exited and was gone long enough to water roses in the alley, thought Bianca. He returned in an even fouler mood.

Eventually, Jane Clewes and Huet trailed toward the exit, in no rush to let the men resume their discussion. Clewes seemed to relish everyone's notice, proceeding at a measured pace like a bride walking down the aisle.

Minutes later, Father Rhys emerged from the confessional looking unmistakably troubled. His preoccupation lingered as he apologized for the interruption and for his long delay getting to the church. Bianca wondered over the reason for his unease.

Constable Patch didn't wait for Berwick to take control. He had his own questions to pose.

"Father, the boy is in the crypt. He has not yet been identified. You must go look at him. Mayhap ye've mets the lad, or knows his family."

"Of course. But if no one here has recognized him, then I doubt he is associated with our church." Rhys looked to his church official and Father Foxcroft, who both agreed. "Mind you, our church is not so far from the cathedral. Paul's Walk is overrun with begging orphans. It would make sense to inquire there, too."

"Aye," said Patch. "Though I'd like to begins with ye."

Father Foxcroft sided with his counterpart. "If no parishioners come forward with information, I agree that you should focus your attention at St. Paul's. The cathedral has difficulty keeping out thieves and other rascals. While it is our most sacred monument, St. Paul's is also party to society's most profane elements."

Berwick disliked Patch taking the lead on what should rightfully be his matter with which to deal. He sallied up to Patch, making the most of his superior height by throwing back his shoulders and looming large as he looked down at him.

"I believe we no longer need your assistance, P…at…ch," he said. "All the necessary parties are here. You may return to your ward, now. Those rascal bakers might need lording over." Berwick's derision was only matched by his thoroughly sozzled state.

Father Rhys squinted, catching a whiff of Berwick's fetid fumes, and exchanged places with his church official.

Father Foxcroft's patience was at an end. He pinned the two lawmen with an unamused stare and bristled, "I remind you that the objective here is to find a murderer and identify a victim."

Father Rhys chimed in. "How you achieve that can be decided elsewhere. I pray thee, leave off your sniping. There is no place for it here. Now, show me this unfortunate child."

Patch had no intention of leaving, and Berwick—momentarily chastened—followed the sexton as he led the group past the sanctuary and down a set of winding stone stairs to a cool room where the body lay on a trestle. Phinn was already there lighting lanterns, and brought one to set on the table next to the body. They gathered round the boy as Phinn talked about hangings, as he had firsthand knowledge. He'd transported criminals from the gallows at Tyburn to graveyards.

Father Rhys interrupted Phinn's morbid recollections to suggest they pray for the boy's soul. The silence evoked a grim reality and sadness to their proceedings and managed to sober even

Constable Berwick. When finished, Father Rhys lifted the lantern to better see the child's face.

"The boy needs his face cleaned. However, I do not recognize him," he said.

Father Foxcroft leaned close, taking advantage of the light to get a good look. "Nay," he said. "I don't recall ever seeing him."

Bianca watched the two priests examining the paternoster twined around the neck. "It is for the coroner to decide, but we feel the addition of the paternoster is irrelevant in his cause of death," she said.

"Obviously it appears the boy died from hanging," said Father Rhys.

Bianca wished to move the questioning along, and she didn't trust that either Patch or Berwick would ask what she wanted to know. "Have either of you any thoughts as to why the death occurred here?"

"I have no idea why my church was involved," answered Rhys.

"Might you have incurred some debt against someone?"

"Nay, certainly not," answered Father Rhys.

Patch could not keep still. "Might someone harbor black thoughts against ye?"

"Rancor, toward you or the church?" added Bianca.

"I should think not. It is for me to instill peace in my parishioners, not loathing."

The vestry official confirmed there was no known animosity directed at St. Mary Magdalen's church, though it would have surprised Bianca if they had admitted otherwise.

When they were collecting themselves to leave and the sexton was pulling a winding sheet over the body, Bianca held up her hand.

"Wait," she said, looking over at Father Rhys. "May I remove the paternoster to take a closer look?" They had left it twined around the child's neck, bewildered that its role to comfort had been so abominated. If there was even a small bit of sacred purpose left in the beads, then let the boy's soul benefit some from it.

"They should be left alone for the coroner to see," said Constable Berwick.

"But the boy was not strangled with them, he was choked by the noose," said Patch.

Father Rhys addressed Bianca. "If there is some use you might gain from their examination, I have no objection."

Bianca carefully unwound the prayer beads and brought them closer to the lantern. She studied the simple cross carved from wood then turned it over. Three letters had been carved on the back. They were too small to discern, even with the help of the lantern.

"If no one has an objection, I would like to take these to Paternoster Row."

"As long as you return them," said Constable Berwick.

"I merely wish another opinion," said Bianca. "I shall return them afterward."

Berwick opened his mouth to argue but was warned off by the two priests glaring at him.

Rhys directed Phinn to inform the coroner of the finding, then turned to Bianca. "Take them, child," he said. "They no longer serve this unfortunate boy."

CHAPTER 7

Bianca left the church and walked toward St. Paul's Cathedral where, between the old Grayfriars and Blackfriars defunct monasteries, curved Paternoster Row. There was a time when, on procession, the clerics recited the great litany, and the opening line of the Lord's Prayer was as far as they got on this short stretch of lane. More likely, thought Bianca, the road was named for the abundance of bead makers, stationers, bookbinders, and text writers who sold their religious books and paternosters within the holy shadow of the venerable cathedral.

Either way, she expected to find someone knowledgeable, someone who might be able to tell her about this particular rosary. As she neared the corner of St. Paul's, she spied her young friend and sometimes accomplice, Fisk—a ten-year-old imp.

Fisk didn't see her fall in behind a horse and rider. When she was nearly opposite, Bianca leapt out, tackling him around the waist. The boy yelped in fright and his thin frame shuddered for a few seconds afterward.

Bianca smiled broadly. "I couldn't resist," she said.

Fisk collected his wits and grinned, revealing the gap between his front teeth. "I nearly jumped out of my toenails."

"It has been awhile. You are nearly as tall as me."

Fisk flattened his hand, palm down, and ran it off the top of his head, drawing it in a dubiously straight line to Bianca. He announced he was taller, which he was not.

"I thought you moved back to Gull Hole," he said. "What reason have you to come up here?"

"I'm looking for someone to tell me about this paternoster." She held it up and Fisk took it, laying it out in his hand to study.

"Nothing special by my eye," he said, giving it back.

"Neither of us are expert." Bianca remembered it was not so long ago that she had posed as his mother and pretended that he was her wayward son needing the guidance of a priest at St. Vedast church. What she had really wanted was for him to spy on the clerics there. And he had been a great deal of help in doing so. "Tell me how you fare these days."

Fisk shrugged. "Father is away in France fighting for the king. Mother has trouble keeping us fed. 'There's too many mouths,' she keeps saying."

In many ways, being the daughter of an alchemist was not so different. Every groat went to buy her father's ingredients or the elaborate equipment that would finally succeed in transmuting base metals into gold; all to no avail. Bianca felt a certain kinship with the little waif, having known what it was like to scrounge and steal for food. She suspected he was out doing just that.

"Mind you, watch your back," she warned. "It matters not to vendors and shopkeepers that you are a starving child. Everyone is treated the same in the eyes of the law. You could lose a finger … or worse."

"I won't get caught," said Fisk, brushing his dark hair away from his face. "I'm too quick."

Bianca shook her head. "I thought the same about myself. And if John had not distracted the constable who had me by the ear, today I would have four fingers instead of five." The two moved to the side of the lane out of the way of a horse-drawn cart. "Watch yourself. That is all I am saying."

Fisk shrugged off her concern. "I had a fellow ask me to work for him."

"Did you now. Doing what, I wonder?"

"Helping him help others. Giving food to the poor. He said he could help Mother."

"It sounds like a noble cause."

"He nearly scared the wits out of me," admitted Fisk, casting a sheepish glance at her. "A big galumphing fellow was after me and I'd just got free of him when this man crossed my path."

"You were being chased?"

Fisk didn't answer. He wasn't going to admit he was up to no good.

"So, who is this fellow who wants your help?"

"Brother Ewan."

"A monk?"

Fisk's bony shoulder met his ear. "I do not know."

"Does he remind you of one?"

"He reminds me of a stubble-chinned coot of the street."

Bianca's brows furrowed in thought. Mayhap the fellow was a pensioned monk, forced out of his old way of life into a new. She wondered how he was able to give food to the poor. She didn't know how much stipend a monk was given when the king dissolved the monasteries, but certainly it was possible he still followed his vow of charity and poverty.

"So where does he get this food to give to the poor?"

"He didn't say. He just told me to think about it."

"Know you where he lives?"

Fisk shook his head.

"Then, how are you to find him?"

"He said he'd find me."

"When?"

Fisk shrugged. In the typical carefree world of a young boy, this was not a concern of his.

"This sounds odd," said Bianca. "If you see him again, go the other way."

Fisk picked up a stick and threw it at the wheel of a passing cart. "I can take care of myself," he said.

"Fisk, a young boy was found hanged at St. Mary Magdalen's church this morning." Bianca had no qualms mentioning the awful crime to her little friend. He needed to understand that the streets were not safe.

"I heard."

Bianca gave him a stern look, hoping to convince him of the seriousness of the hanging. But boys pretend bravery when they are told about danger. And boys learned early to practice wearing a brave face.

"Mind you, be careful."

Before they parted, Bianca invited him to visit her in Gull Hole. She gave Fisk a penny for the boat ride which, by the way his eyes lit up, made her wonder if he wouldn't spend it on dried currants instead.

Bianca left the immediate area of the cathedral with its myriad displays of humanity, well intentioned and not. An insistent pamphleteer followed her, waving a broadsheet of lyrics to a popular street ballad. She didn't stop long enough to hear why she should buy it.

At Paternoster Row, Bianca slowed to look in windows at stationers and beadmakers. The lane was not a long one, but there were shopkeepers there who catered to the more ecclesiastical desires of the community. She stopped outside the first shop that sold the prayer beads and, upon entering, noticed several elaborately decorated prayer books on display.

The shop owner looked up from reading one of his offerings and bid her welcome.

"I wonder if I might have a moment, sir?"

The man removed his reading spectacles and closed the book. "Certainly."

"These are lovely," she said, referring to the prayer books. "Do you make them yourself?"

"Nay. I do not craft any of the items in my shop. I collect exquisite books and pieces. There is a select group of wealthy clientele whose preferences I try to fulfill. Yet for the interested buyer I do offer the objects you see here." He spread his arms, inviting her to look at all he had to offer, then lightly pressed his fingertips together and smiled solicitously.

Surely he must have noticed her common kirtle, her lowborn status, thought Bianca, but he seemed not to care and indulged her curiosity—at least for the moment. A particularly lovely book of hours caught her eye and she admired its embroidered cover. A smooth tulip was stitched in the center, its petals highlighted in shades of pinks and cream. Mossy green swirls of stems and leaves encircled the flower, branching out in a pattern of spirals.

"Owning such a book would be a privilege," she commented, clasping her hands behind her back to keep from running her finger over the handiwork. "Indeed, its beauty speaks to the power of its content."

The proprietor appreciated her saying this and invited her to look at another even more elaborately stitched cover. It was covered in black silk with a theme of Tudor roses. Silver and gold threads outlined the flowers and then twined away in a pattern of stems and ivy. The entire cover shimmered, reflecting light off the fine metal threads. Bianca, who had never learned the finer art of stitching, could only imagine how time-consuming such a work would have been to make.

"It is a beautiful sight." Bianca had to drag her gaze away as she remembered the reason for her visit. "Perchance, sir, do you recognize the maker of this?" She removed the paternoster from her pocket and handed it to the man.

The shopkeeper was charitable enough not to deride its simple craftsmanship. He laid it on a tall table next to a candle and put on his spectacles. "It is common, of no artistic value," he said. He identified the materials used to carve the beads and crucifix, confirming what she already knew.

"But the cross, sir. Can you read the lettering on the back?"

The man bent over the chain so that the smooth black silk rim of his cap came dangerously close to the lit candle. After a moment of squinting and manipulating the cross, he retrieved a thick weight of blown glass and held it over the questionable characters. "I believe the letters read, Y, H, S." He slid the beads over to Bianca and handed her the magnifier.

"The letters look worn," she said. "I suppose that is a Y, though it could be a V. Do you know a maker with these initials?"

"A paternoster maker would not leave his mark on such a common prayer set. However, the owner of the paternoster might have carved his initials into it."

Bianca handed back the lump of glass.

"There is one other possibility," said the man. "It might represent the cult of the Holy Name. A secret handshake for Papists, as it were."

"So the owner may not have accepted the king's reforms?"

"Possibly."

Bianca thought about this. "But it may not be so unusual," she said, looking up from the beads. "I suspect there are people who keep using their old paternoster. It is an item of personal attachment."

"True. These days, it is His Majesty's wish that mechanical recitation be discouraged in favor of mindful petition." He picked up the rosary and fingered the individual beads. "Why so interested? From where did you get this?"

"Sir, this morning a boy was found hanged from a dripstone at St. Mary Magdalen's. It was wrapped around his neck."

The shopkeeper handed Bianca the prayer beads as if they were hot coals burning his palms. "Unfortunate child," he said. "But I am afraid there is nothing more I can tell you."

CHAPTER 8

When one loves another, how many lives are touched? Twenty years ago, the king fell in love with Anne Boleyn. A not-so-simple romance that set in motion seasons of change, cascading, corrupting, affecting, and reshaping lives, molding fate and an entire nation. No group felt the change more than the thousands of religious men and women wrenched from their ecclesiastical paths. Thousands of monks, nuns, friars, and canons were evicted and left without purpose. Acquiescence got them a small pension; refusal was an act of treason.

London was party to any number of these castaways. They found comfort in their numbers, found pallets on which to sleep in crowded rents, replaced nun habits with kirtles and aprons. Some were easily absorbed into the fabric of this congested city; others struggled for direction. However, this aged monk had found his mission, so to speak.

Unable to subsist on his allotted pittance, the man had scrabbled to survive. The skills he'd acquired at the monastery were useless outside its walls. No one needed a lector to read Bible passages aloud while others ate.

He had to do something to stop the hunger pangs.

Arriving at the door off Old Change, he gave his signature four knocks. He waited an equal measure of time during which he checked his knuckles for splinters, then gave another four raps. In response, the door cracked open and a blue eye appraised him.

With the broad flat of his hand, he pushed open the door, thwacking the gatekeeper's forehead.

"Where's Luke?" His stentorian voice filled the hollow space. Neither warm nor cozy, the room stretched the length of the building, an abandoned tannery that still reeked of the tubs of urine and tannin permanently absorbed into its daub.

A few boys looked at each other, then glanced around and found the missing pixie curled on a bench, sound asleep with his arm for a pillow. One of them stalked over and pulled it out from under his head.

"Aws, what?" complained the drowsy lad.

"I'm speaking to you," said the man, his burly voice vanquishing Luke's slumberous state.

Luke sat bolt upright and sprang to his feet. "S-sir," he stuttered.

"Did you carry out your task?"

The boy nodded without hesitation. "I dids."

"You dids what?" said the man, purposely toying. The child was really no trouble and practically shook in fear. He didn't have a mind to lie even if it would save his own skin. Still, he couldn't help himself. All those years being deferential and obedient had not made him kind.

"I did as ye asked of me," answered Luke.

"Come here, boy." Above his closely shorn beard, the man's ruddy cheeks had been rouged by the raw weather, and the boys gathered there wondered if this ruby flush might also have been caused by too many ales.

Luke hesitated, looking uncertain.

"Did you not hear me?"

The boy reluctantly came over. He stared at the ground.

The man tipped the boy's chin up so that he could look him in his eye. "You took care of it?"

"I did!" exclaimed Luke.

"You would not lie, would you?"

"Nay, never," protested the boy.

For added effect, the man eyed him with a pitiless stare. The other boys shifted uncomfortably; any one of them could be Luke, expecting to be thrashed. But he let go of the boy's chin and sat in a chair, the only one in the large empty space.

Luke stood a moment, expecting some sort of remonstration—for what, he did not know. When he saw his master sigh and close his eyes, he slipped behind the others and hoped he was as forgotten as the wall behind him.

The man launched into a well-practiced diatribe. "You lads." He shook his head as if weary of constantly reminding them. "Ye be sinners, do you not understand? You are here because God has sent you." He swept his gaze over them. "He has entrusted me with turning your hearts to Him. Unto Him our acts do honor."

The boys' eyes began to glaze. They dreamed of gleaming armor and fast steeds. Climbing oak trees in Smithfield and pelting passersby with acorns.

"These are difficult times. We live under a shadow of evil. Demons vie for your soul." He leaned forward and clawed the air with one hand. "I must lead ye away from temptation and make ye see what love there is in charity."

His coarse woolen tunic did not conceal his broad chest. He wore a woolen cap and never removed it even on the warmest day. In spite of an unlit brazier in this dank room, drops of perspiration trickled down his temples.

"I am your shepherd and you are my flock. Our service is for the greater good. We distribute the wealth so that all may know a respite from suffering. For what we do is our secret." And here he paused for effect, waiting for them to squirm. "God sees into our hearts and you shall be rewarded for your good acts."

One of the boys, a new charge who had not experienced the tangled argument of his logic, asked in a crystalline voice that sang several octaves higher than his master's, "Sir, what shall be our reward?"

The monk leaned forward, looking for the owner of the question. When he found the boy he echoed the question in a barely restrained voice. The kind of voice promising an eruption. "Reward?" he said. "You ask what is your reward?"

He rose from his chair and the boys collectively shrank back. "Why, the kingdom of heaven is your reward!" His booming voice filled the empty space. He glowered at the boy until the child visibly shook. "And that is enough!" He held the silence until he saw every boy in his charge too terrified to blink. He sat down again.

To this group of coltish boys, heaven seemed an obscure and meaningless trophy. No matter how many times he told them, all that really mattered to them was that they were fed and had a dry place to sleep. They willingly did anything for those creature comforts. They stole for him, brought him the filched goods, and they endured the few times they were beaten for the small measure of security that he offered.

The man scrutinized his questioner. "Come here, boy," he said.

The child tentatively stepped forward.

"Do you, child, understand the sacrifice Our Lord made to free you of your sins?"

The boy didn't respond. Though his naïvety had made him bold, his instincts told him to be wary.

Here stands the spawn of a heathen, thought the former monk. His eyes narrowed and he saw the nebulous gray aura of an infidel standing before him. He wondered how the boy had managed to avoid exposure to the church for so long. Well, it was his mission to make the child know God.

"Our Lord died for your sins," he began. "He endured the excoriating ridicule of hanging on a cross for you. He wore a crown of thorns and never spoke against the men who did this to him. As Christians, we, too, must suffer the calumny of misunderstanding as proof of our faith. We gladly welcome the opportunity to prove our love of God." His voice had softened, lulling the boys into false tranquility.

"Luke!" the man's voice boomed. "Come here."

The group snapped alert. Luke hesitated. He knew how this would go. Others nudged him forward—the sacrificial lamb.

"Luke," said the man when the lad cowered before him. "So it is written, *triginta vulneris absterget mala et plagae; purgatis plagae in secretioribus ventris.*" He then addressed the group, noting their petrified faces. "And what does that mean?"

An unenthusiastic murmur recited in unison, "'Thirty blows that wound cleanse away evil; beatings make clean the innermost parts.'"

When they had finished, the man nodded in approval. "What is your name, boy?" he asked of the newcomer.

"I am Thomas."

"Thomas, you shall come to know your God by our works. What I do, I do in the name of Our Lord, for Him, so that you will be welcomed into His kingdom."

The man rose from his chair and went to a tall ledge and retrieved a carved wood stick with leather strips attached. At the sight of the implement, the boys' eyes grew round and there was a collective intake of breath.

"Luke."

The child trembled.

"You do not want to end like the boy at St. Mary Magdalen's church."

"Nay, sir," Luke vehemently confirmed.

He addressed the group, "Each of you must do penance with a chaste heart." He looked at Luke. "Remove your jerkin and smock."

The child closed his eyes a long second, then did as he was told. He handed his clothing to the new boy and began shivering.

"Turn around, boy."

With tears already streaming down his cheeks, Luke faced the coterie of cutpurses.

Then came the sickening sound of whip to skin. Luke cried out and reaped a second, ferocious blow for his outburst.

Thomas stood openmouthed, stunned, too scared to move. He snuck a glance at the other boys who were staring at the ground in front of their feet. No one came to Luke's rescue. No one questioned the monk's harsh handling.

Halfway through the beating, the lashes lost their crisp violence, but continued until thirty strokes had been delivered. When finished, the man dropped into his chair and bowed his head. His lips moved as if he was talking to himself.

Luke, having braced himself against the sting and impact, remained standing throughout the ordeal. He had difficulty straightening, but took his clothes from Thomas without meeting his eye. The boys parted to let him through.

Feeling as if he were to blame for Luke's punishment, it was with some relief for Thomas when his master spoke.

"Thomas," said the man, finally looking up. "Dress Luke's wounds and give him drink."

CHAPTER 9

While some boys watched vendors and streetsellers for the chance to steal, some watched others for the chance to roll an iron hoop off a broken barrel. A ruckus of shouts and heads bobbing past his window drew Huet from Jane Clewes's rent. He followed the noisy boys down the lane and around the corner, delighting in their sport.

As best as he could tell, the object was to keep the hoop rolling. They chased after, whacking it with a flattened plank of wood to keep it spinning. Huet watched as the ring gathered speed down a smooth stretch of road and became excited when it got away from them and headed straight for a water bearer.

The unsuspecting woman labored under the weight of her yoke and jugs. Even if she knew she was headed for disaster, there was not enough time for her to change course. Huet understood this and thrilled to see what would happen next.

One valiant dark-haired boy ran after the hoop, his arms flailing as he tried to control the added momentum from the pitch of the road. The other boys stopped in their steps, anticipating an impending collision.

At the last second, the woman realized her misfortune, and her only reaction was to try turning away from the iron ring. The boy ran up just as the hoop hit her side, upsetting a jug of water, which spilled in the lane.

The force caused her to slip and she landed on her side, both jugs toppling over. She cursed after the boy and the wasted effort of toting two heavy jugs.

Aware that he was the cause of the woman's distress, the dark-haired boy had not the courage to own his part in the mess. He recovered his hoop and ran back up the hill in pursuit of his friends, who had stayed long enough to get an eyeful and then abandoned him.

Torn between watching the woman curse and following the mischievous boys, Huet chose the more merry of the choices and with a hopeful smile loped after the ragamuffins in pursuit of their next adventure.

Huet found them one street over, laughing and imitating the woman. The dark-haired boy who had gone after the ring stood a little to the side, a half smile on his face, watching.

"I think we should go back and help her," he said.

"Aws. Ye know how heavy them jugs be?" noted one of the imps.

"That is why we should help her. No doubt she filled them from the conduit at Charing Cross. It's a trek."

Another lad piped up, "People are always getting knocked over. It could have been anyone who'd made her spill."

The boy protesting the weight of water jugs grabbed the ring and shooed him away. "If ye be so concerned, then go help her. Ye can be the kindly neighbor. But don't be surprised if she curses ye instead." With a dismissive toss of his head he set the ring to rolling and the hellions instantly forgot the incident to follow after.

The dark-haired boy watched them go, then looked back as if

trying to decide what to do. He noticed Huet standing in the middle of the road staring at him. "What do ye want?"

Huet didn't respond. He just stood there. He watched the clutch of boys disappear around a corner.

The boy frowned, scrunching up his eyes with distrust. "Ye thinking of following them?" he asked. He tipped his head sideways like an inquisitive dog. "Methinks ye is too old to run with the likes of them!"

Huet blinked at the rascal who had just rejected him. His gaze dropped to the ground. The cruel sting of disappointment made his gut begin to churn, urging him to lash out. He resisted its rebuke, but it gnawed and scolded him.

He looked up, ready to lunge for the dark-haired boy.

But his questioner had already gone.

Fisk ran to the end of the road looking for his band of friends, and, not seeing them in the crowded streets, abandoned them to listen to his guilty conscience. It sat on his shoulder and boxed his ear to the point where he circled back to find the water bearer whose load he had caused to spill.

She was nowhere in sight.

Relieved of an unpleasant hour refilling and toting water jugs, he instead trekked beyond Newgate to Smithfield, where he collected arrowheads and sold them back to an arrowsmith on Bowyer Row. With coin in hand, he bought himself a roasted chestnut which he gobbled. Afterwards he felt remorseful having indulged, so he spent the remainder on bread for his mother. His adventures over for the day, he headed home.

At the head of Ivy Lane, Fisk slowed when he saw his mother talking with a tall, coarse-looking man outside their rent. His jerkin was worn and soiled. His beard was in need of a trim. Fisk had never seen the fellow before. His instincts told him to slip into the shadows and listen.

"Think on what your husband would say if he knew the truth."

"And shall you sail to France to tell him? Take yourself and your threats elsewhere. I've no time for this." Fisk's mother started to close the door but the man planted himself firmly on the threshold.

"The war is over. He shall soon return," he said.

"The skirmish in France will continue," said Fisk's mother. "Mayhap you hear the news from Scotland and think it is of France that they speak. I will not listen to hearsay, nor should you. Not until I see him with my own eyes will I believe the fighting is over. The French are as stubborn as our king. My husband is not coming home anytime soon."

"All the more reason for you to consider my offer." He rocked back on his heels in a superior stance. "What man abandons his wife to feed four mouths with nothing but her wits to keep them alive?"

Her voice rose. "He did not abandon me. He did as much as he could. Children grow and they eat more."

"Two hands to work, one mouth to feed. Send him to me. I will make more and you shall receive his wages."

"I will not. You had better leave."

"Fool woman. Do ye not trust me?"

"Ha! I trusted ye ten years ago and then ye left me to mend the damage."

"I was a reckless man. But that is in the past. I have come to make amends."

"Ye have come to take advantage. Now, get away. I'll hear no more of it."

The man's tone became threatening. "Ye will regret this," he warned.

But Fisk's mother had heard enough. She gave him a forceful

shove and slammed the door in his face.

The man cursed and beat on the door.

If Fisk were older he'd demand the fellow to leave. If the man refused, he would have punched his face and sent him running instead. But the man dropped his arms to his sides and stood a moment. He stepped back and studied the front of the building. Fortunately, the shutters were lashed from the inside so there was no easy entry for the man to exploit.

Fisk watched the cozen from his cover of shadow, and saw the man's dark eyes and the weary circles under them. What had this man done ten years ago that had made his mother so bitter? And what did he mean "two hands to work, one mouth to feed"? The man had long limbs and a narrow chest, reminiscent of his own gangly physique. It was difficult to tell, but the man's hair looked black. As black as his own.

A thought occurred to Fisk that fell into the pit of his stomach.

He was ten years old.

This man was so unlike the father who had gone to fight Henry's war in France. This man was coarse and slippery. The visitor turned and started up the lane in his direction. Fisk decided too late that he should have run. Instead, he crouched behind a barrel and listened to the man's steps squish in the fetid mud, then stop.

CHAPTER 10

Jane Clewes felt for loose strands of thinning hair and tucked them under her coif with trembling fingers. She set down her reading, a pamphlet she'd purchased near St. Paul's. She opened her door a crack and stuck her nose out, her pale eyes darting about, checking for passersby. Satisfied that no one was about, she took her trowel and stepped out upon the row of moss-mottled bricks that constructed her stoop.

She and Huet had the corner rent on a well-traveled lane. The entry was on the side of the building along a narrow path that ended at the back door of a second tenement broadside to their own. This dour rent was all she could afford. For a while she'd earned a little extra with her stitching, but now her shaking hands made it impossible to thread a needle. Instead, she'd recently taken up spinning wool. She was quick at it and had already finished the batts she'd been given.

Jane kept a wary eye out for inquisitive neighbors while searching for a spot where she could dig a hole, given her limited strength. She found an area partway down the path toward the back residence and knelt to scrape away the layer of rotting leaves to get to the spongy ground beneath.

They had not lived there long. She wanted to avoid the gossip that would certainly have circulated had she stayed in her previous residence. A woman such as she, living alone, then suddenly and inexplicably accompanied by a young man, had stirred people's notice. People with their spiteful stares. She feared their questions and had successfully avoided them by moving when she felt the heat of their curiosity warm her face. How would she explain it? She wouldn't. And her silence would have incited hurtful speculation—the kind she could no longer endure.

To her way of thinking, she had spent a lifetime paying for her sins, and she saw no need to compound her sorrow now.

Jane heard voices in the lane and got to her feet, hiding the trowel behind her back. If anyone asked what she was doing she would say she was planting an acorn. Let them think she was mad. Better that than the truth.

But no one cared. No one even noticed.

"There," she said, sizing up the divot she'd dug. She went back inside and returned carrying a squirrel, its limp body draped across the blade of her trowel. Despite her efforts, the hole was not long enough, so she curled the animal into a ball then covered it with the damp, cool soil. Even animals deserved a prayer. She recited a short one, then tamped the ground with her shoe.

"You'll not be bothered anymore," she said. "I warned ye." She pointed the trowel at the mound of dirt. "I told ye not to bite him. He knows not the nature of beasts." She clucked her tongue, staring down at the little grave, thinking *What a shame.*

A gust of wind channeled down the narrow path and the cold seeped through her layers, through her heavy woolen kirtle, and straight to her bones. She hurried back to the tenement and put the trowel on the stoop, needing both hands to release the stubborn latch. The door finally gave. She bent over for the implement—and a small leather pouch caught her eye.

It lay against the bricks as if purposely placed there to escape the notice of anyone passing by on the lane. It could only be seen from the other side of the stoop. Jane glanced around. No one was near to claim it, so she snatched it up. She cautiously loosened the drawstring and poked her finger inside.

She gasped. Five crown! She cinched the pouch tight and clenched it in her fist. What she could do with that. She hurried inside and secured the door.

Never in her life had she found a sum of money. Was it a gift? She glanced up, half expecting to see an angel smiling and applauding her. Or had someone put it there for safekeeping? Surely if it were the latter, whoever left it would soon be back to collect it. She checked the door again and threw the second bolt. What if they broke down her door and accused her of stealing?

But how would they know that it was she who had taken it? Her legs shaking, she went to a rickety stool and sat. Someone else could have taken it just as easily, she reasoned.

Jane shook her head. Nay, she must give it to the parish. She'd give it to Father Rhys. That was the gracious way to handle this. Though she desperately needed the funds, she remembered that a heavenly reward must take precedence over an earthly one. She must be charitable. "Faith must be shown by my good deeds," she declared.

But what if someone *gave* it to her? What if someone left it there for her to find? Jane furrowed her brow, thinking. Then she should keep it. But who would be so kind? Who even knew that she was there? She gasped. Someone knew her situation, she had been found out! Her body tensed. She'd been so careful.

She went to the window and cracked open the shutter, searching the lane. A cat slinked along the building opposite, keeping to the shadows. The bells of St. Andrew's chimed in the distance. She then went to the window on the side of the more traveled road. No one paid any notice of her.

Jane turned her back against the window and leaned against it, clutching the bag of coin to her bosom. For the time being, she could hide the purse of money. She would keep it safe. Besides, she didn't have to decide what to do that very moment. After all, God took seven days to create heaven and earth. She could take her time, too.

And she would watch. She'd find out who left the purse of coin by her stoop. She'd be ready when they returned.

Bianca left the shop on Paternoster Row and sought Meddybemps at Newgate Market close by. If she hurried, she could catch him before he left for the day. Not only did she want to see how her new tincture was selling, but she wanted to find out if he had heard about the boy at St. Mary Magdalen's.

She picked out Meddybemps's ubiquitous red cap in a sea of brown and black toppers, and, when she neared his vending cart, she heard his familiar voice trying to charm a woman into buying one of his talismans.

The final sale of the day often brought out the poet in him, and he threw propriety to the wind as he pattered—

> A maid did sleep in her good man's keep,
> Notta me, notta yew, notta too,
> When at her door, came a knock of four,
> Notta me, notta yew, notta too.
> Open maid and let me in
> Notta me, notta yew, notta too.
> For your true love I hope to win.
> Notta me, notta yew, notta too.
> Oh nay, my man would like it not!

Notta me, notta yew, notta too.
He'll see the soup gone half a pot!
Notta me, notta yew, notta too.
Some warmth I need, I speak this true.
Notta me, notta yew, notta too.
Look on my feet they are doth blue!
Notta me, notta yew, notta too.
The maid obliged and let him in,
Notta me, notta yew, notta too.
And half the day they spent in sin.
Notta me, notta yew, notta too.
I've never ate such lovely stew
Notta me, notta yew, notta too.
My feet are warm, no longer blue
Notta me, notta yew, notta too.
He wiped his mouth, and bid farewell
Notta me, notta yew, notta too.
Her pot still full, but she won't tell.

Meddybemps covered his mouth in a coy pretense at surprise, then with a hint of glee grandly bowed before the goodwife. "This one doth suit the apple blush of your cheek, m'lady." He removed a necklace from his display and laid the locket against his dark sleeve. It had a red rose painted on its surface—a finer item than his usual fare of turtle skulls and iridescent beetles preserved with lacquer.

The woman swelled from Meddybemps's attention, and after some flirtatious dickering parted with her coin.

"Goodwife, none shall wear it better than you. Forsooth, our queen in all her riches, dressed in a hundred emeralds and rubies, does pale by comparison. You shall regret it not." He then hung the pendant about her neck and stood back to admire her. He pressed a hand to his heart as if she took his breath away. "Exquisite," said he. "Fare thee well, fine beauty. This charm shall bring you much pleasure." He watched her leave, waiting for her to look back one last time, and when she did, he blew her a kiss, thus sealing the deal.

"You are a master of false flattery, sir," said Bianca, watching his performance.

"But no one returns the goods, unsatisfied." Meddybemps's wayward eye danced. "My method benefits you. Those skeptical of a liquid in a bottle are convinced once I finish wooing them. Though I admit, it is a rare person who does not know about the remedies that I sell. If needed, a little persuasion tips the scales."

"You do not tell them my name, I hope," Bianca reminded him. King Henry had deemed it treasonous to practice witchcraft or conjuration. She didn't want her work to be misconstrued.

"It is our agreement," assured Meddybemps. "I should not like to see you hanged for sorcery."

The two had known each other for years. On the surface one might wonder what the unlikely pair saw in each other. Originally, the streetseller had noticed Bianca trying to steal one of his amulets from his barrow. It was a dragonfly with delicate lacy wings and bulbous blue-green eyes. She had watched him from a discreet distance, and when she finally made to nab the piece, Meddybemps caught her by the wrist and wouldn't let go. She struggled, and after enduring an impertinent stream of name-calling from a seven-year-old girl, he managed to convince her that he had no intention of turning her over to the uncertain mercies of a constable. What became clear to him and what he found admirable was her boundlessly inquisitive nature.

She didn't ask the questions most children asked, such as *Why is your eye crooked?* or *Why do you sing to customers?* Instead, she studied his offerings with a studious eye and asked questions that had never occurred to him, nor could he answer to her satisfaction.

For such a young mind, he felt challenged by her, which intrigued him.

As for Bianca, Meddybemps's appeal was more difficult to understand. Perhaps she appreciated his wiliness, or his irreverence for authority. Perhaps she admired his skill in convincing customers to buy his goods. More likely though, Meddybemps was the surrogate father she had always longed for.

Whenever her own father, Albern, met someone, he immediately determined that person's usefulness to him. He collected and categorized people like they were containers in his alchemy room. Some were utilitarian and could hold anything. He could fill them with all kinds of caustic material and they never visibly suffered from their burden. Others were too fragile for such, but perhaps they were pleasing to look at or had another specific purpose. Bianca's usefulness was somewhere in between. She could work hard and was of some intelligence, but Albern had never appreciated the pleasures of watching her grow or rediscovering the world through a child's eyes.

So it was that Bianca relied on Meddybemps for her livelihood, for advice, and, though neither of them ever mentioned it—for love.

However, an iciness had developed of late, stemming from Meddybemps's involvement with Bianca's mother and her father's discovery of a dangerous element. Meddybemps insisted he had acted to protect Bianca and her mother. Bianca listened to his argument and understood it, but the layer of lies she'd struggled to peel away had shaken her faith in him. She was certain that the truth, or the semblance thereof, still eluded her, and perhaps it always would.

So for the last ten months a layer of ice had glazed the foundation of their friendship, and they stood on its slippery surface—for they each carried the knowledge of the other's secret.

Secrets that could ruin either of them.

"Have you sold any bottles of my remedy for spring sniffles and sneezes?" she asked, looking over his cart.

"Indeed! Those beset with the annual nuisance have taken kindly to its purported benefits. It may be weeks before we see the grass turn green, but they snatched it up and will try it at the hint of itchy eyes and unremittingly drippy nostrils."

"I delivered ten bottles last week."

Meddybemps pointed to the two bottles he had left. "See there? I do not say it just to please you. I shall soon need more."

Bianca sighed, wondering if she had enough dried butterbur root to make another batch. She didn't fancy tromping through the muddy lowland beyond Paris Garden to dig it up.

Meddybemps secured the contents of his cart. "Methinks you should consider hiring someone to help you with your remedies. There are enough earnings you can pay someone a few pennies. She could collect ingredients, or bottle your medicines. Even deliver them to me. You might think on it." He took up the handles and looked up at the sky. "God's foot, the day is gone by. I've sold well enough to leave."

Bianca followed Meddybemps as he maneuvered his barrow through Newgate Market past other merchants closing for the day. His cart showed signs of wear, and creaked loud enough for people to part and let them through. Its wheels were not true, and the streetseller's life would be easier if he would take the time to replace the cart's axle. Bianca thought of mentioning it, but Meddy was the sort who would not lose a day of sales unless he was on his deathbed, and even then he'd try to sell the priest an amulet.

Once they were free of the bustle of market, Bianca joined his side and the two made their way toward the Cockeyed Gull, Meddybemps's boozing ken of choice. The ale was potable and the wenches tart, just to his liking.

On a quieter street, Bianca asked if he had heard what had happened at St. Mary Magdalen's.

"Nay," said Meddybemps. "I never pay any mind to parishioner gossip."

"It is not gossip. A boy was found hanged from a dripstone."

"God's blood. Over a window?"

"Aye. A dragon grotesque."

"Jesu," said Meddybemps. "How did he get himself up there?"

"I don't believe it was self-murder."

"How now?"

"He had a peaceful look on his face."

Meddybemps stopped pushing his cart and leaned against it. He took off a shoe and turned it upside down, dislodging a pebble. "Mayhap he was glad for it. If he was a street boy then he had a hard life."

"By appearance he looked to be a street boy. No one knows who he is, so mayhap he was on his own. But that area is overrun with thieves."

"Bands of thieves run by driggers."

"Meaning someone is in charge?"

Meddybemps stamped his shoe back on. "I doubt there is one overseer for all those boys. Likely there are several, each with their own crew. It would be a difficult task finding out who was with what group. Then, too, these driggers keep out of notice. And the little rascals are a changeable lot."

"Why do you say that?"

"Because street boys are not constant. Their loyalty is to their next meal. It is a matter of survival."

Bianca thought on this. "Let us say that the victim joined a circle of cutpurses run by an overseer—a drigger—mayhap a man, but possibly a woman."

"I see no reason why it is a man's exclusive expertise. A

woman could just as easily control a clutch of rascals," he said.

"How would *you* go about finding that overseer?"

"Those sorts expertly disappear when they sense they are being sought. As I said, it would not be easy." The street vendor's strange eye quivered with anticipation. His skewed eyeball was his most noticeable trait. How rapidly it moved was a reliable gauge of his interest. "But I shall stay mindful of it. That is what you are asking of me, is it not?"

Bianca's mouth slid into a crooked smile. "Aye, it is." The frosty discontent that had plagued their friendship began to melt—if only just a little. "No one else has bigger ears than you."

"I shall make it my priority."

"One more thing," said Bianca, putting her hand on Meddybemps's arm. "Have you ever heard of a man named Brother Ewan?"

"Nay. Should I have?"

"Only if he is notorious."

Meddybemps left off at the Cockeyed Gull and Bianca hailed a ferry at Castle Baynard Stairs. The boatman eased them into the current and Bianca watched the sun drop behind a low bank of clouds. Until last year, she'd never felt particularly concerned crossing the river. It was just a matter of convenience, a relatively quick mode of transport from London to Southwark and back again. But since her accident, she could never step into a skiff without remembering that night. The night she nearly drowned. Or as Cammy insisted, the night she did drown.

Bianca still remembered the strange visage she saw under the water, the glowing green eyes that seemed to look into her soul and (for she was certain) had saved it. She would never tell anyone of the haunting dreams she had had when she was with child. Nor would she admit to anyone that fragments of those dreams still tormented her whenever she gave them thought. She still pondered their import, whether they were a message from beyond. But if a message—then what did they mean?

She touched the scar that ran across her cheek, now healed and faded to a thin, pink line. Another reminder of that fateful night—a visible scar along with the ones she suffered inside.

When she landed, she quickly stepped on solid ground, banishing her ruminations in favor of more practical matters. There was a boy's murder to explain and more medicines to make. Having help in her room of Medicinals and Physickes might benefit in more ways than one. Fisk needed to make money for his family and it would keep him out of trouble. Tomorrow she would seek him out at his mother's near Ivy Lane and ask if she might employ him.

She passed by the South Gate, where the portcullis was being closed for the night, and listened to the slow, steady creak of iron and chain. She considered the St. Mary Magdalen's murder earlier in the day. The boy's serene expression confounded her. Usually the final moments of life are a battle to forestall and prevent death. A child so young in years had vitality. The will to live was implicit at that age. She didn't agree with Meddybemps that a child living on the streets would choose to end his own life rather than continue to live it, struggling day to day. To Bianca's thinking, only when death snuck up and caught someone at slumber could a victim appear peaceful. But here was a child that showed no indication of illness or serious injury other than a broken neck. Why did he not struggle? She could think of no explanation.

Bianca sighed, imagining John admonishing her for getting involved in yet another murder. Certainly, if she had delivered their baby she would be home caring for their child instead of involving herself in an investigation.

"John, I do hear you," she said aloud, seemingly to a tree she was admiring. If someone had overheard, they would have thought her dotty. She picked up a fallen branch still covered in crisp leaves and pointed it at the sky—"I just don't always listen"—and she tossed it over her shoulder.

For now, she would ignore her nagging conscience and try to ignore her enigmatic dreams. Maybe she would never understand why they still haunted her. Dreams were phantoms—real at night and gone by day. And they left behind feelings of ambiguity. At least when she contemplated a murder, she knew an explanation was possible.

CHAPTER 11

Bianca woke to the insistent purr and pawing of Hobs trying to burrow under the covers. The black tiger had returned from his nightly exploits and had squeezed through the warped back door to find warmth and attention from his mistress. He flopped over appreciatively and submitted his striped belly for a good rubbing.

With John gone, the chill of the morning was only marginally improved by the cat's warm body against hers. She lay awake ordering her day and mustering the motivation to throw back the blankets and get dressed. She should at least make a tincture of the remaining butterbur, and once that was done she would go up to Ivy Lane and ask Fisk's mother if the boy could work for her. True, it would be a long walk and boat ride for him from their home near St. Patrick's Cathedral to Southwark and Gull Hole, but she decided to give him money for the boatman in addition to his pay.

Bianca teased Hobs into rabbit-kicking her, then leapt out of bed, leaving him wondering why the tussling could not continue. He indignantly jumped down and stayed underfoot until she gave him a slice of cheese.

Without John, Bianca had taken to talking to her immortal

companion, explaining her concoctions to him and telling him why she must mix septwort with meadowsweet and not mullein. Hobs listened, or gave the appearance of interest, but really he was just keen to be close by in the event that a crumb of the bread she was eating might fall to the floor.

She spent the next hour grating roots into a pile and preparing the herb to macerate with aqua vitae on a dark shelf until she needed it. When she had finished, she doused the fire in the calcinatory stove, dropped the paternoster in her pouch, and headed out the door.

The day was not so cold, and Bianca made the time to visit John's master, the French silversmith Boisvert. His residence on Foster Lane was near Ivy Lane where Fisk lived, and she strolled past St. Vedast church, the site of several unfortunate deaths she'd helped investigate. Scaffolding clung to the sides of the building, an elaborate crisscrossing of timbers and planks. The caved-in bell tower and roof were under repair and she was glad to see an effort being made to keep the church from falling into complete ruin. She wondered if the parish had undertaken the expense, or whether a wealthy merchant or nobleman had chosen to fund the project.

Arriving at Boisvert's address, Bianca rapped at the door and in a moment was greeted by the avuncular Frenchman. His round little body seemed even more so, and at the sight of her, his small eyes disappeared behind his plump cheeks as he smiled.

"The Bianca!" he exclaimed, effusing joy at the sight of her. "Come in, come in. Have wine with me."

"That is gracious of you, Boisvert, but I cannot stay. I am on my way to Ivy Lane." Bianca stepped inside to warm her hands. "I plan to take on an apprentice of my own."

Boisvert shut the door behind her. "To assist in making the remedies? Or are you loneful?"

"Truth be, it is both. I plan to ask Fisk." She unwound the scarf from her neck, then rewound it. "I shall teach him what plants to collect and have him fetch other ingredients."

"This is the same boy who helped you at St. Vedast?"

"Aye. He has helped me on more than one occasion."

"*Mais oui. Bon.* You should not be by yourself so long." He gave a wistful sigh. Bianca thought the silversmith was remembering his own betrothed, who died suddenly at their wedding celebration. He had never been interested in marrying until he met her, and his happiness had been painfully short-lived. However, it seemed that Boisvert had immersed himself back into his work and was none the worse, despite losing his two closest contacts.

But he surprised her. "I miss John's company," he admitted. "Have you any news of him?"

"Only that there are rumors that the fighting in Scotland is drawing to an end."

"Ah! Then he may return home in not so long?"

"I cannot say. I should like it to be so." And this time Bianca sighed.

Boisvert tilted his head and looked at her fondly. "We must believe it to make it so."

A shift in the wind greeted Bianca as she stepped back onto the street. She crossed her arms and tucked her hands under her armpits to keep them warm for the short walk to Ivy Lane. Once there, she remembered the added element of cold in that neighborhood, with its overhanging second stories and lack of penetrating sun. The tenement where her mentor Ferris Stannum had lived appeared now to be occupied again. A sliver of light from a lantern glowed from within, shining through the gap between shutters. The excessively uneven stoop out front had been replaced with a level stone.

As Bianca approached Fisk's door, the piercing cry of a child and the muffled voice of an adult carried through the thin walls to the street. It was no wonder that the boy preferred to spend as much time as he could outside. Indeed, that is how she first met him.

He had been sitting outside on the stoop when Bianca had investigated Ferris Stannum's unexpected demise. An innocent child can be easily ignored by adults. Children tend to blend into the background—but Bianca had discovered that Fisk possessed an observant eye and curiosity that reminded her of her own. Indeed, he'd been instrumental in providing information that had helped her solve her mentor's death, in addition to helping her solve the deaths connected with St. Vedast church.

With her first knock, the door abruptly swung open as if someone had been expecting it. Fisk's mother stood inches away with a crying toddler balanced on her hip. Her hair was unkempt, she wore no coif, and both her eyes and her baby's were swollen from crying. No doubt they had been upset for different reasons. The expectant look on the woman's face startled Bianca, but was quickly replaced with recognition. Fisk's mother had characteristically regarded her with a level of suspicion or, perhaps, distrust. However, today, that palpable wariness fell away.

"Bianca Goddard," she said. "Have ye news of my boy?"

"News? Are you referring to me speaking with him yesterday?"

"He never came home last night. He left in the morning and that be the last I saw of him."

Bianca had always thought poorly of the woman's indifference toward her son. In many ways, their relationship echoed that of Bianca and her father. Perhaps with the husband gone to war, mayhap she had come to rely on her son more. Bianca had gathered that Fisk had matured a little and was taking his responsibility seriously.

"Then you are concerned that he was out all night?" asked Bianca.

"He has always come home for bed." She set her toddler on the ground, and the child hid behind her skirt.

Bianca remembered what Fisk had told her about Brother Ewan, and worried that he'd ignored her warning to avoid him. The sight of the street boy hanging from the dripstone flashed through her head.

"You gave him no cause to stay away for the night?"

The woman's voice turned dark with anger. "What do ye imply?"

"Could there have been a squabble that upset him enough to stay out? Mayhap his absence is purposeful. Mayhap he would like to be appreciated more." Bianca wished no ill will between the mother and son, but she preferred this explanation over Fisk missing because of this monk he told her about.

"Have ye a child?"

Bianca's eyes dropped and she replied softly, "Nay. I do not."

"Then methinks ye should not speak of what ye know nothing about."

Bianca realized she must have sounded accusatory, and tried a softer tone. "Goodwife, I mean no disparagement. You manage better than I under such difficult circumstances. When I saw Fisk he told me his father is fighting the king's war."

"Aye," she said in a small voice and glanced away.

"If no harsh words were between you, then there must be a reason for him staying away." Bianca didn't mention the monk. She thought perhaps she should keep that to herself in case there was more to be learned from Fisk's mother. As she stood there watching the woman push her hair from her face, Bianca noticed a fair-haired girl watching from across the room. She assumed her to be

Fisk's younger sister. The last time Bianca had seen her it was she who had hidden behind her mother's skirt. The girl had lost some of that early innocence and from the look on her face, Bianca sensed she had something to say.

"Remind me of your name," asked Bianca to the child, offering her an opportunity to speak.

The girl opened her mouth, but cast an anxious glance at her mother, who must have warned her off with a stern look.

"That is Anna," said her mother. Her voice became stern. "Anna, come take your little sister and leave us be." She pushed the toddler in the girl's direction. "This is a matter for grown women."

Anna pinched her lips into a tight line and dutifully led her sister from the room.

"I have to remind her that she must help me. It is different for a girl. She can't go wandering off like her brother. She needs to understand that."

"Did she have any thoughts about Fisk's disappearance?"

"Nay," the woman scoffed. "Ye can't believe half of what she says. She's full of ideas and all of them are preposterous."

"When was the last time she saw Fisk?"

The mother thought a moment. "Yesterday. She said Fisk had been chased at market."

"Chased. Did Anna see who chased him?"

Fisk's mother hesitated before speaking. "A man."

"Did Anna say why he chased Fisk?"

The woman wasn't going to admit that her son had been stealing, even if Bianca suspected it to be true. The mistrust the woman had previously felt toward Bianca rekindled. Bianca could read it in her face.

"Likely he got himself underfoot," said his mother. "The boy is always going where he shouldn't." Despite the intentionally diverting answer, Bianca could hear the worry leaking from the corners of her words. If Fisk's little sister had any useful information, it would have to wait until Bianca could speak to her alone. From the way the woman's eyes avoided hers, Bianca sensed Fisk's mother was holding something back. What that was, Bianca didn't know.

Realizing she would learn nothing more, Bianca got to the reason for her visit. "The reason I stopped by was that I wanted to offer Fisk work. I'd like him to help me in Southwark."

"Doing what?" asked the mother, suspicion in her voice.

"I need someone to help collect plants and assist me in making remedies."

"The child cannot distinguish the leaf of a sage from a daffodil."

"It would not be difficult for him to learn."

Fisk's mother snorted with doubt.

Bianca thought it unforgiveable that she would so underestimate her son's abilities. No wonder Fisk preferred being outside to listening to her hurtful remarks.

"Goodwife, I can see that you are worried he has not come home," she said. "But boys often make mischief and forget themselves. When he returns, will you send him to Southwark to talk to me?"

Fisk's mother gave a quick nod, but her distraction gave Bianca cause for doubt.

For whatever reason Fisk had not come home, something was amiss. His mother's peevishness alarmed her. Fisk was a bright child, and though Bianca wanted to believe there was a reasonable explanation for him to be missing, she could not dismiss the notion that he might be in danger. She had warned him away from this supposed monk and she wondered if he'd run afoul of the character. But neither could she dismiss the notion that his mother knew more than she was willing to tell.

Chapter 12

Father Foxcroft left the printer on Old Change, and, once in the lane, crossed himself and took a calming breath. He had struggled to keep an even temper, and the chance to slam a door behind him would have left no doubt in the fellow's mind as to where he stood on the matter. But, thought Foxcroft, he needed to be more careful. A man in his position aspiring to a greater one needed to watch himself.

After all, every word he spoke could influence his future. One never knew who might overhear and go galloping to Bishop Bonner in the hopes of crushing his ambitions. But one thing was for certain: If he was ever appointed archdeacon, he would put an end to these printers spreading ideas of religious reform.

To be honest, the call for reform was nothing new. Clergy had always been accused of abusing their wealth and power, and of profiting at the expense of others. These accusations were not unfounded. He knew of priests and even monks who had taken women into their beds. And, true, he had enjoyed some wealth and had partaken of sumptuous meals paid for by the hard work of parishioners, tenant farmers, and sheep herders, and had enjoyed the extra money he'd got from reciting prayers of indulgence. He knew he was not completely innocent but, thought he with a self-righteous lift of his chin, *his* transgressions were of the standard order; he was only following tradition. *His* excesses were not nearly as detestable as some.

In fact, since Cromwell's reforms, Foxcroft's efforts to lead his parishioners to salvation had been curtailed like all the others. Worst was that he could no longer collect for prayers of intercession for sinners. His relic of St. Stephen's index finger—that brown, leathery monstrosity—had been absconded with by Cromwell's commissioners. Father Foxcroft cursed the chief minister under his breath.

Before the king got it into his head that marrying his brother's wife was a sin, and therefore God was punishing him by refusing him a son, the priest had enjoyed a comfortable life and never wanted for anything. These people, these printers fomenting their ideas of reform—especially those extolling that heretic Martin Luther—were ruining hundreds of years of precedent.

And now this particular fellow he glimpsed over his shoulder at the shop's door—dispensing pamphlets to keep the names of their supposed "martyrs" fresh in the memory of naïve Londoners.

Still grumbling over their heated exchange, Father Foxcroft sought a colleague at St. Benet's church. If Father Wells was not of similar mind, at least he would be a man of similar principles with whom he could commiserate. He trudged down Bennet's Hill, passing what appeared to be three more printers. At one of these he stopped long enough to peer through the window fogged with condensation. Between the streams of water coursing down the glass he got a better look, but he couldn't see what that fellow was busy printing. He riled, thinking that it was probably another pamphlet inciting the masses to gossipmongering. No doubt the fellow printed a treatise of lies intended to stir religious dissent and to encourage people to be suspicious of clergy. There seemed to be no end to the number of people willing to spread malicious content.

Arriving at St. Benet's, Foxcroft strolled into the apse and, not seeing Father Wells, sought him in the sacristy. There he found the man organizing his vestments, smoothing out a silk stole and laying a second one on top.

The men greeted one another. Father Wells took a chair and invited Foxcroft to sit.

"I wanted to share my concern with you about the unfortunate event at St. Mary Magdalen's."

"It is a sad occurrence," Wells agreed.

"Have you heard if they have learned the name of the victim?" asked Father Foxcroft.

"So, it is determined the boy was a victim? This was not self-murder?"

"They think it unlikely that a boy would climb to such a great height for the purpose of hanging himself."

Father Wells nodded.

Foxcroft repeated. "Then you have not heard if they have discovered his name?"

"I have not," answered Wells.

"We must reassure our parishioners that such an evil deed will not go unpunished. If the murderer is not found, we must remind them that he will ultimately face judgment before God."

Wells pressed his lips together and closed his eyes in assent.

Father Foxcroft could not be sure whether Wells's tranquility wasn't ennui. In fact, Wells appeared to have dozed off. Foxcroft's eyes dropped to the man's jeweled fingers. A large ruby graced his stumpy forefinger, though it could have been a garnet, he supposed. The priest's chin disappeared in a mound of jowls and his cheeks glowed from a healthy blush. Obviously, the man had enjoyed the benefits of a church under Rome and had refused giving up all the material gains he had accrued.

"I worry there will be more murders," Foxcroft said, attempting to spur the conversation.

Father Wells's eyebrows jumped and he opened his eyes. "What would lead you to think that?"

"I have a feeling."

"A premonition?" asked Father Wells, his eyes going slanty with suspicion.

Foxcroft ignored Wells's disapproval. Premonition, intuition, gut feelings—weren't they all the same? And what were they if not God's inchoate nudging? "What if it should happen again?" And here he leaned forward, staring intently at his fellow priest. "What if *your* church was targeted?"

"St. Benet's?" scoffed Father Wells. "Why would my church be the site of a murder?"

"Alas..." He leaned back. "The next murder could just as easily happen at St. Andrew's," he suggested charitably.

Wells tutted. "Why distress yourself unnecessarily, Foxcroft? All we can do is hope that they find the perpetrator and pray for protection from this evil."

"Father Wells, praying for protection from evil does not always prevent it from happening."

"What else do you suggest?" said Father Wells, eyeing his guest.

"I believe we must warn our flock against the vicious untruths that reformists and others are spreading."

"And how do you propose to do that? You cannot stop what has been put in motion."

"We must continue to refute the constant charges of corruption against us."

"The people will believe what they want," answered Wells. "It is the opinion of our king and his minister and it serves them well. The wealth no longer flows to the Continent or to us. We must live with this fact, sir, if indeed we want to survive."

Foxcroft thought what a blithe fellow this Wells. How accepting, how complacent. Foxcroft drummed his fingers on the armrests of the chair, feeling peevish.

"Wells, have you given any thought as to why the murderer chose St. Mary Magdalen?"

"Nay, I have not. It does not make sense for me to wonder why it occurred there. I do not think that Father Rhys is to blame—if that is what you are insinuating."

"I agree Father Rhys is blameless. However, it is human nature—and I am speaking here of our parishioners—to find someone to blame, whether or not they are culpable. And because the murder happened at his church, they may think Father Rhys is, in part, responsible for the incident."

"How do you mean?"

"Think on why the murderer chose his particular church. Of all the churches in London, he chose St. Mary Magdalen."

Father Wells squirmed in his chair. "Mayhap it was a matter of convenience," he suggested. "The church may have been close by. I cannot imagine carrying a body, even a child's, any distance. And then getting the body up to a tall window ..." He crossed himself and shook his head. "The church may simply have been a random choice."

"You think it random?" Foxcroft sniffed. "I disagree. Have you wondered whether the murderer harbored a grievance toward Father Rhys? Choosing St. Mary Magdalen's may have been the murderer's way of pointing a finger at Rhys—a finger of accusation."

"I have known Rhys for years. He is a virtuous man and a faithful servant," said Wells, rallying in his colleague's defense.

"There is no evidence for such an assertion." Irritated, he glared at his cohort. "I do not know what you are trying to foment here, but your allegation is unfounded, and if I may be frank, it is insulting."

"Oh, I am not accusing Rhys of any misconduct." Foxcroft waved his hand as if shooing away a fly. "I am only thinking out loud."

"Your line of thought troubles me, Foxcroft. These questions are better left to the magistrate and constable of the ward."

"I only wish to make you aware, Father. I believe we must prepare ourselves should any priest in Castle Baynard find himself in a similar circumstance."

Father Wells sat quietly. He pressed his fingertips together, considering his visitor over the tops of them. "Foxcroft, are you truly concerned for the priests of this ward, or is your distress due in part to your aspirations?"

Foxcroft jerked his head to attention. How tart of Wells to mention his ambition. He felt himself revealed, vulnerable that his objective had been sniffed out by his passive counterpart.

"I don't know what you mean," Foxcroft replied, then just as quickly regretted saying it.

"A man who worries over how he might appear is a man who believes he is being watched. And I wonder, Foxcroft, who do you think is watching you?" Wells's mouth turned up in a half grin. "Is it Bishop Bonner whom you wish to impress?"

Foxcroft squeezed the armrests of his chair. It was true that he aspired to become archdeacon under Bonner. With the position came wealth and prestige. The benefice he received for his duties at St. Andrew-by-the-Wardrobe was measly by comparison to what he could earn under Bonner. Who wouldn't want that? Was Wells jealous? Father Foxcroft did his best to feather his fall.

"Wells, it is our duty to offer our parishioners reassurance and solace. I cannot pretend that nothing has happened in Castle

Baynard ward. Mayhap your parishioners can ignore this tragedy and sally on, but I doubt that mine will.

"Times are uncertain and we both know it. We both know how careful we must be. Neither of us wants to be accused of resisting the king's mandate. He *is* the supreme head of our church. I am simply here to encourage you and our fellow priests of Castle Baynard that we must be careful. That is all."

Father Wells got to his feet and walked to the door, indicating his desire for Foxcroft to leave. "Sir, it is a caution of which I need no reminding."

Bianca left the neighborhood off Ivy Lane and walked to Constable Patch's office in the adjacent ward. Even though Patch had no authority in Castle Baynard, Bianca's concern was strong enough to keep working with him to find out what had happened. She had no intention of consulting Constable Berwick, preferring Patch's pretentious nature to a bombast and a sot.

So, in the interests of satisfying her curiosity and seeing a murderer brought to justice, she continued her investigation partnering with Patch. He did have some authority, she told herself, where she did not, and this often proved useful, but working with the man was never easy. He just couldn't stop himself from being a nuisance at the wrong time, and he managed to irritate nearly everyone he came in contact with.

Patch was busy goading a fellow he had locked away for skipping out of the Fell Inn one too many times without paying his tavern tab, when Bianca stepped through the door.

"Alewife Beth would like to see ye thrown in debtor's prison, Malloy. She says ye've run a string of promises for two weeks now. Ye owe a prodigal son."

The man closed one eye, momentarily confused. "I tolds her when my note comes through I'd pay her," he slurred, still sloppy from drink. He clung to the bars on the door in an effort to keep himself upright. His attire, while filthy from a street brawl, was of some station, so that his story might have had some truth to it. But neither the alewife nor Patch had any more patience.

"Patch," said Bianca, letting him know she was there.

The constable looked over his shoulder and expressed surprise. "I didn't expects to see ye so soon. Have ye anything for me?"

With a clatter, the prisoner collapsed in his cell and lay in a heap. The stool that had been placed there lay on top of him. After a moment the man emitted a pitiful moan.

Patch nudged him away from the door with the toe of his shoe.

"Claims he has a note from Edward Clinton, the first Earl of Lincoln, for services rendered." Patch snorted. "But the earl is on a galleon rocking back and forth off the south coast somewheres and can't honor it right now. He'll be going to Marshalsea debtor's prison until then." The constable sauntered back to the table that served as his desk and dropped himself into a chair with comfortable leather padding. He enjoyed the amenities of his office in London—a far cry from infamous Southwark where he had first started.

"I visited a shop on Paternoster and showed the proprietor the rosary. He thought it a common piece, of no particular value." Bianca withdrew the prayer beads from her purse and showed Patch the tiny carved letters. "I noticed letters carved in the back of the crucifix. I couldn't make them out on my own and I wondered if they had any significance. He believes it is a Y, an H, and an S."

Patch looked at the print and pulled his scraggly chin hair. "Did he know who made the paternoster?"

"He didn't think the letters were the initials of the maker. He thought they might be the owner's initials."

"That is not so helpful."

"He mentioned one other possibility. They might represent the cult of the Holy Name."

"The cult of the holy who?" Patch's brows met in a furrow. "It smacks of subversion."

"He said the cult is a group of Papists. Men whose loyalties remain firmly with the pope."

"So's we have a group of murdering Papists? Why, pray tell, would they murder a young boy and string him up?"

"I admit the idea is disturbing. If the boy's murder is meant as a message then I haven't any idea what their intent is," said Bianca.

From the back cell they heard the odious sound of retching. Patch scrunched his face in disgust.

"Have you learned if the boy has been identified?" asked Bianca.

"That beslubbering lump, Constable Berwick, refuses to share any information with me. I hads to find out by going back to ask the sexton. But, alas. No one knows his name. However, it is rumored that the boy was a filcher. Hisself was seen frequenting St. Paul's Walk to pick pockets. Justs another youth surviving by his wits. He likely got hisself in trouble and his death is probably his comeuppance."

"I wonder if he might have been a lone boy or whether he could have been with a group of cutpurses run by a drigger."

Patch shook his head, dismissing the notion. "It would surprise me not if driggers lived in Castle Baynard ward. But I've never heard tell of them here," said Patch, making a point of it.

"Mayhap we should find out more about these groups," said Bianca. The idea that another constable could be so remiss as to have bands of cutpurses running amok must have pleased Patch, for Bianca saw a glint in his eye. She quickly put an end to his arrogance. "I think, too, we should make sure there are none here."

Patch ignored Bianca's comment as if he hadn't heard it and

stared down at his popingay-blue doublet to brush off a minuscule piece of lint.

"And we must learn more about this cult of the Holy Name," added Bianca.

"Indeed, we must," said Patch, with tepid enthusiasm. "But let me remind ye that the city runs rampants with swindlers and people who exploit others. Driggers or nay."

"There is something else," said Bianca. "Fisk has gone missing from his mother's."

Patch stared at her with a blank look. He then realized who she was talking about.

"The boy who lived across from the old alchemist?" he asked.

"Aye. We had spoken earlier in the day. Apparently, a fellow named Brother Ewan asked Fisk to help him distribute food to the poor. In return he would take care of Fisk's family."

"Take cares of his family?"

"Give them food, I suppose. A young boy seeing his mother struggle to feed his siblings would be tempted. Have you heard of this fellow?"

"The Deft Drigger," spouted Malloy from under the stool. "There's a retched fellow. He should be sitting here in this cold, cruel cell—not me!"

"Stop ye nonsense, ye pribbling cur," said Patch.

Alarmed by the prisoner's outburst, Bianca thought it worth pursuing. "Sir, do you know of this Brother Ewan?"

Malloy, having snared her interest, attempted to stand. He only got as far as his knees before flopping over again. Bianca approached and looked down at him.

"Sir, I mentioned Brother Ewan. Is he known by another name?"

The sot rolled onto his back and blinked up at her. He motioned Bianca to come closer. Patch warned her off but she bent over, careful to keep back from the smell and his reach should he try to grab her ankle through the bars.

"Nay," said Malloy, attempting to sound serious. Then he broke into laughter with a loud guffaw. "Nay, I do not." He screaked in delight.

"Sir, you do not … what?" prodded Bianca.

"I do not …" His eyelids drooped heavily and he fought to open them.

"Ye do not what?" shouted Patch.

"… like yer face!"

Patch shook his head in disgust. "Worthless tosspot."

If Malloy hadn't passed out, Bianca would have pressed him for more. She wondered if this "Deft Drigger" was one and the same as Brother Ewan. Patch denied the existence of organized bands of thieves in his ward, so she would have to go elsewhere for answers.

Bianca left the ward office and searched the market for Meddybemps to tell him what she'd learned. The streetseller was nowhere to be found, having probably quit early. More than likely he had retired to the Cockeyed Gull. She could hardly fault him wiling away the day in a dry tavern rather than sit in the cold drizzle. With a mind for warming up before a boat ride home, she sought Meddybemps at his favorite boozing ken.

Through the mist of the soggy day, the carved likeness of a seagull decorated one side of the tavern's door. As if that were not enough signage, a placard swung from an iron bracket of a tipsy-looking bird, its one eye as crooked as the signage hanging by one hook. The other hook had been sprung free and whether caused by wind or by prank, Bianca appreciated the impertinent message.

She pushed open the door and the blue haze of smoke hovered over the seated clientele like a low-lying mist. In the corner a hearth coughed up the unhealthy smaze, logs smoldering and wheezing, too damp to burn properly. Meddybemps's red cap stood out in the gray brume like a beacon in the night, and Bianca followed it until she was sitting opposite the storied street vendor.

"Ho now," said Meddybemps. "I've seen you twice in as many days." He waved over a wench and ordered Bianca an ale and a trencher of stew.

The men at the table ogled Bianca appreciatively, and Meddybemps reminded them that she was too virtuous for the likes of their filthy hides and to stare at someone else.

"From the serious look on your face I fear there is important news," he said.

Bianca unwound her scarf and wadded it into a ball. "Fisk has gone missing."

"The young lad?"

"He never came home last night—so says his mother."

Meddybemps studied Bianca's face. "And you worry he might become a victim like the boy who was found at St. Mary Magdalen's?"

"I don't have any evidence or reason to believe that another murder like that would happen. But it gives me pause. He's not come home and the weather is not so mild. He's a stubborn boy; however, I think he would not willingly stay out in this cold and damp. And I still wonder who this Brother Ewan is and whether he has had any part in this."

"I am sorry that I have not learned anything about the man."

The wench arrived and set an ale before Bianca with a round loaf of bread scooped out and filled with vegetable stew. Bianca drowned a carrot bobbing on the surface. "However, it is possible that I have learned something. I visited Constable Patch, and he had a fellow named Malloy in a cell. Patch and I were talking about the possible driggers in Castle Baynard …"

"And did Patch deny knowledge of driggers in Bread ward?"

Bianca took a spoonful of stew and smiled as she blew on it. "He did. But while we were talking about Brother Ewan, Malloy suddenly said, 'The Deft Drigger—now there be a wretched fellow.'"

"He said that Brother Ewan was the Deft Drigger?"

"Not exactly. But it has got me wondering if they are one and the same."

Meddybemps took a sip of ale. "But you said this Malloy fellow was silly with drink. Such a man can babble on to no purpose and not remember a word after."

"Aye, he was squiffed beyond reason. But sometimes a person forgets himself and becomes less inhibited. A drunk spills secrets that he would otherwise keep."

"He may be less inhibited and more inclined to lie," said Meddybemps. "A drunk mind speaks a potty mouth."

"What I am saying is that if there is a connection, I need to find out what it is." Bianca's stew had cooled to where she could eat it without burning her tongue.

"I did learn," said Meddybemps, his eyes beginning to jitter, "that the boy found hanged had stolen from one of the butchers. Alas, I do not know which one. There are several at Westcheap Market and at any one time they may or may not be selling that day. This may not be so helpful, though."

"It is a start. I shall ask around. One might have heard of Brother Ewan or the Deft Drigger."

"Or mayhap one might know where you might find a band of young thieves living."

CHAPTER 13

Jane Clewes peered out the window of her rent searching the road for Huet. She'd sent him to the baker, a short distance away, confident that he could manage the errand without mishap. Yesterday, he had taken her basket to market and got eggs for dinner. It didn't matter that he would not speak, he was getting better at making himself understood.

But a big boy like him could become distracted. She stared out the window, trying to calm herself and the apprehension that needled her, for he was taking longer than she expected.

Huet had made great strides since he'd come into her care nearly a year ago. Seventeen years of neglect would be difficult for anyone to overcome. Providence had guided her to save him and Providence continued to guide her now. She relied on her faith, and she never missed a day of mass. To think Huet had never known the inside of a church until she came along. Verily, he had never prayed! Sometimes it was hard for her to comprehend. Odd, given that his care and placement had been undertaken by nuns.

She had searched for years, and when finally her path had led to London she had taken up residence in a tenement that had once been an old tavern. The building had partially burned, and a wealthy merchant bought the damaged building and converted it to accommodate the tide of newcomers, the country folk, the immigrants with hope in their hearts and only a penny in their pockets.

Jane came grudgingly to London. She'd heard stories of its grand bridge, of its fine palaces, and numerous, handsome churches. By all counts she should have been awestruck. But Jane cared not for the crowded city. The stench of its open-ditch latrines made her nauseous. And what good were awe-inspiring sites when she had to keep her head down to avoid stepping in rotting piles of food scraps dumped in the streets?

She believed London encouraged the worst in human nature. Everywhere she looked she saw evidence of excess and poverty at odds with one another—indeed, despising one another! Noblemen on their handsome mounts rode through town with their chins held level, ignoring the beggars running alongside them. All over was the rampant evidence of a struggling populace. And that struggling populace had no choice but to lie, cheat, and steal just to eat.

Though churches were on nearly every corner, and good parishioners followed their king's wavering ideas of religious reform, confusion and even indifference tainted their belief in God and pulled them further astray. Jane witnessed their infidelity. Her difficulty in finding anyone of pious disposition, or for that matter finding anyone trustworthy, had imbued her with a crippling sense of distrust. She kept to herself, went to confession, and tried to right the many wrongs done to Huet.

And Huet had flourished under her care, she reminded herself. Though he remained quiet, indeed silent, his eyes showed that he understood. He might always be mute, she told herself. She did not know if his silence was by choice or otherwise.

Jane felt a swell of pride thinking how much he'd improved under her care. When she first saw him, Huet was so dirty she could smell him across the room. His hands were meaty paws that held the stench of bowels and excrement that he had been made to scrub away. His hair hung in thick mats, crusted with sweat and infested with lice. The boy owned no change of smocks so that he always wore the blood-stained issue he'd been given nearly two years before. His jerkin was similarly christened and his soiled hosen were ripped at the knee from constant bending and washing. What did it matter that his clothes were not fine—they would be ruined after an hour of labor. For Huet had been tasked with cleaning scaffolds and platforms—those grim stages for executions.

She supposed with repetition came tedium and acceptance. One became numb to the gory details and probably no longer saw them as such, though she wondered what effects that exposure had on a person. If one had never known any better, one would not question his lot in life. He would not complain. And there lay the benefit in hiring such a boy.

Unfortunately for Huet, his nature had been exploited in a series of unfortunate circumstances that had finally led to Jane finding him in the service of the executioner at Tyburn Hill. It was hard for her to fathom the convoluted path, the detours and experiences that must have been his long journey. She only knew the gist of it, the few leads that had any credibility and that had aided in her search. The prioress had placed him in a loving home to start, but how was she to know that the parents would die of the pox and leave the babe with no one to care for him?

As Huet grew in physique, his head must have suffered from a lack of humors. Maybe they flowed abundantly to his lengthening limbs, and the ventricles of his brain lacked the fluids to nourish it. She did not know; she accepted the physician's explanation as plausible. It certainly might account for his refusal to speak. He might never partake in the joy of conversation, but she suspected he might know more than he was able to convey. With so many disappointments the frustrations must have been overwhelming, and Huet responded in the only way that managed to serve him.

If Jane crossed him, Huet would storm. His violence frightened her. She'd hide beneath a table, which was no easy task given her increasingly stiff joints. From there she would watch Huet lash out like an injured bear. Only this bear did not roar. Uncertain of the extent of his fury, she would watch in fear, daring to wonder if her death would one day be by his hands.

So she took care not to cross him.

Jane pulled a chair next to the window and began praying the rosary. She had almost finished her Hail Marys when she heard scratching from under the floorboard. Sparing a quick glance out the window, Jane went toward the sound and pushed aside the rushes covering a trap door. She'd found the hiding place by accident. At first, she wondered how it had come to be there and supposed it was born of seditious intent. Mayhap it was a place to hide Anabaptists or heretics.

Then she began to appreciate the security such a secret hideaway could offer. The more she saw of London and its abundance of strange people and its immorality, the more she questioned living there. Besides, one could never be sure which side of religion a person was on and whether it was a favorable position or not. It seemed to Jane that allegiances and the king's dictates changed as often as the seasons. Like Cromwell's commissioners, authorities could arrive unexpectedly and wreak havoc on a person's life.

She carefully untied the rope that held the door closed, then drew back the lid on its creaking hinge. She kept back, enough to avoid any surprise lunge, and peered into the dark recess.

"Ye shouldn't make trouble," she said, then skittishly glanced over her shoulder toward the door. Not seeing Huet, she continued, "There now. Be good. You know what happens when you make him angry. You saw the squirrel. It bit him. He didn't like that."

She went to her chest and tossed a small blanket into the hole. "There. That's something for now. Ye can stop yer shaking."

The words were no sooner out of her mouth before she heard Huet on the steps. She slammed down the lid and hurriedly tied the rope.

With a disquieting rattle of the door, Huet stepped into the rent just as Jane's toe kicked the last of the rushes into place.

While his prisoner slept off the effects of too much drink, Constable Patch left Cyndric in charge, instructing him to promise Malloy bread and water and then not bring him any. Cyndric needed to learn the finer points of making life miserable for any scoundrel who had the misfortune of being confined in his ward. In Patch's opinion, his associate lacked the necessary spine needed to be an effective keeper of peace and order.

Also on his mind floated the seriously neglectful Constable Berwick from Castle Baynard ward. Patch hated sots, and he especially hated men of authority who were sots. In a sense, he thought it his public duty to expose their incompetence—for there was no such thing as a competent drunk, thought Patch.

So it was with pleasure and a bit of simmering meanness that he decided to seek out the man and pester him.

Berwick's office was not so far from Bread ward. Patch strode down Knightrider thinking about Berwick's lack of cooperation and the man's refusal to inform him of any relevant news regarding the recent death. He found the man eating his dinner and eyed his spread of fare, the slab of roast beef smothered in ginger sauce, a bread pudding with sliced apples sitting prettily in a dish, and a bottle of wine uncorked and half gone. What constable could afford wine? Patch's irritation percolated. If he could contribute to a mighty case of indigestion then he would consider his visit a resounding success.

"Good day, sirrah," said Patch. He leveled a weaselly stare at the man.

"It was," said Berwick. He patted his mouth with a napkin draped over one shoulder, then took a sip of wine. "I would offer you some, but then, I only have this single goblet." His mouth curved into a specious smile. "You understand."

"I cames because there is talk of the victim at St. Mary Magdalen's running with a band of thieves." Patch's toes twinkled with joy. "After all, Castle Baynard is rife with filchers." He paused, letting the words soak through Berwick's wine-induced haze. "I was thinkings ye might have heard of a fellow called the Deft Drigger. He has a certain reputation."

Berwick set down his drink. "Nay, I have never heard of the man. It is a man, I assume?"

"We believe it to be." Patch continued. "Ye have lots of problems on the streets around St. Paul's. Ye have orphans and beggars sleeping against the cathedral walls at night. All sorts of mischief thereabouts."

Berwick pressed a fist against his chest and coaxed out a burp. "Every ward has its disreputable areas. Even Bread Street ward has its share of crooked broderers."

Patch remained unfazed. Crooked broderers were highly unlikely, and the insult fell flat. Patch never laughed, even derisively. One might think him incapable. But he afforded his comrade the vague hint of levity. He parted his lips and rocked his head forward and back in some semblance of mirth.

"Broderers, sirrah?" he responded. "The only offense those mousy needle-wielders are capable of is mayhap forgettins to pay their landlords. My ward is respectful and law-abiding."

Constable Berwick poured himself more wine. He swirled his goblet. "I seem to have forgotten the purpose of your visit, Patch."

Annoyed that he was not particularly succeeding in vexing the fellow, Patch repeated his desire to know if Berwick had any knowledge of the so-called Deft Drigger.

"I am sorry to disappoint you, Patch, but this fellow, this Deft Drigger, as you will, is the collective name of all successful overseers of cutpurses. There is no one conspicuous or noteworthy perpetrator for you to single out."

"So says ye," said Patch. The fellow likely didn't trouble himself with making the slightest effort to finding out. Either that, or he had a vested interest in ignoring the offender. Patch chose the latter—culpability over laziness. It seemed to suit Berwick's character. How else could the fellow afford wine with his dinner? "Methinks it is convenient for ye to want me to think that."

Berwick chuckled. "I wonder why you are so interested in this boy's death? Granted, it was unfortunate and a bit of a spectacle. It does raise questions if one gives it any thought, but the likelihood of his death mattering appears remote. I doubt such an incident is likely to repeat itself."

Patch glared at the arrogant sluggard and felt a wave of heat roll up his neck. His desire to prove Constable Berwick incompetent grew. Men such as he should not be tasked with keeping order in a ward.

"Berwick, I am interesteds in doing the duty vested in me by the Lord Mayor and his aldermen. It is a responsibility *I* take seriously." He was intending to remark upon Berwick's apathy when he was interrupted by a formally dressed young man entering the office abruptly. He had a protective hand on the flap of a satchel slung over his shoulder and across his chest.

Berwick held up a finger to silence Patch and motioned the

courier forward.

"A missive sir," said the fellow. He removed a sealed letter and handed it to Berwick, then left.

Berwick turned the letter over and noted the owner of its wax seal. "Bishop Bonner," he said. "I wonder what he could want." He laid the petition on the table next to his plate and continued eating. "Continue, my friend. I should not want to miss a word of what you have to say."

Patch watched distractedly and forgot his line of thought, so impressed was he by the Bishop's seal, its scarlet-colored wax looking so conspicuous and official.

Constable Berwick suppressed a smile, sensing Patch's jealousy. "As you were saying?" he prompted.

Flustered, Patch had no further words, but vowed silently to ruin this man. Colleague or not, at the very least he would see him humiliated.

Bianca left the Cockeyed Gull—frequented mostly by locals in its unassuming neighborhood in London, and went to the Dim Dragon Inn—less discreet, but also frequented by locals, this time in Southwark. Her kirtle and scarf were wet from the constant mist, and she submitted to the lure of friendship and a warming tankard of ale near home.

Though she could have walked back to Westcheap Market and started questioning the numerous butchers there, she felt perhaps the weather might be better tomorrow for traipsing around London. Realistically, she didn't know if Fisk was in danger. She sensed his mother was withholding information that might have informed her. But children could be sensitive and their feelings easily bruised. He could be intentionally staying away to worry his mother in the hopes that she would appreciate him more.

Once, when she was his age, Bianca had been upset by her

father's poor treatment of her mother and she ran off, so angry she didn't want to return. She spent a night near the derelict docks off Castle Alley, staring at the star-speckled sky and the lone wherries plying the river. That had been a warm summer night and this a cold, late winter one, but Fisk was of rugged stuff and, if given a good enough reason, she had no doubt that he could easily survive a night in the poor weather.

Bianca came through the door and saw Cammy eating a meat pie near the window. Her friend looked up and waved her over.

"Have a bite? It is freshly made."

"I've already eaten." Bianca sat down opposite.

"Then prepare for good news," said Cammy.

"Do tell," said Bianca, cheering at the idea of ending her day on a hopeful note. "I am eager for it." She waved to the tavern wench for an ale and gave Cammy her full attention.

"A ship arrived in port from Scotland. They say it is filled with plunder from the army's campaigns on the border. The army is strong with English Borderers. And the commander has successfully gotten the border Scots to swear their loyalty to the king."

Bianca's ale arrived and she took a drink, then cupped her hands around it.

"Should we assume the men are victorious?" she asked. "I suppose plunder is proof of their success."

"Aye," said Cammy enthusiastically. "The war is nearing an end. The men shall soon return!"

"That is our greatest hope," said Bianca. "But we mustn't expect it to happen just because a ship arrives with Scottish plate and sheep."

"There are sheep?" asked Cammy, taking Bianca seriously.

Bianca smiled. "Cammy, I know nothing more than what you told me. Granted, the news sounds promising, but we should not think that Scotland will bend easily." Cammy's expression fell, and Bianca felt sorry that she did not share her friend's optimism. One ship toting plunder was hardly worth getting hopeful about. "Mayhap, though," she added in afterthought, "they *have* been gone for months, and the numbers of men are in our favor."

Cammy, ever hopeful, spoke. "Bianca, John may soon come home. Do you not wish for him in your bed?" Then, not giving her friend time to answer she added, "Not a day passes that I don't fervently pray for Roger's safe return."

"Cammy, I wish for nothing less," said Bianca. Much to her dismay, her restraint was often mistaken for indifference. "Who brought word of this?"

"A crewmember. Who else would know better?"

Bianca kept her suggestions to herself. "It *is* cause for encouragement," she said.

Cammy finished the last of her meat pie and pushed her plate away, setting her empty mug on top. "I think of nothing but Roger," she said with a feathery look of love.

Bianca was less inclined to spells of wistful reverie, and Cammy's preoccupation wore thin as she considered Fisk and the unfortunate murder victim. "Cammy," she said, with the intent of returning her friend to a state of useful practicality, "have you heard of the cult of the Holy Name?"

Cammy's brow furrowed. "Nothing good comes to mind when I hear the word 'cult.'" She wiped her nose on the inside of her wrist. "It makes me think of ranting followers of God."

"Cults are convinced of their righteousness."

"Aye." Cammy nodded. "I saw that you were called away yesterday." She propped her chin in her hand. "A murder?"

"Constable Patch wanted my opinion in Castle Baynard. A boy was found hanged outside St. Mary Magdalen's church." Bianca informed Cammy of the findings and her friend listened intently. Details rarely upset Cammy, and Bianca attributed her friend's strong stomach to a childhood spent in the country. The only aspect of the murder that drew a reaction was learning that the victim was a child.

"'Tis a shame that," said Cammy, shaking her head. "A young life taken. It is difficult to understand."

"We've not identified the boy. Some say he ran with a group of filchers organized by a man named the Deft Drigger. Perchance have you heard of him?"

"'Tis a boastful name. I wonder who perpetrated that shameful badge? The man himself, or a victim of his conniving?"

"No matter. He is rumored to keep his infamous crew near St. Paul's."

Cammy rubbed her neck. "I do not travel across the river much. I work long days and nights. In all my time, I've never been to the cathedral." She looked up at Bianca. "But I can see its steeple from here." She finished the last of her ale. "If this Deft Drigger lived here in Southwark I might be able to learn something useful for you. The Dim Dragon is a kettle of scuttlebutt." Cammy glanced around, then leaned in. "There is no one with whom ye might inquire?"

"Oh, there is," said Bianca, getting to her feet. She straightened her coif. "I just wondered if you'd heard any talk."

CHAPTER 14

Bianca wrapped her arms around her drawn-up knees. She stared through the grainy darkness at the silhouette of an alembic, with its long spout like a bird's beak. There they were, the accoutrements of her craft, leaning against the cracked walls, looking as tired as strumpets after a night of whoring. A variety of still heads for distillation, some irreparably dented or missing a critical juncture, were piled in a corner waiting to be given a bit of care and concern. Bowls littered the table, jars of dried rue, bladderwort, and yarrow lined the shelves. Sprigs of teasel and gathered bunches of cohosh hung listlessly from pegs pounded into the overhead beams. The faint smell of burnt sage still lingered, reminding her of the promised tincture she must finish for Meddybemps. Everywhere the evidence of her passion—her madness? She almost felt as if those crocks, those cucurbits and mortars, lived a life beyond the one that included her. They sat in silent judgment, contemplating, forming an opinion. She gave them life, but for now they sat waiting.

The space where John had slept beside her lay empty like a wide expanse of sea, calm and uninterrupted. Hobs heard her stir and jumped up to join her, chortling in question, *Why do you wake?*

Again, the dream. It had slipped its hand around her throat and squeezed hard enough to rouse her from slumber. She had lost her life and then regained it, but the cost was a soul waiting to be born. The child would have been three months old if it had lived. It would have been a winter baby, born during the coldest days of the year. Destined to be a reticent and resourceful child, she imagined.

From the murky depths of the river Thames, she'd seen (or had she dreamed?) the green glowing eyes of the one who had saved her. The one who had seized her lifeless body and pushed it to the surface. *Who* had saved her? *What* had saved her? *Why* had she been saved? The questions tumbled through her mind and landed in a heap. She did her best to sweep them into a corner of her brain where they might be forgotten, but always the dream would remind her.

A child was not meant to be. John would ask. She thought about John's return and envisioned his face full of expectation. He would glance beside her, behind her. He would look for a swaddled bundle with creamy pale skin and rosebud lips. Then, not finding his child, his face would change and he would ask.

She would tell John that she had lost the baby. Many women do, it often occurs with first pregnancies. He would want to know what had happened. What would she say? How would she answer? How could she tell him that she had pursued a murderer on the river—a man intending to kill the king's army, and by association, him? Could she even get far enough in her explanation to mention the river before John would assume she was remiss in putting herself and their child in danger?

Bianca fell back on the bed and burrowed under the covers. She forced herself to think on the smell of a rose and how one might describe it. What *were* smells, she pondered? Smells were invisible, but present. They were definitive, but intangible. One could easily describe the look of a rose, its color, the shape and size of its petal, the prick of its thorn, but the scent? A rose could only smell like a rose, but why was that smell so singular? It was not like any other flower. It was not like any object. And why were smells unique to one thing? Before long, Bianca had distracted herself long enough to fall back asleep, and when she woke in the morning the dream had been forgotten.

Doing as her mother bid, Anna answered the insistent knock at the door. She hoped to find Fisk on the other side of it, but then why would he bother knocking? He could just come inside. Whatever the reason for his being gone, she expected him to embellish the tale and skew it to his advantage to avoid a beating—which he roundly deserved for being gone so long and making everyone worry. However, the visitor on the other side was not her brother.

"Anna, who is it?" asked her mother, coming to see.

The girl shrank from the door, leaving it ajar. The man took advantage and forced himself into their rent.

"Oh. 'Tis ye again," said her mother in a voice that had dropped from the more cheerful tone of her question.

Anna retreated behind her mother.

"A good day, Meg," said the visitor, a man Anna instinctively disliked.

He received a not so kind retort. "Why are ye here?" asked her mother. Then, assuming the fellow had no honest purpose for his visit and was probably complicit, she demanded, "Where be Fisk? What have ye done with him?"

The man scoffed, disparaging the notion. "Meg, why do you accuse *me*? If he were with me, would I be coming 'round? I'd be gone to the West Country. Do favor me with more sense than that."

"Yet ye show no surprise that he is missing."

"I show no surprise because I know where he is."

"Where? Where is my boy?" She took a step forward.

"He is safe for now. But I cannot say if that will change."

"What? Oh, ye scoundrel. I will not play your game. Ye are cruel to tease me so. Out with it! Be forthcoming, or I shall have no reason to believe ye!"

The man shook his head somberly. "If I said and ye sought others to help rescue him, it would put his life in danger. Neither of us wants that. But, I do regret to say, that if ye desire him home, it will cost you."

"Ye be a cunning knave, Geve Trinion. Such flip-flap. Ye think to take me boy *and* wring money out of me purse."

"Meg, I am not the heartless cullion ye make me to be. I come here because I haven't got the money to see him home myself."

"See him home? Well now. That has changed. Before ye wanted 'im for yeself." She got into his face and pinned him with a dagger eye. "Are ye sayin' he be held for ransom?"

Geve Trinion nodded.

Anna saw her mother's mouth fall open. From across the room little Janeth began to wail. Anna went to her little sister and tried to shush her so she could hear what her mother had to say.

"By who?" her mother asked.

"Good Meg, alas, I am sworn to silence. But there be a fellow with whom I can negotiate for his safe return. Unfortunately, I only have partial moneys." He held up his purse and shook the coins. "More is required."

"God's blood. It is a poor world when a mother must pay for her son's life. It is unthinkable!"

"It is sad that it has come to this. But if we do not give the man what he wants, we may never see Fisk again."

"How do I know ye are not scheming with this person to get my money?"

"Because, if I should succeed in bringing him home, then by rights, ye should be indebted to me." The man licked his lips as if he was slavering over a juicy roast beef.

Meg stood her ground, defiant. "I do not need your help," she said. "Fisk will come home."

The man shrugged. "Ye may be naïve in thinking so."

She read his face, then turned away from him. Anna held her little sister, balancing the girl on her hip while worrying that her mother would do nothing to save Fisk.

Finally, her mother spoke. "What is the cost?"

"Five crown."

"Five crown!"

"We speak of the boy's life, Meg."

Anna knew her mother could be hard on Fisk, but surely she was not so heartless as to do nothing. The family depended on him. Especially with Father being gone. She searched her mother's face, hoping for a pinprick of care to show itself.

"Bring me proof that ye know where he is."

The man pressed his lips together. "It would be impossible. I am not so clever as to sneak in and steal his shoe."

"But ye say ye know where he is. Surely if this rogue expects payment then he would part with a lock of Fisk's hair."

"It is not so simple."

"What say ye? If what ye tell me is true, the man will agree."

"Nay, I think not!" said the man, refusing explanation.

"Ye are surely lying." Anna's mother placed her hand square on the fellow's chest and pushed him backward toward the doorway. She had nearly succeeded in pushing him out when he grabbed the doorjamb, preventing her from shutting the door.

"Truth be," said the man, "the money is to pay a fellow who

will risk his life to rescue Fisk."

"What? And ye cannot find it in yerself to do so on yer own?" She gave him a shove in disgust. "I rue the day I ever met ye, ye white-livered coward. Get out!"

"Do not dismiss me," Trinion implored. "I cannot promise that Fisk won't be sold ... or worse."

"What? Sold?"

"Meg, must I tell you the sordid details? There are those with an unsavory appetite for young boys with which to take their pleasure."

"It is a treasonous offense!"

"Oh aye, it is. And those who participate are surely more evil than the devil."

Anna felt a stab of terror. She watched this man, the way his eyes slid over to look at her and then moved back to her mother. She saw the fingers twitch on the hand that hung by his side.

"Then ye must find a way," said her mother. "Tell whoever has Fisk that I will not part with a penny until ye prove to me that ye speak the truth. Tell him I must have this because ye is a reprehensible liar and I do not believe ye. And even then, Geve Trinion, I could call the constable and have him tend to the matter." She pushed his chest and he stumbled out the door. "I see no cause to believe you. Away. I will have no more of ye."

Bianca had wagered that the weather would be better than yesterday for being outside and going into London. The day remained overcast and cold but gone was the persistent cloud spittle, so in that sense, she had been right. She rose to finish more remedy for Meddybemps and set the bottles aside on shelves until the streetseller's next visit.

The roads remained muddy, the tacky, thick plodge that ruined shoes and hems of kirtles. A few months before, Bianca had purchased a pair of wooden pattens that lifted her a few inches, but they provided no purchase in the slippery slur. The fripperer had told her the previous owner was a fishwife who wore them to market so she could be lifted above the fish heads and tails that littered her stall. Unfortunately, the woman had recently met her demise choking on a perch bone and her husband had no need for the petite pair of lifts.

Turning down Ivy Lane, Bianca wished to visit Fisk's mother to see if he had come home. No one answered her knock. Waiting another moment, putting her ear to the door to listen for movement, proved fruitless. No neighbor peeped out a window to offer an explanation or suggestion, so Bianca continued on to Westcheap Market. For all she knew, mayhap Fisk had returned.

She arrived well into the selling day. The better weather had brought out more customers, and already there were gaping spaces where vendors had sold all their wares and had packed their carts and left. Bianca surveyed the several butchers. She decided a methodical approach was best, and started at one end of the market.

Bianca approached the first butcher, a man with a decidedly broad nose and snaggle tooth. She waited until he finished filling a basket for a servant maid.

"Good day, sir," she said, dipping in a slight curtsy. "I'm asking after the young boy found at St. Mary Magdalen's two days back. I heard he may have frequented the market."

The butcher's eyes flicked over her while he cleaned a bloody blade on his apron.

"I can't be sure if the lad was one and the same," he said, laying the knife on the cart. "Not without seeing the body." An array of cuts of pork and beef were spread before him. Bianca caught a whiff of slightly rancid meat and took a step to the side.

"Know you his name?" she asked.

"Nay," he said. "I only knew the boy by sight." He kicked a dog who roamed too close.

"What did he look like?"

"He looked no different from any other waif trying to get on." The butcher wiped his hands. "He had dark hair. Was quick on his feet. The lad could run faster than a greased piglet."

"The victim had dark hair," confirmed Bianca. "It would be helpful if you would view the body. It might stir your memory."

"I think not," said the butcher. "Like I said, I only knew him by sight. I do not know his name."

"What else can you remember?"

"Methinks he was part of a group of boys who frequent Paul's Walk. They work in pairs, sometimes a group. They be clever. One of the boys makes a distraction, runs into someone, or runs through the apse hollering, his voice carrying to the rafters, making a commotion like his arse is on fire. Disrupting the polite gentlemen's discourse." He gave a quick mocking smile. "I grant ye, there are plenty of filching boys, but when this group appears in market ye might as well loose wild dogs for all the havoc they cause. He used to come with one other boy, but since the hanging, I haven't seen either of them." The butcher scratched his stubbly chin and his snaggle tooth protruded between his closed lips. "Then too, they do not dare."

"Why do you believe that?"

"Me, the cord vendor, and the woman selling apples watch out for one another. If we suspect boys will make trouble, we let them know we be watching. If they try to steal and we catch them, we make sure they understand that they are not welcome." His words hung in the air, as rank as the meat on his cart.

"How do you . . . convince them?"

The butcher moved to the side of his stall and tightened the rope securing his awning. "We take them to the constable," he said without looking at her.

"Constable Berwick?"

"He be the ward lawman," answered the butcher.

"These groups of stealing boys," said Bianca. "You say they are common?"

"Aye."

"Think you that they are organized by an adult?"

"It would surprise me not. Some people are too lazy to earn their own way, but they have no qualms manipulating others to do their work for them. The streets run rampant with those who exploit others."

"Have you heard tell of someone called the Deft Drigger?"

The butcher snorted. "Ah, a fellow christened the king of all thieves?" He rubbed one side of an eye. "There is the Deft Drigger, the Sly Snatcher, the Cunning Cutpurse . . . shall I continue?"

"Then, the name is not unique to a particular man?"

"A scoundrel by any name is but the same."

"Perchance, do you know where these bands of thieving boys might live?"

"They live on the streets. They sleep in abandoned warehouses and under empty street stalls. You'll find them in the shadow of St. Paul's or in graveyards next to tombs quiet as the night sky."

"But, surely the man called the Deft Drigger or the Sly Snatcher would have his own quarters."

"I do not know, nor do I care. It is not for me to find these men. But a man who uses others for his personal gain would not sleep slumped against the conduit at Charing Cross."

Bianca lost patience with the butcher's vague answers and, with a mind for talking with the cord vendor and apple seller, Bianca asked the man to point them out.

The butcher stretched his neck looking for the apple seller. "There she be," he said, pointing to a woman wearing a russet-brown waistcoat and bird-turd-green flatcap. A basket hung from her crooked elbow. "Goodwife Beatrice. Derdwin was late to market and took a spot on the far side. She can show you."

Bianca picked her way toward the woman strolling through buyers, calling out her wares. Her voice had a warm flavor like mulled cider, unusual given that most vendors screeched like a rusty hinge.

"Goodwife Beatrice," called Bianca, waving at her. She caught up to the woman and the smell of apples lured her into buying one. "The butcher said you might know about the cutpurses at market. He said you and the cord vendor keep an eye on them."

"Ha!" said the woman, taking hold of Bianca's arm. "Let us speak over there where I can hear you." She guided her to a less congested area. "What is this about cutpurses?"

"Do you know about the boy who was found at St. Mary Magdalen's?"

"I heard a boy was hanged there."

"The butcher said he'd seen him here at market. There is mention that he belonged to a group of organized boys. Specifically, a band run by a fellow called the Deft Drigger. Have you heard tell of them?"

"I walk this place nearly every day. For cert I recognize many faces. I might even know the names of a few. But the boy found hanged—I do not know him."

"Had you seen him here? The butcher told me that he noticed when the boy was gone."

"The boys who come through are a changeable lot. I don't know how he can distinguish which one suddenly does not come around." The woman made a face like the butcher was daft. "Methinks that after an absence, then one might remember when once again one sees." The woman clarified. "You remember when you are reminded."

"Methinks the boy has not been buried," said Bianca. "Might you take a look at him?"

The woman reared away from Bianca and crossed herself. "Nay. That is a dark undertaking. The souls of the murdered look to haunt the innocent living. Ye'll not get me in there."

"Then, did you notice where these boys run to?"

"Well!" said Goodwife Beatrice. "You might ask Derdwin. He makes it his sport to chase them."

Bianca followed Goodwife Beatrice across the market to a barrow next to a fellow selling rabbit pelts. The fur trader enjoyed a steady business, whilst the cord vendor entertained one customer, finally convincing her to buy a lengthy hemp rope to hang her laundry.

"Derdwin," said Goodwife Beatrice. "The wench wants to know where the cutpurses go when you give them chase."

The cord vendor was a large man and Bianca likened him to the king (whom she'd glimpsed once on procession) in matters of size. She had a difficult time imagining him chasing young boys and having any success at catching them. He returned her stare, visibly unimpressed.

Bianca introduced herself. "The constable would like to know where these dens of thieving boys be."

"Constable Berwick?"

"Constable Patch, sir."

"Who be Patch?" the vendor asked.

"He is assisting Berwick in the matter." She forgave herself this small untruth.

Derdwin exchanged looks with Goodwife Beatrice, and Bianca supposed they passed some sort of unspoken message.

"I've run them as far as the alleys off Old Change, I have. The area has plenty of derelict buildings. Also near Paternoster Row."

"That is a large area to search." Bianca knew how twisty and dark those alleys could be. How one rent abutted another and doors opened on alleys, providing quick exits for fleeing criminals. "You cannot be more specific?"

Derdwin shrugged.

"I was told that the victim at St. Mary Magdalen's may have been part of the Deft Drigger's band of boys."

His forehead creased from one side to the other in a scowl. "Pah, Deft Drigger," he muttered. "I would say look to the back alleys near St. Paul's, I would," he said. "And say it, I did."

"You've seen this fellow?"

"The Deft Drigger? I have not seen him. I've heard tell of him, though. If I ever got me hands on the cullion I'd squeeze 'im till his pips squeak. But methinks he works his boys near the cathedral."

"Do you know if he is a monk? If he might call himself Brother Ewan?"

The cord vendor said firmly, "I'll say no more, because I know no more. I said it, and that is what I said." He grabbed a nettle stalk from a pile behind his barrow and vigorously began separating the pith from the stem, stabbing his knife into its spongy tissue with a viciousness undeserved by a humble plant.

Bianca left Westcheap Market and wandered down Paternoster Row. She had no idea where to look for this supposed Deft Drigger, or Brother Ewan if they were indeed one and the same. Then again, she thought about the drunk Malloy, and reminded herself she was acting on information given by a drunkard.

She surveyed the shop fronts, and noticed the owner she'd spoken with in his establishment talking to a customer. As far as she could tell, there were no young boys milling about or even walking up the lane. Perhaps she might discover a group of cutpurses if she strolled the neighborhood around St. Paul's and meandered down its popular walk. After all, she was familiar with a thief's method and she knew what to look for.

Near the front of the cathedral's entrance, she spied two boys listlessly sitting on the stone steps and she slowed to observe them. Neither seemed lively enough or even interested in doing anything other than sit with their caps extended, begging for pennies. It is a sad predicament to be dependent on the pity and charity of others, thought Bianca.

Where once the charity of parish churches might offer help for the disadvantaged, now they could barely maintain their buildings. The king had wrung every groat from every parish and every citizen to fund his senseless wars. All the more reason to cease the subjugation of Scotland. "We cannot even take care of our own," muttered Bianca.

She walked up to the boys and dropped a penny in each of their caps, asking if they'd heard about the boy at St. Mary Magdalen's. The boys had heard, and wary looks spread across their faces. Bianca assured them that she was only trying to find the boy's mother, and might they know his name? Both claimed ignorance, and Bianca asked if they'd heard of Brother Ewan. Bianca saw no flicker of recognition on either of their faces. The two gave the impression of staying clear of thievery, relying instead on their plaintive looks for help.

She trudged on to visit Paul's Walk, when a man stepped in front of her and waved a broadside in her face. The print was too close to her nose to read, and before she could object, the fellow launched an explanation that tumbled from his mouth with such speed that she could do nothing but stand there, dumbstruck, and wait for the man to run out of breath.

Bianca had no interest in learning every word to the most popular bawdy song in London, but she could not get away from him. When she went left, he did the same. And a fake to the right, then a quick dodge was matched expertly.

"Leave me be!" said Bianca, exasperated. "I do not want it!"

"But think on the next time ye hear the laddies sing. Do you want to be sitting by like a mouse? This is a delightful ditty," he said, and the man began to croon. "'As I was a-walking down a London street, a pretty little oyster girl I chanced for to meet. I lifted up her skirt and boldly I did peep, just to see if she'd got any oysters ...'"

Bianca nearly slapped him as much for his failure to take no for an answer as for his impertinence. The fellow tilted his head back and boisterously sang, "'O oysters, O oysters ...'"

Bianca took the opportunity and got well away.

She had not gone far when another chapman offered her *his* latest edition. He was considerably more mannered and accepted her refusal to buy his broadside, a rhymed account of the eight laws of villainy, including an illustrated example of each. But a few steps past she came to a halt. A thought occurred to her. She turned and looked at the man. He wore a plain fig-brown doublet with no defining trim, and his sturdy build, neither thin nor stocky, was evident in the way his hose clung to his calves and defined them. His chin ended in a pointy beard that divided the small ruffle on his smock collar. She had seen him before, frequenting this area around the cathedral.

"Do you have others?" she asked, walking back to him.

The man removed a satchel containing an array of printed material. He ticked off the titles of several rhymed compositions, while thumbing through his offerings.

"Are you ... Clement Naylor?" she asked, seeing the name on some of the printed material.

"Aye," he said, and he continued making suggestions from his selection.

A pamphlet caught her eye, and she stopped him before he

skipped over it to read the titles of more broadsides. She reached in and withdrew it.

"What is this one about?" She read aloud the title and looked up for an explanation.

The chapman hesitated, but lowered his voice confidentially. "It is a defense written to the king."

"By Robert Barnes. Was he not burned at the stake for heresy?"

"Aye," said Naylor. "It happened a few years ago. But there was a time when the king found his words useful. He used to preach at Paul's Cross. His sermons always drew a crowd. Unfortunately, when the king's chief minister fell from favor, so did Barnes."

"You speak of Thomas Cromwell's demise?"

The printer nodded.

"Two others burned with him," Bianca recalled. "All three maintained their innocence."

"They never received a trial," said Naylor.

"They took their sentence bravely. I remember people talking about it," said Bianca. "Three Papists were hanged, drawn, and quartered for treason at the same time." She flipped through the pamphlet and scanned a page, then handed it back. "Mind you not draw attention circulating this. The king might have your hands cut off."

The printer stuffed the pamphlet back into his satchel. "The king was once sympathetic to these ideas, when it served him to do so. Goodwife, I only seek to remind."

"I think there is much that our king wishes to forget."

The printer did not argue. He gave a quick smile in acknowledgment. "I wish to remind the people."

"You might profit more from bawdy broadsides," said Bianca, turning her back on the oyster man, shielding herself from his blatant glare. "That fellow makes good coin from it."

"We live in dangerous times. I believe matters of our immortal soul are more important than frivolous revel."

"I think you brave to sell this chapbook."

"I believe in what I do."

"Sir, can I find you here most days?"

"I have several commitments on my time. But I often sell my works here. The gentlemen who frequent Paul's Walk are men of some money and education. They wish to stay informed."

"Perhaps you have noticed the boys who disrupt Paul's Walk to pick purses?"

"They arrive in drifts and waves."

"I am looking for someone called the Deft Drigger. He may be organizing these bands of young cutpurses."

"Search the alleys off Old Change. I've seen them run through. There is a fellow there who lives in an old tannery. He may have something to do with it."

"And the name—the Deft Drigger? Does it sound true to you?"

"As true as day," said Naylor

.

CHAPTER 15

Melrose, Scotland

They camped on the south side of a ridge and waited for nightfall. Sheep had been slaughtered to feed the men. John finished his portions then spent his time near a fire, packing his shoes with the fluffy seeds from bulrush. The leather suffered from being constantly damp, and since there was no time to let them dry, he made do with the absorbent plant that he collected from riverbanks.

"They say Sir Eure is especially keen to march on Melrose," said Glann McDonogh, joining his friend. The pikeman laid his weapon beside him.

"Has Melrose not already suffered from our Lord Lieutenant's hand? Pray tell, why should we return? What makes it special?" asked John.

"Ah," said McDonogh, glad to inform. "Because the heart of Robert the Bruce is buried there."

"Who is this Robert the Bruce?"

"Tsk, his name ye do not know?" McDonogh could scarce

believe it. "Sirrah, he is held in great esteem by every Scot in the land. There is scant a fellow north of the Tweed who doesn't tell his story."

"I am scarcely a Scot. Why should I know of him?"

"Because knowing who our enemy reveres is useful in defeating him."

John broke apart another bulrush head, and the seeds like dandelion poured out and made an ample pile. He grabbed a handful and pushed it down his shoe.

"Robert the Bruce was king of Scotland some two hundred years ago. He murdered his rival for the throne and was banished from the church because of it. He fought you, the English, over and over, and never defeated them. He became a fugitive. Then, while hiding from the enemy, he watched a spider try to anchor her thread. She tried six times to hitch a strand to a beam. On the seventh try, she succeeded. He took it as a sign. He rallied his men and defeated the king's army and won Scotland's freedom."

"Which king was this?"

McDonogh shrugged. "Methinks Edward the second."

John tried on his shoe and stomped his foot on the ground. "I like it not," he said.

"Wot, it is a great story!" cried McDonogh.

"I speak of my shoe." John removed it and stuck his hand down to the toe to manipulate the makeshift padding. "So, he learned from a spider and all of Scotland thinks him a hero."

"There is wisdom in it."

"Staring at a bug? You could stare at cow shit to greater effect—and learn a greater lesson."

McDonogh held his hands toward the fire to warm them. His gloves were worn through at the tips and his thick fingers were grubby, and red from the cold. He was the only foreigner sitting with English billmen, but they didn't mind. The Irishman had a quirky way about him and loved a good story. His English was better than most because he liked to talk. He especially liked to talk with John. For his part, John welcomed McDonogh's good cheer and wry commentary.

"I hope the Scots hid well this Robert's heart," said John quietly enough so the others would not hear. "I should not like to see a people's sacred relic abominated."

"In truth we do not know what he would do with it. But disturbing its rest is a cruel act." McDonogh scratched his arse. "Then, too, it might hasten this war to an end that much sooner."

"I should think it would rouse every Scot from every kirkton and brae to avenge their hero—if this fellow, this Robert the Bruce, is of the mettle you say."

"The future comes a little at a time," said the Irishman. "We shall soon know."

"I should think you would want this war to go on," said John. "The inconvenience of it lines your pocket. You are paid and you are fed."

"I have no wife to return to, but even I wish for an end to this. I should like to go home. I've killed enough Scots."

The two watched a fellow pikeman feed the fire. The sun was pitching toward the west and it would soon be nightfall. They would wait until the village of Melrose was asleep in their beds. They would wait for cover of darkness to do their worst.

There wasn't much money in what he did. Hauling batts of wool around London and dropping them off with spinners, then delivering the skeins back to the clothier, earned him enough for one meal a day and his portion of rent for a shared room. But tromping around London did give him time to think. Geve Trinion trudged up the lane to his last stop of the morning.

He thought about Fisk. He couldn't understand why the boy's

mother opposed his offer. It seemed a good solution to both their problems. With such a brood, one less mouth to feed would have been helpful, he thought. And, the offer to send home the boy's wages would have been better than the child stealing on the streets of London. He took offense that she did not trust him. But then, when he really thought about it, why should she?

As it was, this was an opportunity to make twice the money on Fisk. His scheme might work out quite handily.

To his advantage, Meg appeared genuinely distressed. The lines of worry dug deep into the skin around her eyes; she had lost that saucy glint that had once so beguiled him. But, he was too clever to let her fool him again. It was his turn to deceive.

He knew she was capable of more than she let on. She squawked over the ransom money, but Geve knew that she would find a way to get it. He didn't care how, but she was a master of double-handed deals and if she really wanted Fisk returned, she could do it. He just needed to be a little more patient. And if she came up with the money, he would disappear from her life forever, without another word.

Trinion dreamed of getting rid of the pack basket that he lugged all over London. When he first took the job, he had looked forward to meeting women. He imagined he would go from one to the other, engage them in some witty repartee, then if one of them were amenable … maybe a little rumpy-pumpy. But the spinners he dealt with were too old to care about anything other than their next meal, or they were harried mothers with children hanging on their hems. No opportunities presented themselves and, after two years, he had grown weary of it all.

He approached Jane Clewes's tenement and saw her peeping at him from behind the shutter. Didn't she have enough spinning to keep her busy? Maybe he should leave her more batts. She was a new spinner and he had been to her rent only twice before. She'd hardly said a word to him when he first met her. He'd confirmed who she was and told her when he'd return to collect the skeins. She just snatched the batts out of his hands and closed the door in his face.

Such a fearful lady with her dim hazel eyes appraising him, and that jutting chin turned up like a crescent moon nearly touching the tip of her nose. Did she think he did not see her watching him? He doffed his cap and she ducked out of view. He believed her quite mad.

Trinion went around the corner of the building and met Jane already standing on the stoop, waiting. She ran her twitchy gaze over his person.

"G'day, Goodwife Jane," he said, ignoring any implied animosity from her thorough examination.

"It is if you like dreary, gray ones." She offered him the door to come inside, but even on a day such as this, he preferred the cool unforgiving climate to the one inside her rent. He compromised by straddling the threshold, one foot in and the other outside on the stoop.

Jane hurried off to get her skeins, and he thought she must be feeling spry this day. She usually had a pronounced hitch to her walk. Usually it pained him to watch her cross the room to fetch her finished work, but today she didn't seem troubled by her handicap. "Ye must be feeling nimble of joint today," he said.

She greeted his observation with a cold stare. "Today be no different than any other," she replied.

If she wished to say so, he could not be troubled to argue.

Jane gathered an armful of yarn to her chest. She had made it halfway back when the sound of something scratching stopped her. She listened, as did he. Their eyes dropped to an area of the floor.

"That one sounds sizeable," he said. "I know a good rat catcher." Manners aside, he saw no harm in broaching the subject when it came to getting rid of vermin. They were a nuisance to both rich and poor. "I can send him by."

Jane stomped the floor and the scratching ceased.

"'Tisn't necessary." She dumped the spun wool into his arms. "There are seven."

His mouth must have gaped for she pointed to the yarn. "Skeins. There are seven skeins."

"Oh. Aye." Geve Trinion looked over the quality of her spinning and found it quite good. He stuffed the skeins into his pack basket and removed the last of the batts along with her earnings. Despite his counting it out for her, she snatched it away and began recounting it.

"I shall put these by your stool," he said while she mouthed the count. She could have managed the batts herself but he felt generous. He crossed the room and deposited the pile of carded wool on a stool near her hearth. Running his eyes around the interior of her rent, Jane Clewes didn't seem to have but the bare essentials to make herself comfortable. She had a wobbly table and a bench, a small cupboard, and a few pots for cooking. No fire burned in the hearth; she probably saved her fuel to cook her meals and hoped that would generate enough heat to take the chill out of the air. He wondered where she kept her savings.

He was walking to the door when the strange sound began again. It sounded as if it was coming from directly beneath him.

"Ye must have holes in the foundation," he said, stopping to listen. "They don't need much. I've seen them squeeze through a hole the size of an angel."

Jane Clewes's eyes darted to the floor and back again. The scraping clearly unnerved her.

"I've a knife. I could pry up a board and see what be under there." Maybe she kept her money down there.

"You will do no such thing!" she said. Her sharp rebuke made him jump. "Leave it be!"

"I do not mind, goodwife," he assured. "I hate rats. Ye should know how many ye got. Then I can send a fellow round to take care of your problem." He knew who to ask. And he would be there pretending to help while scanning her rent for a hidden stash of coin. "Ye wouldn't want them getting loose in here."

"There is no danger of that, sirrah. This floor is as solid as the ground out my window." She then escorted him to the door and practically shoved him out it.

If that were not peculiar enough, a thickset young man stood on the stoop staring at them with his mouth slightly open and his crooked teeth pointing north, and south, and in between like a compass rose. The lad showed no signs of moving aside to let him pass.

"Huet. Come inside," admonished Jane.

The lad closed his mouth, releasing Geve from its spell, and squeezed through the door, his large size filling its frame.

Jane Clewes ignored common civility and did not introduce him to the new arrival. Nor did she offer a hint of explanation as to who this was. The two exchanged awkward glances until Geve could bear it no more.

"And who might this be?" he asked, since she was disinclined to introduce them.

"Huet," answered Jane.

"Huet ..." he prompted her, fishing for a last name.

"Huet," she said.

"Huet Huet?"

"Huet."

"Huet Clewes?" He didn't want to insult her, but her ambiguity thoroughly rankled.

"Huet."

He stared at her.

Jane Clewes stared back.

"Very well," he said, closing his satchel and securing it. "I will return for your work at the end of the week." He was cutting her allotted time in half. He didn't give her an option. Churlish women don't deserve one.

CHAPTER 16

Bianca walked down the narrow alley off Old Change, grateful there was still enough light left in the day that she didn't fear what could be lurking in the shadows. She happened to notice that Naylor's print shop was just around the corner. She supposed he probably had a good view of anyone running past his window.

Her keen sense of smell was useful not only in her work creating medicinals, but in identifying any unique odors that could lead her to a desired place or outcome. In this case, the lingering smell of urine on rotting hides (used to remove hair), led her to a location where she suspected there had once been a tannery. Some smells just never go away.

No loitering boys populated the narrow alley. Several rats fed on a pile of refuse, untroubled by her approach. She stopped in front of a building whose frontispiece next to the door had a carving of a man holding up a fox hide.

For as dilapidated as the building appeared at first glance, the wood of the main door was of new ash, barely weathered. Perhaps it had been recently built to replace an old punky one, but it gave the impression of being impregnable.

Bianca knocked and waited. When no answer came, she tried the latch and, to her surprise, the door yielded with her slight push. She checked over her shoulder, then peered inside. Mindful she was trespassing, she took a cautious step over the threshold.

A small entryway opened into a sizeable space, its length greater than its width. The suffusive damp accentuated the lingering smells from the tannery. At the far end a brazier glowed. Its burning coals washed the area in a pleasant orange color and almost masked the holes in the crumbling wall. A warming fire went a long way making a place feel welcoming.

"Who goes there?" asked a baleful voice from the other side of the glowing coals. The words bounced off the bare walls.

Bianca squinted to see beyond the fire. A figure sat directly behind the brazier, the iron stand and bowl blocking her full view.

"My name is Bianca Goddard." She took a few more steps, watching the dark corners for signs of movement. A few long benches and a table were pushed to one side.

"Have we met before?"

"I think not." Bianca stopped.

"Come closer, I cannot see you."

As Bianca neared, she saw an older man sitting before the brazier, the firelight exaggerating the puffiness under his eyes. His cheeks were scarred from a bout with smallpox.

"What brings a maid knocking on my door? Could she be lost? Perhaps she is new to the city and has nowhere to go."

"Nay. I am not lost and I am not new to the city. I am looking for the Deft Drigger."

"Deft Drigger?" said the man, baffled. "Meaning a fellow versed in the finer art of thieving?"

"Aye. A fellow who could be instructing a group of boys to steal for him."

The man chuckled. "People's baseless conclusions always

astonish me. Is this what you heard on the street?"

"There is talk that his boys are more skilled than others. People say they have been organized to help one another steal. They have not gone unnoticed by vendors and shoppers."

The man returned his gaze to the glowing coals. Bianca noted his cowled, rough woven tunic that stopped at his thighs. A leather belt cinched his waist. His dark hosen ended in scuffed, worn shoes and he wore a rustic woolen cap—the style favored by shepherds.

"There is no one here by that name. You have wasted your time."

Bianca hesitated. The printer had directed her here. There could be no denying that this building had once housed a tannery business.

"Someone has seen several rowdy boys run this direction. Boys who have stolen at Westcheap Market and Paul's Walk."

"Boys run. It is their nature. But if those lads are stealing, it is not me who has put them up to it."

"Might you be unaware? We know that boys beget mischief. They don't always admit their misdeeds."

"I do shelter boys when they need it. But they are not thieves." He pushed a coal scuttle with his foot and it scraped along the floor. "No boy under my tutelage breaks God's commandments."

"Your tutelage? What instruction do you give?"

"I teach them that the kingdom of heaven is earned through sacrifice." A mouse scurried across a beam, showering them in dust, and the fire snapped in protest. He waved at the smoke and particles falling in front of his face. "We can no longer rely on the church to undertake the care of its young flock. Where can a child—one who is abandoned or orphaned—learn about the glory of God?" He looked at her as if she might know. "Who educates these children in justice?"

"They are left to learn it on their own," said Bianca. "I suppose they learn on the streets or from their parents by example."

"Aye!" The man agreed, meeting her gaze. "Too many children have no home and no guidance. So, I do what I can. I see that they eat and that they have shelter if they require it. I provide what the parish can no longer give."

"Your mission is commendable, sir." She ran her eyes over the cracked walls, and single brazier heating a large space. "But your property is in poor repair. How can you afford to help?"

"Charity. There are those who give of their food and money."

"And by what name are you known?"

"Brother Sedar."

"You are a monk?" Bianca's eyes dropped to his tunic, realizing it could have once been a robe.

"I *was* a monk. I use my pension to support this endeavor. A monk is accustomed to having little. I have no possessions and I know how to live on nearly nothing."

"Are there others like you, similarly inclined to guide wayward boys?" Perhaps there was a community of dispossessed monks and she had only found one of several.

"It is possible. But I do not concern myself with other pensioners."

"Have you met Brother Ewan?"

Sedar frowned and shook his head. "I do not recognize the name."

"Perchance might you know a boy named Fisk? Might you have taken him in?" Bianca described her friend, but Brother Sedar claimed ignorance.

For a shelter for boys, Bianca wondered over the strange lack of them. "Sir, where are the boys now? I've not seen any come or go."

"They are completing their given tasks. At the end of the day, they will return for camaraderie, a lesson, and a meal."

It seemed the boys had a choice and were not being held against their will. Perhaps the real Deft Drigger was not so lenient. Bianca loosened her scarf. The brazier warmed her side as she studied him. "How long have you been in London?"

"About three years. I came from Faversham."

Bianca wondered if there were any records that could corroborate his story, but those records were probably lost during the dissolution and the confiscations. Besides, she didn't expect that the chief minister or any other official from the Court of Augmentations would give audience to a woman of her station. She doubted that Patch would have fared much better.

Brother Sedar took a rod and poked at the coals in the fire. His answers were clipped and vague, but at least he was talking.

"Brother Sedar," she said. "Three days ago, a boy was found hanging from a dripstone at St. Mary Magdalen's."

"I saw the body before he was cut down." His eyes never left the fire.

"Was he a boy under your care?"

Brother Sedar's head jerked up. "I gave him a meal and a bed, once."

"The constable has not been able to identify the victim. Do you recall his name?"

"His name was Peter."

"Know you his surname?"

"I do not recall. I only knew his acquaintance for one night. He did not stay."

"If the boy had any relatives they must surely be wondering where he has gone to."

"If the boy had any relatives would they not have heard by now? They would have come forward. I can think of no reason why they would not. Unless, of course, he had no family." Brother Sedar got to his feet. He had a broad chest and gave Bianca the impression that he must have been a muscular man in his youth.

What chores as a monk would have favored strength such as his? She also wondered if it was true that Peter had no family. The child could very well have relatives who, perhaps in some way, felt responsible for the child's death. Or were, in fact, responsible for it. Whether through negligence or complicity, guilt could silence even the most innocent. Bianca studied Brother Sedar's face. Could *he* be feeling the burden of guilt?

Bianca withdrew the paternoster from her purse and presented him with the beads.

"This was found twined around the boy's neck. There are some letters cut into the crucifix," she said, pointing them out.

The monk shook his head. "I cannot read them."

"The initials are Y, H, and S."

"Are you suggesting that the initials belong to the owner?"

"Aye."

He handed back the prayer beads. "I do not agree."

"What else could they mean?"

Brother Sedar returned his gaze to the fire. "It could simply be the Greek initials for Christ."

Bianca nodded then asked, "Brother Sedar, do you think that the letters might mean the owner belonged to the cult of the Holy Name?"

The monk pressed his lips together, making a vein in his temple bulge. "It is possible. But why would anyone advertise that he is a Papist?"

Indeed, why would the murderer condemn himself by deliberately leaving proof of his association with a religious group so vilified by the king? Was it done intentionally or by accident? Bianca thought on this. She even thought the most likely group of clandestine Papists would be the pensioned religious. She could see several possibilities, each more confounding than the next.

"It will be dark soon," said Brother Sedar, motioning toward the door. "The area is not safe at night. I do not want to be responsible should you encounter trouble on your passage home."

CHAPTER 17

The priest at St. Benet's, Father Wells, began each day with a meal of poached quail eggs. While he waited to be served, he studied the silvery gray light outside his window, which overlooked a long stretch of enclosed garden—alas, still dormant and showing no signs of waking. The overcast sky promised another dreary day, and he felt his mood adversely affected. It made him think—why was it that one associated sunshine with a sanguine disposition? He tapped his spoon on the table as he considered this, then the spoon stopped midair. Likely, it was because sunshine was so uncommon. It was like a gift from God every time colors were lit to their full intensity. He nodded, content with his explanation.

Finally, his meal arrived. The platter was lowered in front of him and his wine refreshed. His cook had arranged the twelve eggs—one for each disciple—around the periphery of the plate; an artful attempt to symbolize the seating at the Last Supper. In the center was a slice of bread, toasted lightly on one side—Jesus.

He scooped up an egg and deposited it on one corner of the toast, then raised it level with his mouth. "Peter," he said, naming the first apostle, and he bit off the corner. With each successive egg he named a disciple and ate "him" along with "Jesus," saving "Judas Iscariot" for last, taking the time to bite "Judas" in half and watch his little yolk bleed.

His meal done, he pressed his napkin to his lips and rose from the table. His back ached and he grimaced as he made his way to the door to don his hat and gown. It was such a brief walk to the church it was hardly worth the effort of dressing for the weather. If he was younger, he would have made a dash for it and not bothered.

Wistfully remembering days of his lost youth, he lifted his gown off its hook and reached for his paternoster underneath, but it was not there. Had he dropped it the night before? He looked around on the floor, forgetting his aching lower back, but his search proved fruitless. Perhaps he had taken it to bed. He returned to his palliasse and threw back the blankets, but his prayer beads were not there. He stood a moment, trying to remember. There were bits from last night that remained a mystery. In fact, he couldn't even recall coming through the door and going to bed. Well, mayhap they would be found. He began walking the short distance to Thames Street, pausing briefly on Addle Hill to order his thoughts.

The previous night had been difficult. He'd stayed out far too late and the wine he'd been served had made him feel queer. He was not certain and could not remember to what, exactly, he had agreed. His recollection of the gathering was fraught with missing moments, and if he had not been accompanied home by the younger cleric in service to Bishop Bonner and Father Foxcroft, he might not have gotten there without mishap. As it was, he had had trouble keeping up with the two men, and he'd been approached by a young thief thinking him an easy target. If his escorts had not answered his calls for help, he might have been knifed in the liver and left to wallow in his own blood. The whole incident was a blur of confusion, but he remembered the shouting and the terrible fear he felt in those precarious few minutes.

His annoyance with Father Foxcroft persisted past the meeting, even though the man had insisted on seeing him home safely. Foxcroft's ambition to earn a position under the bishop was on full display, his obvious fawning after Bonner a disgusting show of obsequiousness. Being a fellow priest in Castle Baynard, Wells felt in some measure responsible for Foxcroft's behavior. He knew Foxcroft didn't care for him and cared even less about what he had to say, but he had pulled the lackey aside and told him there was nothing worse than a groveling priest.

"As humans we may grovel before God," he had lectured. "But do not flatter Bonner to gain office. Earn it through scholarship and exemplary character." Even though the wine had loosened his tongue and dulled his judgment, he remembered he did not reveal his own shady past with Bonner, which had been handsomely rewarded. (At least to the point where he was able to eat quail eggs every day.)

Foxcroft had become strident and advised Wells to mind his own affairs and keep out of others'. Wells snuffed cynically, remembering this. He stopped walking to blow his nose, the cool morning air causing a tiresome nasal drip. Foxcroft's terse response was as he had expected. Men like Foxcroft never see themselves in the light that others view them.

Thames Street was practically empty this early in the morning. Dogs outnumbered the people and rats outnumbered the dogs. Father Wells could see his breath—the puffs billowing like smoke from a miniature serpent, the kind drawn in the margins of a book of hours.

The timber construction of a lender's residence turned into the stone façade of St. Benet's church, and Father Wells walked alongside the familiar building to the arched entry. It occurred to Wells that when the church bell rang, its tolling probably shook the lender's furnishings and his building's foundation since the two buildings practically touched each other. He imagined the usurer sitting over his important papers, a quill poised, and then the rattling chime shaking the ink from the nib, ruining his numbers. He wondered if the man had grown used to the interruption or whether he anticipated with dread the jarring reminder calling God's flock to prayer. Either way, the man never complained.

Indeed, in these times it was a prudent man who kept his opinions to himself. Lamenting his own poor decision, he thought that perhaps he had been wrong to reprimand Foxcroft. Father Wells pushed open the door and stepped inside the narthex, where the cavernous silence and cool air enveloped him. Perhaps he should have let Foxcroft be; let him make a fool of himself. Aye, he decided in regret—in this environment, a man was better served staying his tongue, and keeping his secrets.

Father Wells was the kind of man who kept his head down.

After informing Patch of the victim's first name and returning the paternoster, Bianca spent the next few days working on her remedy for spring sniffles and visiting Cammy at the Dim Dragon Inn. No word had arrived from the northern border regarding the king's army or the supposed end to the king's efforts to suppress Scotland.

She had visited Fisk's residence every day and never found his mother or his family at home. It was too far and inconvenient to visit more than once a day. She had tried early in the morning, thinking she might catch them home, and had received no response. The family's absence troubled her and she had no way of learning whether Fisk had returned. For all she knew, the family could have hurriedly left for some unknown reason—perhaps failure to pay their rent. She continued looking for him on the streets and asked at market, but no one had seen him. Even Meddybemps had nothing to report.

Her efforts to learn more about the boy named Peter at St. Mary Magdalen's had also reached a standstill. Even Patch, with all of his pestering and prying, was unable to garner any more information from Constable Berwick or the church officials. Nor was he able to learn anything about Fisk's disappearance. Bianca's suggestion that Brother Sedar's quarters be watched received an unenthusiastic response from Patch and plenty of grousing that he didn't have the men to devote to such an undertaking. He argued the address was in Castle Baynard and it was Berwick's responsibility. For the next few days, the series of obstacles forced Bianca's inquiry into stalemate.

She occupied her time with her chemistries, studied her notes for past concoctions and devised possible new ones. During swaths of quiet when she tended the fire in her calcinatory furnace and watched the alembics rattle from the heat, her thoughts ran through what she knew about the victim at St. Mary Magdalen and her visit with Brother Sedar.

Sedar did appear to have been a monk. Certainly, a friar would be able to tolerate the bare necessities of life and teach that sensibility to others. A pensioned monk would have some resources, but she didn't know how much, or even if it was possible to stretch those resources to provide for others. Mayhap he held connections with those of wealth who could help his cause.

Perhaps he was correct in identifying the initials to be the Greek letters for Christ. But would he say that because his own name, Sedar, matched the last initial?

Brother Sedar's reaction to her question about the "cult of the Holy Name" had made her think. *Why would anyone advertise that they are a Papist?* Why, indeed, would anyone in this king's London flaunt their affinity for the pope?

Was the murderer a Papist—a follower of the pope and the traditional beliefs? Was it his way of flouting his allegiance to the old religion? But why would such a person murder an innocent boy?

Or, perhaps the murderer had left the paternoster as a talisman, a conscious effort to wish no more harm on the child's soul than had already been done. In which case, its significance might only be religious.

However, what if a murderer wanted people to *think* a Papist perpetrated the crime? Leaving the paternoster with the initials representing the cult of the Holy Name might successfully implicate the group in the murder. Then again, Brother Sedar and the shopkeeper might be wrong—the letters might actually be someone's initials, and by coincidence were the same as the Greek letters for Jesus.

Bianca turned each possibility around in her mind, holding the choices up to the light to try to see through them to some sort of truth.

It was on one such morning that she had begun to distill peppermint, when she went into her back alley to refill a jug with rainwater. She had left the door ajar and upon filling her crockery she heard movement inside her room of Medicinals and Physickes. Thinking she had an intruder, she peeped through the crack in the door. Not seeing or hearing anyone, she waited and listened. Nothing.

She stood back, wondering if perhaps Hobs had brought her a mouse, but when he appeared next to her with the hair on his tail standing on end, she knew it was something more.

She quietly poured the water back into the cistern and, wielding the empty jug, crept around the corner of her rent and poked her head out to see the front entrance. The door to her hovel was left ajar. Someone was inside.

Bianca tiptoed toward the door and quietly pushed it open to better see, glad that the hinges didn't creak. Someone was looking over her latest experiment.

He wore a grubby jerkin and Bianca caught a whiff of perspiration. There was also a miry smell of river about him and she guessed he might be a muckraker from the trail of silty clay tracked across her floor.

She hesitated, trying to decide what to do, but when he found her strongbox with all of her savings and banged it with a pair of iron tongs, she'd seen enough. She raised the water jug and rushed forward to strike him.

But he was a man practiced in defense. He dodged her blow and caught her arm as it came down. In one smooth move he twisted it behind her back, and the jug fell to the floor.

"Zounds, ye could hurt someone with that!" he said. He nudged the pottery out of reach as Bianca struggled.

"I'll not have my earnings pilfered!" And Bianca kicked his shin.

The fellow let go of her and clutched his throbbing leg. "Hear, hear," he said, hopping backward and raising a hand in a show of surrender. "I'm not here to steal your money."

"I trust what I see. Unless my eyes deceive me, you hit that box with a pair of tongs!"

"There was a mouse on it. I was doing ye a good turn!" The fellow was as ugly as he smelled. His upturned nose with hairy nostrils was the first thing she noticed.

Bianca snatched the tongs off the floor and pointed them like a knife. "Methinks that is a quick excuse. Who are you?"

"They call me Brian Bindle, my lady." He took off his soiled flatcap and swept it low across his body as he bowed. He watched Bianca from under his ridge of brow until she bid him rise.

"Why are you here?" Bianca liked him not. And she trusted him even less.

"Constable Patch sent me. I am to bring ye acrosst the river.

There is something he wishes ye to see."

Constable Patch's emissary insisted that Bianca not delay. A second victim had been found, this time at St. Benet's, another church located in Castle Baynard ward. St. Benet's was not far from St. Mary Magdalen and had in common a similar size building, typical of a parish church. It had been a week to the day of the first boy's death.

Bindle and Bianca hailed a wherry, and when she asked if Patch knew the victim, Bindle shrugged. "We couldn't see who it was. They were working to get 'im down when I left."

"Was he hanged from a height?"

"He was."

"Did the victim have dark hair?"

"Goodwife, in truth I could not tell."

Bianca thought about Fisk and worried what she might find once she got there. She sat in silence for the ride across, twining a loose lock of hair around her finger and fidgeting in her seat.

They landed near Paul's Wharf next to the old ship cranes and the ward's namesake, Castle Baynard, inhabited by one of the king's courtiers. From there the church was only a short walk.

Unfortunately, St. Benet was located on Thames Street, one of the most heavily traveled lanes in London. There was no shortage of interested spectators and Bianca arrived to a scene much like the one before at St. Mary Magdalen. This time, however, the body had already been recovered. The crowd had not yet dispersed and there was an anxious collection of locals milling about. Speculation ran rampant, theories abounded as witnesses tried to make sense of yet another distressing death.

Bianca arrived just as a well-dressed fellow was taking Constable Berwick to task. The man looked to be of money, likely a nobleman, wearing a smartly tailored doublet and fox-lined gown. Constable Patch stood by, snickering in delight as his peer received a condescending haranguing, the likes of which only a man of education and higher standing could successfully deliver.

"He likes this not," said Patch to Bianca's questioning look. "He heard of the other boy's hanging and is threatening to take the matter to the Lord Mayor."

Bianca had no interest in Patch's gloating. Foremost on her mind was learning the identity of the victim. She steadied herself, trying to prepare for news about Fisk.

"Patch, did you see the victim?"

"I dids, it is another nameless boy."

Bianca felt uneasy. "You would recognize Fisk if you saw him?"

"I believes I would." He read the concerned look on Bianca's face and put her at ease. "Nay, 'twas not yer young friend."

Bianca closed her eyes in relief. She resolved to do more to find his whereabouts. Fisk was not her family—but in a sense, he was. When she opened her eyes she took up the nobleman's cause. "Mayhap telling the Lord Mayor would be a good thing. He may dispatch more help to find the murderer."

"Naws," groused Patch. "Berwick woulds make a pidgy mess of it. He can barely manage his own sorry group of men."

"Well then, this may be your chance to show them of what you are capable." Bianca said this lightly. She wasn't in the least bit serious. She was curious, though, to see if Patch would think it a good idea. His arrogance never failed to astonish her.

Patch grew quiet, as if gauging the right moment to make himself known.

Politicking aside, Bianca got on with her work. "First, though, tell me what happened." She gripped Patch's forearm, snapping him out of his reverie.

"Another boy was found dangling from a rain spout." He

pointed at a stone gargoyle at the edge of the roof.

"The murderer, if he is the same one as before, is not content to hang the boy from a tree," said Bianca. "He always chooses the side of a church."

"'Tis a lot of effort to dispose of a victim," said Patch.

"It is not so much disposing of the victim as it is displaying it," observed Bianca. "Why does the killer choose parish churches in Castle Baynard ward, and hang the bodies on the outside of the buildings where they can be readily seen? It is a pattern." Bianca scanned the side of the building, pondering how the murderer managed this feat. "I think it is to prove a point."

Constable Patch followed her gaze to the side of the church. "And whats point do ye think the killer is proving?"

"That is the question." Bianca ran her eyes around the spectators again. "At the least I am hoping we might be given allowance to view the body."

"Wells, if not while Berwick is around, then after he takes his leave. Which may be soon judging by the color of his face." Patch scurvily smiled as he glanced at the red-faced Berwick. "He will want to be gone soon enoughs to retire to his ill-gotten stash of wine."

"While we wait, tell me what you know about the victim," said Bianca.

Patch tugged at his chin hair. "He looks to be the same age as the other victim. Tattery clothes. No bloods on his person that I saw. A skinny child."

"And the priest? Who is the priest here?"

"Father Wells. He is inside. I imagines he and the churchwarden are discussing what to do. He says he arrived per usuals this morning and dids not notice the body."

"I suppose if you didn't look up you would not see it."

"He says he approached from Thames Street. The body was

on Bennet's Hill."

"So, who first reported it?"

"I do not knows. I only came to learns of it from Bindle, who happened to be in the neighborhood."

"Who is this Bindle fellow? Do you trust him?"

"Aws, I might take him on. He's suitably menacing. Used to shovel the ditch latrines when they overflowed. Would be a promotion of sorts."

Bianca studied the bystanders, looking for any familiar faces from the incident at St. Mary Magdalen's. She'd known murderers to assimilate in a crowd for the strange pleasure of viewing the reaction to their crime. To the best she could see, there was no one in common.

"I would like to speak with whoever discovered the body," said Bianca. "And I'd like to search the grounds, but this crowd makes that impossible right now."

The sudden absence of the nobleman's loud ridicule drew Bianca and Patch's notice. He had finished berating Constable Berwick, who quickly turned heel and stalked off.

"A tall bottle calls to 'im," said Patch.

"We must thank him with another," said Bianca, and the two seized their chance to get into the church without being stopped.

Inside, they followed the sound of voices to Father Wells, a parish priest flagrantly beringed with gemstones on his sausage-sized fingers. Both his manner and his speech bespoke a man used to the privilege of his office and then some. His grave discussion with his sexton and two laymen was interrupted by his notice of Patch and Bianca crossing the nave.

Patch introduced himself and told them that Bianca would serve as a witness to whatever was said.

"Are you the constable of this ward?" asked Father Wells.

"He be indisposed," said Patch. "I am with Bread ward, but we work together."

"And this woman's name?" asked the priest, looking at Bianca.

"She be Bianca Goddards—a woman of exceptional memories," boasted Patch. "She can recall conversations word for word, a second set of ears, an asset to my infestation." The men ran their eyes over the uninvited pair and exchanged looks.

"Very well. I have no objection to a woman of sharp wit, provided she can tolerate what most would call a deeply disturbing sight," said the priest.

A course of action was decided, and the men dispersed. Father Wells gave permission for Bianca and Patch to view the body, then excused himself. The two followed the sexton across the nave to the chancery—a temporary resting place until the initial examination was complete. Faced with finally seeing the victim, Bianca tensed, hoping that Patch had not been mistaken. The thought of Fisk murdered momentarily paralyzed her. She froze before entering, staring at a wide beam of sunlight streaming through a high window. There would be no question, no trying to see in a dimly lit room and coming to an eventual realization. She made a quick sign of the cross.

The body lay on the tile floor. The sexton had taken care not to handle him any more than was necessary. Bianca sighed audibly at the sight of the poor child. It was not Fisk, but the boy's peaceful expression and tragic death tugged at her heart. This was a young life, someone's child, a life extinguished too soon, for no apparent reason.

"The coroner has been summoned, but he is delayed," said the sexton. "I see no harm in ye looking him over, so long as ye don't disturb him." He then stood aside and watched as Patch began examining the body. Bianca crouched beside him, playing the role of assistant.

To his credit, Constable Patch had watched Bianca enough

times to know how to appear credible. But Bianca basically ignored his yammering and concentrated on silently conducting her own examination.

First, was the paternoster coiled around the boy's neck. Immediately Bianca could see a difference in the way that this paternoster had been used. The prayer beads dug into the boy's skin, indicating he had been strangled with it. Also of note was the quality of the paternoster. The beads were polished silver, an expensive set owned by someone of wealth or importance.

"Should you look to see if they have letters carved in them?" asked Bianca, giving a slight nod to Patch that he should do just that.

Constable Patch looked at the sexton for permission. "I likes to look at these beads more closely."

The sexton nodded. "Put them back like ye found them."

Patch began unwinding the prayer beads from the child's neck and got them tangled, frustrating himself. In her impatience, Bianca took over and gently removed the paternoster.

"I don't see any carving on these," she said, turning them over and carefully examining them. "They are entirely different from the set at St. Mary Magdalen's." She slid some beads to see the cord and rotated several beads, looking for letters. The cord was of some strength and there was filigree and some embellishment on the crucifix, but no letters.

She handed it to Patch and sat back on her heels. "The paternoster is a strange choice for the murder, is it not?" She thought a minute. "The first paternoster was simple, common on most counts except for the lettering. This one is more elaborate and made of silver. Why the change?"

Patch could offer no explanation. He blinked at Bianca, then stared up at the high window as if the answer might fly through it.

Without thinking, Bianca took over examining the child's

body while Patch looked on.

"Ot, she seems to have the gentler touch," commented the sexton, mocking Patch, who grumbled under his breath.

Again, the boy showed no signs of poisoning. His eyes were slightly open. He still looked relatively peaceful, but less so than the first boy. The sexton had removed the noose and the child's skin showed the furrow from hanging. But there was one difference. The silver paternoster had been used to kill the child; it had cut into his skin.

Like the boy at St. Mary Magdalen's, he bore the telltale signs of a life lived on the street. His face had a few streaks of grime. His shoes were too big, probably stolen then stuffed with grass to make them fit. They found a penny, a dice, and a length of thin cord in his pockets.

"Not much in the way of possessions," said Patch.

"Nothing of much purpose," said Bianca, looking over the paternoster one last time. She lifted the child's head to receive the cord of beads and looped them around his neck for the coroner to see. Returning the murder weapon to the victim—the mere act of twining the paternoster around the child's neck in imitation of the murderer's work—gave Bianca pause. It was as if she'd assumed the role of killer and her hand began trembling. She finished and quickly got to her feet.

For once, Patch sensed her disquiet. He saw her hand shake and the troubled look on her face. Her unease became his.

"I thinks we have finished here," Patch said to the sexton.

CHAPTER 18

Bianca followed Constable Patch through the nave of St. Benet's Church and exited onto the street. The crowd had dispersed, leaving no trace of the tragic murder the church had been involved in.

"I needs to get back to my office," said Patch, then added, "by way of Constable Berwick's."

"What do you propose to do there?" asked Bianca.

"I just wants to see if he knows anything more."

Bianca gave him a skeptical look. "And you believe that he will gladly tell you?"

"Naw, no," groused Patch. "But ye can learn a lot from a man when he doesn't like ye."

Bianca watched him saunter up the street, then turn the corner. Left to her own, she went back inside and waited for Father Wells. Church officials surrounded him, discussing the unfortunate incident, and Bianca bided her time until she could speak to him alone.

At last the men dispersed.

"Father Wells," called Bianca, catching up to him. "Have you time for me?"

The priest stopped and turned, a little surprised to see her again. "Of course."

Bianca noticed something off in the way he was dressed. He wore the customary black cassock and skull cap. His shoes were remarkably clean given the soggy state of the roads of late. She couldn't place what didn't seem right, but she knew from past experience that when she felt this pinch of awareness, it usually warranted cause for explanation.

"I am wondering sir, if there are any disgruntled parishioners who might have reason to make trouble for you?"

The priest's eyebrows raised in offense.

"Have you had any conflicts of late?" asked Bianca.

"Conflicts?" questioned Father Wells. "Nay! I am just a vessel for God's work. What cause would anyone have with that?"

"I agree it seems unlikely that anyone would wish ill of you, when obviously you devote yourself so completely to your parishioners' needs. However, it would be impossible for you to attend to every matter concerning St. Benet. I wonder if someone is upset with any change? Perhaps there is a member associated with the church who has caused some discontent?"

Father Wells rejected the notion. "All decisions are made in the church's best interest."

"I imagine it is difficult changing and conforming to the king's wishes. There are many who are uncertain about his reforms. They may not understand or agree with all the decisions. Some think these reforms go against God."

"The reforms are the king's. And he is the defender of the faith." He said this woodenly, as if he no longer believed it but was obliged to say it.

"Then, you believe the king is God's appointed representative?"

163

The priest's voice lowered to a hiss. "Goodwife, what are you insinuating here? Your questions could put us both in peril." He took her by the arm and guided her beyond earshot of anyone in the apse. "If this is about the unfortunate debacle this morning, then I am unable to give you any more information. I have already told you and the constable everything I know."

"I understand, sir. But mayhap you might consider why St. Benet church was singled out. I only ask that you consider the possibility. Think on it, and if anything occurs to you, let me know."

"If choosing St. Benet is part of the killer's design then I haven't a notion why. You are asking me to look inside a killer's heart and surmise what is in it."

"Is that not a priest's domain?"

Father Wells's face turned puce. He opened his mouth to dismiss her, but Bianca interrupted.

"I understand you did not see the body when you arrived this morning. I was told that you were alerted by a parishioner who first saw it."

"That is true," he said, his tone evening out.

"Who was that parishioner?"

"Why should that matter?"

"I should like to ask him some questions." Bianca thought it obvious. She didn't want to sound coy, but something about Father Wells's defensiveness didn't sit well with her.

"I fail to understand why you are asking me these questions. Is it not the responsibility of the constable or magistrate?" His hand went to his side as if seeking something and, not finding it, he then pressed his hand against his side awkwardly. It occurred to Bianca what had caught her notice but had escaped her realization. Most priests wore a paternoster around their neck or waist, or even strung across their chest like a bandolier. Father Wells had none to wear. And by the way his hand moved, it appeared that touching his beads was a habit that had suddenly been balked. Father Wells continued, "Constable Patch said that you were a kind of witness. A person to help him keep his facts sorted."

"It is my duty. However, I also find people for the constable to interview. People whom he might overlook."

Wells glanced away from her and after a moment relented. "I was informed about the body by a woman," he said. "Her name is Jane Clewes."

Bianca remembered the name. The woman insisted that Father Foxcroft hear her son's confession the morning of the first murder. "Is she not a parishioner at St. Mary Magdalen's?"

Father Wells was curt. "I did not say that she was a parishioner here."

"Do you know where I might find her?"

"Father Rhys would know. However, it might benefit you to question Father Foxcroft about this matter."

Bianca detected a cool edge in the way Wells mentioned Foxcroft's name.

"Does Father Foxcroft know what happened this morning?"

"He has been over to express his grief. He appeared while they were cutting down the victim. Father Rhys, however, might still be unaware of the death."

"Word travels fast in Castle Baynard ward," said Bianca.

"Indeed," agreed Father Wells, meeting her gaze. "I would have thought Foxcroft would have slept in this morning."

"He is a late sleeper?"

"I do not know what his habits are, but he was out late."

"Were you with him last night?"

Father Wells answered without hesitation. "There was a meeting with Bishop Bonner and it went on for some time."

"Longer than usual?"

Father Wells snorted. "Aye."

Bianca suspected from his reaction that Father Foxcroft might have forestalled the meeting.

"Father Foxcroft appears exceptionally interested in matters concerning the other parishes in Castle Baynard ward," said Bianca.

"Aye, he does," said the priest. "His interest goes beyond what is required of him."

"He has ambitions?"

"Ambition makes for a good servant, but a bad master."

Bianca was unfamiliar with the inner workings of power and position in the king's church. But she seized the priest's willingness to talk. "Then you worry his desire is misplaced?"

"Goodwife, we all have ambitions." He tucked his chin, making his point. "Since the king and his chief minister closed the monasteries and stripped them of their valuables nearly eight years ago, being a priest is less attractive and it is certainly more dangerous. We are restricted from many of our previous duties."

He did not come out and say that he, as well as other priests, had lost a significant source of income, but Bianca suspected this to be true. Religious relics had been confiscated, pilgrimages banned, indulgences forbidden. (Even though the king had ordered several thousand masses to be said for Jane Seymour's soul.) Priests were required to follow the king's doctrine and those who were reluctant to change, or who remained reticent about supporting the reforms, or who were presumed sympathetic to the old ways—or to the pope—were threatened and often punished.

The king's condemnation of the pope—that "Roman bishop-usurper"—was so convincing that people grew indifferent to the plight of the clerics. Indeed, there was a general lack of sympathy, and even outright animosity, toward them.

But while the people of England mused over the reforms and

wondered what effect the changes might have on their everlasting souls, many were certain that the clerics had enjoyed a life of unwarranted privilege. Cardinal Wolsey (though quite dead now) had built a home rivaling anything owned by the king, and was eventually shamed into giving it to His Majesty. So, why not give their money to His Majesty instead of the profligate clergy and a foreign pope?

"So, you see, being asked to assist Bishop Bonner is an honor to which we might all aspire."

"Because he is God's noble servant?"

"Of course."

Bianca had seen enough to know that men of position were unlikely to have gotten there by being exemplary models of piety. She doubted Bishop Bonner was any closer to God than any other priest, or for that matter, any other person. More often than not, circumstance and opportunity made the man. Not merit.

"And Father Foxcroft aspires to this as well?"

"Most decidedly so. He wishes to be archdeacon."

"What benefit is there in that office?" asked Bianca. She figured the benefit was more money, but she wanted to hear how he would answer.

Father Wells smiled as if he needed to exercise patience. He explained in simple terms. "As priests, we are called by God to serve Him and His people. We all welcome the chance to shepherd a bigger flock."

Bianca said nothing in response, but she could have predicted such an answer. Still, she was preoccupied with the two murders occurring not so far apart, and decided to leave matters of church politics alone.

"Have you any thoughts as to why two churches in this ward have been the sites of such a heinous crime? Why is this area plagued with this problem?"

"Mayhap the murderer, assuming it is just one murderer, lives nearby."

"You think it a matter of convenience?"

Father Wells nodded. He looked to take his leave, but Bianca had not finished questioning him.

"Is Bishop Bonner specifically looking at the priests from nearby parishes to make his appointment for archdeacon?"

The priest's face lifted with recognition. "I do not presume to know the bishop's intent. But, of late, he has taken an interest here."

Bianca thought a minute. "Remind me, sir, what other churches are in the ward?" There were over a hundred parish churches in London, and it was impossible for her to know the names of all of them.

"There is St. Andrew-by-the-Wardrobe, Father Foxcroft's church," said Wells.

"Any others?"

"Well, there is St. Paul's."

The cathedral didn't fit the murderer's pattern of targeting smaller parish churches. Not only was it massive but it was almost constantly occupied. Beggars slept against its walls, and there seemed to always be thieves and charlatans looking for an opportunity. "And who is the priest there?"

"Several men handle the position."

"And were those men present at the meeting?"

"They were not. The bishop separates the business of the cathedral from that of the parishes."

"I see," said Bianca, thinking.

"If that is all, I have a mass for which I must prepare," said Father Wells.

Bianca startled out of her thoughts. She would not let him get away without asking one last question. "Father Wells, you are not wearing a paternoster."

The priest appeared flustered and his face began to pink. "I seemed to have misplaced it." He craned his neck, looking past Bianca at someone entering the apse. "I must excuse myself now." And Father Wells left her to wonder.

Near Melrose, Scotland

They waited for night to settle. They did not move until all trace of day was swallowed by a vast silky dark above. The king's army had turned southern Scotland into a bare and blackened wilderness and before them lay the sleepy hamlet of Melrose, waiting to be feasted upon, to be pillaged, for havoc to be wreaked.

As the men descended upon Melrose, John could see the outline of its abbey in the moonlight, shaped like a fluted cross—an Amalfi cross, he would later be told. With its beautiful stones and elegant east window, Melrose Abbey was considered one of the most beautiful in all the land.

Sir Eure and Sir Layton took up where the Earl of Hertford left off and made Melrose suffer a second time. They took whatever booty they could find.

Between the burning and the destruction, Sir Eure launched a search for the embalmed heart of Robert the Bruce. Sepulchers were overturned and smashed. Flagstones pried up and sacred rooms plundered. John had been entailed to search the graveyard, and this he did with a listless spirit of indifference. He studied markers and lent his muscle when told, and luckily for him, in the ensuing mayhem, his lack of wild rabble-rousing was taken for methodical efficiency.

For all of their thorough ransacking, they did not find the hero's heart.

Instead, they found something of even greater value. They

discovered the Earl of Angus's family tombs. In two crypts near the high altar lay the esteemed members of the Douglas clan—the sacred resting place of the erstwhile defenders of the region and Melrose Abbey.

Meanwhile, the Earl of Angus, England's sworn enemy, watched from Eildon Hills with his men. And in his darkest moments of despair, the earl never could have imagined the blasphemy perpetrated upon his kin by this cruel agent of King Henry—Sir Ralph Eure.

Eure ordered the tombs defaced and the bodies dismembered. His men hacked apart the limbs and scattered them on the ground. The transgression pleased Sir Eure, a man with a heart as black as the graves that he desecrated.

As the turmoil raged around him, John left Melrose Abbey and stood guard on the outskirts of town. If the Earl of Angus and his men were anywhere near, surely he would not stand by as his family's honor was profaned.

But the Scottish army did not come.

John stared at the distant hills but was unable to distinguish an outline of horses from a ridge of trees. While the fires burned behind him and the crash of falling timbers merged with the exultant cries of looting soldiers, John lifted his eyes to the night sky and dreamed of his lover's soft embrace. There was comfort there, even if it was just a memory.

Later, Sir Ralph Eure boasted that he had conquered all of Scotland from the Tweed to the Forth. And the king saw fit to reward him with his conquests.

Eure grew fat with confidence. It was a conceit that the Earl of Angus would make him regret.

CHAPTER 19

Bianca left St. Benet's church and walked to the side street where the victim was discovered. The usual bustle of commerce had resumed and pedestrians wandered past, some stopping to gape at the rain spout where the body had been. A couple of hours had passed since the body was recovered, and Bianca, aware of the unfortunate lapse of time, searched the area for anything that might have been dropped by the murderer.

The cobble street made it easier for her to notice anything unusual, and Bennet's Hill was particularly tidy, being home to several profitable businesses as well as the church. The light was such that she didn't have to pick through the shadows, and she could see fairly well. However, all that she found, besides a few pennies, was a length of cord, a comb, and a strip of leather, probably from a bridle. She stuffed them in her purse and was about to leave when she spotted a rag next to the wall.

It was a dirty piece of linen, probably used to wipe drips, as it was stained with splotches of black paint. The cloth was still damp and gave off a sweet odor. She couldn't place the smell, and stood a moment sorting through her memory of scents with which she was familiar.

But she'd never come into contact with a smell such as this. Perhaps it fell from a painter's cart and had nothing to do with what happened earlier that morning. Still, she found it unusual and her curiosity was stirred. She gingerly dropped the filthy rag in her apron pocket to think about later.

Next, she wished to speak with Father Foxcroft. Bianca made the short walk to St. Andrew-by-the-Wardrobe in the hopes of finding the priest back at his church. She wanted to learn his whereabouts for the night before, but, more importantly, she wanted to get a better sense of the man. A layman informed her that Foxcroft was busy but if she could wait, he could speak with her between appointments.

Bianca wandered around the interior of the church, listening to the faint murmur of pigeons cooing in the rafters. She gazed up at the soaring buttresses, a majestic sight. She wondered if the great heights were meant to remind sinners of how small they were compared to their almighty God. It made sense that a church would be designed with that in mind—with soaring heights meant to humble the wicked.

"I understand you wish to speak with me." Father Foxcroft appeared from across the way. His voice boomed in the vacant space, jarring Bianca from her thoughts.

Bianca curtsied. "If you have a moment."

"I do not, but what do you want to speak with me about?"

"I was told that Bishop Bonner convened a meeting last night."

"He did."

"And you were present, as well as Father Rhys and Father Wells?"

"That is correct."

"Did you talk about the recent spate of murders?"

Father Foxcroft did not immediately answer. When he did, his response was curt. "The deaths are a grave matter of concern. However, if you expect me to tell you the details of what was said, it is a confidence that I will not break."

"Perchance, did you notice when Father Wells left the gathering?"

"All of us left around the same time once the meeting was over."

"No one lingered?"

Father Foxcroft shifted his weight. "Well, mayhap me," he said. "I attended His Grace to the road."

From what Father Wells had implied, Bianca supposed Foxcroft was ensuring his good favor with Bishop Bonner. She didn't expect he would be forthcoming about this or their discussion.

Obviously Wells and Foxcroft were at odds with one another. Perhaps theirs was a competitive relationship, a rivalry. Their rivalry, she intuited, was not a friendly one.

Bianca studied Father Foxcroft, a younger man to Wells by nearly a decade. Bianca placed him in his thirties. He appeared of sturdy build and his hands were not soft like most priests'. In fact, they looked strong from physical labor (perhaps manual labor in his youth).

"I wonder, sir, what do you think of Father Wells?"

"What is my opinion of the man?" His mouth curved into a half smile. "He is a good servant of the church . . . a faithful follower."

"A faithful believer in the king's supremacy?"

Father Foxcroft hesitated. "Aye, he is."

The hesitation caught Bianca's notice. For the most part, priests instinctively protected one another. Only the bravest and most devout would make their conscience known. But the way Foxcroft answered left room for doubt. Whether his pause was meant to imply Wells's duplicity or an attempt to make himself appear more devout, she could not be sure.

"Sir, do you think Father Wells is to blame for the recent murder at his church?"

"What? Father Wells committing such an abominable crime? Nay! Certainly not!"

"I am not suggesting that Father Wells is the murderer," said Bianca. "I am wondering if you think he may be remiss in some way. Perhaps his sincerity or his integrity is suspect. Mayhap he is being called into question either by God or by the murderer. Could there be cause for him or for St. Benet to be used by the murderer?"

Father Foxcroft thought for a moment. "I suppose it is a possibility," he ventured. "As priests we are representatives of our church and its parish. And certainly, God protects those who are sincere." Foxcroft's tone changed to one more insinuating. "Is Father Wells less earnest? Only God knows what is in his heart. But, aye, perhaps he is being punished for some flaw of character."

"And the same could be said of Father Rhys?"

"For cert. It is feasible."

"What flaw would be worthy of their being punished?"

"That is between them and our Maker," answered Foxcroft.

Bianca waited for him to offer an example, but he kept his silence.

"Do you worry that St. Andrew-by-the-Wardrobe might also be victimized?"

"How could I not worry? I live a righteous life devoted to my king and our Lord. But I have lived long enough to know that no man is without fault. Even though I have opened my heart, I am still guilty of sin in His eyes. What man is not?"

"Might you say that a priest is a church's public conscience?"

Father Foxcroft tilted his head, contemplating Bianca's logic. "I believe parishioners believe it so," he answered.

"A pious life is a commendable one," she said. She sensed Foxcroft was anxious to get on with his day, but a thought occurred to her—what if *he* had perpetrated these murders in an effort to besmirch the priests of the afflicted parishes?

How easily could he have gained access to the interior of two churches and executed a heinous crime? A priest might be admitted without question. A priest might even know how to gain entry without anyone knowing.

"Father Foxcroft, I know you must attend to your duties. But do you think someone might want St. Benet and St. Mary Magdalen to suffer? Mayhap it is not so much about murdering homeless boys as it is about denigrating the reputation of those churches. Because if I understand you correctly, if the church is ruined—so, by association, is the priest. And it appears that Father Wells and Father Rhys have both fallen from grace."

"Who would scheme such a horrible crime just to destroy a priest?" He looked askance at her, clearly disgusted. "I wonder, Bianca Goddard, what church do you attend?"

Bianca had not expected him to round on her. She had not expected a question about her own religious habits. She said nothing in response to his question, fearing if she named the nearest church, he might make it a point to inquire after her. She was not a regular churchgoer; her negligence could be cause for trouble.

Father Foxcroft's face turned sly. "I should think your priest has some work to do on you."

Bianca left St. Andrew-by-the-Wardrobe, and, rather than dwell on the priest's insinuation that she was a lost child of God, she turned her thoughts to finding another lost child—her rascally friend, Fisk. The day was not so inclement that she couldn't walk to Ivy Lane to see if the family was finally home.

The walk gave her time to think about Father Foxcroft and Father Wells. She supposed men of God were just as prone to envy and the sins of pride and greed as any other man. Priests assumed a superior morality; they knew what to say and how to keep adherents mystified and in awe. They were trained to do so, but were they any better than the rest of humanity struggling to find purpose and meaning?

Bianca shoved her hands in her apron pocket to warm them and felt the coarse fabric of the rag that she'd found. She thought back to Father Wells and his missing paternoster—how flustered he'd become when she mentioned it. What if the paternoster twined around the victim's neck was his? Certainly, he would not admit it. No one else in the church—the sexton, or the churchwarden—seemed to notice that he was not wearing one, nor did they discuss the paternoster's fine quality or recognize it as belonging to Father Wells. If they did, it was not mentioned in her presence. Bianca skirted St. Paul's Cathedral and turned down Paternoster Row, stopping to peer inside the window of the shop owner she had spoken to days before. He was engaged with a customer, a wealthy merchant from the looks of him.

Could Father Foxcroft be carrying out the murders in order to destroy the reputations of his fellow priests in Castle Baynard ward? Was he capable of such treachery? It was astonishing to think of a priest taking a person's life, or—even more disturbing—taking the lives of children. It was a crime of unconscionable evil. Bianca stepped up her pace. The years of deducing people's motivations in committing the ultimate cruelty of murder had hardened her to every possibility. Bianca believed that, if given a strong enough reason, anyone could kill.

But what if Father Wells had orchestrated the deaths? He

never could have managed hanging a child, given his age and round physique. He would have needed an accomplice.

But who?

Perhaps someone indebted to him? Someone whose secret he knew and who feared what could happen if that secret were divulged? But what would be his motivation? A raven cawed overhead from the roof of a stable. Bianca watched its head bob up and down in warning. Another scenario even more disconcerting occurred to her.

She remembered the priest's thinly veiled contempt for Foxcroft's overtures to win favor with Bishop Bonner. Wells had said that all priests had ambitions. Perhaps Wells plotted these murders at various parish churches and included his own so that no one would suspect him. People would wonder why St. Andrew-by-the-Wardrobe and Father Foxcroft had remained untouched. Bianca pondered this idea as she continued walking. Whereas Foxcroft connected the murders with a priest's guilt, mayhap Wells wanted to draw attention to a priest and a church that had *not* been affected. If St. Andrew-by-the-Wardrobe, Father Foxcroft's church, remained untouched by this spate of murders, people would wonder why.

Bianca considered this for a bit. The murders had occurred one week apart—a long time to wait to prove her theory. Plus, another life was a high price to pay.

But if the paternoster belonged to Wells, why would he use his own?

A nobleman approached on his handsome mount. Bianca stopped and watched him pass, so proud and unapproachable. She reasoned through a possibility. Wells could claim his prayer beads were stolen. He could claim someone used them to make it appear as if *he* had committed the crime. Bianca groaned at the tangle of explanations. And these only included the notion that either

Foxcroft or Wells was the murderer.

Bianca reached Fisk's neighborhood and turned down the cheerless lane, its sour tenements moldering in the relentless damp. She hoped to see Fisk sitting on the stoop—but alas he was not. It had been seven days since she'd heard word of him.

The shutters on his mother's rent were closed against the chill, and Bianca listened for sounds of activity as she stepped up to knock. This time, she received an answer. The door opened and Fisk's bleary-eyed mother peered out at her.

"Goodwife, are you well?" asked Bianca, concerned over the woman's harried appearance.

"Oh, it is you," said Meg, throwing off her cloak of suspicion and replacing it with one of passivity. She stuck her head out the door and looked past her visitor down the lane. "Come inside."

Bianca stepped into the darkened room. A single tallow lit the interior, filling the room with a disagreeable smoke and stink. She looked around at the young children, searching for Fisk among them. Not seeing him, she swallowed before asking, fearing what she might learn.

"I've come by a couple of times," said Bianca. "No one was home. I thought you had moved."

"Nay. I was out."

Bianca's eyes fell to Fisk's little sister, Anna. She stood to the side, listening. The girl had an intelligence that matched her brother's.

Fisk's mother spoke. "I heard another boy was hanged at St. Benet's."

"Aye. It is true. I am grateful it was not Fisk," said Bianca.

"But my boy is still not returned."

"I came to find out if he had come home," said Bianca. She lowered her voice in regret. "I've not been able to trace him."

Meg sniffed and gave Bianca an irritated look. Bianca

wondered why the woman was so terse with her. After all, she had Fisk's best interests in mind, and wished to work with her to find him.

Bianca decided to ignore the woman's pettish humor. "Have you learned anything that might help me in our search?" she asked.

Meg was momentarily distracted by her toddler standing with her arms raised, demanding to be held. She hoisted the child onto her hip.

"I was told he was being held for ransom," she said.

"Ransom?" exclaimed Bianca. "How did you learn of this?"

"A fellow came by. He said he knew where Fisk was and for five crown he would return him to me."

Bianca stared in surprise. "Who was this person?"

Fisk's mother shrugged. "He is a scoundrel of the worst kind."

"You do not know his name or where to find him?"

"He knows where to find me."

This was a surprising turn of affairs. Bianca wondered if the other victims had been put for ransom. "Do you have the money for Fisk's return?"

"Do I look as though I do?" She glared at Bianca. "Besides, I do not trust the skate to be telling me the truth. For all I know, he learned that Fisk had gone missing and is looking to take advantage of me."

"Did he say who had Fisk? Did he give any hint to where he might be?"

"Nay. He said that he expected they would sell my boy if I didn't come up with the money."

Bianca's stomach turned. The thought of Fisk enduring such a harrowing experience petrified her. Boys could be sold for any number of reasons, and none of them good.

"Sell him?" she repeated. She could barely get the wind to ask, "For what purpose?"

Fisk's mother replied, "I was told for a man's perverted pleasure."

Bianca closed her eyes. It took her a moment to respond, and when she did, she spoke in anguish. "We cannot let this happen."

"And how do ye plan to stop it? I don't have the money," said Fisk's mother in exasperation. "But, as I said, the rogue might have heard my son had gone missing and is playing me for the money. I told 'im to bring me a lock of Fisk's hair or a piece of his clothing to prove what he said is true. He hain't done that." She wiped her nose on the back of her hand and pushed the hair out of her toddler's eyes. "I don't know what to believe anymore."

At least the man hadn't threatened to hang Fisk if he didn't get his money, thought Bianca. "And this man hasn't been back since?" she asked.

"Nay. Like I said, I told 'im not to trouble me unless he can prove he knows where my boy is."

"Did Fisk ever tell you he was approached by a man to come work for him?" In truth Bianca was at a loss. Either Fisk's mother didn't know who this fellow supposedly collecting ransom was, or she didn't want to say. She could ask Patch to intervene, perhaps post someone to keep an eye on the place. If this "rogue" showed up again, then he could be followed.

Fisk's mother shook her head. "Nay, he never told me that."

Bianca thought it very much like him not to mention such an offer to his mother. Fisk had taken on the responsibility to help his family and he would not say anything to worry her. But if there was a way for Fisk to have come home by now, he would have done so. He would not have wanted his mother or siblings to wonder after him.

It gave her all the more reason to find this Brother Ewan. Whether he was the infamous Deft Drigger that Patch's prisoner suggested, she did not know.

Chapter 20

Ancrum, Scotland

It would be wrong to think that a Scot would let his family's tombs be desecrated without a fight. While Sir Euce boasted of his land acquisitions, the man from whom he'd taken the land quietly amassed an army with the help of a former rival, the Earl of Arran. There was no shortage of volunteers. They came from Fife and the borderlands. They brought their bows, their arquebuses, and their pikes. One quarter of them were mounted. Though they lacked the number of their enemy's forces, their determination made up for their lack of men.

After Melrose Abbey, the king's army, lazy with plunder, retired south toward Jedburgh. They set up camp near the village of Ancrum.

John had removed his jack and was repairing a loose plate when he caught sight of Glann McDonogh returning from the latrine. His friend looked as pale as frost on a shepherd's purse. He waved him over.

McDonogh shambled toward John and dropped himself on

the ground next to him. He immediately lay back and closed his eyes.

"You look poor, my friend. What ails you?"

"The flux." He threw his arm over his eyes.

"Be it bloody?"

"Nay, it be much."

John dug into his sack, rooting around the bottom to pull out a stoppered jar. He opened it and took out a pinch of something waxy. "Here, take this with a drink of ale. It may do you well."

McDonogh didn't bother sitting up, but reached out his open palm. "Is it poison? I hope it be."

"It is my wife's concoction. She insisted I take some of her medicinals."

"She be a witch?"

"Nay," said John. "She be a white witch." It was easier to call her that than explain Bianca's deviant obsession.

"If it should work, then I shall name my firstborn after her."

"And if you have a son?"

McDonogh propped himself on an elbow and smiled. "I shall call him . . . a miracle. There is little chance a maid will submit to me long enough to sire a child."

"You are not so ugly that there isn't a woman who would have you."

Glann motioned for John's flask of ale and washed down his medicine.

"Assuredly you are not such the licentious villain as yonder Roger," said John, tipping his chin at the repugnant archer slapping knees with his like-minded cohorts.

John took umbrage with Roger. He'd seen the swasher infected with the remorseless fever born from pillaging and laying waste to a village and its people. Not only did he revel in the destruction but Roger had taken pleasure with maids and mothers alike. Odious behavior was expected—indeed, it was encouraged—but John only kept his sights on the enemy in front of him. Not his enemy's women.

McDonogh looked over at the archers, and unfortunately made eye contact with one of them. Their jesting aside, they saw fit to take issue with the lowly billman and sallied over. Glann moaned and laid his head back, dreading the impending confrontation.

Roger spoke first. "Did I hear my name?" he asked.

"If your name be villain," answered John.

Roger's cohorts let out a long, sarky whistle. Glann moaned a second time and remained lying on the ground.

Roger scooped up a handful of mud and packed it into a ball. "What say you, Irishman?"

Glann shook his head. "I say nothing of use." He remained supine with his eyes closed, wishing the archer and his band to go away.

"Nothing of use? Yet your friend, here, calls me villain."

"Let him be," said John. "He has the camp runs, and if you linger you might catch his bad air and infect yourself."

"It takes a stinking billman to sit with a stinking Irishman," said Roger, and his friends tittered.

John returned to mending his jack. He worked on stitching a plate in place and kept his tongue. Bianca would have been proud.

But Roger edged for a rise. "Stand up and call me villain . . . drudge." He was tossing the clod of mud in the air and catching it while keeping his eyes on John.

John continued to repair his jack. He would have continued to ignore Roger if the cullion hadn't called him a "yellow-livered wally." With a long exhalation, John put aside his stitching and slowly stood. McDonogh sat up and struggled to stand—he was not about to leave John to face Roger alone. But John didn't wait for help. He took a step toward Roger while McDonogh still tried to steady himself.

A humorless smile spread across Roger's face as he waited for John to respond.

"Villain!" shouted McDonogh, trying to push his friend out of the way and get in front of him.

Roger's eyes shifted to the Irishman. He glanced back at John, and, in one smooth move, he advanced on McDonogh to seize his collar. He pulled the Irishman forward and stuffed the Irishman's mouth with the mud ball.

McDonogh spat out the dirt and sputtered, "Ye reeking rot of a..."

But John delivered a punch to Roger's gut, and McDonogh's curse was drowned by Roger's gasps for air. The band of rogues came to their leader's defense. They grabbed hold of John's arms and pulled them behind his back, exposing him for Roger to punch.

It took a moment, but Roger straightened. His breath was still heavy. "Well, John Grunt," he managed. "It seems ye need to be reminded of your rank." He looked at McDonogh, whose face was smeared with the remnants of mud. The Irishman had moved in front of his friend again in an attempt to take the blow. "Step aside, Irish. Ye look unfit to handle what I am about to deliver."

In spite of his wobbliness, Glann McDonogh took a defiant stance. "Ye have to strike me first," he dared.

With a weary smile, the archer shoved McDonogh aside, which was not so difficult given the Irishman's feeble health. He drew back his fist and landed a punch to John's ribs.

The crack could be heard ten feet away.

John doubled over, and Roger's rogues held him for a second blow.

Which Roger gladly delivered.

But billmen take issue when one of their kind suffers at the hands of an archer. The unspoken resentment that festered between the two ranks instantly rekindled. Even though a billman's duty was to protect the archers, it didn't preclude reminding an arrogant man of superior rank that he should appreciate his billmen every once in a while.

Roger saw, too late, the hulking pikemen who descended upon him. They tackled his legs and brought him down like a felled tree. Once on the ground, they took turns kicking him until he could do nothing but curl into a ball. Nor did his coterie of scum-hearted routers fare any better.

The stifled rancor of the lowly soldiers erupted in an impressive tangle of gut punching and wrestling. Pikemen piled on, getting their chance to even the playing field before eventually getting pulled off by men of more stolid nature. Ultimately, the latter prevailed and the more impetuous pikemen were restrained. Luckily, no other archers entered into the fracas. Instead, they watched with interest from a distance away. Apparently Roger had few allies.

In the end, John suffered a cracked rib. Every breath sent a sharp pain through his chest.

Roger's torso and legs bloomed in a panoply of purple bruises. And of course his most vulnerable organ was suitably and irreparably bruised—his pride.

Meanwhile, as the sun began to sink in the west, a small contingent of Scottish horsemen appeared near Peniel Heugh Hill. The English watchmen saw them ride northwest and alerted Sir Eure and Sir Layton. The two officers, fat with plunder and confidence, decided to pursue them. It should not take long to subdue this small militia of the earl's forces and deliver them a final, crippling blow.

A call to arms was sent through the camp at Ancrum Moor.

Cracked rib and flux be damned, John and McDonogh prepared to fight.

Before Bianca returned to Gull Hole, she made one last visit within London. The mention of Jane Clewes as the first to report the second victim's body was worth a talk with the woman. Bianca remembered how insistent she'd been that Father Rhys hear her son's confession.

She took a narrow path between two residences that ended on Knightrider, and following the curving road to St. Mary Magdalen's saw a young girl near the entrance of the church. She sold tied bunches of dried mint and rue from a basket. The herbs were much sought after this time of year to freshen well-worn rush mats and discourage biting fleas. Bianca had plenty of each, but gave the girl a penny for a bunch of rue anyway.

Inside, she did not find Father Rhys. The churchwarden told her he was not expected in until later.

"Then I wonder if you could tell me about Jane Clewes?" she asked.

"Jane Clewes?" said the churchwarden. "She has only recently come to St. Mary Magdalen's. I believe she is widowed, but in truth I do not know."

"The young man she was with," said Bianca. "He is her son?"

"She is his guardian. She has never said that he is her son. The circumstances there, I do not know. She does her best by him. Defends him against any perceived slight upon his person, either spoken or insinuated. She keeps to herself. I've never seen her mingle or enter into gossip. Jane Clewes is a very pious woman."

"Where did she live before coming here?"

The churchwarden shook his head. "As I said, she keeps her counsel. I do not know."

"Might you know where she keeps house, sir?"

"Is your intention to visit her?" asked the churchwarden.

Bianca nodded. "Aye."

"Then, I doubt that you will be successful. She is quite distrustful. But she lives in a tenement off Knightrider, on Sermon Lane or thereabouts."

A soft drizzle greeted Bianca when she exited the church and walked to Sermon Lane. She pulled her scarf over her head to warm her ears. She didn't know how she would find Jane Clewes given the vague description by the churchwarden. She would probably have to ask neighbors. However, luck favored her and, as she neared the corner of Sermon Lane, she noticed a woman at a window on the end building. Bianca slowed and recognized her distinctive profile. It was Jane Clewes.

To her surprise, Jane quickly opened the door to her knock.

"A good day to you, Goodwife Clewes," said Bianca. The woman looked stunned, as if expecting someone else. Bianca introduced herself. "I was at St. Mary Magdalen's when a boy's body was discovered there."

Jane Clewes ran her eyes up and down Bianca. "What need have you with me?"

"I was told that you were the first person to come upon the victim at St. Benet's."

"Was I?" Jane Clewes scowled.

"Father Wells told me. He said you were the first to report it."

"Father Wells of St. Benet's Church?"

"Aye," said Bianca.

Jane Clewes neither confirmed nor denied the assertion. The drizzle that had beset the day turned into a downpour. Bianca pulled her cloak closed at the neck to shed the sudden rain pouring off the roof. The woman grudgingly let Bianca inside.

"You are kind, goodwife. I have a long walk home." She glanced around the small rent, noticing a feeble fire twitching in the hearth. "Do you stay warm here?"

"I manage," answered Jane. "I make enough to buy a faggot every day."

On the bench next to the fire was a pile of wool and a distaff.

"Ah. Do you spin?"

"Aye," said Jane, brightening. "I work with Geve Trinion. He brings me fresh batts twice a week. He used to only come round every Tuesday. But I am quick on it."

"The work serves you well," said Bianca, sensing the woman's pride. "And a lap of wool keeps you warm while you spin it."

Jane Clewes's face relaxed a bit. Bianca thought the woman might even go so far as to smile. But alas, she did not.

"You are a parishioner of St. Mary Magdalen's?"

"I am."

"The area around St. Benet's is not your neighborhood," said Bianca.

"It is not so far afield," said Jane. "There is no law that says I must stay near home."

"Well met. The latest body was reported in the early morning hours." Bianca tried to sound conversational. "That is an unpleasant time to be out. It being the early chill of a damp morning."

Jane's face tensed. Bianca waited for the woman to answer.

"When is the weather not chill and damp?" said Jane. "I frequent a baker by the Wardrobe." "Be there issue in that?"

"Nay," said Bianca, waving away the woman's concern. "One is free to buy bread wherever one likes. But what unfortunate luck to stumble on such a sight when only a week ago your church was the venue of another such murder."

"It is by accident that I came upon the second victim."

"And did you see anything unusual? Other than the body, of course."

"I did not," answered Jane.

Bianca glanced around the room and took in its joyless interior. "Where be your son? He is not here?"

"You stand corrected. I am Huet's guardian. He is running an errand for me. I expect him soon."

"It must be a blessing to have his help. Have you lived here long?" asked Bianca.

"It has been a few months."

"I have met quite a few people coming here from the country," said Bianca, hoping to prompt Jane to say where she was from without pointedly asking her.

Jane Clewes crossed the room, favoring one leg with a slight hobble, to toss a few more sticks on the failing fire. "I only just came to London." She gathered several skeins of wool and put them in a basket next to a bench.

Bianca gave up trying to induce Jane to talk and asked directly, "Oh. From where?"

Clewes straightened and placed a hand on her hip. "You haven't told me anything about yourself." Clewes walked back to Bianca and stood squarely in front of her. "What is it that you want?" She looked for all the world like she would not say another word until Bianca answered.

"I forget that people are sometimes interested to know about me. My life is taken up with keeping a home. I am married to a silversmith's apprentice," she said. "He's gone to the border with the king's army." She gave a rueful smile. "I'm here because the constable hires me to learn what I can to help him find who murdered those two boys." Bianca made it sound as though she was not the one investigating these crimes. "So he wanted me to ask if there was anything strange you might have seen or remembered when you discovered the body?"

"Nay," she said. "Nothing gave me pause. Except of course, seeing a boy's life ended so grievously."

"It is a great sadness. I am certain you can sympathize with his mother."

Jane Clewes did not respond.

It was in that odd silence that Bianca heard a strange scratching. She looked across the room and thought it came from behind a wall, but then she located the sound near the center of the room, under the floor. Jane Clewes started coughing.

"What is that noise?" asked Bianca.

"My hearing is failing me. I did not hear anything."

"It sounds as if something is under your floor."

"Well," said Jane, tossing off Bianca's concern, "this is not such a fine place." She went to the center of the room and stomped the floor. "I have sent for a ratcatcher."

"You can scarce afford their fees. I can do it for you."

Jane Clewes looked horrified. "Nay, I think not!"

"I have done it before," assured Bianca. She refrained from mentioning any details.

Clewes crossed the room and opened the door. "The rain has lessened, I think." It was still raining heavily. "My problem will be taken care of shortly. Huet shall soon return. You should not be here. He gets confused about young women. Now, I ask that you take your leave." She held the door for Bianca, giving her no choice.

The weather was too poor to spend any time outside, so Bianca hailed a wherry to take her back to Southwark. As she waited for it to draw alongside the stairs, a rat slinked past, disappearing between some barrels on the docks where merchant vessels unloaded. Bianca wondered over Jane's peculiar situation. Was it vermin under her floor or something else? And what did Jane fear Huet might do if he saw her there?

Bianca stepped on board and sat beneath a tarpaulin, tolerating the smell of its tar coating for some protection against the rain. In the distance a new ship arrived in port, a galleon, and she wondered from where it had come. She wondered if someday John might return on a similar one.

Arriving at the stairs in Southwark she hitched up her kirtle—the roads being even muddier than in London—and ran all the way home to Gull Hole. There she found Hobs curled in a tight ball on a blanket, sleeping away the day and now the evening, his ambition to hunt in the cold and wet replaced by a desire to stay warm. She hung up her cloak and scarf, shed her soaked stockings and changed into dry.

The activity woke Hobs and he blinked at her, as if he'd just been subjected to a blinding beam of sunlight. "Here be the slugabed of Gull Hole," said Bianca, smiling at her favorite feline. She opened the firebox of her calcinatory furnace and cleared out the ashes to lay a fire. In her haste to leave with Brian Bindle, she'd neglected to bring in sticks to dry. It would be useless to try to start a fire using the wet wood. However, her failure was to the Dim Dragon's advantage, and the opportunity to warm up with a steaming bowl of barley stew was added motivation. She wiped her hands on her apron and remembered the rag she'd found on Bennet's Hill. She pulled it out and gave it a sniff, given pause by such an unusual smell. It was something she'd never encountered.

It was not floral, but its scent was sweet. What other substance could yield such a smell? Honey? Nay. Bianca shook her head. Wine? Doubtful that. Puzzled, she tossed the rag on her pallet to think about later.

Before she left, she shaved some cheese for her immortal cat, even though there was the possibility that he could never starve. But she loved Hobs enough not to subject him to a wretched night foraging for mice in the rain.

"Stay home, little friend," she advised. Then, shaking the rain from her cloak, she threw it on again. She secured the shutters tight and grabbed John's flatcap to keep her head dry.

Despite the wet night and the sinister dark, Bianca looked forward to seeing Cammy. If her friend had time, she would discuss some of her findings with her. She appreciated Cammy's level sensibilities—though to be honest, Cammy's infatuation with Roger was difficult for Bianca to understand. Her friend had no assurance from Roger that one day they would marry, yet she remained as loyal to him as if she had been spoken for.

The maid from the country was strong and knowledgeable about farm animals, but men who grew up in London were a different breed. Bianca hoped, for her friend's sake, that Roger would return and ask for Cammy's hand, even though John cared for him not, and truth be, she found the fellow a bit too proud to be trusted.

As she neared the popular boozing ken, Bianca could hear the boisterous whobub of its clientele seeping through the mud-spattered exterior walls. She hauled open the door and stood a moment, locating a trestle where she might sit. There was the usual coterie of regulars planted about the room, and always a goodly number of new customers trying out the fare either through recommendation or coincidence; more often, thought Bianca, probably the latter.

Across the room sat Mackney and Smythe, the motley pair of thieves, and Bianca decided to join them until Cammy was free.

"A good night, Bianca Goddard," said Mackney when she settled in next to them.

"A good night for a barley stew and the company of friends," said Bianca. She removed her flatcap and shook out the droplets of rain on the floor.

"Aye, that," said Smythe. He had finished a trencher of said stew, and Bianca wondered how the gangly thief could eat so much and still remain as thin as the Dim Dragon's ale on a Saturday night.

"Word is," said Mackney, "a ship is in port from the borderlands. There is news of a recent rout near Jedburgh." He looked down into his ale and said in a quiet voice, "It is not in the king's favor."

Bianca suddenly lost her appetite. "What do you know?"

"Roy the Robber has gone to see what he can learn. He's been away for some time now."

"No doubt waylaid by opportunity," said Smythe with a snide lift of his eyebrow. "Roy can never do just one task without first doing two others."

"Mean you, finding a gull to nip and foist?" Bianca referred to Roy's sneaky tactic of pretending to faint; when someone (usually from away who didn't know any better) came to help, Roy would slice the strings of the man's purse and run off with it.

"He can't stop himself," said Smythe. "He keeps a running tally."

Bianca caught Cammy's attention and the wench made her way over, toting several empty tankards. "Did they tell you a ship has come in?" she asked Bianca.

"I saw a galleon when I came back from London. Do we know for sure that it sailed from the borderlands?"

"Aye," said Cammy. From the serious look on her face, Bianca knew her friend was worried.

"Well, it will do us no good to fret until we learn what has happened. Roy shall return soon enough. Mayhap he will have solid news."

"Last week they said the war might be over, and I had hopes for Roger's return."

"As did I for John," said Bianca, trying to allay her friend's fears, "but we shall know soon enough. This may only be a rumor, and you know how unreliable the first reports are."

The serving wench looked away, and it appeared she was trying to keep from crying.

"Can you bring me a bowl of barley stew?" asked Bianca. She hoped her friend might benefit from her personal adage that keeping busy was the best remedy for keeping brave.

"Aye, and an ale as well?" asked Cammy.

As Cammy moved away, Mackney and Smythe watched the backside of her before turning their attention to Bianca. "She puts too much faith in this Roger fellow," said Mackney.

"She has pinned her heart on him," said Bianca.

The portly curber did his best to turn Bianca's thoughts to matters not so troubling. "Did you hear, pray tell, about the monkey that got loose at Westcheap Market the other day?"

"A monkey?" asked Bianca. Such sights were rare, especially this time of year.

Smythe started laughing, a chittery kind of laugh in which his teeth tapped together. He insisted on telling the story, and elbowed his partner, who yowled from its bony sharpness.

"It were a tawny Moor who had the beast tied with a rope round its neck. He was walking it through the market for a show at one by the clock next to the conduit. It would cost a penny to see. But a lady with too many questions beset him, and, unbeknownst to either of them, the monkey worked the knot at its neck and slipped away. A moment later they heard an ear-cracking scream. The monkey had jumped on a vendor's back and stole her basket of walnuts. The thing ran like a demon—jumping stall to stall, upsetting turnips and plums, upending barrows, climbing to a roof and running along its eave, all the while screeching like a madman! The entire market was in an uproar. I've never seen such confusion. And all of it from a creature no bigger than a cat." Smythe began laughing again in that strange way he had, and Bianca found the sight of him more amusing than imagining the turmoil from the monkey.

Mackney laughed, too. "And then the little demon, with the basket of walnuts in the crook of its arm, jumped from one building to the next, all the way down the row with the tawny Moor most sorry and running alongside beneath. Finally, it reached a tree and the tawny Moor tried coaxing it down. All the merchants gathered round, demanding payment for the damage it had caused."

"Such a quivering sack of bones," said Smythe, taking a swig of ale.

"But the monkey sat in the tree and bared his not so small teeth at the crowd," said Mackney. "No one could get him down. There was much shouting."

"It must have been a sight," said Bianca.

"Oh, it was!" said Mackney. He continued the story: "The monkey took issue with everyone shouting at his master, and aimed a walnut at Tuck the turnip farmer. Hits him on the crown! The monkey found great sport in that. He hit one person after another. Walnuts showered down and the sellers went antic picking up the walnuts and throwing them back at the monkey."

Bianca grinned. "Pray tell, how did it end?"

"Why, the silly beast ran out of walnuts. When it realized it had no more, it threw down the basket. Then it climbed up the tree and jumped to a roof, scrambled to the peak and disappeared over the top. They be looking for it still."

"There is a monkey on the loose in London?"

Mackney and Smythe both smiled.

"God's tooth. That should give some a fright."

"Indeed," the thieving pair chimed. "Everyone is lashing shut their windows tonight."

Cammy arrived with Bianca's stew and ale and joined them at the table.

"Alewife Frye is letting me take time to eat," she said tearing off a hunk of bread, then dipping it in a bowl she had brought for herself.

The weary maid had barely finished her stew before they felt a draft on the back of their necks. A whoosh of air threatened to extinguish the tallows in the wall sconces. They turned to see who'd opened the tavern door. Roy the Robber had returned.

CHAPTER 21

Geve Trinion tucked his knife back in his waistband and examined the lock of hair in good light. He ran a finger over it. This should be proof enough for Meg. After all, it was what she asked for. He tied the lock with a strand of undyed wool, wrapped it carefully in thin cloth, and placed it in his pouch. He would have to be mindful when removing coins so as not to ruin the fragile bundle. He didn't want it to fall apart before she'd seen it.

The day seemed interminably long with all the stops he had to make. His list of visits was made up of old women, spinsters looking for income to eke out their meager existence. They all wished to be complimented on their skeins, as if their self-worth depended on the quality of their spinning. He wearied of throwing them crumbs of praise and watching them peck at the bits like sparrows outside his door.

He told himself that he didn't have long to wait. He would get his money and then he could start a new life. Leave London, with all its filth and the insidious reach of its truculent king, behind. He could almost smell the green scent of freshly scythed hay and the faint hint of smoke drifting across a field from a cozy hearth in a warm stone cottage. Perhaps the world was not so wretched if he could still dream such notions.

When at last he stepped up to Meg's door, he took a moment to smooth down his hair and straighten his cap. He adjusted his codpiece to calm an "itch" he had there. Truth be, he still found her attractive.

"It is you," she said upon answering the door. His heart sank. There were many ways those three little words could be said, and she had voiced them in a not so welcoming way. His hopes for amorous comport dashed, his mood turned black.

He pushed his way into her rent. Her daughter with her puling mouth fell instantly silent, eyes all agog, staring slack-jawed at his person. He looked around the room. Where was the pretty fair-haired one? He could have growled like Gorgeous George at the bear garden and made the little one cry. But he refrained from being needlessly dramatic.

"I've brought proof," he said over Meg's protests to get out. "It is what you wanted."

Meg's face turned pale. She searched his face.

The corner of Trinion's mouth turned up. His eyes dropped to her bosom and crept around its shapely contour. He thought back to a time long ago, and his mind could have lingered there if not for a sudden sharp sting planted on his cheek.

"God's blood, wench!" He raised his hand to return the favor, then stopped himself. He was running afield of his purpose. Let her husband beat her, he thought; it was not his place. But her husband was busy stabbing his way through France. He almost reconsidered. "Do you want to see proof, or not?"

Meg's angry brow changed to worry. Her eyes searched his face. "Aye," she said, softly. "Show me."

Geve Trinion removed the sack of wool and uncinched the pouch dangling from his belt. It was empty from paying out coins to the spinners, except for the lock of hair. He removed the sample from his purse, and, before he could even present it to her, she snatched it out of his hand.

Meg turned away to unwrap the thin square of linen. Such a lovely curve to her neck, he thought as it bent to examine the lock of hair. Her own splendid mane remained covered beneath a loosely tied headrail. He was so close he could have whipped it off her head and watched her silky, custard-colored hair tumble out. He could have swept her up and forced his lips on hers. She would eventually relent to his wiles. Aye, he could have taken her, right there with her pathetic spawn watching. It would suit him to do so, and it would serve her right for all of her doubting and disrespect.

But he didn't.

To his dismay, her shoulders began to shake. Aw. She was crying. He'd seen before how a woman could be so overcome with grief that they were rendered speechless. Then the wails of despair would come pouring forth. He reached out a hand to comfort her. He would let her weep into his shoulder. Oh, it would have made his deceit even more believable.

But, at the last second, he drew back his hand as if it had gotten too close to a flame. Instead, he appealed to her maternal instincts to convince her to part with her money for Fisk's safe return.

"Meg, Meg," he began. "This is the proof that you wanted. I placed myself in great danger to secure it. The heartless cur has agreed to part with Fisk. But it comes with a price. Fear not—Fisk is safe. At least for now. Your money together with mine will be enough to secure his safe return. Do this, and bring your boy home. Never will you be apart from him again." He paused, waiting for her to speak, then added, "Unless, of course, you decide it so."

But Geve Trinion would be rudely reminded that a woman could be full of surprises.

Little Luke was so distracted that he never heard the shouts of a drayman hollering to move lest he be trod upon. One moment he was walking, and the next he was sitting on his bum. He blinked up at the fellow who had seized his arm and yanked him aside.

"You nearly ended under a horse's hoof," said a fellow with a red cap and queer-looking eyes. One peeper focused on him and the other looked over his shoulder so that Luke turned around to see who else he was talking to. No one was there. He turned back, and the man held a sly smile on his face. "You must be more watchful," he warned, and he leaned into his cart festooned with swinging talismans and clacking bottles.

The boy got to his feet and brushed himself off. He looked about as if surprised to see where he was. He didn't like running this errand for his master. The lane where he was supposed to leave this purse of coins was unnaturally dark even on the brightest day—but he hadn't seen one of those for weeks it seemed. He wondered if the clouds had swallowed the sun, and would he ever see it again?

Luke glopped through a woefully thick patch of mud that nearly sucked the shoe off his foot, then crossed to the other side of the lane where the road looked less gluey. The monk's words kept rattling around in his head. He made it very clear that he *and* God would be most angry if Luke did not follow through. Luke knew firsthand the pain of the monk's wrath, and could only imagine what God's would be like.

The faint glow of a candle shone through the window of the tenement on Sermon Lane. Luke slowed and approached cautiously, looking to see if the woman was watching out the window. Last week he had seen her sitting there, staring, her sharp nose sloping down to nearly touch her chin. She might have been a kindhearted woman for all he knew, but since he didn't know he associated her unattractive profile with a nasty temperament.

This time Luke did not see her by the window. He cautiously crossed the road once he was past its line of sight and circled back. He pulled out the purse of coins, their heavy weight a comfort in his hand. Part of him longed to take the coins and never return. But where would he go? He had no family that he wished to stay with—his uncle was meaner than the monk, if that was even possible.

Luke hesitated beside the building across from the woman's tenement. The purse of coins sang to him. If he kept the money he could leave London. The thought of it gave him a thrill of hope. But as he contemplated the idea of being on his own, he remembered stories of forest spirits and devils lurking behind cairns and scary creatures that could eat him for dinner. He realized he was not so brave.

With a sigh, Luke resigned himself to doing the monk's bidding. He crept forward toward the stone stoop, careful to look down to the dead end of the alley where it was the most dark and dangerous. No one was around and the door to the tenement remained closed. Luke tiptoed to the step and gently laid the purse of coins on the ground beside it. Still facing the door, he walked backward, mindful not to snap a twig or disturb a single fallen leaf. He listened, staring at the rent as if that would help him to hear. No sound stirred within.

On all counts, he believed he had successfully completed his task. He turned to make away, but had only taken a single step when, suddenly, the door banged open and a monster flew out after him.

Luke ran for his life, for surely, he thought, he was going to lose it. He'd never seen such a brute. It was taller than a tree, and Luke was certain it was bigger than one. It silently trundled down the stoop and gave chase, its eyes bulging and as vibrant green as scum on a pond.

Instructed never to lead anyone back to the old tannery, Luke turned up a short lane and headed for St. Paul's Cathedral.

Paul's Walk would be crowded. It would be difficult to find him among the people, and he could hide behind the massive columns lining the way. But before he disappeared into the cavernous nave, Luke stole one last look over his shoulder. To his horror, his pursuer had gained on him. Luke bit his lip and dove into the popular hall.

To the men of station, the men wearing their scholarly gowns and chains of office, nothing was as important as news mongering, be it truth or simple fancy. Practically any amount of mayhem could be tolerated at Paul's Walk so long as it didn't disrupt their cherished discourse. But Luke made such a commotion that conversations paused and attendants turned to watch him run frantically through the apse, upending stalls and crashing into people.

The learned men sighed. When would the commoners stop using Paul's Walk for their frivolous scuffles?

Luke was too frantic to stop running and find a place to hide in the great nave. He exited the other end, just as his stalker began navigating the havoc he'd left in his wake. Not only the annoyed men of station, but booksellers whose businesses had been toppled took issue with the causative agent. They blocked and admonished the hulking figure. They let him know they were none too pleased. And as the men of station delayed his pursuit, the goliath's frustration began to mount.

The men soon realized they had angered someone who should not have been provoked. His neck and face pinked and he wrawled like a bear, lashing out in frustration. Perhaps the soonest way back to normal was letting him through. Stands could be righted, books picked up, conversations resumed. The educated men of Paul's Walk stepped aside and let him pass. They pointed the way out.

Along the edge of the courtyard where priests delivered their sermons in the high pulpit at Paul's Cross, little Luke hid behind a bushy laurel and gasped for breath. His lungs heaved. He peeped between the branches to gauge whether it was safe to return to the tannery.

Next time, Luke would insist someone else deliver the money to the lady. Besides, it was time for someone else to take a turn. Why did he always have to do it?

When Luke's breathing calmed, he quickly grew bored crouching behind the bush. Only parishioners and men in scholarly gowns walked past. After a few minutes of watching, the threat appeared over. He popped his head up and looked around. He saw no sign of the giant.

Luke's belly grumbled, reminding him of a bowl of soup awaiting him. If he got there in time, he'd get an extra slice of bread for a job well done. With nary another thought, the boy skipped down the walk and made for the tannery.

He kept to the shadow cast by St. Paul's, that ever-present shade, and speculated about what kind of soup he would get. Mayhap one made from the drippings of the monk's roast chicken.

Luke envisioned the steam tickling his nose and anticipated the contentment of a full stomach. He stepped up his pace and began whistling. A perfectly straight stick lay in his path and he picked it up and ran it along the iron posts surrounding the small graveyard he passed. Its rattle so engaged that he didn't hear the ponderous steps approaching from behind. From the corner of his mind came a warning that he was not yet in the clear. He dropped the stick and listened. A glimpse over his shoulder confirmed his worst fear.

Luke ran straight for the tannery. It was a matter of survival and he'd gladly take thirty lashes compared to being eaten alive.

He dove down an alley that served as a public latrine, a dark and putrid place between buildings with no windows on either side.

Luke slopped to the end and turned the corner onto the lane. He could smell the acrid taint of the building nearby. Only a quick dash and he would be safe. He'd pound on the door and they'd let him in.

But perhaps it is when one is so close to success that one takes the least care.

Refuge within his sights, Luke burst into the lane and sprinted to the tannery door. He gave the signal knock. Four quick raps, a pause, followed by another four quick raps.

But when the door opened, the monk's brows pulled together in a scowl. He scratched his head. Did he imagine hearing the requisite knock? No one was there.

The door closed behind Roy the Robber and he met the clientele's stares at the Dim Dragon Inn. Mackney waved his curbing hook, hailing him over.

Bianca made room for Roy, watching as he leisurely navigated between tables, greeting some patrons and shaking his head in answer to others. The somber look on his face did not change and Bianca sensed his news was not good. He greeted everyone before sitting down, giving her a nod, but his eyes avoided hers when she returned the greeting in kind.

Word had circulated that Roy had left to learn more about the recent report regarding the king's army. Soon, half the customers of the Dim Dragon had gathered around their table. Cammy hurriedly delivered the ales in her order, then stood behind Bianca to listen.

The group impatiently watched Roy shake out his wet cap and set it on the table in front of him. Mackney, unable to wait any longer, spoke. "Pray thee, quench your thirst, Roy. Partake of my ale and enlighten us."

Roy helped himself to Mackney's tankard, drinking long while a dozen eyes watched with anticipation. He finished the ale and wiped his mouth on his wrist.

"I found a boatswain," he said. "The fellow was securing the ship to the bollards at Romeland. He said they had returned from Eyemouth where they heard tell what had happened. They brought a few men home from the conflict in Ancrum Moor."

"A few? How many be a few?" asked Cammy.

Roy did not know.

"Did ye ask?" Cammy's frustration began to mount. When she got a shake of the head from Roy she persisted. "Where is Ancrum Moor? Be it near Edinburgh?"

"It is a large heath near Jedburgh—south of Edinburgh on the borderland."

"Let him tell the story!" exclaimed a patron, keen to hear the tale.

Roy the Robber wiped his nose on his sleeve. "February began favorably. The king's army was boosted in numbers with Spaniard mercenaries and others. They had over fifteen hundred English Borderers and assured reivers—though truth be, the reivers are an untrustworthy lot."

"But they swear allegiance to the crown," said another serving wench who'd come over to listen.

Roy snorted. "Ye think it matters to those lawless rebels?"

"How do ye know those numbers?" asked a patron from the far end of the table.

"I am telling ye what the boatswain said and that is all. I have no cause to disbelieve him. I saw with my own eyes the men on board that ship. They were subdued. Demoralized and tired."

"Can we go there?" asked Cammy eagerly. "Mayhap Roger .. ." She leaned down and spoke into Bianca's ear. "Mayhap John!"

Roy the Robber scowled. People were loudly speculating and drawing their own conclusions. He held up his hands to silence them. "If ye want to dither on, then do so. But if ye want to hear the gist of it then let me speak!"

The patrons murmured. They nudged each other to quiet.

Roy continued. "The army had just taken Melrose and their abbey and left them in ruins. This came after a long bout of plundering Scottish villages south of Edinburgh. They'd done what Henry wanted. They brought the Scotch to their knees." He looked up at Cammy. "Have you a meat pie for my trouble?"

The serving wench, loathe to miss a single word, looked irritated.

Bianca put a hand on Cammy's. "I will tell you what you miss."

Mackney piped up. He had Scottish blood in him, but he was a loyal Englishman, having come to London as a lad. "And this be the army led by the Earl of Hertford?"

"In truth I do not know," replied Roy. "They are all one and of the same. The Earl of Hertford commands the forces but there are commanders under him. They treat every village with the same cruelty as Dunbar." Roy shook his head.

"And what of Dunbar?" asked a patron.

"It was an act of savagery, that. They struck at night while families slept, burning houses to the ground. Raping women and killing those who tried to escape."

Bianca winced. Even though she promised she would tell Cammy everything, the girl did not need to know the wicked details.

"But the Scots fought on," said Roy. "They hid behind rocks and knolls. They picked off the English one by one."

"Oh, aye," said Smythe, who had remained quiet until now. "They be a feisty lot and there be no rules of war that they follow."

"'Tis because there are so few Scots by comparison," said Mackney. "What chance have they against the might of the English army?"

Cammy returned from the kitchen with a pork pie and ale. "What have I missed?"

Bianca shrugged. "Nothing of mention."

Roy took a hungry bite of pie and washed it down with another long drink.

"So, the men felt invincible and they headed south toward Jedburgh to camp on the Ancrum Moor. But on Peniel Heugh Hill they spied a Scottish cavalry and they took chase after them."

"Oh, why could they not let them be?" asked Cammy. "I fear to hear what happens next."

Roy the Robber broke off some crust and pushed his cheek out with his tongue. His hesitation unnerved Bianca. She felt her neck tighten as she waited for him to continue.

"The king's army did not know that the Scottish army lay in wait, out of sight, over the hill." Roy took another drink of ale.

Cammy dug her fingers into Bianca's shoulders.

"There be two battles. Both with the same result. One force of two thousand spearmen, hagbutters, and archers started shooting at the cavalry but the wind blew the smoke back into their eyes, blinding them. The cavalry had led them into a trap. The horsemen disappeared over the hill where the Scottish army lay in wait. The Scots crested the hill with the English below them and rode down into the English vanguard and pushed them back. The smoke was so thick the English could not see and they retreated into their line. Confusion ensued, and the line collapsed."

"How many Scots *were* there?" asked Cammy.

"They estimate twenty-five hundred Scots, including border reivers. Plus, the Scots had cannons."

"And we did not?" exclaimed Mackney.

"They were in pursuit. Cannons can't be toted about so easily."

Smythe sucked in his breath. "Ye cannot trust these Scots.

These reivers. How will there ever be peace in that land?"

"Indeed, when it looked like a rout, the assureds tore off their red crosses and fought for the other side."

"Treason!" a patron shouted.

"Eight hundred Englishmen died," said Roy.

Jaws dropped. The disaffection of the reivers was often talked about. Their treachery was legendary. But to hear that it may have resulted in the slaughter of so many countrymen boiled the blood of every Englishman and iced the blood of the Englishwomen in the Dim Dragon Inn.

"The army broke and scattered through the countryside." Roy's eyes scanned the bewildered faces, still stunned.

"A hostile countryside," said Mackney. His words sat heavily in the air.

No one said a word. No one moved. Eyes blinked. People stared.

"Did the Scots take prisoners?" Cammy asked in a small voice.

"Aye, they did. The boatswain said a thousand men were captured."

More silence.

"It was a rout," concluded Smythe.

"Where is the army now?" Cammy wanted answers. "Are they coming home?"

Roy could not say. "Good wench, I have no more information."

"Surely, the king can send ships to bring them home," said Bianca.

"If the laggards knew where the ships would be. And then, it would depend on whether they could stay alive long enough to get to them," said Roy.

Bianca's heart sank. The odds were against John. Even if he had survived the battle at Ancrum Moor and had avoided capture, how could he possibly get home? What if he was injured? She had no idea where this moor was, or how close it was to the border. And then, even if John was able to cross into England he would still be in danger. It was a long walk home.

Chapter 22

Bianca had one too many ales with Cammy. The two spent the next hour apart from the rest of the clientele, discussing Roy's story. Goodwife Frye saw the look on Cammy's face after Roy finished and knew the wench would be useless serving any more customers. The goodwife was wise like that, and sympathetic to the fears of a young woman's heart. She had not forgotten what it was like to love a man and to be hopeful for him.

The two friends came to no conclusion, no recourse. After all, what could they do? They were left to carry out what women were destined for since time immemorial—to wonder and to worry.

With the assurance that the two would always comfort one another no matter what the future held, Bianca walked home to Gull Hole. It was so late and rainy that the lanes were empty of ne'er-do- wells. Even miscreants had the sense to stay dry on such a night.

Too many ales kindled Bianca's raw emotions, thoughts that were better left suppressed. The good part, if there was any, was that she did not mind walking in the pouring rain. As she passed her neighbor's coop of hens she reached through a slat and pulled out an egg. The ale had dulled her conscience and she figured he owed her at least that for as many times as she'd had to kick one of his chickens out of her rent. She fiddled a bit with her padlock, and once inside her room of Medicinals and Physickes lit a tallow.

She thought it too late to start a fire in her stove, so Bianca opted instead to strip herself of her wet clothing and bury herself beneath her covers until morning. Normally, her return would have woken Hobs, who was sleeping on the bed, and he would have at least roused long enough to greet her and expect his belly to be rubbed. But the black tiger didn't budge, even with Bianca kicking and rustling around to get warm and comfortable.

She leaned over to blow out the flame when she caught sight of him. She sat up and put her hand on his side. His chest barely moved. He barely breathed.

"Hobs," she said, shaking him gently. She repeated his name and shook him more vigorously. In that brief moment it occurred to her that maybe her immortal cat was not ageless after all. Maybe the elixir of immortality was no better than any other medicine. Perhaps her old mentor, Ferris Stannum, had not discovered the elusive philosopher's stone. Without having to put her beloved cat to the test, the feline had resolved the question for her.

Bianca's heart fell. Having Hobs underfoot, her little "house spirit," had been an inconvenience that never truly irritated her. The cat was just reminding her that he was there, and no matter what she might have found so absorbing at any given time, it wasn't nearly as important as he.

"Oh, Hobs," she said, stroking his side. Perhaps her repeated petting might stir him. Though he was just a cat she never felt completely alone as long as he was around. She breathed into his ear, calling his name, trying to rouse and urge him back from whatever "world" he was in.

Now with John being gone and learning the news from Roy

the Robber, she felt a painful vacuum in her life.

What if John never came home? Bianca contemplated whether she would continue to live in this derelict room with only her herbs and a cache of supplies and instruments to keep her company. Would she grow old here? Would people continue wanting her concoctions? Or would she be that odd, rumored woman—more interested in plants and chemistries than the desire to keep a comfortable home? A woman eventually forgotten in time. For what woman can claim her place beside men of similar inclination and not be denounced for it?

Was all this for naught?

Meddybemps would have cautioned her against entertaining such thoughts. Aye, she had too much spleen, she could not deny it. Therein festered those melancholic, uneasy feelings. The black bile that normally coursed through her veins multiplied twofold. But in the silence of her room, in the pitiless and expansive night, she could not help herself. Moreover, she did not want to.

If left on her own, how would she fare with no one to love? Without John to challenge and tease her? Without John ...

Her morale spiraled and she added another thought to the mix. What if something happened to Meddybemps? What if he could no longer sell her medicinals? What if *he* died?

The two of them had been careful around one another since the incident of her father's stolen *lapis mortem*. Rebuilding her faith and trust in the streetseller had come in fits and starts. So, too, had she distanced herself from her mother. The deception and lies had shaken Bianca more than either of them would ever fully know.

In the quiet of her thoughts and in the hushed lull of contemplation, Bianca rolled onto her back and let sadness consume her. She gave over to sorrow and her tears flowed.

After a time, her sobs turned to snuffles and she blew her nose and wiped her tears. She sat, quietly staring at a trickle of water coursing down the wall. The roof over her head needed repair. One of these days she would scramble on top of it and patch the leaks. As she listened to the rain and wind continue to beat against her little home, her mind emptied of everything except for the sound of weather. That, and a faint sound of life beside her.

Bianca turned and stared down at the black tiger. Was he purring? "Hobs?"

The cat made the effort to lift his head and gave a short mew.

Bianca stroked his fur. "Hobs! What happened?" She rubbed his back as if the act of doing so would reinvigorate him.

The tallow spewed a smoky stream in their direction, and Bianca waved away the smelly haze, then moved the chamberstick. When she turned around, Hobs was sitting.

"God's blood, Hobs! One moment you could have passed for dead and the next ..."

He blinked at her, then yawned.

Bianca grinned. "Come, you slyboots. Let me give you some dinner." She pulled a blanket around her shoulders and in the dim light cracked the egg she'd stolen from the neighbor.

Outside, the rain literally caught its second wind and pelted the door and shutters. Her door had never been plumb and water soon streamed down the inside and pooled on the floor. There was nothing Bianca could do to stop the leaking. No amount of straw stuffed in the crack would prevent the wet from getting in again. With a sigh, she remembered Boisvert's quarters in Aldersgate; and even though she had not liked living there, she did appreciate its better construction. Looking back, she regretted not letting John find them a better place to live. Why had she always resisted his wanting to improve their lives? What was she leery of?

She decided she must be more willing to please her husband. She needed to trust that his eagerness for their mutual comfort might actually be ... a desirable quality. Another gust of wind blew open a shutter and it clattered against the wall, startling her. Hobs, having devoured every drop of egg, sprang from the table and ran behind the stove.

"Hobs, it's only the wind." She pulled the shutter closed and lashed it with a length of rope, but it continued to rattle, and Bianca knew she would have difficulty sleeping with the banging. With a sigh of resignation, she moved a pail under the window to catch the drips. "It will have to do for now."

***

Constable Patch had waited for this moment.

He found out the name of the nobleman who had berated Constable Berwick from Castle Baynard ward, and with a carefully rehearsed plea for help (or rather, a carefully rehearsed complaint regarding Berwick's indifference), Patch succeeded in making his counterpart look incompetent. After explaining the dire circumstances of two boys whose deaths had been as good as ignored, the nobleman sought assistance from the Lord Mayor's aldermen.

"Most lawmen would have made an effort to find the culprit, but I don't sees that Berwick has lifted a single finger, exceptin' to pour more wine," he told Sir Edward Craven. "It is his sworn duty to puts an end to such terrible crimes when they occur in one's ward. He's refused my help and has refused my good faith efforts to advise him." Patch went on to explain that he had personally solved no fewer than four murders and had risen through the ranks to the position he now held in Bread ward. His expertise was indisputable.

The point taken, Sir Craven duly noted Patch's achievements and relayed his concerns to the appropriate alderman. Apparently, said alderman had spoken to Constable Berwick, and had made an impression, for now the ineffectual Berwick stood before Patch in his office in Bread ward.

"Patch," said Berwick, forgoing wishing him a good day, or evening, or anything. His ruddy complexion seemed even worse than the last time Patch saw him. His face appeared nearly purple.

"Berwick," returned Constable Patch in a measured tone, which was difficult for him to manage. He could hardly wait to hear what the rotten cur had to say.

"I've heard tell that you have been critical of my handling in the recent deaths."

"Deaths?" said Patch. "I call them murders." He leaned back in his chair. "Mayhap it is a difference in opinion."

Berwick's expression was unmoved. Patch wondered what was going through the fellow's mind. Obviously, the man had been spoken to, maybe even chastised for his anemic response in the matter.

"The aldermen have requested that guards be posted at every parish church in Castle Baynard ward. They fear an epidemic of sorts."

"Epidemic?" inquired Patch.

"A scourge of murders."

"Ah." Patch had informed Sir Craven that the bodies were found one week apart, and if the perpetrator was following a pattern, they might expect a third victim within days. "Is a third death inevitable?" asked Patch. He had only been speculating by suggesting it to the nobleman. He now wondered if Berwick or the aldermen were privy to news that he had not yet learned.

"If inevitable, then it must be preventable. At least that is how the council views the situation."

"And how long do they propose to continue this watch?"

"Until the murderer is caught."

Patch pulled his scraggly chin hair. "Methinks posting men will discourage a murder. It will not work in catching a perpetrator. He will see the guards and leave."

"That may be the aldermen's intent."

"But thens, the murderer might go somewheres else." The closest ward being his own, thought Patch with a rill of alarm.

Berwick's mouth turned up in a wry smile. "Tut-tut, Patch. What was once my blemish might soon become yours."

Patch examined a brass button on his doublet then looked up at Berwick. "What are ye proposing?" he asked.

Berwick picked up the quill on Patch's desk. He rubbed its nib between his thumb and forefinger while contemplating his peer. "I am here because I value my position in Castle Baynard. I need more men to post at the churches. I do not presume to know whether St. Mary Magdalen or St. Benet will be the scene of another unfortunate crime, but I must take precautions so neither will become the site of another murder."

Constable Patch had never heard the man sound so reasonable. Apparently, he was experiencing Berwick in a rare moment of sobriety.

"The murderer might take aim at St. Andrew-by-the-Wardrobe, since it is the last remaining church in the ward," said Berwick, pointing the feather at him. "I want you to send men there. I've run out of men. I want more."

"There is St. Paul's," reminded Patch.

Berwick dismissed his suggestion. "It is prohibitively large and almost always occupied. A murderer would find it too risky."

"Ye say that like ye know the man," said Patch, eyeing Berwick.

"I will pretend ye did not say that," said Berwick, unruffled.

"It is a matter of being thorough," responded Patch. "Why takes the chance?" He was surprised how cooperative he managed to sound. If he had been Berwick, he would have thought himself a right chummy fellow. Very accommodating, indeed.

"Do ye have the men to post at St. Andrew's?"

"I can find them," said Patch.

"Then I shall expect you and your men one night after the morrow. I will tell them where they need to stand guard." He tossed the quill onto Patch's desk.

Patch didn't like that Berwick was directing *him* rather than it being the other way around. The fellow needed a lesson in humility. Berwick had better show more deference if he expected his full cooperation.

Constable Berwick turned to leave, his request delivered.

"Berwick," said Constable Patch. "Why do ye ask me for helps in this? Why nots ask another constable in another ward?"

Berwick faced him, an arch look on his face. "Because if this plan does not work, if there is another murder, I can blame you."

Chapter 23

Ancrum Moor

Because John had suffered a cracked rib, he was not in Sir Layton's vanguard sent in pursuit of the sighted Scottish cavalry. He was still required to wield his pike under Sir Euce's command—as long as a man was breathing, he was expected to fight. He would be in the larger of the two divisions with the spears in the center. The archers took one flank and the arquebusiers took the other.

While Layton and his men chased the Scots over a plateau and marshy landscape, John fell into line beside his friend, Glann McDonogh—still stricken with the flux—and, together with the remaining army, Euce marched them forward.

It is a sorry disadvantage for a man to enter battle suffering illness or injury. But John and Glann were of sturdy stuff; they had learned to scrap for their lives, placing themselves at a greater value than did the commanders or men of higher rank. They would not be left behind to nurse their wounds or to perish on their pallet. Let them scrabble until their last dying breath, for that is what a soldier did. In the months since he had left London, John had internalized this code of honor. It had replaced some, but not all, of the resentment he held toward the higher-ranking archers. Defending his honor to the death was not just a quaint adage to voice or to follow, but instead it had become a guiding principle instilling itself into John's every fiber.

Be that as it may, both John and Glann were not as able as they had been an hour before.

They followed their vanguard and marched west into a brilliant setting sun, squishing across fields muddy with days of rain.

"We keep apace of each other, but not so well with the line," said John, recognizing that he and McDonogh were both lagging behind.

"Wot, I hope neither of us will see the bottom of our brother's feet."

"Forsooth, we are fading to the back. The archers will be none too pleased."

"It cannot be helped," cried McDonogh. "Neither of us are well."

"Methinks this battle will be about staying alive," said John. "I can barely raise my pike."

"There be no apologizing or complaining," said McDonogh. "Doing either is a wasted effort. Keep God in your heart and all will be right." They took a few more steps—then McDonogh stopped and laid a hand on John's arm. His face turned a bilious green.

"Irish, speak to me!" John stood with his friend and let others go around them.

McDonogh doubled over and puked.

"You can't keep on," said John. "You may not die by the sword, but this flux will surely level you."

McDonogh leaned on his pole and wiped his mouth on his sleeve. He reeked of human sick and shit.

"You can't carry on like this," repeated John. He looked down the line at the hundreds of men pushing forward. For a moment he wondered what difference two men could make in this sea of soldiers. They barely had the strength to defend themselves, much less attack the enemy. If he had to, John could fight with the stabbing pain in his chest. The frenzy of battle made a man forget everything except getting out alive. But as John looked at his friend, he was sorry that Glann was at a sore disadvantage.

"I have to, John. I have no choice in the matter."

"You could fade to the back," said John. "Let others go before you."

"The archers will shoot me in the back." Determined not to hold anyone up lest he be trampled himself, McDonogh shambled forward. "Go," he admonished John, waving him on. "I cannot keep up. I won't be the reason for both of us getting killed."

John knew he had to keep moving. "It is not dishonorable to save yourself," he said, hoping his friend would take his words to heart. There was no time to advise and no time for farewells. The archers kept moving forward, and as he looked back at the rank slogging toward them, he saw Roger, recovered from their fight and wearing his war face.

John turned away and pulled McDonogh about so as not to make eye contact with the rake, but it was too late.

"Get back to your rank," said Roger, and he shoved John into Glann.

John swung about and pulled his dagger from its sheath. He pointed the blade at Roger's face.

"Get back to yours," John threatened. He could ill afford another scuffle with the archer.

But neither did the archer want another tangle with John.

Instead, Roger smirked and pushed his thumb between his first and second finger, giving John an obscene "fig of Spain" as he marched past.

"I would so enjoy seeing his unblinking eyes staring up at the sky," said Glann.

The words had barely left his mouth before the hagbutters began firing, emitting loud cracks of sound.

"It has begun!" shouted John.

"Go!" cried McDonogh, waving his friend forward. "*Faoi fhothain a chéile mairfidh muid!*"

"Can you not tame your tongue?" shouted John, primed with emotion. "It may be my next life before I learn yours!"

"Under the shelter of each other, we will survive!"

John hoped it to be true. There was scant little he could do for Glann, and in the scrabble of sweat and shouts, the two men became separated. The unrelenting advance of soldiers swept John forward, carrying him to his fate and deciding it for him.

As Sir Euce's contingent crested Palace Hill, they were suddenly set upon by their own men in frenzied retreat. The vanguard, unable to see their enemy with the wind blowing smoke from their own arquebuses back into their eyes, rushed at them.

They slammed into their own men and in the confusion, no one knew which way to go.

The sun had been blinding. Men shouted that they were unable to see. Cries went out that it had been a trap. The whole Scottish army had been lying in wait.

But before John or any of Sir Euce's men could understand what had happened, the Scots tore into the confused mass.

Swords slashed, pikes stabbed, halberds struck.

The Scots possessed pikes three feet longer than the English weapons. John forgot the pain in his ribs as he fought for his life. In the ensuing brawl, he killed men who were his own. He knew not if he succeeded in killing a single Scot.

This time, the archers did not have the advantage of distance, nor did they have the protection of a line of billmen in front of them. John saw them impaled just as easily as billmen, and he stepped on their bodies to leverage his pike into his enemy. But as the Scots advanced and infiltrated, and the men fought hand-to-hand, John abandoned his pike in the skewered body of a dying man, and pulled out his dagger.

In the throes of battle, there is no time to think. The sounds of sword on metal and the jarring percussion of cannon and arquebus, an unnatural cacophony of death, permeated John's brain. And mixed with the sound of weapons came the sound of men in their last throes of disbelief. Incredulous that *they* were the victims and that this bloody horror is what *they* yielded.

The impassioned pleas to God fell on His deaf ears, as did the brutish oaths and grunts and screams. And it occurred to John that an injured and dying horse screamed as loudly as a man.

Time lengthened, and yet it seemed so short. Every moment felt like his last. The exhaustion consumed him, it swallowed him whole, and still he fought on. At his feet lay the evidence in his fallen brethren that the slaughter they sustained was real.

As the sun began to set, it became glaringly clear that the day would not be theirs. England would not claim victory. The "assured men," those Scottish reivers with red crosses on their sleeves, ripped them off their jackets and joined their Scottish kin in attacking the English. If earlier the confusion was crippling, now it was disastrous.

John looked about him and saw no line of billmen, no line of defense at all. Men ran, they fought others to get away or to get to the back of the field. He heard no orders being given, he saw no men on their mounts. It was stay and be killed, or run and maybe be killed.

So, John ran.

CHAPTER 24

The next morning, Bianca rose well after the neighbor's cock had crowed. Her mind had finally let go of her troubles long enough to allow some much-needed sleep. Too many ales and worries had left her head aching. She listlessly set a fire in her calcinatory furnace and made an infusion of peppermint and willow bark to relieve the pounding in her head and parched mouth.

She sat at her table with her hands cupped around her mug, watching the steam rise, then curl and twist before disappearing. Her thoughts drifted to John, and she rehashed Roy the Robber's news about the rout up north. Part of her reasoned that the news might just be hearsay, and that until the story was confirmed she shouldn't waste time believing it. Besides, the crew member might have gotten his facts wrong. Roy said the ship had brought home the wounded, but he didn't know where they were taken or who was caring for them. It might be a few days more before she learned any additional news about Ancrum Moor. Bianca lifted the drink to her lips and took a sip of the hot brew.

Then again, the crew member could very well have been telling Roy the truth.

Realistically though, she could not be certain that John was involved in the skirmish. She'd received no word since he'd left and, in truth, she had no idea where he was. All she knew was that he had been headed for Scotland. She didn't know who his commander was—whether it was the Earl of Hertford, or someone under him. Nor did she know whether John actually made it to Scotland. She'd heard plenty of stories about sickness and treachery on board the king's ships ferrying the men north. The more she considered all the possible ways that a man could die, the more she realized how even making it to the battlefield was in and of itself an accomplishment.

Bianca finished her tea concoction and resolved to busy herself in matters where she might have some influence on the outcome. Even trying to figure out what had become of John felt like a useless exercise, and would only make her feel worse. Eventually, she would know.

Setting her mug aside, Bianca pulled on dry stockings and immediately felt the comfort of warm feet. The end of winter is the bleakest time of year, when patience wears thin and the desire for sun and color made every day of brown mud increasingly less tolerable. Bianca unlashed her shutters and dumped the pail of collected drips out in the already saturated lane. The sun made an effort to force itself through the clouds, but only succeeded so far as to marginally brighten the sky. Still, it was enough to inspire Bianca to make a balm for the inevitable insect bites that would menace citizens when the weather improved.

She searched through her stoppered pots and found a stash of witch-hazel bark and dried comfrey leaves and, satisfied that they were not too old to use, made a pile on the table. Her supply of beeswax was enough for now, but soon she'd have to trouble the beekeeper near the orchard on Horsleydown Road to raid his skeps for more. She also found tansy and, remembering her mother rubbing it on a wasp bite she'd gotten when she was young, decided its fairy buttons were worth adding to the mix.

Hobs returned from his morning foray and leapt upon the board to sniff the selection of herbs. After concluding that none of them were delectable, he gave himself a bath.

"You're feeling back to your old self," said Bianca as she rummaged for the pieces to her distillation apparatus and laid them one by one on the table. She began fitting them together, aggravated at herself for not taking the time to clean the junctures before storing it. She sat down and spent the needed time scraping off residue and dissolving hardened bits with oil of turpentine, a solvent that made her nostrils burn.

It came as a welcome distraction when she heard a small voice at her door.

"Goodwife, may I speak to you?" A wisp of a girl stood outside, peering in. She appeared uncertain about entering Bianca's room of Medicinals and Physickes, but who could blame her with the place smelling so foul?

"For cert," answered Bianca, beckoning her inside. "Granted, I am using a very disagreeable liquid, but it doesn't mean that I do not welcome visitors. Come in."

The girl carefully crossed the threshold, acting as if a sea serpent lurked just beneath it and would rear its ugly head to swallow her whole.

Once Bianca got a better look, she realized this was Fisk's younger sister. The child had markedly different coloring from her brother. Wispy gold hair framed her petite face and her eyes were a bright chicory blue. Her grungy coif was too large for her head and her kirtle showed no cleaner.

"Remind me of your name?" asked Bianca.

"Anna," answered the girl. Her head barely moved, but her eyes roamed the room, rolling up to see the herbs overhead, then down to rest on the copper apparatus spread across the table.

"Welcome, Anna," said Bianca, standing and ushering the girl to sit. "Come. I shall get you a drink of cider."

Anna did as she was bid. She sat rigidly, self-consciously, while Bianca fetched her a bowl of drink.

"You are Fisk's little sister," said Bianca.

The girl said nothing but gave a quick nod.

Bianca stoppered her noxious solvent and settled across the table from her guest. "I am surprised to see you here. Did you come across the river on your own?"

"I crossed the bridge."

Bianca blinked in surprise, thinking that the dark, narrow byway was not the safest route to Southwark. She'd give the girl a penny for a return wherry. "And no one troubled you?"

"I am a fast runner."

"A useful skill for a young lady."

Anna almost smiled.

"How did you know where to find me? Did Fisk tell you where I lived?"

"I followed you home."

"Did you, now." The child was full of surprises. "When might that have been?" The last time Bianca had visited Ivy Lane was yesterday. If Anna had followed her, the girl must have traipsed all around London, over to St. Mary Magdalen's, then to Jane Clewes's tenement . . . by the time Bianca returned to Southwark it was nearly dark and several hours would have passed.

Anna shrugged. "Once when you came by."

"Ah, so not yesterday?"

The girl shook her head. "When you came the day after Fisk didn't come home."

Bianca studied her little visitor. She had something of her brother's fearlessness about her. She could see that the two weren't so very different in temperament.

"Gull Hole is not so easy to get to. It is a distance from Ivy Lane."

"I wanted to talk to you." Anna had not touched the cider.

Bianca pushed the drink toward Anna. "Have some. It is not so poor. I only work with bad- smelling liquids. I don't serve them to my guests."

Anna took a tentative sip and must have deemed it potable, for she visibly relaxed and gave over to gulping down the entire portion.

"Would you like more?"

Anna nodded stiffly. Still, she remained reticent.

Bianca filled her bowl and gave her some bread and cheese, which was received with wide eyes and, this time, an eager and grateful smile. The poor girl was stick thin. Without a father to bring in a wage, and now without Fisk's help, it was obvious that Anna's mother was struggling to feed her children. Bianca waited until the girl had finished before prompting her to speak.

"I have more if you want it." But Anna shook her head. It didn't take much to fill a tiny stomach. The girl ran her gaze around the room, gaping at the strangely shaped instruments and bottles lining Bianca's shelves.

"I wanted Fisk to come and help me with my work," said Bianca, conversationally. She guessed Anna was there to tell her something in regards to her brother.

Anna's eyes settled on Bianca's. For as young as she was, the child possessed a maturity or awareness beyond her years.

"I know the name of the man who spoke to Mamma about Fisk."

"The man who told her Fisk was being held for money?"

Anna nodded solemnly. "His name is Geve Trinion."

Finally some information that may be of use. The name

sounded familiar. Bianca couldn't place where she'd heard his name and tried to remember.

"He came by the day Fisk went missing and then a second time. He says he knows who has Fisk."

Bianca sat up. This, was of inestimable value. Anna's mother had not told her the fellow's name. Why had she withheld the information?

"Did he say who has Fisk?"

"Nay. He said the rogue was keeping him until Mamma gave him money. Then he'd give Fisk back."

Bianca already knew this, but she hoped Anna knew more. "Do you know where Fisk is being kept?"

Anna's face clouded over and she bit her lip. She shook her head.

"Know you where this Geve Trinion might live?" After all, the girl had successfully found her across the river in Southwark.

Again, Anna did not know.

Bianca sat a minute, coiling her hair around a finger, then uncoiling it. She tried remembering where she had heard of this Geve Trinion.

"And he has visited twice?"

"Aye."

"But you don't recall ever seeing him before?"

"Nay," said Anna. "But Mamma called him a rascal and wanted him gone."

"How do you think she knew him?"

"I do not know. But she likes him not. She mentioned about the damage he'd done."

"Damage? To what?"

"I do not know. But she was angry about it." Anna peered into her empty bowl of cider, then looked up at Bianca with soulful eyes. "Could I have more?"

"Oh, aye," said Bianca, springing from the bench and refilling her bowl. Anna continued.

"The first time he came to the house, he wanted to take Fisk," she said.

"Take him?"

"He said he would take Fisk with him to work in the tin mines."

"And this was before Fisk went missing?"

"Aye. He said he would send Fisk's wages home to help Mamma so she could feed us. That it would be better than letting him steal."

Bianca sat down heavily on the bench. Being a cutpurse was fraught with danger, but working in a tin mine was also a perilous occupation. The ever-increasing need for the metal attracted a steady flow of unemployed men to the West Country, all willing to toil long hours. Whether they worked underground or outside in the weather, Bianca feared a young boy such as Fisk would be taken advantage of. Who was this Geve Trinion? What man would take a boy to the stannary to work beside him without exploiting him in some way? Likely he would garnish the boy's wages and keep them for himself. An even more odious thought occurred to her, and her stomach turned at the thought of it.

"You say he has visited your rent twice? Once, to ask your mother about taking Fisk to the tin mines and then a second time, after Fisk had gone missing, to tell your mother he knew who had him."

"Aye," confirmed Anna. "And if Mamma gave him the money, he would give it to the man and then Fisk would come home."

"But your mother doesn't have the money."

Anna shrugged. "She doesn't believe him. She says he is lying and is just trying to get her money."

Bianca mindlessly picked up a joint from her disassembled apparatus and tapped it on the board. Anna finished her cider and watched Hobs parade across the table, stepping between the copper tubes without disturbing a single one. He sat directly in front of the girl and stared at her. Anna stroked his back.

"Geve Trinion!" exclaimed Bianca, making Anna start. She pointed the piece of pipe at her. "He brings wool to Jane Clewes." Bianca rose from the bench and tossed the pipe on the table. "Anna, you have been very helpful. Can you describe this Geve Trinion?"

"He was tall with dark hair. He had a beard. I couldn't see a lot of his face."

Bianca went to her purse hidden under her bed and gave Anna a penny. "Keep this if you ever need to visit me again. It's safer to take the ferry than walk across the bridge. Come, I'll take you back to London."

CHAPTER 25

It was Anna's first ride across the river and she sat stock still, as if frightened to move for fear she would fall in. Bianca remembered the first time *she* had stepped foot in a wherry. The boat had wobbled so badly that the boatman had shouted at her to crouch and took her hand. She had plopped herself down as soon as she could. It had only been a few years ago, so she was quite a bit older than Anna was now.

Bianca admired the girl's determination to visit Southwark and find her. The South Bank's salacious reputation was deterrent enough to keep most away. But Anna loved her brother. And she put herself in harm's way to try to see him home.

A larger wherry angled past, loaded with revelers impatient for the opposite side. Men frequented Southwark to drink and be merry, to gamble, to watch bearbaiting and bullbaiting, to cheer at cockfights, and to foin. That Bianca chose to keep her room of Medicinals and Physickes in the sordid ward might at first seem counterintuitive, but it served her purpose.

Locating her hovel near a chicken coop helped mask the smells caused by her experimentation. What could elsewhere have been cause for alarm was effectively smothered by the overriding stink of chicken droppings.

Secondly, there were any number of peculiar goings-on in the borough at any given time, and the constant distractions of rowdy drunks, knifings, thievery, sodomy, rape, murder, street brawls, arrests, gambling, chases, skullduggery, biting dogs, dumped chamber pots, rats, cats, bats, church bells tolling, night watchmen calling, and visitors shouting for boats, shouting for constables, shouting for the hell of it, all took precedence over the occasional foul odor wafting into a lane and catching anyone's notice.

"Only walk the bridge if you have no choice," Bianca told Anna as they reached the other side. "The first ride is a bit disquieting, but you shall get accustomed to it. It is not very common that anyone falls in." That last bit was not entirely true, but Bianca's intent was to reassure Anna.

They disembarked and Bianca accompanied the girl up to Knightrider, where they would part ways.

"You're nearly home," said Bianca, looking in the direction of Ivy Lane. "You were brave to seek me out and I am grateful you did. I want to see what I can learn about this Geve Trinion. Mayhap he will lead us to Fisk." Bianca straightened the coif on Anna's head. "It is better if you do not mention our talk to your mother. She may not want me interfering."

Anna nodded, and Bianca was moved that the girl trusted her. The child put on a brave face, but she could see she struggled to conceal her worry and fear.

"Anna," said Bianca, bending down to her. "I love Fisk, too. And I will do everything I can to find him."

Anna bit her lip and Bianca straightened. She pulled the girl against her and felt Anna's shoulders shake as she began to cry. "You must not fret," said Bianca. "All will be fine." She said this as much to assure herself as the young girl. She wiped away Anna's tears and tried coaxing a smile from her. "Take this," she said, giving Anna another two pennies once she settled. "Get yourself something to eat at market, but save the penny I gave you if you need to see me again."

Bianca continued on to Jane Clewes's rent, wending past the drays and vendors moving their wares to market. After hearing the news from Roy the previous night, she was heartened by this bit of information from Anna. Between worrying about John and feeling helpless regarding Fisk, she had tossed around in bed restlessly, even though she had drunk enough to have dropped a man her size. Now she had hope, and she would ride its wings to see where it took her.

Bianca slowed as she neared the tenement, wondering if Huet might be outside on the road. She wondered what he might do if she asked to speak to Jane. But after surveying the area and looking into the side alley, she found that either Huet was inside or he was out running an errand. Bianca stepped up to the door and knocked.

"I've taken care of the rats," was the first thing Jane Clewes said at seeing her.

"Marry, I am glad to hear it," said Bianca. "But that is not why I am here."

Jane made no offer to invite her inside.

"Is Huet home?"

Jane's eyes slid to the side, then settled on Bianca's. "He is." She kept the door nearly closed.

Bianca looked past Jane, trying to see into the dimly lit interior. She thought she saw movement.

"The man who brings you batts of wool to spin. What is his name?" She wanted confirmation that she had remembered correctly.

"He be Geve Trinion."

233

"And, this Geve Trinion … do you know for whom he works?"

Jane's brows furrowed in thought. "I do not recall."

"Might he have mentioned it? Do you know where he takes your skeins?"

"So long as I am paid, it matters not," said Jane.

For a moment, Bianca feared this was all for naught. She had been so hopeful that finding Geve Trinion would lead to Fisk.

"Does he give you coin or perchance a note for your work?"

"He gives me coin, of course. I have no use for a note. What good is a square of paper with scratching on it?"

"Goodwife Clewes, it is a matter of importance that you try to remember. A child's life may be in danger." Bianca thought she saw Jane Clewes start at this mention. "Surely you must understand a mother's heartache when a child goes missing."

Jane grew quiet and rubbed her chin while studying Bianca's face. Her tone was softened when she finally spoke. "Methinks he takes them to a clothier near St. Antholin. I remember he said the man had spinners in thirteen wards. It was Trinion's task to collect skeins in Castle Baynard and Bread wards. But, to be true, if he mentioned the clothier's name, I do not recall it."

"If I mentioned the name do you think you might recognize it?"

"Possibly."

"Well, no matter, Goodwife Clewes. You have been helpful." Bianca hesitated, her mind slipping into contemplation.

"If that be all," said Goodwife Clewes, growing impatient and moving the door to shut it.

"Oh, aye," said Bianca. She had just snapped out of her thoughts when she heard scratching—similar to the other day. "What was that?"

"I don't hear anything," said Clewes. "It is your imagination." And she slammed the door and shot the bolt.

Bianca remained on the stoop, blinking in surprise. She pressed her ear against the door. Unfortunately, any sound on the other side was effectively muffled, and to her disappointment the shutters were latched. Bianca knocked again, but Jane Clewes did not answer.

Bianca returned to Knightrider and walked toward Friday Street with a mind for finding the clothier who employed Geve Trinion. Unfortunately, there were plenty of clothiers near St. Antholin. Their shops ran along a lengthy stretch of city from Tower Street up along Eastcheap to Candlewick and Budge Row, and Watling all the way to St. Paul's. She had a formidable task armed with only the name of a worker delivering batts of wool.

She decided to begin her search at the Red Lion, a large courtyard of shops. It was a random choice, but Bianca hoped that through inquiry, observation, or just mindless luck she could find someone who would lead her to the clothier who employed Geve Trinion. Inquiring at the guild would not offer anything helpful. They were unlikely to keep lists of a clothier's employees.

Bianca passed under the fabled "Red Lion"—the currant-red timber over the gate of the cobbled area off Budge Row. The entire square was taken up with the busy commerce of well-established shops involved in the manufacture, but mostly the display, of broadcloths and draperies. Merchants and noblemen, lords and ladies, entered and exited the shops, some with servants in tow carrying bundles.

At first, Bianca anticipated being poorly received, but then she saw a goodly number of commoners also engaged in some purpose. They appeared mindful of their superiors but were not cowed by their lack of privilege. This she took to heart, but still, the task before her was a daunting one.

Bianca adopted a plan and decided to keep to it however she was received. She would enter each shop in turn, beginning with the one closest to the gate, then work her way around the periphery. Surely she might learn something of use.

In front of the first shop, Bianca paused to straighten her coif and waist jacket, then hauled open the door. The smell of wool and a hint of smoke from a fire in a hearth gave the room a comfortable and distinguished feel. Bolts of woolen cloth in an array of colors lined the walls and were stacked on tables. This was not the rough kersey she was accustomed to wearing, but the finer worsteds and scarlets intended for the middle class and the wealthy.

Bianca eyed a couple dressed in the subdued colors of the merchant class. They perused the selection, talking with the proprietor, who looked over at her standing by the door. He excused himself and walked over.

"Good day, sir," she began, and curtsied. "I seek a man who might be under your employment. It is of utmost importance that I find him."

The proprietor looked her up and down.

"Utmost importance?" he said. "Might I ask, in regards to what?"

"A missing child." Bianca saw no reason to be evasive.

The man looked surprised, but he declined from asking more details. "What is the fellow's name?"

"The man is employed by a clothier who collects skeins from women in thirteen parishes. His name is Geve Trinion."

"I deal in finished cloth. Mayhap ye would be better served asking weavers."

"I mean no impertinence, sir, but I was told he worked for a clothier."

The man sighed, then glanced over his shoulder at the couple who were awaiting his return. "There are a few clothiers with larger operations."

"Would they have shops in this area?"

"Not in the Red Lion. There is a clothier named Bridgton who has a warehouse off Budge Row near St. Mary Aldermary. Also, William Dayton keeps shop next to the Stout Swan."

Bianca thanked the man and exited to the courtyard. She stood a moment studying the remaining shops, realizing that perhaps it might be better to abandon her inquiry there and instead seek the men with larger operations on Budge Row, first.

In the vicinity of the church the shopkeeper had mentioned, she eventually found a warehouse that looked promising, and after several unanswered raps on the door, and being unable to slide it open, Bianca was about to give up. But luck turned in her favor, and a drayman arrived with a cart of fleece to offload.

He gave her a curious look and hopped off his wagon. "Ye be seeking your wage?" he asked, thinking her a spinner.

"Nay. I am looking for someone who might work here."

"Who?"

"Geve Trinion," she answered.

"His name is not familiar. However, Master Bridgton employs lots of people."

She stood back as he opened a well-hidden panel and reached inside. She heard the ringing of a clamoring bell and was glad she was not close to its jarring sound. In a moment, the warehouse door slid open, revealing a somber-looking man with a ledger tucked under his arm.

He scowled at Bianca as if he couldn't be bothered, and looked past her and the drayman at the dray.

"Where from?" he asked.

"Hoddesdon."

The man brushed past Bianca to inspect the fleece in the cart. He pulled back the canvas and riffled through the exposed wool.

"Good. It is of quality," he announced. He returned to the warehouse, walking past Bianca without so much as a look and called to a worker in some dark recess of the building. "Winslow! There be a delivery to stow."

He retreated to a broad table, where he opened his ledger and asked the vendor's name. The two discussed matters of business and Bianca waited patiently. Finally, the drayman, having attentively watched his cart be emptied, brought Bianca to the dealer's attention.

"Sir, this woman wishes a word with you."

The man looked up and then over at Bianca. "Ye are not his wife?"

"Nay, sir. I am not." Bianca approached, speaking over the echoing clamor of the busy warehouse. "I am looking for a man named Geve Trinion. He works for a clothier who collects spun wool from thirteen wards."

"Our operation is a great deal larger than that. Indeed, we are one of the largest and most profitable in all of London. No one else matches the quality of our woolens."

"It is possible that the number is incorrect," said Bianca. "Perchance, do you have a roster of names?"

"I do. But I remember the name of every worker in my employ. This Trinion is not one of them."

Bianca doubted a clothier so boastful of the size of his operation could recall every man who passed through his door.

"He has a rough beard," she said. "It covers most of his face."

"I told you," he said. "This Trinion is not one of my men."

She was about to ask if she might look at the roster anyway, when he snapped his ledger shut and tucked it back under his arm.

"Try Dayton," he said, dismissing her.

"Next to the Stout Swan?"

"Is there another?"

Anytime Bianca felt curtly dismissed, instead of retreating she would do her best to irritate. "Would you mind if I looked over your roster of laborers?"

"I do mind. I have already said this fellow does not work for us." He turned on his heel and stalked off, leaving Bianca in his wake. She immediately followed, but after a few angry and determined steps, she realized it was not worth another moment trying to deal with this tactless snouter. She would return later if she had no better luck.

On Budge Row, Bianca's irritation worked to speed her on to finding Dayton the clothier. She headed to the Stout Swan and slowed to study the signage for any hints that might indicate the whereabouts of the man's establishment. In spite of being invited inside the boozing ken by a bleary-eyed chapman, Bianca managed to find the carved wooden likeness of a man wielding a teasel comb against a length of fabric. No nameplate hung near the entrance, and since it appeared to be the only shop of its kind in the vicinity of the podgy swan, she took her chances and entered.

Instead of a spacious warehouse, this was a simple shop, adequately stocked with a selection of woolens catering to a customer of more modest means. She did not feel out of place standing there; she could have been fetching an order for her master.

A backroom conversation grew louder until a pair of men discussing a possible shipment to Antwerp entered the room where she stood. She waited until they had finished, then introduced herself and asked after Geve Trinion.

"Geve Trinion," repeated the man who called himself William Dayton's assistant. "He collects skeins, say you? I should think Enfield would know." He excused himself and returned to the back room again, leaving Bianca alone with his associate, who spent his time moving fabric off a table onto a wheeled cart.

Bianca remained hopeful that she had stumbled upon the right clothier. A part of her bristled at having to sift through these various wool establishments. It was taking far too long when every minute mattered when it came to finding Fisk. But, she reminded herself, she had little choice given the frustratingly few pieces of useful information. And, if this clothier yielded nothing worthwhile, she would have to persuade Patch to place a watch at Jane Clewes's tenement. Going to every clothier in London would take far too long.

A customer entered the shop, and as the worker abandoned his cart to tend to him, Dayton's associate returned along with a distressingly thin older man, stooped to the extent that his spine resembled a ram's horn. His eyes peered out from the bottom of his forehead so that his face remained hidden.

"Enfield here says Geve Trinion is under our employment."

"He covers the spinners in Castle Baynard, Bread, and Vintry wards," said Enfield in a clear and strong voice. For as disconcerting as Bianca first found the man's appearance, she was pleasantly surprised to hear he had healthy lungs.

"When do you expect him back?"

"When his sack is full. But that is unpredictable, good lady."

"Would you know where he lives?"

"It is in the records. If you wait, I shall find out."

"It is a matter of importance. The constable of Bread ward would like to ask him some questions."

"Oh!" said Dayton's associate. "What has he done?"

"Sir, I am not here to accuse him of mischief. I merely need to find him so that he can be properly questioned."

He and Enfield exchanged looks and the latter retreated into the rear of the warehouse, returning shortly with a pile of papers stuffed into a leather binder. He went to the table and untied the cord holding it together, then proceeded to turn over several pages before running a bony finger down the list of names and addresses. After a few pages his finger came to a stop.

"He lives on Friday Street just beyond Mayden Lane." Enfield stared at the entry a minute, his finger remaining on the page as he thought. "Next to a fishmonger." He looked up. "He mentioned this once and I remember he liked it not." He turned his head to address Dayton's associate. "'Twas the smell of it. He said the stink got in his clothes and the ladies complained."

Bianca thanked him and a lift of optimism made her an inch taller. She should have no trouble finding Trinion now. She started for the door.

"Eel bait," Enfield blurted.

Bianca stopped. She turned around, thinking he insulted her. "I beg your pardon?"

Enfield lifted his head. He grinned—a gesture that did not favor his withered face. "It is what we call him."

CHAPTER 26

Bianca wished to avoid confronting Geve Trinion alone. If the man was sinister enough to kidnap boys, what could he do to her? Constable Patch resignedly gave up his anticipated nap and followed her out the door.

"The deaths occurred one week apart," said Bianca. "Our time is running out. I don't know if Trinion intends to hang Fisk, but if we don't find him soon it may be too late."

At Friday Street near Mayden, they easily sniffed out the fish shop. They studied the entrances on either side of the fishmonger. Neither door hinted who might live inside, and without any other choice, they would have to inquire at each. It saved them some time when one of the doors swung open and a man stepped into the street, pulling the door shut behind him.

"Sir," said Constable Patch before the man got away. "I be looking for Geve Trinion."

The fellow looked at Patch and then Bianca. "Geve Trinion?" he asked.

"He works for Dayton, a clothier, collecting wool from spinners," said Bianca.

"Oh, aye," answered the man. He gestured to the door on the other side of the fishmonger. "He lives there. But I don't expect you'll find him home, it being a day of work." He started to leave and Bianca hurried after him.

"Sir, if he is not here, could you tell us if you've seen any boys with him?"

The man looked from Bianca to Patch. "Of what concern is this?"

"We be trying to finds a missing child," said Patch.

Bianca added, "Or, perhaps you might have heard boys' voices? Especially at night?" The doors were crammed against each other—a sure sign that the walls in these tenements were thin.

The man shook his head. "Nay, he shares his room with two men. I've not heard any child." He tipped his cap at Bianca and nodded her a good day.

"We mights find someone home," said Patch after the man turned the corner. He stepped up to the other door and banged on it. "Manners be damned," he said over his shoulder.

In a moment, they heard someone yelling and the clumping of a heavy footfall. The door jerked open enough for two narrowed eyes to size them up.

Bianca inquired after Trinion.

"He's not here," said the man. His unbuttoned doublet hung open over his half tucked-in smock. He had the bleary-eyed appearance of a person disturbed from sleep.

"But ye know the man?" asked Patch.

"He shares a room with us."

"And how, sir, do you earn your living?" asked Bianca.

"I am a cobbler." He looked at them with a level of distrust. "Are ye here to ask him questions, or me?"

"Well, since ye be available . . ." said Patch. He tugged on his popingay-blue doublet with shiny brass buttons.

243

The cobbler liked him not.

Constable Patch straightened and lifted his chin. "We wish to come in."

"For what purpose?" asked the man. "Ask me what ye will, here. Whether inside or out, the answers shall be the same."

Bianca gave Patch a warning look. They needed to see the room. Besides, what would stop the cobbler from lying in order to get rid of them?

However, she needn't have worried. Constable Patch's suspicious nature never faltered. "Methinks ye might be hiding something," said Patch, his hackles raised.

The man's drowsiness vanished as he took umbrage with the accusation. "I haven't anything to hide. Forsooth, I hardly own but the clothes on me back."

"Then ye shouldn't mind us looking around." Patch laid his hand on his rondel dagger. "Ye can comply now, or I will be back with a few more men . . . and a smote less patience."

"Make it quick," said the cobbler, realizing that sometimes the fastest way to get rid of constables was to just give them what they wanted. "I have somewhere to be." He stepped back and opened the door, revealing a dark stairwell.

Bianca and Patch followed him up the stairs to a landing, which opened into a room with a narrow window at both ends.

"How many live here?" asked Patch, running his eyes around the periphery.

"There be three," said the cobbler, tucking in his smock and buttoning his doublet.

The walls showed nothing in the way of openings or hideaways. Three pallets lay on the floor, three stools surrounded a table. A chest was pushed against one wall and Patch wandered over to give it a kick. He threw back the lid, then pawed through a pile of smocks and hosen.

While Patch asked questions, Bianca studied the rafters and beams, listening. There were no muffled sounds of struggle coming from anywhere inside the rent. If Geve Trinion had abducted Fisk, he was not hiding him here.

The cobbler grew impatient and wished them done. "I need to make my day's wage," he said. "If your argument is with Trinion then ye should let me be."

There was no excuse to linger. They wished Trinion had returned while they were there, but they would have to keep watch on the place until he returned. Reluctantly, Patch and Bianca descended the stairs, following the cobbler. None of them spoke, only their clomping footfalls sounding in the empty stairwell. They had just got to the bottom when the door opened from the street.

"Trinion," said the cobbler. "You have company!"

Without introduction, the cobbler left the two with a man who fit Anna's description. His beard was broad and unevenly trimmed, covering most of his face in thick brown hair—distinctive for its untidiness. A lumpy satchel was slung across his back, and he hesitated before entering the tenement, looking from Patch to Bianca.

The pair blocked his entry.

"Ye be Geve Trinion?" Patch asked.

The man looked uncertain as to whether to admit it.

"We wants to ask ye some questions. It should not take long." Patch straightened his doublet and tipped his head. "Ye distribute wool for Dayton the clothier?"

Again, the man hesitated, then responded with a drawn-out, "A . . . y . . . e," like he could change the answer by shaking his head if he needed to.

"You collect skeins of wool from Jane Clewes, do you not?" asked Bianca.

Changing the focus to the spinner loosened his tongue. "Odd

woman," he commented.

"How so?" asked Bianca, curious what he thought of her. Perhaps his response might reveal his own character.

"She be taking care of that lad like she does. I heard tell she got him out of employ at Tyburn. Why she would bother, I wonder. He seems well-suited for the chores of the gallows there. So long as a bowl of porridge waits at the end of the day, his kind will do as they be told."

"You think him unworthy of a better life?"

"I fail to see how living with a peculiar woman is better than what he had."

"At least he is not sweeping the guts of dead criminals to dogs," said Patch.

Trinion exchanged a callous smile with Patch.

Bianca shot Patch a disapproving look, prodding him to get back to the subject at hand.

"How do you know Meg?" she asked, putting an end to the men's mean-spirited remarks.

"Who? The name is not familiar."

Bianca, annoyed with his evasiveness said, "She lives off Ivy Lane. She has a son named Fisk."

Trinion continued to act ignorant, furrowing his brow as if trying to remember.

"Sirrah, I have it on good word that you have spoken to her. And on more than one occasion. You expressed interest in taking Fisk to the West Country tin mines."

Geve Trinion's disingenuous expression lifted as if he had just remembered. "Oh!" he exclaimed. He shook his head, feigning nonchalance. "The woman with fair hair. Of course." He offered no more explanation, but Bianca and Patch glared at him, waiting. The wool collector shifted the pack on his back and, seeing that they were not going to let him through, acquiesced.

"I knew she be struggling to feed her brood. I simply offered to take the boy with me to the mines and send her his earnings."

Bianca tipped her head. "It is odd that you would not remember this."

Geve Trinion cleared his throat. "Well, she is not the first woman I've made that offer to."

"This 'offer' is a habit of yours?" asked Bianca.

"I . . . I intend to seek my fortune there, and I am a generous man. The woman's husband has gone to war and truth be, she can ill afford taking care of her brood. The boy is of good age. If he can benefit his family, then he should."

"And what did Meg say?" asked Bianca.

"Tssk. She did not take an interest." He gave a smirking laugh. "She would rather have the boy filch at market and risk him losing a finger than give him up to earn money through honest means."

Bianca tipped her head. "Honest means? What would prevent you from keeping the boy's wages for yourself?"

"I would never do such a thing!"

"Yet you expect Meg to agree to this with only your word as assurance?"

Trinion glowered at Bianca. "Are you questioning my honor?"

"You say that you have made this offer to other women?" asked Bianca, ignoring his question.

Trinion studied her a moment before responding. "Of what do you accuse me?"

Patch was anxious to have his say, and interrupted. "There have been a number of boys gone missing. Unfortunately, they turn up dangling from churches."

"That has nothing to do with me," said Trinion.

"But methinks ye have something to do with Fisk being gone," said Patch.

"Oh, nay! Not on my life! I have no hand in that!"

"But you told Fisk's mother that you knew who had him," said Bianca. "And you told her you could negotiate his return."

Trinion avoided her eyes. His mind flitted back to the day he'd brought Meg the lock of Fisk's hair. He had been so sure she'd be convinced. He would have pocketed the money and been on his way days ago. But he hadn't expected her response. Meg threw the lock of hair at him and called him a scoundrel. "Do ye think me so remiss that I would not know my own son's hair?" she had shrieked. "Ye snipped a lock from your own head, ye slug-witted cullion! A ten-year-old doesn't have gray hair!" She then cursed him with a savagery that left no room for misunderstanding. She liked him not, and his scheme had failed.

Trinion glanced from Bianca to Patch and back again. He needed to put an end to this ruse.

"Truthfully, I do not know where Fisk is."

Bianca and Patch stared at him.

"Why woulds ye tell his mother otherwise and raise her hopes?" said Patch. "Ye makes a mockery of motherhood."

"Did you expect to profit from his disappearance?" asked Bianca.

Geve Trinion did not answer.

"Ye are a shameless conniver," said Patch. "I should haul ye in for being despicable."

"When I first approached her, my intent was to save the boy from starving," said the now contrite Trinion.

Patch stepped directly in front of the man, inches from his face. "Do ye think we be daft? Ye have as much care as a rat in a store of grain. Ye can't save yer arse by continuing to lie."

Trinion had no more spleen for manipulation or for a weasel-eyed constable insulting him. "Who are you to enter into this matter?" he said, glaring at Patch. "Ye should mind your own ward and stay out of personal affairs. That boy is my son!" The two locked eyes.

Bianca shook her head. Another exceptional child born to a loathsome parent.

"I do have care," Geve Trinion insisted.

"Ye are a sorry excuse for a father," said Patch, disgusted.

Trinion's eyes ran over Patch in his handsome doublet. "Ye have done well of it, I see. What would ye do if ye didn't keep the law for the ward? How would ye earn your keep? You have some position and a nice doublet. But what about a man who hasn't any luck? What is there for a man like me?" he complained.

"Well," said Patch. "For cert I wouldn't be exploiting me son, no matters how desperate I was or however much I didn't like 'im."

"'Twas not about the boy. I would like him fine if I knew 'im. But Meg kept me away. She never gave a twig's snap for me. I tried with her years ago. Besides," he said, feeling the heat of their judgment, "it ain't for cert that Fisk is mine. Meg said he is, but she be a woman who could not content herself with only one man. She had her beauty then, and didn't she know it. Enough to make a man distraught. Got her in mounds of trouble, it did. But I say this now and there is no shame in saying it, one less child to feed would be helpful to her."

"Tell me how it benefits Meg to take her last few coins? Do you seek revenge for her lack of interest in you?" Bianca's voice rose. She could not let this losel go without a word. "You sought to lure her with false promise. You told her you knew where Fisk was." She'd met morally reprehensible men before, but she found this one especially difficult not to slap. "You saw this as an opportunity to profit."

Geve Trinion looked down at the ground.

"For shame," admonished Patch.

CHAPTER 27

It was as if she'd been thrown down a well. Bianca lay at the bottom of a black, sullen disappointment that she was no closer to finding Fisk than when she first learned of his disappearance. Geve Trinion proved to be nothing more than an opportunist, a scoundrel willing to capitalize on his old lover's misfortune. She was sorry she had spent precious time uncovering his deceit, and sorrier still that he had turned out to be Fisk's natural father. She hoped that if she ever did find Fisk that the two would never chance to meet.

If she ever did find Fisk ...

With every passing day it seemed more unlikely. He had been gone nearly a fortnight. Too long for a child to leave home in the hopes of returning better appreciated.

Bianca's anxiety mounted. With no new leads to follow, she spent her time rehashing what had happened and what had been said in her search for Fisk. Nothing pieced together.

Finally, with one day left before another possible murder, Bianca woke in the night, her heart pounding in her chest. It beat so forcefully that her entire body shook. Perspiration dampened her smock and she sat bolt upright, trying to catch her breath. She pressed her hands against her chest for fear her heart might crack her ribs and beat its way out. Panicking exacerbated the problem, but she could no longer prevent her growing trepidation. For all she knew, she had lost John and now Fisk. There was no evasion of that pain. There was only the realization of her intense grief and her attempt to accept it.

Bianca stared at the shutters, closed against the night. One hinge had pulled away from the window trim, letting in a splinter of moonlight. The beam splayed across the floor and the covers of her bed, highlighting the uneven textures of strewn rushes and a lumpy blanket. She searched for Hobs and saw him nestled in a pile of dirty clothes on her chest. He had abandoned her to turn restlessly in bed by herself.

The latter part of the night was spent gazing up at the rafters. Nearly sleepless, she rose early the next day. She had decided she would go to St. Paul's and spend the day in Castle Baynard ward. She might visit Fisk's mother and find Constable Patch to see if plans had been made to post watches at the parish churches.

Hobs remained peacefully sleeping, content and warm on the chest. She dropped her woolen kirtle over her head and tugged at the apron he was lying upon, urging him to move.

"Hobs," she said. "Come now. I need this." But as she attempted to pull the apron out from under him, the cat offered no resistance—his body was completely limp.

"Hobs!" Bianca swept him up and held him close against her. She stroked his face and whispered in his ear. "I cannot bear it. Why you?"

She sat on the bed with him in her lap, petting his lifeless body. Whatever malady had caused his previous episode had now returned in full strength. Remorse, that bittersweet pain of regret, settled in her hollow gut, making her feel utterly alone.

Normally, Bianca would not connect unfortunate events with

a spate of bad luck. Nor did she believe life's inexplicable mishaps were a predictor of more misery to come. But her broody state of mind prevented her from considering a reasonable explanation. Life, or rather death, seemed to demand her attention.

She cradled the black tiger in her arms, rocking him, and cried. His presence had always comforted her; he had always reminded her of life's simple joys when one can love. In some way, taking care of him had given her purpose beyond making medicines. He had given her a reason to hope that life might return to some semblance of normalcy when John returned to her side.

But the only certainty in life was death. And while Bianca had clung to Hob's possible immortality, she realized that there was really no everlasting life in the sense of breathing and being. Death was our ultimate immortality.

Bianca sat, giving no thought to time. She kissed Hobs and thanked him for his love. She thanked him for sharing his life with her. Eventually, she cried out her tears. She supposed she must have been sitting there for half the morning. She heard the soft clucking of hens outside her rent and her mind began moving past her grief. The pain was still there, it would always be there, but she could not let it color what needed to be done. She wiped her face and laid Hobs's body back on the chest. There would be time to bury him later.

"Blessed be, my sweet friend," she whispered, smoothing the fur between his ears, and kissed his head.

She straightened and took a long breath. She would dress and ride a wherry to London. She would find Constable Patch and urge him to set up guards at St. Paul's and every parish church in Castle Baynard ward. If she had to walk the circumference of St. Andrew's, she would do it.

As she busied her thoughts with what to do, her mind crawled out of its haze and she noticed that next to Hobs was the stained cloth she had found on the street by St. Benet's.

"God's blood," she said, picking it up, then looking at the cat.

She raised the grimy rag to her nose and smelled its peculiar scent—a smell like no other.

She had meant to try to find out what that smell was, but had forgotten about it. With all the other worries crowding her mind, this may have been something critical staring her in the face. She took another whiff of the cloth, bunching it up to her nose and taking a deep breath.

Its effects were immediate. Her vision began tilting and she became dizzy. She tried steadying herself and stumbled backward onto the bed.

Overhead, the beams circled like carrots being stirred in soup. Bianca spread her arms on either side, hoping to make the whirling stop, and groaned with nausea. She closed her eyes, waiting for her head to clear.

"God's tooth! What is that?"

In some ways the rag's sweet smell reminded her of her father's room of alchemy. Its scent was sweet, but it had an overtone of a more acrid creation. Its unique odor completely eluded her. She had never encountered it before.

After some time, the spinning stopped. Bianca cautiously opened her eyes and blinked up at the ceiling. It looked as solid as before. Still wary, she propped herself on her elbows and looked around. All was still. The effects were gone, she was none the worse.

She picked up the rag and held it out like a dead mouse. "I don't know what you are, but you're coming with me." She folded the filthy rag inside a clean cloth and stuffed it in her pocket.

Borderlands Scotland

As night fell over his shoulder, John put as much distance as he could between himself and the battlefield at Ancrum Moor. The slash of swords and the groans of dying men began to fade, though he could not help but relive the distressing sounds whenever he thought of it. With the cover of dark he decided to trek south toward the border of England, where he hoped he might find refuge. But for now he was in hostile land.

He didn't know the terrain with its monadhs and streams, nor did he know if and when he would cross the border. He reckoned he might be a solid day's walk if he followed the River Tweed. But even if he were to head south, the northern reach of the kingdom was as rough and duplicitous as its neighbor. He could head southeast toward the sea, toward a port, but there was no assurance that he would find an English ship there. And if he didn't, how would he survive until one arrived … *if* one arrived?

He stood still to get his bearings. He sighted the setting sun and distant hills and corrected his course, trudging on.

The battle had been a slaughter.

The Scots had lain in wait. The king's army began to scatter. The men realized the futility of fighting and abandoned their injured comrades. Everywhere John had looked, men were being captured. He held no illusions that they would be spared in prison. They would suffer misery commensurate with the torment that they had been guilty of inflicting on the Scotch. John would rather die than be taken prisoner.

Ahead, an outcrop of ledge offered protection and a place to catch his breath. He loped toward it to lean against its lichen-covered stone, glad for the chance to rest out of sight. A man on a moor cannot escape notice, and he'd been fortunate so far. He'd not taken a straight path south, but veered east, away from the battlefield. He slid down the face of the rock and sat. His jagged breathing sounded loud in his ears, and in this rare moment of rest every breath inflicted a stabbing pain, reminding him of his injury and his folly fighting the rattlepated Roger just before the battle.

He wondered what had become of the arrogant archer. Had he suffered an agonizing death, or had he been fortunate and had a quick one? Then again, Roger might have been taken prisoner. The charging Scots with their long pikes had skewered plenty of men, and John had fought doubly hard to keep from being stabbed. He had not dropped his weapon and run like many of his rank, but had stayed on, trying to keep his wits about him. Through no fault of his own, he was pushed backward into the line of bowmen, who then panicked to see their protection fall apart before their eyes. With no time or distance to use their bows, the archers tried fending off their foe by using their arrows to jab enemies in the neck.

John took off a shoe and rubbed his sore foot. Scenes of the battle played before his eyes. He never saw what became of his friend, Glann McDonogh. The Irishman had been at a sore disadvantage with his flux plaguing him so. He should have stayed back with the supply wagons, but John suspected even they had been ruined and their supplies confiscated. No one had escaped the Scots' furious retribution. With a sigh of regret, he hoped Glann had died quickly. The mercenary would not have survived long in prison in his condition, and he would have hated to shit himself to death.

John cautiously peeked around the corner of the ledge. As far as he could tell, no one was in sight, so he used the remaining daylight to remove his jack and examine a wound. His left arm had been sliced, and rolling up the sleeve of his blood-soaked smock, he found that the slash still bled. He tore a strip of fabric from the hem of his shirt and wound it around his arm. The applied pressure helped to distract from the sting.

Soon, night would fall, and John would need to keep moving to assure his safety. If he kept the mountains over his right shoulder and followed the river, eventually he would reach the ocean. Once there, he could follow the coastline south until he found a friendly port. It was his only hope, really. Looking out over the vast, wild terrain, his chances of surviving a walk to London were poor. What roads were there—what thieves preyed on men such as he, ignorant of the terrain and the rules of the road? Either way, he would have to rely on the charity of strangers to shelter him and point him in the right direction.

John closed his eyes and leaned his head back against the ledge, inhaling the smell of damp earth, both comforting and disconcerting. Comforting in the sense that now he could rest. Disconcerting in that he was not home in London. He wondered what Bianca was doing. He wondered if she struggled under the responsibility of motherhood, or whether she reveled in the challenge and joy of seeing their son grow. He sat for a time, waiting for night to fall and for the Queen Moon to show her luminous face. He would travel by the light of her gibbous smile, enough for him to see his way. With luck he would be near the ocean by morning.

Bianca cut through alleys and gardens on her way to the stairs at Winchester Place. Her first matter of order was to find Constable Patch and see what, if anything, was being planned to thwart another murder. She stood with three other women waiting to take a ferry across and listened to their chatter about Goodwife Hayden's goat getting loose and eating the flowers off Alewife Bently's witch hazel.

"I look forward to them bloomin' ever' year," said one woman. "I know then that spring is not so long afar."

"I cut the branches and bring it inside. It makes for a smite better smellin' room," said another.

The mention of witch hazel called to mind other uses for the bark, and Bianca remembered that her own supply was running low. When she had a chance, she needed to forage for more, but first she needed to get through this day and night.

As she watched a wherry float toward the stairs, she made out the telltale red cap of Meddybemps sitting among the passengers. He caught sight of her as they neared, and rather than disembark and wait for a second boat, he stayed seated and waited for Bianca to board.

"What brings you to the South Bank?" she asked as she sat down beside him.

"You, my dove. I haven't saved a fare, but at least you have saved me the walk to your room."

One of the women concerned with Alewife Bently's witch hazel sat down next to them. She could have chosen a seat by her friends, and Meddybemps tartly pointed this out.

"I have private words for this lady," he said, pointedly.

The woman gave Bianca a snide look. She did not argue, but got to her feet in a great show of inconvenience and moved ahead to share a seat with the other women, whispering so that each of them, in turn, snuck a glance over her shoulder, then shared comments on the inscrutable pair.

Meddybemps rolled his eyes, which, given their independent orbits, looked freakish. It was good that only Bianca saw the gesture.

"I'm guessing you don't need any medicines for market," she said.

The boatman collected the fare and poled the boat back into the current.

"Nay, I've got some news of interest regarding this possible monk you mentioned." Meddybemps lowered his voice as he noticed the three women in front of them leaning back to better hear. He cupped his hand to Bianca's ear. "I have found out his name."

"Do tell," said Bianca. "I wish to know."

"Apparently, he was a monk from Kent. His name is Ywan Hanks Sedar." Meddybemps spelled out the first name. "Y, W, A, N, pronounced Yiwan. Y . . . H . . . S. Are those not the initials on the paternoster?"

"Where did you learn this?"

The boat began to rock as the wake from another wherry broke against their hull.

"A man came to my cart for a remedy to ease his sore joints. He told me he was once a religious man, but had taken a pension and shared humble quarters with two others. I asked if he found it difficult to live on the pension he was given. He jested that he was used to having very little being from Faversham monastery. I asked where the monastery was located and he told me Kent."

"That is where Brother Ywan told me he was from," said Bianca.

"I asked if there were any other monks from Kent who had come to London but who did not live with him. 'Oh yea,' said he. 'One monk was fortunate to secure a position in a parish church in Broad Street ward.'

"'Were there any others?' I asked. 'One more,' said he. 'Brother Ywan came to London and has not been heard from since.' He said the monk would have seen his end soon enough if Cromwell's agents had not closed the monastery. This particular monk believed his personal remorse could not be appreciated without chastening the flesh.'"

"Chastening the flesh?" repeated Bianca. "And how does one chasten the flesh?"

Meddybemps leaned close so the women in front of them

could not hear. "Self-mortification."

"By knife or by whip?"

"A whip, apparently," answered Meddybemps.

Bianca sat a moment. "One should embrace good health when one has it," she said. "Why would God want someone to harm their own person?"

"Flagellation is severely frowned upon by the church," added Meddybemps. "What was once accepted as a show of empathy for Christ's suffering is now reason for being ostracized. When I heard him mention Brother Ywan I asked for his full name and he told me."

"Has Brother Ywan been ostracized?"

Meddybemps bit a hangnail. "Possibly. It makes me think that a monk who is shunned and on his own must find other ways to make money."

Bianca sat quietly, listening to the boatmen call to one another as they passed. So, Brother Ywan and Brother Sedar were one and the same. Certainly, the monk had not told her everything about his shelter for boys. From what Meddybemps had learned, if three pensioned religious men were struggling to survive on their pooled resources, how could Brother Sedar help several boys *and* himself on a single pension?

"I was on my way to see Patch, but I think I must first visit a monk."

Chapter 28

Meddybemps accompanied Bianca to the abandoned tannery off Old Change. Brother Sedar had been less than welcoming the first time she visited; he was the sort of character who guarded his privacy, but with a house full of boys how could he expect to remain unnoticed? They passed Naylor's printing shop en route, and Bianca, noticing its darkened interior, took it to be closed.

Turning down the narrow alley, Bianca caught a whiff of the pungent tannery. How anyone could live there puzzled even she, who was more accepting of disagreeable odors than most.

"Fie upon it!" exclaimed Meddybemps, stopping to look around. "That stink! What is it?"

"He lives in an old tannery."

"I hope for not much money." Meddybemps waved his hand in front of his face as if it would replace the foul smell with something better. "If I succumb to this smell, drag me out to the road before I die. I should not like my last breath to be of this."

Bianca knocked at the sturdy ash door and received no response. She tried a second time with the same result.

"Let me rattle it," said Meddybemps, ready to take his turn.

He proceeded to pound the door, then kicked it with the ball of his foot.

"There is no need to destroy my door, sirrah. I must ask you to cease," said a sonorous voice at Meddybemps's elbow. There stood Brother Sedar, looking vexed. "If you have business with me, then out with it."

"You told me you were not familiar with the name Brother Ewan," said Bianca.

The monk looked at her. "I do not recognize EEE-wan," he said, emphasizing the pronunciation. "If you are referring to my first name, it is pronounced Yi-wan, with a beginning sound like the word 'if.'"

"Your initials Y, H, S are the same as those found on the paternoster used to hang a boy at St. Mary Magdalen's church."

Before the monk could answer, Meddybemps spoke. "You are the Deft Drigger—the man who runs a thieving ring at St. Paul's and its side streets."

Brother Sedar calmly ran his eyes over the two of them. He showed a surprising lack of emotion at being so bluntly accused.

"These are serious allegations," he said. "And they are unfounded." He made a move toward the door and was blocked.

"Methinks you should tell your story to the constable," said Bianca. "If you are as innocent as you claim, then you should not object to this minor inconvenience."

Constable Patch looked up from his oversized desk and perked at the sight of Bianca entering with two men in tow. He recognized the streetseller bringing up the rear and stiffened at the sight of him, but in between was a third incomer, a man he'd never seen before.

"Wells, now. I was just wondering if I might sees you today, Bianca Goddard," he said. "The day may be significance."

"This is Ywan Hanks Sedar," said Bianca. When she noticed Patch's expression remained unmoved, she added, "His initials match the letters we found on the paternoster at St. Mary Magdalen's."

Patch stared a moment, still unable to grasp the connection. Bianca was about to explain when suddenly Patch's face bloomed like a rose on a hot summer day and he quickly assumed his usual bluster.

"By my beard. Wells now. Let's hear what he has to say." Patch leaned back in his chair and folded his hands on the desk, an expectant look on his face.

Bianca stood aside and the monk stepped forward to address Patch.

"It is true," he said. "My name is Ywan Hanks Sedar. I am a pensioned monk from Kent. I moved here with three others after Cromwell's agents closed the monastery. We had a difficult time adjusting to London, but it was either this or a more uncertain future in the nearby village. The town folk did not take kindly to men of cloth after the king and his agents embarked on their campaign to denigrate the church." Here, the monk's tone turned accusatory. "But I ask you, Constable, who do you think is more corrupt? The king or the pope?"

Patch squirmed in his chair. He wasn't about to answer that one.

"Sir, yer bitterness is glaring," said Patch. "Ye tread on dangerous ground." Patch did not overtly discourage the man from voicing a treasonous opinion. If the fellow chose to incriminate himself, Patch would be more than happy to refer him on to the magistrate.

"I speak on grounds of truth," said the monk. "It was a difficult adjustment coming to London and living outside the routine and protection of the monastery. Indeed, one of us refused to leave, and he did not accept the king's supremacy. He was punished as a heretic."

Bianca spoke. "We understand, it must have been difficult to change your way of life. But if surviving in London is so difficult an adjustment, why would you leave the support of others sharing a similar predicament?"

"We cannot live companionably."

"Yet you got on well enough at the monastery?"

"We had our separate quarters. And our life there was completely given over to serving God."

Bianca wanted more of an answer. "And so you ventured out on your own, knowing that it would be more difficult to afford a place to live?"

"I am accustomed to having few possessions."

Until now, Meddybemps had been content just listening. "Yet you found living in London on your own was too difficult. So you enlisted a tribe of boys to thieve and support you."

"They are not thieves," responded Sedar.

"Then what are they?" asked Meddybemps. "They menace Newmarket and Westcheap. There isn't a vendor who hasn't had an incident."

"I do not tell them to steal."

"Yet they do."

"If they need to steal in order to survive then it says more about the state of affairs of this man's kingdom than it does my efforts to advise them. I ask that they seek God's guidance on a daily basis."

"You want us to believe that you manage to feed and shelter these boys with just your pension?" asked Bianca.

"I accept the charity of others."

"And who might be these Good Samaritans?" asked Patch.

"The boys are instructed to help people. Perhaps they carry

something for an elderly woman who looks in need of assistance. If they are given a penny or an apple in return, they bring it back for the general welfare of the group."

"Then can you explain why they might steal?" asked Bianca. "The boys are rascals and we can trace many of them back to you." This was a fabrication, but Bianca hoped it might jar him into explaining more.

"As I said, I instruct them to help others."

Bianca considered a different angle. "What happens if a boy is unable to find someone needing help? What if he comes home at the end of the day and has nothing to contribute?"

"Then that boy has failed to find a way to show kindness. Opportunities abound. I want them to see and to understand that. Our way to salvation is through our good acts. It is not by faith alone. A boy who fails even one day is expected to look into his heart and ask himself why he did not do better."

Meddybemps squinted one eye in disbelief. "These are young lads, sirrah. Do you truly expect them to consider their failings?" He snorted, incredulous. "When I was that age, I would do anything to keep from being beaten."

Brother Sedar kept his counsel. Bianca found his reticence telling in itself.

"Brother, do you beat the boys if they return with nothing to offer?"

"They learn discipline," he said calmly. "There is a difference."

"Ah," said Bianca. "But do you think the boys are mature enough to understand?"

"It is a small discomfort for their failure. Our Lord suffered a great deal more for our sins. I instruct and teach them empathy."

Bianca and Meddybemps exchanged looks.

"It is understandable with young boys," said Patch. Everyone became quiet and cast long looks at one another.

"I met a boy named Luke," said Meddybemps, breaking the silence. "If I hadn't pulled him to safety he would have been trampled by a dray. He looked distracted for a young boy. I took him to be eight or nine years old. There was a haunted look about him. Mayhaps he was consumed in thought. Distracted. I kept an eye on him.

"He was near a corner tenement near Sermon. He seemed on edge, like he was scared. He cautiously approached the door, then left a purse on the stoop. He had no more turned to make away when the door flew open and out came a young man, rather large in build. He chased the boy—with what intention, I do not know. But the boy was terrified."

"That is where Jane Clewes lives," said Bianca. "That would have been Huet who gave chase."

Meddybemps continued. "I know the shortcuts through the alleys and lanes and I saw him enter Paul's Walk. I waited at the other end and saw him exit. He hid by Paul's Cross. I wondered if his pursuer would give up. The boy had the advantage of being fleet of foot. But nay, his pursuer flushed him out from behind a bush and Luke took off again. But, as I said, I know the cutbacks and short paths between these lanes. Now it was me who pursued the boy and I followed him straight to your door, sir."

Brother Sedar listened stoically to Meddybemps's story. He gave no hint of surprise or consternation hearing this. The only one showing surprise was Bianca. So, Meddybemps had been to the tannery before.

"I pulled Luke away and questioned him," said Meddybemps. "I asked him, was this where he lived? You have taught your boys well, sirrah. He did not answer for the longest while. But I know a hungry lad when I see one. After a trencher of beef stew, I asked what he left on the stoop.

"'A bag of coins,' said he." Meddybemps's errant eye began to dance. "A bag of coins? The boy claims he was ordered to deliver the money. And that it was not the first time he had done so." Meddybemps's confidence soared as he continued to question the monk. "So, I wonder, Brother Sedar," he said, "if, as you say, you struggle on a measly pension, why do you instruct this boy to leave money there? What secret do you keep?"

Constable Patch's eyes doubled in size. He delighted in Meddybemps's clever handling of the man, even though he still thought the streetseller a shady fellow.

Brother Sedar simply stood there, his expression passive.

Patch spoke. "Sirrah, ye may think ye should nots have to answer, but I assure ye, ye most certainly do. There is the matter of young boys being murdered and ifs ye think ye can remain smug and refuse to cooperate, I shall turn ye over to someone who makes his reputation getting men to talk." Patch leaned forward in his chair. "So, listen close to what I says. If ye be innocent of these heinous crimes, then proves it."

Brother Sedar dragged his eyes from Patch and took in his surroundings before answering. He nodded almost imperceptibly, as if he was having an internal conversation with himself.

"I am an honorable man," he told Patch. "It is my earthly journey to right any wrongs that I may have either willfully or unknowingly caused. But I tell you now and I will tell you true—I am not behind the deaths of those boys.

"I am at a loss how to convince you that I am not a murderer. You have my word as a man of God, but you doubt even that. The king has succeeded in making every cleric, every servant of God, vulnerable to suspicion. It grieves me that I cannot protect the innocent from having their most tender secrets divulged and judged by men like you. No one but God should know what is in a man's heart. You tread on ground most unnatural for those of your rank."

Constable Patch's eyes narrowed into mean little slits as he listened to Brother Sedar.

The monk continued. "I cannot take back a mistake. As I said, my purpose is to make amends." He paused, then continued. "But before I tell you, I want your sworn word that this remains private. I ask all of you to keep your wise counsel." He looked round at each of them, seeking their promise.

"If what ye tells us is of no use," said Patch, adding a caveat to his promise.

For once, the monk showed some emotion. His face pinked and he struggled to continue.

"Get on with it, man," said Patch. "This yammering on to no effect is wasting precious time."

Brother Sedar closed his eyes as he began. "Years ago, when I was at the abbey, I would travel to Davington Priory to bring them foodstuffs from our stores. Davington was not a rich priory. The nuns had a small bit of infertile land that could not be cultivated. Their prioress struggled to prudently administer their meager funds. Jane Clewes was the cellaress and as such, was charged with procuring food and supplies. Often, they lacked the funds to sufficiently feed the sisters and obedientiaries. Also, the buildings suffered from a number of maintenance issues. The roof leaked in the sleeping quarters, posts rotted, hinges broke. The steward neglected to make repairs, given the lack of resources to properly do so. Faversham Abbey was not so far away, and we helped them when we could.

"The duty to deliver them food often fell to me. I had numerous dealings with Jane Clewes and we became friends. She often told me in confidence the troubles Davington was facing. It was not just that their money was in short supply, but their prioress spent what money they had on plate and religious objects. It was her assurance against Cromwell and the king dismantling the religious houses. Jane told me this having followed the prioress one night to a strong box buried outside the priory, covered in a rubble of stone. The cache was filled with glittering gold plate, silver vessels, and pyx boxes. Jane knew not what the prioress planned, but neither could she broach the subject to her superior. She kept quiet, but it gnawed at her.

"But the prioress continued to spend lavishly, putting the rest of the household at risk. Food fell in short supply.

"She confided this to me and I have kept silent until this day." A look of regret came over Brother Sedar's face. He dropped his head and stared at the ground.

Bianca prompted him to continue. "We wish only the truth insofar as proving your innocence, sir. You have our oath that what you say will go no further than this room. If you are blameless, then tell us all."

The monk stared at the floor a moment longer, then glanced up at Bianca and sighed. "I admit I felt a concern and care for Jane Clewes that went beyond my duty." He paused, then said, "We had become familiar with one another."

Constable Patch's eyebrows shot up. He looked to say something and Bianca pinned him with a sharp look and a shake of her head. Patch reluctantly shut his mouth.

"Indeed, on more than one occasion," said Brother Sedar.

Patch couldn't contain himself. "Ye being a monk? A man of faith and vows! For shame. Can ye not see why the king and his agents dissolved these so-called holy houses?"

Bianca and Meddybemps looked at Patch in horror. The constable's words fell like a black soaking rain. There was no taking them back now.

But Brother Sedar did not flinch. He probably had expected the reaction, for while the outburst obviously pained him, he continued on.

THE LOST BOYS OF LONDON

"Indeed, she got with child."

Patch groaned. "Sos, what happened then?"

"When the prioress pressed her to disclose the identity of the father, she kept our secret. She used her knowledge of the prioress's spending as leverage."

"She blackmailed the prioress?" said Patch.

The monk ignored Patch. "Jane had the child. Of course, she could not keep it. The prioress placed the baby in a loving home and life returned to its routine.

"When the commissioner and auditors from the Court of Augmentations visited Davington, they saw little of value beyond the small landholding and buildings which could be stripped, torn down, and sold off to a wealthy nobleman with an interest. They began seizure of the property.

"Each of the nuns were given a small pension. Some chose to live with family, others went into service with the wealthy. Jane sought to find our son.

"I never expected to see her again. I never learned what had become of her, or to our son. It was not long after, that the closing of Faversham Abbey began. And I found my way to London.

"But as God deemed, one day I saw the two of them at market. The years have changed her. They've changed me, I cannot deny that. I wanted to go to her. But my profound remorse held me back. Mayhap my shame." Brother Ywan shook his head. "I followed them and discovered where they lived. Since then, I provide for them as best I can. That is what Luke was tasked to do. I had him leave money on her stoop."

"Ye couldn't bring yeself to go knock on her door and just gives it to her?" said Patch. Empathy and subtlety were never his strength.

"It is better that I don't. I have no knowledge of their lives all these years. I am curious, but I do not deserve to know. Sometimes the pains of the past are better left alone."

Meddybemps and Bianca remained quiet while Patch fidgeted in his chair.

What hardships does one undertake when one loves? thought Bianca. Love demands equal parts of joy and sorrow. Love is a balance between the two, but sometimes one weighs more than the other.

"We shall keep your story quiet," assured Bianca. She turned to Patch. "I believe we have no further cause to question him."

"Well," said Patch, believing the man deserved some sort of punishment beyond that of a broken heart. "I will be keeping ye here for the night," he said. "Tonight is of some importance in this matter. I prefer to be safe about it, than regrets it later. I'm sure ye see the sense in that."

Brother Ywan made no argument against Patch's request. "If it should prove my innocence in these horrid crimes, then I submit myself to being held."

Patch had expected some resistance; most men took umbrage with being locked away. He led the monk into the cell that had previously been occupied by the drunk Malloy, who spoke so ill of him.

"There is one more thing I must tell you," he said, once Patch had secured the door. "I fear for Jane's life."

"Why?" asked Bianca.

"Our son … is a violent boy."

CHAPTER 29

Patch instructed his minion, Cyndric, to keep watch over Brother Sedar, then left with Bianca and Meddybemps for Jane Clewes's tenement. While pausing to let a farmer and cow pass, Bianca breathlessly explained that she had heard scratching from under the floorboards and had been led to believe the dilapidated building to be infested with vermin—most likely rats.

Now she wondered if she'd been naïve to think the condition of Jane's quarters was to blame for something perhaps more sinister.

"Her son is formidable," said Meddybemps as they neared the residence. "How shall we manage him if he should become upset?"

"Wells, there be three of us to one of him," said Patch.

"Methinks it would take the king's guard to subdue the likes of a lad as strapping as he," said Meddybemps.

"We must simply be careful not to rile Jane in his presence," said Bianca. She looked pointedly at Patch, who dismissed her warning.

"I worry nots," he said blithely.

"Let me do the talking," said Bianca. "Though if Fisk is being held captive, I've a mind to kick down the door."

They did not see Jane sitting by the window watching the lane, so they had the element of surprise in their favor. Or so they hoped.

While Meddybemps and Patch watched out of sight, Bianca stepped up to the door and firmly knocked. There was no window at the front of the building to give anyone away, and soon they heard a creak and saw Jane Clewes peeping out.

"Jane," said Bianca. "If I may have a word with you."

The woman scowled and ran her eyes over Bianca.

"What is it that you want?" she asked. She must not have seen Meddybemps and Patch hunkering in the shadows. "Why have you returned?"

"Is Huet home?"

"Why is that your concern?" answered Jane, her eyes searching Bianca's face.

"I have news concerning him."

"News? What do you mean?"

"Please, if I may come in." Bianca looked over her shoulder as if someone might be listening. She leaned forward and lowered her voice. "What I have to say must be said in private."

"Say what you must, but you must say it from there. It will be heard well enough and by my ears only."

Bianca needed to gain entry and, without Jane noticing, she slid her foot inside the door frame to prevent Jane closing it. She further distracted by calling into the interior for Huet.

"He's not here!" said Clewes, her voice shaking. "You must leave." She made to shut the door, but Bianca shouldered it open, startling Jane, who stumbled backward to avoid being hit. Bianca stepped inside, and Meddybemps and Patch hurried in after.

To her chagrin, Jane Clewes found herself facing the three of them.

"What is this?" she demanded. As she looked from one to the

other, her bravado fell away and she became fearful. "I'll get you the money," she said, backing away. "There is no need to hurt me."

"Nay, it is not that," said Bianca. "Where is Huet?"

"He has run an errand for me."

"Are ye harboring a young boy?" demanded Patch.

"What?" answered Jane, struck by the question.

"We have reason to believe ye be up to no goods." Patch placed his hands on his hips.

"Nay! What purpose would I have to do that?"

"Mayhap it isn't ye who took the boy," said Patch.

Jane regained her boldness. "What are you saying? Do not speak so twistedly. Say what ye mean!"

"I means, did your son lay hold of any boys? In particular, a lad named Fisk?"

"Certainly not!" said Jane Clewes.

"We knows yer boy, this Huet, is a brute and knows not his own strength. It is said he has some temper about him."

"Who said this?" demanded Jane.

Bianca intervened before Patch could mention Brother Sedar. "He has been seen chasing boys through the streets."

"He chased a lad through St. Paul's," added Meddybemps.

The former nun's indignation could not cover an embarrassment over a matter beyond her control. She made the sign of the cross and offered a quiet prayer, her lips mouthing the words. When she finished she crossed herself a second time. "He has made many strides, but he is headstrong. I have done my best. He has a willfulness that, try as I might, I cannot curb.

"There is a sadness in him," said Jane. "His childhood was spent doing work meant for a grown man. They thought him older because of his size and strength. 'Tis a sorry shame they used him thus." Jane's eyes shone with sudden anger. "They treated him no better than an animal. I have tried to help him overcome his past, but I fear it will take years."

With this admission, Jane's shoulders began to shake. Her emotions now overwhelmed her. "I gave a sacred vow, but our liege willfully changed the course of my life. He changed the course of many lives. What was, is no more. Perhaps some can live without duty, but I cannot. I resolved to find my son and rebuild our lives, together."

Jane's explanation gave insight into Huet's history, but it mattered less to Bianca than finding Fisk. Perhaps Jane told the truth, but perhaps she believed she must cover Huet's actions for fear of what might happen. Bianca had come to search the tenement. The strange scratching she had heard previously could well have been Fisk's desperate attempt to get her attention.

Jane stopped talking and Bianca primed her ears, listening for the scratching. She stepped away from them, following a noise to a floorboard near the center of the room. Trampled rushes covered the floor and she pushed them away with her foot, then knelt beside a plank that wobbled when she pressed on it.

"Here," said Bianca. "Help me." She jammed her fingertips between the slats, and with Meddybemps's help, the two grabbed hold of either end and began lifting it out of the worn nail holes.

Jane broke past Constable Patch in a hurry to reach them. "Stop! What are you doing?"

"I have to know," said Bianca. "I heard the scratching again." She and Meddybemps laid aside the board and peered into the dark space beneath the floor, as black as a dead man's mouth. Bianca sat back on her haunches and surveyed the room for a lantern or a candle. Spying one, she pointed it out for Patch.

"This is an intrusion!" Jane Clewes shook with rage. She glanced over her shoulder at the door, then turned back. "Huet is due to return. Ye should not be here! I beg you, leave!"

Patch was handing the lit candle to Bianca, when suddenly

something leapt out of the crawlspace, making Bianca yelp, then disappeared into a black corner of the room.

"'Tis a cat!" Patch exclaimed. "God's blood—a cat!"

Bianca leaned over the opening in the floor and shined the candle down into the black space. It appeared empty except for a bowl of water. She blew out the candle and got to her feet.

"You are keeping a cat?" she asked.

Jane Clewes had already abandoned the hole in the floor and was attempting to coax the creature out into the open, ignoring them. Her effort was to no avail.

"See what you've done?" she cried. "If Huet comes home, he'll want to play with it. He knows not his own strength!"

Bianca, Meddybemps, and Patch stared blankly at the nun and the terrified cat, then at each other.

Bianca apologized, feeling responsible and more than a little disappointed. The monk's story had given her hope, but now she was no closer to finding Fisk than she was when he had first gone missing. While reprehensible, Geve Trinion had been nothing more than a despicable father. And Brother Sedar was too cowardly to do anything more for his son than give money anonymously, leaving Jane Clewes to fix a broken child. "Let me help you," she said. She couldn't bear the thought of causing more unhappiness for this woman.

Bianca went over to a small table against the wall, beneath which crouched a white and black cat, its mirrored eyes watching. "He is a well-favored fellow," she said, admiring his handsome looks. She put her hand out for him to smell. "Have you a piece of cheese or meat?"

Jane Clewes brought Bianca a small piece of gristle left from the previous night's meal. With some encouragement, Bianca coaxed the cat forward, and after he saw that she meant him no harm, she gently carried him to his owner's arms.

The tension in the nun's body fell away as she held her cat and stroked its fur. Bianca smiled at their compatibility and was reminded of her own raw sorrow losing Hobs. She understood the woman's desire to love and care for another, even if it was a pet.

"I suppose we be done here," said Constable Patch, removing his cap and scratching his sparsely haired scalp. "We've matters to attend elsewhere."

"I know you are disappointed," said Meddybemps to Bianca. "But we shall find Fisk." He knew his words could not put her mind at ease or release her from a burden she willingly undertook. He feared their search would probably end badly. It had been too long. The possible outcome hung in the air, though no one dared mention it.

But Bianca quashed her feelings of defeat. A pamphlet on a small table caught her eye and she picked it up. Mindful not to mention Jane Clewes's previous life at Davington, she read aloud the title of the pamphlet. "*Supplication Unto King Henry the VIII* by Robert Barnes," said Bianca. It was printed by Clement Naylor. She looked at Jane.

"There is no harm in reading," said Jane defensively.

"Robert Barnes was a follower of Martin Luther," said Bianca. "The king does not favor Luther's beliefs."

"He did when it served him to seek a divorce from Queen Catherine," answered Jane. "I read so that I might understand. There is much I do not know about our king's decisions to close the monasteries."

Bianca raised her eyebrows. "Are you agreeable to Barnes's words?"

"I see no point in answering that. Barnes defended himself against England's bishops. They are the words of a man imploring for equitable discourse and consideration. But, our king does what he will regardless of what I or anyone else thinks."

Constable Patch's eyes shifted between the two as he relished the thought of a nun spouting a treasonous opinion of the king.

Bianca noticed Patch's sudden interest. She set the pamphlet facedown on the table.

"I think we are finished here," she said.

CHAPTER 30

Bianca, Meddybemps, and Patch stood outside of Jane Clewes's tenement. The story of Brother Sedar and Jane Clewes had no bearing on Fisk vanishing. Once again, Bianca had reached an impasse. The chimes of church bells announced the hour and soon the sun would set, portending night with its dreaded possibilities.

Although Bianca had no cause to think Fisk would be the next victim, the possibility still troubled her. Another boy had died a week after Fisk went missing, and there was no evidence linking Fisk's disappearance to the church hangings. Still, if the murderer was following a pattern, then tonight was reason enough to be worried about what might happen.

Whether Fisk would be involved or nay, the murderer had not been caught, and until he was, Bianca would continue to work to find the killer.

"I'm meeting my men before we go to St. Andrew-by-the-Wardrobe," said Patch. "I hopes Berwick has the sense to post guards at the other churches and St. Paul's."

"It is a precaution worth the effort. While it seems that the murderer is making a tour of Castle Baynard ward," said Bianca, "he could always repeat his crime at a previous site."

"We don't know what the perpetrator plans," said Patch. "And Constable Berwick is a shiftless lubberwort who can't be bothered doing his job."

"Since the murders happen in the small hours of the night," said Bianca, "we have some time to prepare. I agree that St. Andrew's seems the most likely place for the next crime. I will join you later, Patch. For now, though, I need to eat."

Meddybemps's face cheered at the mention of food. He insisted that Bianca accompany him to the Cockeyed Gull. "They have a flavorsome egg-and-cheese pie. It will do you well to be around others for a spell. You must give your mind a rest."

Borderlands—

Exhaustion demands payment.

John stared at the burnished horizon blooming over a distant ocean. His entire body ached from a consuming fatigue born from months of overwrought nerves and difficult conditions. Having made it this far, he knew his journey home might be within reach. Yet, he could not muster the strength to keep going.

He needed sleep and he needed food. Either one would be helpful, but unless he satisfied both, the final leg of his journey would be impossible.

In the distance, a shepherd's shack stood in silhouette against the sky. From where he stood, no light glowed within the humble bothy, meaning it might be empty. Then, too, night had not quite finished and a traveler could very well be inside, sleeping. Either way, the hope of rest and shelter was too tempting to keep away.

He had stopped long enough for a chill to set in, so he hurried on, keeping the hut in his sights and scanning the landscape for activity. The thought of sleep lifted his spirits and quickened his steps. He imagined a pallet and blanket, dried meat hanging from a beam, and kindling for a fire inside this little bothy, but the reality, he reminded himself, would be nothing like he imagined. In this impoverished land, such necessities were too valuable to leave behind. He braced himself for the inevitable disappointment as he trod ahead.

A crescent of sun burned over a ridge, and it would be a rare late winter day of light and sharp shadows. The clouds would quicken across the sky and there would blow a fierce wind that would fill his ears with a constant roar. Such a day would bring a shift in fortune, all for the good, thought John.

Nearing the bothy, he slowed and adopted a stealthy approach, his ears primed and his eyes straining to take in his surroundings. No dog was tied outside, no horse, no wisp of smoke escaped the chimney. Nothing indicated that there was a person inside. John circled the hut at a safe distance, looking for anything to warn him away.

He crept to within a few feet of the hut, then stopped and listened. Silence.

He approached the ramshackle door and pressed his ear against it. Silence.

He placed his hand against its wood and slowly pushed it open, holding his knife at the ready in the other. Inside, he found nothing but cool, dank air and the quiet of an empty hut. Glimpsing over his shoulder, still leery for anyone about, he cautiously stepped inside.

It was just an empty room. There was no table or stool. No pile of straw to sleep on. A fag of kindling lay next to the hearth. Only abandoned spiderwebs hung from the rafters—not the wished-for smoked meat. A small tallow lay in a pile of ashes from a fire that had long since died.

But the room enticed. He could finally give over to the demanding pull of sleep. The growl in his stomach had not been answered, but because it had been ignored for so long, it had abandoned its insistent yawps.

John searched his pack for a flint and could not find one. He closed the door and removed his jack, rolling it into a pillow. His wound would wait until light. He lay down on the dirt floor. A couple of breaths later he fell into a greedy and capacious sleep.

Constable Patch met his men, and they trudged to St. Andrew's, where they found Father Foxcroft in the chancel. According to Foxcroft, Constable Berwick had not been by, and Patch, irritated by the constable's lackadaisical attitude, left in a huff to find him.

Patch expected to have to search every boozing ken in the ward before finding Berwick, but he began at the ward office on the off chance that the constable might actually be there. To his utter surprise, he found Constable Berwick and three of his underlings sitting around a table playing goose. They sipped Spanish sack and guffawed over sending one man back to "The Grave," where he had to start the entire game over again. A pile of coins sat in the middle, stakes to be collected should a man navigate all the geese and hazards. The king had outlawed the game, requiring men to use their spare time to practice archery instead. Patch could not keep from reminding the scrofulous lawman of his duty and the importance of the evening.

"Patch, you vex yourself with concerns that truly matter not," said Berwick as he shook his die. He dropped it, then moved his piece a number of squares, remarking that he had just missed landing on "The Maze," which would have set him back to square thirty.

"Then I must ask," said Patch, his irritation compounding, "ye think it matters little that we catch a man murdering young boys?"

Constable Berwick took a sip of sack and relished the taste. "Patch, watches are set at the two churches where the fellow struck before. You told me you would bring your men to St. Andrew-by-the-Wardrobe. Are you here to tell me you have not found anyone?"

"I am heres because ye said ye would post *my* men where *ye* wanted."

"And I shall. But it is too early. I shall be by later, after this game. You needn't trouble yourself so."

"Then *I* shall post my men. Ye needn't bother. Play yer silly game and drink yer sack. And ifs the aldermen should ask, I will tell them where to finds ye. Passed out on your goose board!"

Berwick chuckled. He treated his peer like a nigglesome midge. "We have plenty of time, sirrah. I see no sense in attending church for so long."

"It would do ye no harms," said Patch. "In facts, it might favor yer sorry soul."

"P…at…ch," answered Berwick. "We all stand in the mud and gape at the heavens, but it is the dust to which we all return, not the stars."

"I have no doubt that ye, sirrah, shall waste eternity rotting in the ground," said Patch. "But I intend to let my good works speed me to a heavenly reward."

"Ha, goose!" exclaimed one of the men, and at first Patch thought he was being mocked.

"If you roll a seven next time, you'll claim the pot," commented another.

"It is your prerogative," said Constable Berwick to Patch. He poured himself more wine and replenished the cups round the table. "Do your worst, Patch. But I recommend a more measured approach, lest you become mired in onerous discontent. Investing too much heart in a desired outcome will not assure it."

Patch turned on his heel and stalked from the room. He let the door slam and stood on the street, looking up at the sky. "It is a chance I do willingly takes."

Even though John was surrounded by physical beauty the likes of which he'd never seen, it had not been the rolling hills and heather-covered fields that shaped his dreams. Nay, it was the twisty warren of leaning buildings and narrow alleys of London that had influenced his sleep. For that is where his heart lived, and home occupied his deepest yearnings whether he gave conscious thought to it or not.

So, while London was fraught with any number of hazards that could quickly end a man's life, John considered the city safer and more reliable, since he had grown up understanding its inherent dangers. This vast land of Scotland, with miles of territory and scant population, felt unpredictable, twitchy.

But while his heart longed for home, this time his dreams kept him in Scotland. He was running through the countryside chased by a phantom he could not hear nor see. The demon nipped at his heels, its cold breath chilled the back of his neck and stank with hostility. The demon sought his death, his ultimate dispatch.

He restlessly rolled over to start a new dream—a more agreeable one. He fretted, wished for a blanket, listened to the wind accost the bothy with its ill-fitting door rattling on its hinges. Soon he fell back asleep, descending and moving deeper, like tumbling down a well.

He found this dream more to his liking. A door opened and Bianca stepped inside. Her alluring blue eyes found his, and she crawled on top of his chest and leaned down. Their lips met in a kiss. A tangle of wavy black hair hung about them like a curtain, creating a private world, just the two of them. Her skin pressed warm against his. He ran his hand down the slope of her spine and over the curve of her buttocks. She was his bliss. It was so real as to be better than life this dream . . .

But then her mouth pulled away from his. Her lips moved. *Get up. Get up, John.* Confused, he reached out to pull her back, but she withdrew. She stepped back, shrinking, fading, then disappeared. He felt a rush of raw cold on his cheek, its harsh sting startling.

His eyes flew open and in the feeble light of the shepherd's shack, he found himself pinned by the icy steel of a blade at his throat.

"Get up," said a voice. "Or I will kill you where you lie."

CHAPTER 31

Bianca didn't have the appetite that she thought she did. She picked at the egg-and-cheese pie and nursed a single tankard of ale for the entire time she and Meddybemps were at the Cockeyed Gull. 'Twas a lively ken, one where the ale was better than average and the wenches were strong of wit. The servers were used to a salacious clientele, and if they hadn't the grit for saucy banter they would have left long ago.

Meddybemps corralled his usual impertinence out of respect for Bianca and the gravity of the evening, but the boozing ken was, in effect, his second home. The wenches knew him well, as did the patrons, and their meal was frequently interrupted by someone coming over to fill the streetseller in on a matter of personal business, or just to gossip.

In a sense, just being there with Meddybemps distracted her enough to help lift her spirits, but only a bit. Between interruptions, Bianca ruminated on Fisk and the possible danger he might be in. The best she could do now was to meet Patch at St. Andrew-by-the-Wardrobe, and keep her ears and eyes open.

As the clientele became rowdier and the ale visibly dribbled down their chins, Bianca grew impatient to leave.

"We need to go to St. Andrew's," she said, gathering up her scarf.

Meddybemps finished the last of his ale and set his tankard at the end of the table. His hail- fellow-well-met manner fell away, replaced with a more somber nod. Bianca made for the door and the streetseller followed, pausing here and there to bid his friends a good night, but retaining enough foolery to pinch his favorite tavern wench on the arse, prompting her tart reply.

The night was brisk, tolerable, in that the damp air was less bone-chilling than it had been. Still, it would not be pleasant for standing outside for very long, idly waiting for something to happen. In the nearly clear sky, the Queen Moon gazed down at them, hiding only a sliver of her full face. She, too, seemed to be interested in London on this late winter night.

The two kept a quick pace, opting to take a longer way to the church rather than cut through precarious alleys. Passing by the side of St. Andrew's, they saw a man leaning against a tree, blowing into his cupped hands, trying to keep warm.

"One of the appointed guards?" queried Meddybemps, gesturing toward the man.

"I doubt he would be there if he didn't have to be," said Bianca.

The two stepped up to the double doors of the church and went inside. It took a moment for their eyes to adjust to the dark interior, lit only by the glow from a sanctuary lamp and a few scattered candles. Voices rose and fell, echoing from the front of the church where Father Foxcroft, Constables Patch and Berwick, and a few others stood in conversation.

"It is not so very late. Have we missed the culprit?" Meddybemps asked Bianca as they crossed the nave.

"I hope not," she said. "From the sound of it, they are probably bickering over details. I am glad, though, to see Berwick make an effort to be here. He seemed uninterested before."

"I was wondering when ye might show," said Patch, noticing their arrival.

"Was that a watch on the south side?" asked Bianca. She ignored the uncomfortable scrutiny of Constable Berwick's stare.

"Aye. It's one of Patch's men," said Constable Berwick.

Bianca could tell that Berwick's ruddy complexion had not faded. He spoke clearly, though, and perhaps this night might have refrained from excessive drink?

"So there are guards posted at St. Mary Magdalen's and St. Benet's?" she asked.

"We was just discussing thats," said Patch.

"It is futile to outguess the logic of a troubled mind," said Constable Berwick. "But why would the killer repeat his crime at the other venues? I think we should assume he wants every church in Castle Baynard ward to be equally affected."

"Dids ye not just say we cannot guess the logic of a troubled mind?" argued Patch. "Yet ye take no precautions in case ye be wrong?"

"Constable Patch," said Berwick. "If you be so certain that I am wrong, then post your men at St. Mary's and Benet's. I will not stop you."

"Ye told me *ye* was posting men there," said Patch. "That ye didn't have enough men for all the churches and ye appealed to my good natures to take care of what should have been *your* responsibility. Ye want me to shoulder the expense for Castle Baynard's problem!"

"Sirs, we are talking about a child's life!" interrupted Bianca. "If you do nothing to stop the killings, then you are complicit in these boys' deaths."

"Good sirs," said Father Foxcroft, "we benefit from cooperation, not acrimony. I suggest that we take a moment to pray for guidance."

This seemed to catch everyone up and resulted in sheepish looks all around. No one objected; after all, they were standing in a church. They might as well ask God for some help. While the others listened to the priest's invocation, Bianca listened to Patch grumbling under his breath.

She had to agree with him. She didn't understand why Berwick was taking a gamble by not posting men at the other churches. Perhaps he stood to gain the money that would otherwise have been spent on their wages. Then, too, Berwick might just be lazy. He could be inciting Patch to undertake the responsibility and expense so that he and, by association, Castle Baynard ward wouldn't have to.

Father Foxcroft finished and addressed Berwick and Patch. "Now, let us discuss this matter with God in our hearts."

The moment of reflection had no effect on Patch. He took up his complaint where he left off. "I shall see if I might find some guards for the other churches. But it is late and I do not suppose I'll rouse many men out of their beds. However, if I do, sirrah," he said, jabbing his finger at Berwick's face, "I shall send the note to your ward's aldermen for payment." For good measure, he thrust his finger forward a couple more times, pinching tight his lips to keep from adding further insult.

As Constable Patch stalked from the nave, he passed Father Wells arriving from St. Benet's. Wells stopped, obviously uncertain over what must have transpired, then joined Father Foxcroft and the rest of them.

"I am here to lend my emotional support," he said.

"It is unnecessary," said Foxcroft, his conciliatory tone for cooperation gone. "Guards have been posted. I do not see what use you can be. You should return to St. Benet's and make yourself available should the need arise there."

"I was under the impression that the murderer would, most likely, strike here."

It seemed Patch's surly temper was the order of the night. Bianca sought to defuse another spat—now between the priests. "In truth, we do not know where he will strike. Or even *if* he will strike," she said. "But, Father Wells, if you should want to stay, I'm sure there is no harm in your being here."

"Everything is well in order," said Father Foxcroft, ignoring Bianca's invitation. "Too many people will simply get underfoot. It might even discourage the murderer."

"Should we not want that?" asked one of the men.

Father Foxcroft spoke. "I believe the object is to catch him. Forsooth, I do not know what use Father Wells can be in all this."

The churchwarden of St. Andrew's looked uncomfortable and sought to smooth over his priest's contentious outburst. "We are glad to have your added prayers, Father Wells. It is an uneasy time for all of us."

Wells fingered his paternoster, a replacement, Bianca noted, that he wore like a bandolier. "Perhaps, Father Foxcroft is right," said the priest. "I am sure he has the emotional well-being of his parishioners in mind. I see I am not needed here." Wells met everyone's stare, avoiding Foxcroft's mulish glare except for a quick, cheerless glance cast in his direction. His eyes lifted to the rood above the chancel. He crossed himself, then turned to leave.

Bianca watched Foxcroft's face as Father Wells walked to the exit. She thought she might have seen relief in Foxcroft's expression, which caused her to wonder why he did not want his fellow cleric's help. It struck her as odd, perhaps even misguided. Mayhap there had been words between them. Whatever reason Foxcroft had for sending his counterpart away seemed linked with some deep-seated bitterness.

Meddybemps saw it, too. The pair exchanged an unspoken

understanding that came from years of familiarity with one another. Bianca wandered toward the back of the nave and Meddybemps followed.

"What do you make of Wells's terse dismissal?" he asked her quietly.

"The more I think on it, the more I believe there is unfinished business between the two men. Father Wells knows something about Foxcroft that he has not told us."

"Should we go after him?"

"I think we should. I have a few more questions."

The two strode toward the door and no one from the remaining group called after to ask where they might be going.

"They either did not notice us leaving, or they did not care," said Meddybemps once they were on the street.

"I think it is the latter. Which suits me." Bianca looked up the lane and spied Father Wells just turning the corner. "There he be."

The two caught up to the ambling priest, who seemed in no particular hurry to return to St. Benet's. He expressed mild surprise at seeing them, and rather than stand in the street they accompanied him back to his church.

Bianca was careful not to mention the possible enmity between him and Father Foxcroft. Instead, she skirted that topic and hoped to dig into what Wells knew about Foxcroft's past. Jane Clewes's comment about a man wishing to defend himself against the bishops of England had got her thinking. "Father Wells," she said, "Foxcroft was quite brusque with you. It makes me wonder why he was so adamant against your staying at St. Andrew's tonight."

"It is his prerogative," answered Wells.

"Aye, but he clearly did not want you there."

"That may or may not be his reason. It is more likely that he does not wish to be reminded."

"Reminded? Of what?"

"Let us just say that I believe he takes the possibility of being appointed archdeacon very seriously."

"That is understandable. I suppose if a murder occurred at St. Andrew's it would not bode well for him."

"Nay, it would not."

"I understand all of the priests in Castle Baynard are being considered for the position."

"That is true. However, the number of prospects has been winnowed some by this terrible spate of killing. Bishop Bonner views it as a withdrawal of God's blessing on a church and its beneficent."

"Meaning, you are no longer being considered for the appointment?"

"Possibly. But obviously, I do not know Bishop Bonner's mind."

"Are you disappointed?"

Father Wells gave a halfhearted laugh. "I am fortunate to have a position in a church that I care about. I shall leave the honor of appointment to men who are more willing to do what they must to please the bishop."

"Father, if I may ask, what is it that you suspect?"

Father Wells stopped talking. "What is it that you are asking me?"

"Why did you come here? What were you expecting to happen?"

Meddybemps broke in. "You said Foxcroft does not wish to be reminded."

The priest fingered his replacement paternoster before speaking. "I needed to satisfy my curiosity," he said, reluctant to continue.

"Father, we are talking about a life that may be at risk. Do you suspect Father Foxcroft is involved in these murders?" Bianca persisted.

"I have seen Father Foxcroft change his beliefs to curry favor."

Meddybemps had no more appetite for the priest's vague insinuations. "She asked if you suspect Foxcroft of having a hand in these deaths. And what does Foxcroft not want to be reminded of?" Meddybemps was not by appearance a menacing man. However, when faced with obfuscation, he openly bristled and his strange eyes wheeled around. It could put the fear of God in anyone—including a priest.

"Do I think him capable of murder? Nay, I have difficulty imagining Foxcroft carrying out such an act. But, is he capable of scheming a crime that might benefit him? Indeed, I think him extremely capable."

"Are you saying he might have arranged for someone to murder boys and display their bodies at various parish churches throughout Castle Baynard?"

"It has occurred to me. I wanted to see if St. Andrew's would be included in this mayhem."

"And if it is not?"

"Then I believe its omission would be suspicious. Why would every other parish church be targeted, and not his? It is not divine favor that excludes St. Andrew's—it is Foxcroft's."

"This is a serious accusation, sir," said Bianca. "How do we know that it is not you who set this in motion? Could you harbor a grievance against him and hope to bring St. Andrew's and Father Foxcroft's obvious exclusion to public notice?"

Father Wells shook his head. "I have not the heart for such a scheme. But I have seen Foxcroft abandon his beliefs like Judas if it proves expedient for his advancement." Wells addressed Meddybemps. "That is what I believe he does not want to be reminded of. If he is capable of hiding and then handing over a fellow priest to face heresy charges, then he is capable of adjusting his morality to the whims of those whom he wishes to please."

"Meaning Bishop Bonner?" asked Meddybemps.

"Aye."

"Who is the priest that he betrayed?" asked Bianca.

"He was a man of influence on the king. When the pope denied Henry's divorce from Catherine, Henry sent Robert Barnes to the reformists and Martin Luther, to appeal for his favor. But Luther also rejected Henry's case for divorce. Barnes was assured protection while Cromwell was the chief minister, but when Cromwell fell, so did everyone around him."

"You speak of the man who was burned at the stake with two other priests?"

"I do. As I said, Foxcroft once supported him when Bishop Bonner and others saw Henry consider Luther's ideals. Foxcroft supported helping the reformist priest when it served him to do so."

The three had arrived at St. Benet's. Without mentioning it, they walked to the corner and looked up Bennet's Hill running alongside the church.

"The streets are quiet," said Bianca, relieved not to see a body dangling from the dripstone. "Perhaps it is true that the murderer will not repeat a crime at a church he has already touched."

"I can rouse my sexton to keep watch," said Father Wells. He bid them a quiet night. "Let us hope the murderer reconsiders. In which case, the killer may escape his mortal punishment, but his soul will not escape God's."

"You need to speak with Father Foxcroft again," said Meddybemps once the church door closed behind Father Wells.

"If he has set all of this in motion, he need only deny his involvement. Unless we can catch the murderer and he implicates Foxcroft, then I am not sure what use there is to further pestering the man."

"You might be able to tell if he is lying," said Meddybemps. "Or he might mention something, perhaps slip in the mud, so to speak."

They began walking back to St. Andrew-by-the-Wardrobe.

"Then again," said Meddybemps, "Father Wells could have been lying to put us off *his* trail."

"True that," said Bianca. "This business of priests lying is a sorry thing." They both fell silent as they continued down the street.

"The other thought is," said Bianca, rousing out of her rumination, "if Father Foxcroft is complicit and we keep a close eye on him, we might catch him doing something suspicious."

"Like what?"

"Like warning someone off from St. Andrew's."

"We might say the same of Wells. And now we've left him alone to do what he will."

Bianca stopped walking. She looked up at Meddybemps. "I don't suppose you would shadow Wells for the rest of the night?"

"Someone should," replied the streetseller. He looked back in the direction they'd come. "I'll go linger about," he said.

Bianca hurried on, squelching through the mud and rocking wood planks as she passed over the worst bits of road. She sifted through their conversation with Father Wells and remembered the pamphlet at Jane Clewes's tenement. The publication and others like it stoked an undercurrent of fear and distress. She wondered if that was their purpose, or was it merely a means for educating and perpetuating the reformists' ideals? With the king being so volatile, it was an act of bravery to flout Luther's reforms. Henry had once rejected them and had been deemed the Defender of the Faith for doing so by the pope. But several years later and with Catherine unable to give him a male heir, siding with the reformists stood to serve him. He had willingly considered embracing the Lutherans' reforms. But ultimately, he rejected them when Luther and the princes of Germany did not support his divorce. How Henry viewed the Lutherans today was different from yesterday and might very well be different tomorrow.

Bianca turned onto St. Andrew's Hill where St. Andrew's church stood tall against a clear night sky, the surrounding buildings giving place to its divine station. She passed the watch, still manning his post; this time, he acknowledged her with a bow of his head, which she returned in kind. Stepping up to the entry, she was overcome by the urge to say a prayer for Fisk.

Bianca had never ascribed to the tenets of religion, preferring instead to set her course by her own set of morals. She saw more majesty and peace in a towering oak tree and the starry sky than she did in a man lifting a wafer over his head. This religious equivocation that Henry and others squabbled over seemed based on opinion and interpretation that didn't stem from God's word, but from words written and interpreted by men.

Was there a spiritual realm? She believed there was, most decidedly. But she didn't know if the concept of "heaven" or "hell" or somewhere in-between wasn't just man's invention to try to keep people from killing each other. Bianca named *her* heaven "bliss" and *her* hell "hate," and the in-between was "confusion." It served her well enough, and to Bianca it made sense.

So, as Bianca stood outside the door to St. Andrew-by-the-Wardrobe, she sent her thoughts to this entity called God, but she didn't ask for a miracle or for divine intervention. She only asked that she remember what strength there was in doing what was right. That she would know wisdom in judgment to see her through the night, come what may.

After a whispered, "Amen," she hauled open the door and

went inside.

CHAPTER 32

Borderlands—

Even though John had indulged in his first restful sleep in nearly a year, it would take more than a day's worth of tranquil slumber to calm the beast within that came from being a soldier in war. There was no blinking awake and making sense of a cold blade against his neck.

Despite his wound and the bone-weary aches of exhaustion, John rolled and thrust out his legs, catching up his aggressor and throwing him off balance. Though his neck grew wet with blood, he did not stop to think on it. He would fight for his life until it was gone.

In the darkness of that little shepherd's shack, John's instincts told him which way to find the scoundrel. He stretched out his arms and connected with the man, wrapping them around a pair of knees. With a quick tug he pulled his assailant to the ground, the man landing with an emphatic "oomph." The intruder barely knew what happened before John threw himself on top and landed a fist where he suspected the fellow's face to be.

He had judged well. A whump and sharp crack of cartilage told him he'd found the fellow's nose. The man howled in pain, unleashing a torrent of oaths. And in that dim light afforded by a loosely hung door, John saw the glint of metal lying on the earthen floor.

So, too, did his attacker.

They both scrabbled after it, John nearly the victor, but nay. He grabbed the man's wrist and tried pinning it to the ground, but the fellow rolled out from under, and sat back on his knees. He was about to stand, when John leapt on his back and began choking him.

The force of his landing sent the fellow sprawling. The knife flew out of his hands, but John continued digging his fingers into the intruder's neck. The rascal lay face down and John sat on his back, crushing the air out of him. The sound of his own heavy breath and the man's desperate gurgling filled his ears.

As he had once been told … it was kill, or be killed.

Only a handful of men remained in the nave, among them the churchwarden, the sexton, and two others, one associated with the administration of the church and the other a concerned parishioner. Constable Berwick and Father Foxcroft were nowhere to be seen.

"Where is the constable?" asked Bianca, walking up to them.

"He left," answered the churchwarden, offering no further explanation.

"He left? Where did he go?"

"He went to check on the guards."

"Then I need to speak with Father Foxcroft." Bianca turned, looking for him.

"He has retired to the sacristy to pray," said one of the men.

Bianca started in the direction of the room and was

immediately questioned.

"You are not seeking him there, are you?" asked the churchwarden, hurrying after her. "He asked not to be disturbed."

"I must ask him some questions."

"Ask them of us. We can help."

"Nay, the questions are for him only." Bianca made a move toward the sacristy and the churchwarden caught her up by the elbow.

"You do not understand," he said. "He wants his privacy."

"He chooses the worst night to expect it. I shall wait for you to bring him to me."

The churchwarden let go of her arm. "Father Foxcroft will not take kindly to being interrupted. If you found him uncooperative before, then I can tell you, he will not have softened."

"Sir, we are trying to prevent another murder. I beg you, do not deny me."

In spite of his objections, the churchwarden was not a callous man. Bianca wondered if he had children that he held close to his heart, for she saw his resolve begin to waver.

"As you will," he said. He left to collect Father Foxcroft, and rather than return to the group of men who had been listening to their conversation, Bianca wandered after the churchwarden, out of earshot.

While she waited, the chimes of a clock near St. Andrew's tolled the midnight hour. The thick walls and hollow interior of the church could not muffle its grim tidings. A ripple of anxiety rolled down her neck as she realized the next few hours were crucial. If Fisk still lived, he might very well be the murderer's next victim. As she waited for Father Foxcroft, Bianca thought about their conversation with Father Wells.

Perhaps Foxcroft *had* conceived the plan of discrediting all the churches in Castle Baynard ward so that *his* might look special—

graced by God, as it were. But her mind kept wondering about the possibility that the murders were not Foxcroft's doing, but someone else's. Someone who wished Foxcroft to look suspicious. Murders perpetrated to draw attention to Foxcroft's exclusion. The priest had called Foxcroft a Judas. If Father Wells thought that, then surely other priests shared his opinion. But perhaps there were others who had noticed Foxcroft's deceit. Others who wished Foxcroft's disgrace. Others with a deep-rooted grievance against him.

As Bianca pondered this, a wave of realization dawned on her and her heart began to race. A possible motivation fell into place. Bianca snapped to, as though she had been shaken out of a dream. But with this sudden revelation appeared the churchwarden, returning with a troubled look on his face.

"Father Foxcroft is not in the sacristy," he said.

"Did you look elsewhere?" asked Bianca.

"He is not in his office, nor the confessional." He went over to the chapel and searched inside. "He is not here, either." The churchwarden called out to the other men. "Did Father Foxcroft pass by?"

The men shook their heads and offered no suggestions.

"He would not have left without informing us," said the churchwarden, dismayed. His voice was quiet with concern.

"It is a sizeable church. Could there be areas where you might not have looked?" asked Bianca.

The churchwarden sent the sexton to search the church's lower level. He then called out for the priest, bellowing his name so that it echoed off the stone arches of the clerestory, then faded. They held their breath, listening. There was no answer.

"Why would he leave without telling someone?" the churchwarden repeated.

"Has anyone asked the guard outside?" said Bianca.

A strange look came over the churchwarden's face. He started for the narthex door and Bianca, along with the men, followed him into the street.

Borderland—

He felt the man go limp in his hands. John wasn't certain the man was dead, but it disgusted him to keep choking him. He let go and the man's head hit the earthen floor. Had the fellow been alone or were there others? John looked over his shoulder and listened. What if someone was waiting in ambush outside the bothy?

John crawled forward and retrieved the knife from off the floor. It was wet with his own blood. He touched the collar of his smock, also damp with blood. The wound stung but it wouldn't be the death of him. John got to his feet, and after wiping the blade on his hosen, stepped to the door. Odd that the man had closed it behind him when he had entered. Peering out through the crack, John saw no one waiting outside in the twilight. He had slept the entire day, and night was falling. He waited, listening. He heard nothing except the wind lash across the land.

John tucked away the new knife and returned to the body. He suspected the man was a soldier. He smelled of smoke and blood; like a man used to the elements and the hard life of battle. He wore nondescript garb, a padded jerkin, and torn hosen. John rolled him over with his foot. The fellow's face was a mess of blood and dirt hidden by sweaty, matted hair. It was just as well that he couldn't see his victim in the dim interior. He shrugged, figuring the man was probably a Scottish deserter. Perhaps he, too, had deserted the battle and was looking for shelter.

He felt through the man's pockets and found a few shillings, which he stuffed in a shoe. He searched his pack and found some dried meat and bread, and crammed the bread in his mouth, chewing like he hadn't eaten in days. As he savored the taste of food (albeit stale), John sat back on his heels and began viewing the horrible incident a bit more favorably. The extra coin and provisions would help him survive another few days.

And what is this? A flint to set a fire! John decided to take the fellow's pack and leave his empty one.

A sharp wind menaced their faces, funneling down the lane between the buildings on either side, reminding them that winter still held them in her grip. Bianca held the collar of her cloak closed and rewound her scarf against the snap of cold. There was no sign of Father Foxcroft on the street—indeed, no one was about at this late hour.

They walked to the side of St. Andrew's where the watch had been posted. Perhaps he had noticed Father Foxcroft leave. At first glance, he appeared to have left.

"He might have walked behind the building for other reasons, or to get warm," said the church official. But as the branches of the tree dipped in the wind, moonlight illuminated previously dark areas and there, on the ground, was the posted watch.

"Is he asleep?" asked the churchwarden. For all appearances the man was taking a nap. The churchwarden called to him and received no response.

The church administrator pushed past, irritated that the man had taken advantage of the arrangement. "Here, here," he said, nudging the fellow with his boot.

The tree limbs waved from another gust of wind, letting the moonlight through to shine on the guard lying near the trunk.

"He didn't hear you," said Bianca, having reached the spot and peering down at the man. "He's dead."

302

CHAPTER 33

"He's been strangled with a paternoster," said Bianca, crouching to examine the dead guard. The man's final expression was not the peaceful one seen on the boys. He had died struggling, fighting for his life. Why had the offender departed from his usual method of killing? Was he even the same murderer who had killed the boys? Bianca looked up. "We still don't know where Father Foxcroft is."

"Are you suggesting that Father Foxcroft is the perpetrator?" asked the churchwarden.

"Is this his paternoster?" Bianca unwound the string of beads and handed it to him.

He looked them over. "In truth, I do not know," he said. The churchwarden showed it around and scanned the side of St. Andrew's church. "For cert, the murderer wanted the watch out of the way," he said. "He might have wished to scale St. Andrew's, but was thwarted."

"The guard's body is still warm," said Bianca, standing. "He may not have gotten far."

"We scared him off," said the church official, and the men studied the shadows for a murderer lying in wait.

"We'll find him!" enthused the parishioner.

"And if it is Father Foxcroft committing these crimes?" Bianca said to the churchwarden.

The man appeared conflicted, contemplating the alarming possibility.

"Then he must account for these heinous deaths," said the parishioner with no hesitation. "He must face justice the same as any other man."

"Aye," nodded the churchwarden, resignedly. He sent the church administrator and parishioner to find Father Foxcroft, then took hold of the man's feet while the sexton took the man's arms. "And where are you going?" he said to Bianca as she strode toward the street.

"I have a suspicion I need to follow."

Bianca made it to the area near Old Change without a single mishap from tippled revelers stumbling home after an evening of debauchery; nor did she encounter any thieves or gropers. She credited her good fortune to her quick and determined stride—and her serious countenance. One look at her was all it took to put someone off.

She neared Clement Naylor's print shop and pulled the dagger she carried on nights such as this. The shutters were closed and secured from the inside; no light seeped from under the threshold. On the door hung an impossibly heavy padlock. The shop appeared quiet and empty, or at least settled for the night.

Father Wells had got her thinking. She remembered Jane Clewes's pamphlet printed by Clement Naylor, and thought back to her brief conversation with the man. He had mentioned Robert Barnes, and now she knew that Father Foxcroft had turned the priest over to Bishop Bonner. Could this be the underlying motivation?

Bianca looked up at the second story and saw that it was also secured. The shop only had two faces. Flanking it on either side were other businesses—also closed and latched for the evening. Bianca spent another minute studying the building, then skirted its perimeter to an alley running behind. The smell in the alley was rank with the stink of refuse and human piss. No one with any sense would linger there any longer than necessary. She crept from shadow to shadow, calculating the location of the back of the shop.

In the wavering moonlight, Bianca came upon a second, equally formidable lock securing the back door. She ran her fingers over the door's hinges and pressed the wood where they were driven. Both wood and metal were of solid material, no rust or rot to take advantage of. She stepped back and gazed up at the second story. One of the shutters was askew, while the other lay flush against the sill. There was a gap, large enough to wedge a hand under. The only problem was getting to it.

As Bianca studied the window, she noticed a metal ring jutting from one of the construction timbers on the exterior wall. A length of rope hung down, probably once used for a laundry line between the opposite building. The rope had frayed, and she wondered if it was rotten from the rain and cold of winter. With both hands, she grabbed onto the ends and tested her weight. The rope went taut, but it supported her. Hitching her hem above her shoes, she placed a foot on an uneven timber. She then leaned back and pulled herself up the rope, hand over hand, placing a second foot on the exterior wall. She paused to balance a moment, her arms straining, then scaled the remaining distance to the timber with a gouge running the length of the building.

At the metal ring beside the window, Bianca realized how precariously it supported her. With her feet wedged in the divot and one hand grasping the rope, she jammed her free hand under the gap of shutter and wrenched it open. It complained, emitting a creak as the heavy board pulled free of its rusty hinge and clattered to the ground below.

She quickly swung toward the side of the building, away from the opening, hoping to escape notice—for what little good that would have done her. If someone had heard the shutter and decided to have a look, she would have been difficult to miss.

To her surprise, no one poked their head out the window, and no light shone upon the sill. Bianca steadied her breath, then leaned toward the opening to peer inside. The room was completely dark. She held still, her muscles aching, and listened.

A gust of wind blew down the alley, catching the loose fabric of her kirtle so that it flapped about her legs. Below, leaves rustled and swirled against a wall. It was a long way down if she fell.

The rusty edge of the steel ring cut into the rope. A few fibers had frayed and she wondered—could the rope withstand one last feat? She would have to hold it with one hand and reach for the opening with the other, pulling herself through the window to gain entry.

Shifting her weight to one foot, Bianca took a breath and pushed out from the building, swinging toward the opening. She let go of the rope with her right hand, and reached for the windowsill. Having grabbed it, she then pulled herself halfway on its ledge, released the rope, and clung to the sill.

Her feet scraped the side of the building, seeking a toehold. She cursed her skirt with all of its fabric, and thought how much easier this would have been if she were a man. But she wasn't, she told herself. She walked her arms forward and managed to swing a leg up, planting a foot on the ledge. With a bit of struggle, she dropped into Clement Naylor's living quarters, headfirst, and landed with a whump.

She cringed at the sound she'd just made and hurriedly crawled under a nearby table.

Any second someone would come and investigate. She snapped her mouth shut to keep from sounding like a panting dog, and the air passed noisily through her nostrils. Though the interior was dark, enough moonlight allowed her to see across the room. If Naylor was home, he was not asleep in the bed opposite.

Bianca listened to the building settle and the wind ravishing the exterior. No one came to check on the thuds and scrapes, and after a time, she crawled out from under the table and tiptoed across the room. A narrow stairwell led to the ground floor.

A candle would have been helpful, but alas, she would have to rely on her sense of touch to safely descend the stairs. She tested the first tread, laying a hand against the wall, then carefully applied her weight. It eased quietly underfoot. Bianca steadily descended to the bottom where she stood stock-still, surveying the printing shop in front of her.

A hearth's dying embers cast enough light to illuminate the shop, which consisted of a single narrow room. There were no partitions. A printing press dominated the middle—a strange-legged construction with two supporting arms like columns, and a cross member at the top. It reminded Bianca of the scaffolds at Tyburn. Suspended from the center was a heavy cylindrical block with a rod to crank down the weight onto a wooden box beneath. Bianca tiptoed over for a better look. The mechanics of the press intrigued her. She manipulated a hinged frame that bent over on itself, and moved it up and down, marveling at its clever design, when she caught a whiff of something familiar. The smell ran up her nose and she recognized its singular strangeness. It was the same smell she'd noticed on the rag she found beside St. Benet's.

She continued sniffing the air, laying her hand on the flat of the press as she did so. Its surface was wet and tacky, leaving her fingertips sticky with ink. Rather than wipe them on her apron, she looked around and found a rag tossed on a table with tongs and leather ink balls. The cloth was obviously stained with ink and smelled of the same peculiar odor. Not only that, but she felt a stupefying effect.

Bianca dropped the cloth and stepped away from it.

The faces of the victimized boys had been filthy with what she had thought was dirt. Boys living on the streets had no sense of cleanliness and no means by which to remedy the problem. They were notoriously unkempt and no amount of normal scrubbing would have cleaned their grimy faces. But, had the victims' faces been smeared—not with mud and filth—but with ink?

She went back to the cloth and picked it up by a corner. Could the cloth she found at St. Benet's have been from Clement Naylor's print shop?

Again, she brought the rag to her nose. This time, she inhaled long and deep. An almost instant vertigo came over her. Instinctively, she turned away and gasped for breath, steadying herself against the table until the room stopped tilting.

Bianca thought back to Hobs in her room of Medicinals and Physickes. She remembered tossing the rag on the chest and the cat had slept on top of it. Had the smell killed him? Had it incapacitated him that first time, then killed him the second?

She stuffed the cloth in her purse and cinched it tight.

Now with her eyes adjusted to the dim interior, Bianca noticed a rope strung across the room with large sheets of printing pinned to it, like laundry on a line. Turning the damp paper toward the embers illuminated the printing of the first page of a pamphlet.

On the Freedom of a Christian, she read, by Martin Luther. So, it wasn't just a remembrance of Robert Barnes that Naylor printed. He actively championed Luther's reforms. Printing and disseminating such ideas was dangerous, and Clement Naylor appeared to have a steady diet of doing so. Rather than support the king's ideas, this was an indication that he was furtively kindling a resistance.

Bianca read the title and first line of the next sheet and the one after. The sheets were copies of Martin Luther's argument. At the end she came upon a short page different from the rest. She unpinned it and began to read ...

Here hangs the body of a prevaricator and a scoundrel. A man of endless deceit and whose wavering word changes with the hour. Faithful to none, loyal only to one—in and of himself, he would sell his everlasting soul, his God, verily his country, for the fleeting kiss of celebrity granted by one equally unworthy and whose infamy will long outlive his mortal breath. Be in his spectacle this cautionary tale—'tis not what a man does that exalts or condemns him, but what is in his heart.

Father Wells had called Foxcroft a Judas. That he had turned in a fellow priest to please Bishop Bonner. *Here hangs the body...*

Bianca pinned the sheet back on the line. She stared at the ominous message and the treatise hanging on the rope. *Here hangs the body...*

It was then that she heard a muffled cry. She froze, her eyes searching the dark, thinking it her imagination. Perhaps the smell on the cloth had made her delusional. She still felt a bit woozy, and being in Naylor's print shop had spurred her unease. Then, she heard it again.

The sound came from the back of the shop.

Bianca stepped toward the stairwell and stopped. A narrow hallway ran beside the stairs to a back door. The area under the stairs was enclosed with wood paneling. She waited, trying to determine if the noise was Naylor in the alley, working the lock. She was about to bolt up the stairs when she heard a second muted cry and a thump that made her start. Someone was trying to get her attention.

"How now?" she called softly, stepping into the narrow hall.

Another thump rattled the paneling.

Bianca ran her hand along the wood and felt a gap near the edge of the wainscot. She followed the space down to where it ended in a metal hasp and pin. Her heart began thudding in her chest as she tried pushing the pin out. It had been tightly wedged in place and no amount of pushing or pulling was going to remove it.

She hurried back into the shop and looked over the table of tools near the printing press. Next to several leather ink balls lay a mallet. She grabbed it off the table and went back to the hall.

The tool was an unwieldy, cumbersome solution—it was too big to effectively knock out the pin, but after several hits, the piece of metal finally budged. After a few more misses, Bianca hit the pin with enough force to free it of the hasp and it clattered against the wood on a length of chain.

Bianca barely had time to recover her balance before the door swung open with a tortuous screak and out fell a body, landing at her feet.

CHAPTER 34

Borderlands—

John straightened, considering what to do. The ocean and an eastern port were within sight. With luck he might find a British galleon sailing for home. The exhaustion that had consumed him began to fall away like rain shed from a roof. His thoughts went to Bianca. How he missed sleeping next to her. Those mornings when neither of them wanted to get out of bed to tend to the fire. Her smelly concoctions and burnt meals. He smiled. What would it feel like to lay eyes on his son for the first time? How old would he be by now? Well, no matter, the day would be a happy one, indeed.

John looked down at the rascal lying on the floor and the smile left his face. Leaving the body in the shack would be a gruesome discovery for anyone happening upon it, and there was nowhere to hide him. If he were waylaid in port and the body was discovered, in what sort of trouble would he find himself, being a stranger in a foreign town? He could burn the bothy with the body in it, but that would attract attention, and he might be spotted leaving.

John went to the door and cracked it open. He would have the cover of dark by which to work.

Taking hold of him under the arms, John dragged the body across the floor and then outside, laying him beside the shack. He blew into his fists to warm them while scouting for a place to dig a grave. But the ground of this wild coast was dotted with boulders and thin soil. John dug his toe into the ground in despair. Even if he had a shovel, he would be scraping and digging until the sun came up. The wind roared in his ears and he covered them with his hands. Nothing would do but to find a depression in the land. He could place the body there, then cover it with a thin layer of moss and peat, mayhap stones.

John walked the immediate area, and by the light of the moon, began surveying the land. A seeping panic of lost time began gnawing at him. To his mounting dismay, he found no suitable spot where he could put a body that wouldn't be discovered. The best he could do was an area beyond a knoll, out of sight of the shack.

He hurried back to the bothy and began dragging the man across the field, up toward the knoll, stopping twice to get a better grip and to catch his breath. The wind kept up its funereal howl, warning and whipping him, punishing his every step. When he finally got there, he pulled out the man's knife and began cutting the top layer of soil. Stones hindered his progress as his blade kept striking and glancing off them.

When he'd collected enough sphagnum and moss, John rolled the body to its final rest. He knelt to tuck the arms beside it and arranged the legs. The cold made his hands ache, and he stopped long enough to warm them again, then covered the corpse with strips of earth and bits of heath. The wind kept up its gale, blowing away the scraps of placed dirt. John cursed and cut more to replace them, wondering if this was a futile exercise and nearly laughing at the absurdity of it. Perhaps he'd finally lost his wits.

Well, it was the fellow's poor luck to stumble upon the shack with him in it, he reasoned. But it was *his* poorer luck to have to deal with a dead body. As he reached for a stone near the man's head, the wind got hold of the man's matted hair, freeing it from off the bloody face. For the first time, John got a long look at the man's face as the moon shone bright upon it.

John rubbed his eyes as if it was a trick of the night.

He stared, unable to move, refusing to believe. His fellow soldier, knave, archer, pompous Roger, and Cammy Dawny's lover, lay dead by his hands.

"Fisk!" Bianca cried.

The boy had been leaning against the door and landed on his side when it opened. He lay there, motionless, his mouth gagged. His hands and feet were bound and a short length of rope connected them so that he was held in a crouched position with his knees bent. At first, Bianca thought he was dead, but then she saw him struggle against his bindings. She helped him to sit and removed the gag with trembling hands.

"Whatever happened?" she said, untying the knots. She could make quick of them with her knife and impatiently sliced him free.

Fisk rubbed his sore wrists and looked at Bianca. His eyes were wide and his face was nearly black with grime—or, thought Bianca, printer's ink.

"He promised me an apprenticeship," said Fisk, disappointed. "He promised me a bed to sleep in and meals to eat. He said he'd pay me three shillings tonight and that I could give it to Mother tomorrow. I had no reason to doubt, he was so kind to me." Fisk massaged his ankles and added, "Until now."

"Why did you not return home to tell them where you were? Anna and your mother have been sick with worry. And so have I."

Fisk cast a sheepish look at her. "I did not think anyone cared."

313

Bianca resisted boxing the boy about his ears. "How could you think that? You are loved."

"I was scared to go home. I overheard some fellow with a rough beard talking to Mother about how he was going to take me to the West Country and make me work in the tin mines there. I knew she could get more money by sending me away with him. I didn't want to go."

"Oh, Fisk," said Bianca. Truth be, there were times growing up when she felt unloved, as well.

"I don't believe she would have ever done that."

"She didn't want to talk to him and she slammed the door in his face. I didn't have time to run before he saw me hiding, watching him. He grabbed my arm, but I got away. I was afraid to go back. I think he is my father, and not the one fighting in France." Fisk got to his feet, none the worse for being dosed with ink, and offered Bianca a hand up. "I don't look like Anna and them. They have yellow hair and blue eyes. This man had black hair and dark eyes like mine."

"You figured it right," said Bianca. "Geve Trinion is your natural father."

Fisk met her gaze, but before she could read his expression, he glanced around skittishly. "I don't want to be here when he returns."

"You speak of the printer?"

"He came up behind me while I was eating and tried to suffocate me. He must have only half killed me because I woke up in the dark with a gag in my mouth and my hands and feet tied. I didn't know where I was. I didn't know if my eyes were open or closed it was so dark in there. That was you coming down the stairs just now. The dust rained down on me and I realized where I was. I listened, wondering if I should pretend that I was dead in case it was him. But his steps are heavy and he often clears his throat. You didn't do that and your steps were lighter."

Fisk grew thoughtful as he rubbed his wrists and then something must have occurred to him for his face grew anxious.

"What is it, Fisk? What troubles you?"

"There was another boy," he said. "His name was Matthew. I thought he was another apprentice, like me. One day he was here and the next he was gone."

"I believe you have escaped an untimely death," said Bianca.

"The printer told me that Matthew went home. That he didn't want to be an apprentice anymore." Fisk looked at Bianca with wide eyes, as if he had just pieced it together. "It was strange, because we ate a meal together that last night and we went to bed, and in the morning Matthew was just gone." Fisk turned his face to her. "He never said good-bye."

Bianca hesitated, but decided Fisk would find out anyway. "Fisk, you may not be aware, but since you've been missing, another boy has been hanged from a parish church here in Castle Baynard ward. It is possible that Clement Naylor is involved." Bianca saw the horrified look on Fisk's face. "I'll explain later, but we need to leave at once."

If Clement Naylor was the murderer, as Bianca thought, he might very well return—either for Fisk, or for the printed sheet drying in his shop. Perhaps he had scouted St. Andrew-by-the-Wardrobe to make sure he could use it for his next murder. The posted guard might have put him off, but only temporarily. Strangulation with a paternoster followed the murderer's pattern. And now with Father Foxcroft missing, it made her wonder.

"I may need your help," she said. "I'm sorry I can't take you home just yet."

Fisk had barely answered before they heard a sound at the shop's entrance. The padlock was being worked.

Bianca and Fisk ran up the stairs of the print shop just as the padlock scraped and the door began to open. At the window, Bianca reached for the rope on the ring and handed it to Fisk.

"Hang on to this and walk down the wall," she whispered. "Wait for me between the two buildings at the end of the alley."

Fisk got up on the windowsill and looked down.

"Hurry!" Bianca waved him on. "And don't jump!"

The downstairs door clicked shut and footsteps crossed the room. Bianca glanced toward the stairs then leaned out the window to watch Fisk rappel down the side of the building. He got within five feet of the ground and let go, landing harmlessly on his rear.

Bianca grabbed hold of the rope, just as the bottom stair groaned with weight.

"Who goes there?" Clement Naylor had overheard their scrambling.

Bianca gathered up her skirt and got herself onto the sill. The ring and the rope were in poor condition from the evening's use, but with no choice in the matter she had to entrust her weight to the rotten hemp. If she could get halfway down without it breaking, she could survive the fall without too much injury. With a final glance over her shoulder, she swung herself outside, feeling for the grooved timber with the toe of one foot.

Luckily, it didn't take her long to find it, and she began scaling down the wall. Her hands burned from sliding down the rope in her haste to reach the ground. She was halfway down when the rope soundlessly frayed at the ring and the whole thing gave way. The strands of rope suddenly went slack and Bianca landed on her back, the wind knocked out of her. She lay there, surprised, blinking up at the sky, her mouth opening and closing like a fish out of water. Then she remembered Clement Naylor. He would notice the missing shutter. She couldn't let him see her on the ground next to it. She got her breath and rolled up against the building.

Seconds later, Naylor stuck his head out the window and looked down the alley in either direction. He pulled his head back in, and Bianca thought he was done, when half his body suddenly leaned out, looking for the missing shutter. Spotting it in the alley, he gave an audible, "Hmmph," then disappeared.

Bianca got to her feet and flattened herself against the wall. The shadows would give her cover if she clung to them, and she ran for the corner.

"Did he see you?" asked Fisk when she ducked in beside him.

"I think not, but I don't want to wait and find out." She crept to the other end of the gap and peeked around the corner at the front door. It was still closed but she expected Naylor would open it any second. "We need to get out of here, but we can't let him see us on the road." Bianca pulled Fisk after her, back into the alley. "Naylor will see that you're gone. He'll put it together about the noise and the missing shutter."

"Why does he want to kill me?"

"Fisk, I do not know if that was his intent. Understand that it has nothing to do with whether or not he liked you. Now, follow me." Bianca ran down the alley with Fisk close behind, then broke across the road to hide in a dark alcove a distance from the shop. From there they could keep the front door in sight. "I have a sense where Naylor may be going, but I don't know for sure. We'll need to follow him."

They didn't have to wait long before the door opened and Clement Naylor appeared. He secured the padlock and started walking down the street. One hand rested on a messenger bag slung across his chest, and the other swung freely at his side as he hurriedly strode down the lane.

Bianca and Fisk retreated into the alcove and watched him pass.

The two cautiously stepped from the doorway. They trailed

him at a safe distance, dashing from shadow to shadow along the periphery of the lane, careful not to expose themselves in the conspicuous middle. Naylor turned toward Paternoster Row, heading in the direction of St. Paul's.

With the other parish churches previously targeted and by now hopefully guarded, there were no other religious buildings left in Castle Baynard ward but the massive cathedral. But Bianca didn't expect that Naylor would necessarily attempt a murder there. How could anyone hang a body from its formidable exterior without some sort of scaffolding or crane?

However, if the printer was determined to stage his next spectacle at St. Paul's, he would have no choice but to use the church grounds to gain access. At the corner of Paternoster Row, Bianca and Fisk stopped and watched the printer cross the churchyard, a lone figure in a sea of stretched shadows from nearby buildings.

"He's heading for the Cross," whispered Bianca.

Paul's Cross was an open-air pulpit built of timber on stone steps and covered with a lead roof. Affixed to the roof's peak was a large lead cross. The circular pulpit was the site of weekly sermons given by priests appointed by the bishops of London, as well as a venue to announce royal proclamations. Of course, it was also known for a tumultuous history where men voiced their opinions and incited riots. Curiously enough, thought Bianca, the buildings lining the Cross yard contained an ever-increasing number of publishers.

Bianca turned to Fisk. "I need you to find Meddybemps," she said. "He should be at St. Benet's Church. I've asked him to follow Father Wells. But I need him here. Can you do that?"

"What do you think Master Naylor is about?"

"Whatever it is, I do not think that he is up to much good. Now hurry!" Bianca pointed the way and gave him a gentle push.

Fisk hesitated, as if resisting her request. Bianca was about to scold him when, without warning, he wheeled about and hugged her around the waist. Bianca's eyes widened in surprise. She stiffened, not quite knowing how to react, but the boy had weaseled his way into her heart long before this awkward show of affection. Before she could lay her hand on his back, or return the gesture in kind, Fisk took off running, his young legs pumping and his worn shoes pounding the ground beneath his feet.

John felt suddenly ill. He had more respect for his enemies— the Scots—than he did for this man, this English brother. How many times had he wished Roger dead? And now here he lay, murdered by his own hand.

He vomited in the soft sphagnum and retched until nothing more came. Well, he thought, wiping his mouth on his sleeve, what is done cannot be unmade. For now, he must finish burying him.

Using peat and moss was futile with the wind blowing ever stronger. Instead, he ranged the immediate field, collecting stones, and laid them on top of Roger. Once he had finished, it would look like an obvious burial site. Mayhap the stones would be removed and the body discovered, but there was the chance the site would be left undisturbed out of respect for the dead.

John laid the last stone just as the sun broke above the horizon. He stood over the grave. A prayer might speed Roger's soul on its journey. But John didn't bother saying one.

The war had changed him.

* * *

Clement Naylor disappeared behind the pulpit's low wood walls. Bianca wanted a closer look, so she dashed from one of the buildings to a tree within sight of the front of the pulpit. Once there, she made herself slim against its trunk and took a peek.

Naylor's head bobbed up and down as if he was securing

something hidden behind the enclosure. Finished, or perhaps taking a rest, he stood up. Bianca ducked behind the tree trunk. When she dared to look, she saw Naylor standing on the short wall in front of the sermon dais, which served as a narrow divider, a dangerous height if he fell. But from the ease with which he moved, Clement Naylor appeared unconcerned with its possible peril.

He held a coil of rope in one hand, and in his other an attached metal bar. Naylor stepped along the short preacher's wall, angling for a better look. He stopped and wound back his arm, tossing the metal bar onto the lead roof. It made a dull thud. The printer hopped off and disappeared inside the enclosure.

Bianca could see movement on the opposite side, but she couldn't determine what he was doing. If she could reach St. Paul's eastern transept, she could get a better look. She studied the placement of trees staggered across the churchyard. If she was lucky, she could sprint the short distances between them and work her way over. Then she could creep along the transept to the pulpit.

Bianca lifted her hem and draped the gathered fabric over one arm. With Naylor engaged, she ran for the first tree, where she caught her breath and peeped toward the pulpit. Nothing indicated that the printer had noticed her. She then set her sights on the second tree and ran that distance without issue. She could have become too bold, but Bianca had learned not to let success soften her diligence. Caution had come with maturity.

Another few dashes and she made it to the cathedral, where she clung against the building, hidden in shadow. Once she'd caught her breath, she began making her way toward Paul's Cross.

She was nearly halfway there when she heard a second dull thud on the roof of the pulpit. The printer had returned to the front and was again standing on top of the sermon's wall. This time, he was on his toes, reaching for the metal bar. He finally caught hold of it and pulled. He had made a loop around the cross decorating the peak.

Bianca slid silently along the cathedral wall until she reached the side of the pulpit. But the structure's height and her close proximity made it impossible to see what Naylor was doing. She moved on, keeping to the building's dark cover, and circled behind Paul's Cross to a set of stone steps leading up to its base.

It would be foolish to climb the steps and try to stop Clement Naylor without help. She only wished for a better look. As she placed her foot on the first riser, she saw the printer pull the rope. She heard a groan, followed by the sound of something being dragged across the stone floor.

She kept to the side of the stairs and took another step, pressing herself flat against the stone. Again, Clement Naylor reached over his head, taking hold of the rope and Bianca, still hidden in the shadows, wagered another step. Naylor pulled on the length, bending at the waist to make the most of his effort.

A groan of agony came from the pulpit floor, and there lay Father Foxcroft, his wrists and ankles bound, his face smeared with black ink and a gag in his mouth. A noose hung around his neck— the same rope being used to drag him across the floor.

Bianca drew her dagger. She felt no particular duty to risk her life to save Foxcroft, but this was a cruel way to kill a man, even if it was to prove a point—which Bianca believed was Naylor's intent. Constable Berwick was as good as gone, and for that matter, so was Patch. All she could do was hope that Fisk and Meddybemps might return in time to help.

But she could bleat louder than a blaring bagpipe when she needed to, and the churchyard was rimmed by shops whose masters slept content in the upper stories. These men, so accustomed to their peace and quiet, would surely run to their windows if she made a ruckus.

Meanwhile, Clement Naylor continued pulling the rope and

ignored Foxcroft's thrashing and whimpers. The whites of Foxcroft's eyes shown large and wild as every tug worked to compound his pain. If he survived being dragged across the floor by his neck, his ultimate demise was still to come.

Why had the printer not strangled the priest if his intention was to hang him from Paul's Cross? It would have made his work easier, thought Bianca. Apparently, the numbing effect of the printer's ink had worn off. Perhaps Naylor wanted Foxcroft to fully grasp his impending death. Naylor wished to send a message, hanging Foxcroft from the cross atop Paul's pulpit.

Another yank, and the printer pulled the priest to his toes, straining Foxcroft's neck to take the burden of his weight. His chin tipped up as he fought against the noose and this awkward stance. His eyes bulged, trying to see Naylor.

The printer tied off the rope, then reached down into his bag, removing a sheet of paper. He smoothed it out and pinned it to Father Foxcroft's front.

"Would you like to know what it says, sirrah?" said Naylor, admiring the message. He began to read, "'Here hangs the body .. .'"

Bianca had heard enough. "Stay, you," she said, stepping out of the shadows.

The printer turned and his eyes dropped to the dagger in her hand.

"I remember you," he said with a slight wondering tilt of his head. "We once had conversation."

"We did," said Bianca. "We spoke very near here. You sold pamphlets and a broadside of Robert Barnes's supplication to the king."

"Your memory serves you," Naylor answered.

Father Foxcroft desperately tried to see who had so boldly intervened. His garbled moans and whinnies redoubled.

Bianca nodded toward Naylor's captive. "Methinks you have a personal score to settle with this man."

"I do," said the printer. It was as if he was discussing a matter of no particular import. He could just as well have mentioned the weather, or the way the moon shone on the steps. "I should like to get on with it."

"That cannot happen."

Clement Naylor flashed an indulgent smile. "This man must atone for his crime."

"*His* crime? Sir, it serves no purpose to avenge a man's poor judgment with his subsequent murder."

Clement Naylor jerked the rope attached to Foxcroft and the priest squealed in pain. "Then you know."

"I have learned that Foxcroft gave over Robert Barnes to be punished as a heretic."

"A charge unjustly proffered," said Naylor. His eyes slid sideways to Foxcroft, who continued making a fuss. "This man is an unconscionable liar. He is made of the stuff of air—he puffs to condemn others, then disappears like a gust of wind, refusing the burden of his false conduct. His whims, his beliefs, his faith are as changeable as our king's vacillating desires. He is a dissembler—a rascal. He is a poltroon …"

"He gave over your friend," said Bianca.

"That he did." Naylor nodded. "He subjected my friend to a humiliating and cruel death. No one deserves such an end—to be burned alive." Naylor pushed his satchel away with his foot. "The king had listened to Barnes, once," he continued. "He nearly adopted Luther's ideas for reform. But then, as the pope and the Continent turned against our king, Harry could no longer stomach their criticism, and so he took out his frustration on Barnes." The printer pointed his finger at Bianca in warning. "Do not protest too much, for you shall be licked raw by flames."

"It is the punishment for heretics," said Bianca. She wished Meddybemps and Fisk would return.

"He was not a heretic," insisted Naylor. He fixed her with an angry stare. "Barnes and I met years ago at the White Horse Tavern when I was at Cambridge. A group of us often discussed the church, the bishops, the blatant corruption. Martin Luther's writings were of great interest to us and we embraced his ideas for reform. I followed my friend to London and learned my printing skills from Thomas Raynalde. There were several wealthy patrons who wished for reform and who believed it was important to disseminate printers throughout the city. While I worked with the printed word, Barnes bravely urged reform from this very pulpit. He gave many a rousing speech from here." Naylor's eyes surveyed the enclosure with fondness. "But one day he was arrested and placed under house arrest. I continued to work clandestinely with him to distribute Tyndale's translation of the New Testament."

Naylor straightened the note on Father Foxcroft's front, ignoring the priest's continuing struggles. "After two years, Barnes was released, but his incarceration did not stop him from spreading his ideas. He continued urging reform until he learned that the authorities were planning his execution. He fled to Wittenberg, where he studied under Martin Luther. It was there that he wrote his supplication, the pamphlet you saw in my satchel."

The printer sighed. "The king and Thomas Cromwell suddenly realized how he might be useful. Barnes knew Martin Luther personally, and they wanted him to convince Luther to accept Henry's divorce from Catherine. But Barnes failed to secure Luther's approval. He also failed with the German princes. The king's use for Thomas Cromwell and Robert Barnes had come to an end. When the king executed Cromwell, my friend lost his sole protector. The rest you know." He ran his eyes around the vacant courtyard, then looked at Bianca. "You have delayed me."

Bianca played for time. "But why murder young boys?" Foxcroft still balanced on his toes, finding a position that allowed him to breathe. "They were innocent of these deceits!"

The printer remained unmoved. "Their innocence assures them everlasting peace," he said as if it should be obvious. He untied the rope holding Foxcroft hostage. "I should be commended for saving them years of suffering under this erratic king. Their deaths attracted attention—did they not? They were easy victims and their deaths made the priests uneasy. The paternosters twined around their necks are the perverse symbol of a deceptive religion and of those who practice it." He interpreted the expression on Bianca's face and continued. "Come now, be not sad. I saved these boys from the king's muddled religion and from the pope's corrupt one. Fear not, they will experience their reward in heaven."

"But our king shall not live forever. He grows more infirm by the day. He must be carried from room to room. The man is mortal. Another sovereign will rule, perhaps one more just."

"I have grown weary," said Naylor. "There is no justice in the courts. This time, it is left to me to set the balance right." He gestured to the knife in Bianca's hand. "It would be better if you left now, while you still can."

"You strangled the guard at St. Andrew's tonight. You could have used the ink cloth to put him to sleep instead."

"A paternoster was more expedient and I needed the ink for my victim."

Bianca glanced around for Meddybemps and Fisk. She appeared to be very alone.

"The second boy," said Bianca. "You strangled him."

"Something I do regret. I had dropped the cloth and he was waking. I am sorry if he felt pain." For a second the printer was almost contrite, but he roused out of his remorse.

"Was it your intent to hang Fisk like the rest?"

The corner of Naylor's mouth turned up as if she had found him out. "Someone better came along." He looked at Father Foxcroft and gave another tug on the rope to make his captive squeal. "Now enough of this."

Bianca desperately delayed. "You cannot murder this man and think that you will not be punished for it."

"It troubles me not," he said. "I expect to pay for his life by sacrificing mine. I have no illusions. There is no escape for me." The printer's demeanor was one of cold calculation and resignation. He thoroughly believed that his cause was righteous. He showed no faith in his fellow man to exact justice, and he had no patience (or was this also a lack of faith?) that God would satisfactorily judge the man's soul.

"Release the rope or I will scream," threatened Bianca.

Clement Naylor smiled, unconcerned. He reached above Father Foxcroft's head and pulled on the rope, lifting the priest several inches off the ground. The priest began a fierce struggle, a final dance with the noose.

Bianca could not stand by and watch the man suffer. As Naylor reached above his head for more leverage, Bianca tightened her grip on the dagger's handle. With a piercing cry Bianca rushed at Clement Naylor and drove the blade into his arm.

Stunned, the printer clapped one hand to his injury. His determination was impressive, for he did not let go of the rope. He looked at his hand covered in blood.

He said nothing in response to Bianca's attack. The sleeve of his jerkin grew saturated, but the wound seemed to have no effect on him. He turned his back on her and with both hands heaved on the rope, bringing Father Foxcroft partway onto the pulpit roof.

Bianca stared aghast as Naylor ignored the bleeding and continued to hoist Foxcroft across the roof, inching him toward the cross. In desperation, Bianca ran forward a second time. She aimed for his outer thigh—a wound that would slow him; but at the last second, the printer turned to face her, and she stabbed him in his inner thigh.

The reaction was immediate. Clement Naylor screamed. He hunched forward and gripped his leg—and let go of the rope. The priest slid off the roof, the slack rope trailing behind him, and struck the ground beside the printer.

Naylor's wound was mortal. Bianca knew she had sliced an area where blood would drain in a matter of minutes. She had once witnessed the quick demise of a longshoreman with a similar gash. The longshoreman had bled copiously. Naylor would be no different.

Around the perimeter of the courtyard, shutters flew open and the muted glow of candles shone within. Inquiring shouts echoed off the walls of the stone cathedral and built to a manic crescendo.

Bianca answered back, calling for help. Soon the entire courtyard reverberated with voices and the clamor of shutters opening and closing, with doors creaking and the agitated stirrings within.

Despite his heavy bleeding, Clement Naylor retained enough strength and wherewithal to pull his dagger from its sheath. He staggered, already feeling the effects of his blood loss, and looked at Bianca.

"I do not fear my death," he said, dropping to his knees. "I fear the world that is left behind."

Bianca stepped back. She didn't trust that the printer couldn't still lunge for her. But his last act of life was not meant for her.

Mustering one final breath, Clement Naylor raised the dagger over his head, and plunged it into Father Foxcroft's heart.

CHAPTER 35

By the time Meddybemps and Fisk arrived, Bianca was already explaining to a crowd of stunned residents what had happened. Most were hastily dressed, without doublets and hosen, wearing heavy gowns, their legs unconventionally bare. Constable Berwick had been summoned and Bianca requested that Patch be found, but likely he was still rounding up men to guard Castle Baynard's vulnerable parish churches.

Bianca was quite aware of the dubious position in which she now found herself—a woman with a bloody knife and two dead men lying at her feet. She admitted to stabbing Clement Naylor twice in an effort to stop him from hanging Father Foxcroft and explained the printer's final act of retribution.

People stared gape-mouthed up at the crucifix with the rope still looped around it. They shook their heads at the lengths some men take to murder another. But Bianca would save Naylor's motivation and their final conversation for once the constables arrived.

Meddybemps eyed the printer, slumped over the body of Father Foxcroft.

"It appears you have some story to recount," the streetseller said. His eyes went to the bloody dagger in her hand.

Bianca cleaned it off on her apron and put it back in its sheath. "He ignored me when I told him to stop."

Meddybemps's brows jumped. "Indeed."

Bianca's gaze dropped to Fisk, staring at his dead mentor. She was sorry there was nothing covering the bodies. She knew it must have come as a shock to him, realizing the depth and nature of Naylor's hatred. "I am sorry, Fisk." She struggled thinking what to say. She didn't know whether Fisk would accept Clement Naylor's fate and her part in it, or reject her as another murderer. It would serve no use explaining that she had not meant to kill him, only stop him. It was a subtlety she didn't expect his young mind could grasp. But Fisk was wise beyond his years, and his loyalty to Bianca was unshaken. In fact, it grew because of her courage.

"You would not have stabbed him if you didn't have to," said Fisk. He dragged his eyes from the disturbing scene and looked up at her. "I am sorrier for you."

The weight of killing someone was a burden reserved for the unfortunate few. How one carries that weight is a personal choice, a choice that might change over time, but the weight is never lifted for those with a conscience. Bianca glanced at Meddybemps, who kept his counsel, and in the matter of murder probably always would.

In as much a show of affection as it was relief, Bianca embraced her young friend, grateful for his safety and his understanding. She held him, and the emotional strain of the past few weeks, and year, came to the surface, cowing her to tears. Life can be extinguished in a matter of seconds; its brevity a stark reminder to love just a little longer, just a little harder. Bianca reached for Meddybemps and the three clung together, finding solace in a troubled world, until Bianca's tears turned to smiles.

As before, word traveled fast in Castle Baynard ward. Soon Constable Berwick's boisterous voice announced his arrival, ordering people to step aside and let him through. Having earlier shown a remarkable lack of responsibility, he now threw himself into his office with such vigor that it thoroughly rankled Bianca's sense of propriety. She refused to give her full account until Constable Patch, her "employer" and "colleague," as she called him, had been found and could also hear.

Her refusal was one small slight lobbed at a man who deserved a cartload.

But soon enough, Patch arrived. Constable Berwick, whose patience had been readily tried by then, remarked, "Well, sirrah, I see you finally got yourself here."

"If ye had done yer jobs placing guards like I tolds ye, I would have been here long ago," responded a tired Patch, but who still had enough in him to consider throttling the man.

Constable Berwick turned to Bianca. "Now that the requested party is here, suppose you tell us your account?"

So, Bianca told them how the night had unfolded, how she had seen a pamphlet printed by Clement Naylor in support of Lutheran ideas and Robert Barnes. "When Father Wells told me that Foxcroft had given over a former priest who had extolled church reforms, I remembered my conversation with Naylor. There was no indication that he might have been behind this, except I know from past experience that betrayal is an insidious poison. It taints the betrayer as well as the betrayed.

"I went to the printer's shop to see if he was there, to see if there was any merit to my thinking this." She hesitated before admitting she had broken in to his bedchamber—certain such boldness would be cause for scorn. There was some tittering, but they let her continue.

"He was not home." She waited for them to realize the

significance of his absence. If a man is not in his bed at such a small hour—where was he? "I took the opportunity to look through his shop. And I noticed a peculiar smell." She pulled the two cloths from her pouch and held one up. "I found this cloth at the site of the second boy's murder at St. Benet's. I kept it because I had never smelled anything like it." Bianca handed the cloth to Constable Berwick, who ran it under his nose. Immediately he opened his eyes, registering his distaste, and handed it to Patch.

"This," said Bianca, holding up the second rag, "is what I found in Clement Naylor's shop."

Again, Berwick and Patch sniffed the square of linen.

"I feels a bit queer," commented Patch.

Bianca nodded. "I believe there is some element in this printing ink that makes a person queasy, that quiets them to the point of sleep, even death if they breathe too much of it."

"That would explains how he managed to get his victims to the murder sites and hangs them," said Patch.

"He was a strong man, and quite agile," said Bianca. "He came to St. Andrew-by-the-Wardrobe with the intention of committing a third murder. But he was stymied by the presence of a guard. He strangled him with a paternoster."

"But how did he get Foxcroft?" asked Berwick.

"I believe he either snuck into the church and found Foxcroft alone, or else Foxcroft left the church—perhaps to go home. Either way, Naylor subdued the man he blamed for betraying Robert Barnes and decided to exact his own revenge, rather than hope for Foxcroft's downfall. There is a note pinned to Foxcroft's front that I first saw in Naylor's shop. The opportunity to kill Foxcroft presented itself tonight, and he seized it.

"In the end, Clement Naylor got what he wanted—Father Foxcroft's death; but he failed to execute the man's ultimate humiliation—hanging him from the cross where Robert Barnes had gained the attention of an entire world."

"But what about the boys?" asked Patch.

"Naylor's intent was to draw attention to the priests of Castle Baynard ward. He wanted to make them squirm. Make them wonder why their church was targeted. The boys were vulnerable and in his own twisted way, he believed he was saving them."

"From what?" asked Patch.

"From the king's religion and the pope's."

The men exchanged glances but said nothing.

"Did you learn their names?" asked Patch after a moment.

"We know that the first boy's name was Peter—that is all. And I believe the second boy's name is Matthew," said Bianca, looking at Fisk, whose eyes filled, remembering his recent friend. "Naylor lured him to his print shop in the false belief that he would become his apprentice."

"Has he a surname?" asked Berwick.

Bianca looked at Fisk, who shook his head. "That is all we know for now," she said. "It is possible that we may never learn anything more about these boys."

Before long, the sun would banish this nefarious night, with all its grim murders and weary players. The air, heavy with devilment, would vanish with the day. And with good discourse friends would listen and commiserate. They would smooth the rough edges of grief, soften the harsh candor of human beastliness.

With the crowd dispersing and the fresh bloom of excitement faded, Bianca returned Fisk to his mother, Meg. Meddybemps returned to his bed. Constable Patch and Constable Berwick contented themselves with matters of office. And the scourge that had befallen Castle Baynard ward was over.

With night cautiously giving leave, Bianca descended the stairs at Paul's Wharf, where she found a lone boatman asleep in his skiff, his wool cloak his blanket, a thick book for his pillow. He must have heard her, for he rose without a word, and steadied the boat as she stepped on board. She was too tired to think much of his quiet manner or how the river became so smooth that they seemed to float above it. Gone was the lingering apprehension that accompanied her whenever she rode across the river. Her fatigue dulled her memories of that fateful night nearly a year ago, so that she felt a passive acceptance of all that was, and of all that may be.

She dropped a penny in the boatman's cup and stepped onto the wet stairs with the river sloshing over them. Careful not to slip, she climbed to the landing and had only taken a couple of steps, when a strange recognition washed over her and she turned to face the skiff. The boat was gone, vanished. She searched the Thames as far as she could see. But the river was deep and dark, and she always kept her secrets.

Bianca ambled home, and it was with great relief when she turned the corner in Gull Hole and smelled the acrid stink of her neighbor's chicken coop. She stopped to filch an egg, and let herself into her room of Medicinals and Physickes. Though the sun would soon rise, Bianca planned to spend the day in bed. She desired nothing more than a few hours of sleep.

She took a breath of her room's unique odors and closed her eyes, glad to be home. She shut the door and left the shutters closed, wanting the room dark even though it would be a rare day of brilliant sun. Her shoes and stockings were left in a pile as she stripped down to her smock. When at last she fell into bed, her body throbbed with weariness, but her heart was at peace.

As she lay there drifting into light slumber, her mind gradually emptied of all the frets and fears that had trailed her so doggedly. The sensation of falling to sleep, that odd descent into numb awareness, dragged her down and pulled her under. She dreamt of Hobs and a smile tickled her lips. She saw him parade past, stepping across her chest like she was nothing more than a cushion beneath his paws. His tail he held high; his black tiger stripes sailed on like a galleon's flag.

She smiled watching him go by, and remembering his swagger and inexplicable appeal. He was just a cat, her grimalkin, an opportunist that had found dependable food and shelter. He could have left anytime he wanted, but he never did. Her cheek twitched as she imagined the soft touch of his whiskers and heard his quiet, breathy sniff and purr. Brushing it away, she turned over to snuggle back to sleep.

A second later, her eyes opened. She listened, blinking at the empty chest where she had laid Hobs's body. She rolled onto her back, and this time felt a heavy weight compress her lungs. Suddenly she was besieged with Hobs rubbing his face against hers.

Bianca cried his name. She sat up, expecting this vision to fade as dreams always do.

But Hobs did not disappear. Hobs was home.

CHAPTER 36

A month later—

Warm days had settled in, taking precedence over cold ones. With heavy cloaks and thick woolen garb stashed away, the citizens of this fair city moved with a lightness of spirit that only the first inkling of spring could manage to evoke. Puddles shrank and sparrows chirped. Laundry stretched from lines between buildings, the smocks and hosen dancing in the breeze. Pendulous yellow catkins hung from willows along the South Bank, and the fields in Paris Gardens turned green almost overnight.

Relishing this elysian scene was Bianca and her young apprentice—Fisk. They each carried a basket for collecting plants, namely butterbur root that Bianca needed for her spring sneezing remedy. Having already dug a goodly amount, Fisk located yet another plant they could plunder.

"Your mother wondered if you would be able to distinguish between plants," said Bianca. "But methinks you are quite proficient. Eventually, I will send you to scavenge on your own."

Fisk crouched beside the butterbur and poked his spade into

the spongy humus. "I never thought about leaves and plants before. But I like it here. I can see the curve in the river, and instead of smelling London, I smell the river and fields."

"You do not mind the odors of my chemistries?" In truth, some of her concoctions were far more noxious than London's streets.

"It is not so terrible. After a while, I don't notice."

Fisk's mother had agreed to let Bianca employ him to help in her room of Medicinals and Physickes. The arrangement proved so successful that Bianca had offered to make him her apprentice. Both Meg and Fisk accepted.

It was not a usual apprenticeship in that Fisk did not live under the same roof as his mistress. Her room was far too small to accommodate a second pallet. But she clothed and fed him as if he were her son. Even his little sister, Anna, came over once a week to play with Hobs and chase wandering chickens out the door.

At the end of it all, there was no guild to which Fisk could aspire belonging. What he would do with this acquired knowledge was entirely his decision, but Bianca knew this discipline and his curiosity would be to his benefit.

She believed that one day Fisk would further his experimentation. She envisioned him in a well-appointed room surrounded by elaborate alembics and every kind of possible stove, all provided by a wealthy patron, or perhaps a king—though in afterthought, she would discourage any dependence on moneyed patrons, especially royalty. Well, he would make an important discovery and never have to worry about eating again.

The two worked at uncovering the butterbur root, and Bianca sliced off a fat portion for her supply. "We've enough now to make a month's worth of medicine," she said, brushing off her hands and kirtle. "Let's be on our way. I've butter and bread and sage to sprinkle on top."

Fisk patted the pile of earth back over the remaining roots and the two merrily made their way home. They passed the bull- and bearbaiting gardens (busy attracting crowds for an afternoon show), skirted the seamier lanes with taunting wagtails, passed the South Gate with tarred heads on pikes, trod past the Dim Dragon Inn humming with noise, then turned past the Walnut Tree Inn toward Gull Hole.

Once inside, Bianca drew water from the barrel in the alley to wash the roots. She set a bowl in front of Fisk and gave him a rag, then sliced bread for their meal. Hobs heard them return and appeared on the windowsill to keep watch over both of them and the lane outside the rent. Butter being a particular favorite food of his, he made himself a pest when Bianca slathered the bread and sprinkled the sage on top.

"Here you are, my house spirit." She gave him a dollop, and he closed his eyes to lick it one direction, then the other.

Fisk devoured his slices before Bianca had finished her first. She pushed her remaining portion across the board to him. "Eat, you need it if you want to be taller than me."

"I already am!"

"I think not quite." Bianca drew them a couple of mugs of ale with a mind to get more from Alewife Guildford, who made a flavorsome morning brew.

She had just sat down when they heard a knock at the door. Since living alone, so few people visited that when she was interrupted, she immediately grew suspicious. But with Fisk around, Bianca worried less about uninvited callers.

Bianca cracked open the door and peered out.

She blinked in disbelief.

"John?"

A grin spread from behind a shaggy beard. "By my life I thought I would never see you again," he said.

Bianca flung open the door and John reached for her. The weight of care slid off their shoulders. Only the press of body against body would do; the feel of skin, the smell of familiarity.

Finally, they broke apart and Bianca stepped back to look at him.

"You are more disheveled than I could have imagined."

John lightly touched the scar on her cheek. "I fear to ask," he said.

"In good time," replied Bianca.

John rolled up his sleeve and showed her his wound, still wrapped in a length of linen. "It will heal," he said to her concerned look.

"Well, good sir, you have come to the right place." Bianca took his hand and led him inside to Fisk. The boy got to his feet and smoothed down his smock.

John looked at Fisk, confused. "I have not been gone so long," he said. He glanced around the room. "Where is our son?"

Bianca had feared this moment almost as much as she'd feared John's possible death. Her eyes found his, and though she had often imagined and dreaded his reaction, it was not blame or anger that she found in his stare. It was sadness.

John shook his head in question and Bianca's lips moved. "The baby did not survive."

John's head dropped. His finger went to the corner of his eye and he stared at the floor, then he took her in his arms, realizing that his disappointment was also hers. "It seems we have both survived life's battles," he said quietly. "I am grateful that I did not lose you in yours."

Fisk shifted his weight side to side, looking uncomfortable. Feeling as if he was intruding, he made a move for the door. "Mayhap I will go home now," he murmured.

Bianca turned to her young friend and opened her arm for

him to come closer. "I've made Fisk my apprentice. And he is a fine one, at that."

John tilted his head. "And he does not mind inhaling the stink?"

"Nay, sir. It does not trouble me. It is worse along the Fleet."

"Ah, then this is a good match, I see," said John.

"Fisk, come tomorrow and we will start anew," said Bianca. She went to her purse and handed him his pay and a little extra. "Buy yourself and Anna a treat. You have time to make it to market before they close."

Fisk's eyes brightened, and donning his cap he bid them both a good night, eager with thoughts of sweetmeats on his mind.

Bianca closed the door and without a word dragged out the tub that she lined with sheets. She put pots of rainwater on her calcinatory stove to heat. She and John talked while waiting for the water to heat, and John noted the crooked doorjamb and windows in need of repair that he would undertake mending in due time. When the water steamed, Bianca undressed John and placed his war-torn uniform in a pile to be dealt with later. There were no complaints that the tub was too small, or that the water was too hot. John eased himself into the tub with an appreciative sigh.

His arm wound needed attention and this she provided, cleaning off the dried blood to better apply a healing salve. She scrubbed his back, stopping long enough to give him a long kiss. He almost pulled her in with him, but they saved their desires for later. As in battle, John ignored his painful ribs when he needed to.

"When you are able," said Bianca the next morning, "we must go to the Dim Dragon. There are those who will be glad to see you."

John fell quiet, picking at his bowl of oats and chopped walnuts. Bianca noticed his sudden reticence.

"Is it too soon to remember your friends?" She asked this, thinking he must need more time to accustom himself to civilian life.

"Is Cammy still working there?"

"Aye, she is," said Bianca cheerily. "We shared many a meal, commiserating over our lost loves."

John lifted his mug and hid his reaction behind a drink.

"Why?" Bianca searched his face.

"Might she have found a new love, perchance?" He set down his ale, avoiding her eyes.

"Nay. She most fervently pines for her archer. Truth be, I have not encouraged it." Bianca tried masking her alarm. She blotted her lips with a napkin and laid it beside her bowl. "Is it Roger? Do you have news of him?"

John stared down at his bowl. "He won't be coming home."

Bianca felt the blood pulse in her temples. She could barely ask, anticipating the answer. "He's dead?"

"Aye," John said softly. He offered no more and Bianca did not ask. They were both guilty of murder and it was this ultimate transgression that they could not discuss. In time, perhaps they would speak of it, but for now, burying their secrets was easier than telling them.

And so, as a young couple worked to regain their lost time together, a city, oblivious to time's relentless passing, unflaggingly carried on. Citizens would live and die under a king who wrought havoc and prosperity in unequal measure. And while this king refused his mortality, others prepared for it. Such is the way of rule. Such is the way of power.

Some men trust their king. Some trust those of education, or wealth. Some trust God. And when these disappoint, innocence— that treasured gift of faith—is gone forever.

Here ends this story of Bianca and her coterie of misfits, thieves, and friends—the people she called family. And in a world full of lost boys—abandoned children, of men killed in battle, men scarred from war, of boys who grow into petulant kings, and men who forfeit the gift of loving their children, this lost boy of London, this soldier, murderer, apprentice, and lover, found his way home.

Glossary

angel—a coin worth ten shillings

arquebus—early portable gun, forerunner of a rifle

assureds—Scots who had sworn allegiance to King Henry

beadle—a parish officer who dealt with petty offenses

Blackfriars—Dominican monks

bothy—shepherd's shack

brae—a steep slope rising from the water

broderers—those who embroider

cozen—a cheat

cullion—a base fellow

curber—a thief who uses a hook on a line or a curved stick to steal items from open windows

drigger—a person who organizes a band of thieves

Droch áird chúgat lá gaoithe—May he be badly positioned some windy day (Gaelic)

fleering—jeering

foin—thrusts (sexual connotation)

fripperer—one who sells used clothing

God's nails—an oath

Grayfriars—Franciscan monks

grimalkin—cat

hagbut—another word for an arquebus

hagbutter—a soldier armed with a hagbut or arquebus

jack—soldier's jacket sewn with metal plates

jerkin—a man's close-fitting jacket

kirkton—a Scottish village next to a church

loneful—lonesome

losel—good for nothing fellow

lubberwort—lazy, fuzzy-minded person
monadh—moorland-covered mountain
nigglesome—bothersome
parchmeners—parchment makers
pidgy—ridiculous (made-up word)
pizzle—penis
plodge—mud
pribbling—trivial speech or a pointless squabble
puling—whining
quoits—curling stone
rondel—typically a twelve-inch dagger with a sharp point. Reminiscent of a strong ice pick
routers—bullies
sack—Spanish spiced wine
Scotch—Scot
slugabed—an individual content to rise late
snouter—wise-ass
stomacher—triangular boned bodice
sumptuary law—used in reference to control what people wore. A man must not dress above his station.
swasher—swaggerer, a narcissist
tarpawlin—cloth coated in tar
View of Arms—a test and demonstration of men's archery skills
wagtails—whores
wally—buffoon
water roses—urinate
whobub—hubbub

Author's Note

By the late winter of 1545, King Henry VIII had waged war on both France and Scotland. There is nothing like a war to distract a man and his country from his recent cuckolding at the hands of his licentious fifth wife, Catherine Howard. Harry's reasons to invade France were several. Firstly, France had long been England's enemy. Harry argued that while France and Spain wrangled over northern Italy, he could join forces with Charles V, the Holy Roman Emperor, and take Paris. Not only did the aging king pine for military glory but he wanted to force King Frances I to honor pension payments in arrears and other obligations to the British crown under past treaties. Harry just didn't like the French monarch and had always been competitive and perhaps jealous of his successful rival across the channel.

Then, too, there was the not so small matter of subjugating the Scots in the north. Henry sought to punish Scotland for breaking their Treaty of Greenwich in December of 1543, which would have united the two kingdoms through the marriage of the infant Mary (Queen of Scots) to Henry's son, Prince Edward. He also took exception to Scotland realigning with France and feared a French invasion at the northern border. For the next eight years Henry undertook a cruel offensive of death and destruction against the Scots, later known as "The Rough Wooing." Ultimately, Henry's triumph at capturing Boulogne and subjugating the Scots came at a huge financial cost. He drove the Tudor dynasty to the brink of bankruptcy, leaving his heirs to struggle with the crippling burden of his debt.

Chief among my sources regarding the various campaigns in Scotland, I consulted *The Earl of Hertford's Expedition Against*

Scotland—a Tudor narrative of the landing at Granton, the capture of Leith, Edinburgh, the burning of Haddington, Hawick, Dunbar, and the sack of Jedburgh and other places. For the movements and descriptions of the battle of Ancrum Moor I read numerous accounts of the crucial battle and pieced together the main points. Any mistakes in interpretation are my own.

Aside from Henry's political ambitions, matters of religion wavered under the king's final years. The pope's refusal to grant a divorce from Catherine of Aragon had set in motion numerous reforms too involved to go into detail here. Initially, Henry defended Catholicism against Martin Luther's reforms, but when those reforms could serve his purpose, Henry broke with the church in Rome and effectively made himself pope of his own church. He always considered himself a Catholic and toward the end of his life he adopted a more conservative stance on earlier reforms, retreating from the more extreme proposals of his now fallen chief minister, Thomas Cromwell. Perhaps he experienced feelings of guilt toward his treatment of monks during the dissolution of the monasteries, or worried for his soul's afterlife, which may help explain his conservative decisions.

My reason in bringing up religion in this particular Bianca Goddard mystery is to point out the volatile times in which people found themselves. Clerics were required to take the oath of supremacy, swearing allegiance to the monarch as Supreme Governor of the Church of England. Failure to do so considered treason. Reformists who wished changes other than those implemented by the king were treading on dangerous ground.

During the Middle Ages, the Virgin Mary was the focus of devotions for pious Catholics, but beginning in the mid–fifteenth century amid calls for reform, evangelical Catholics shifted their devotion to Jesus. By the sixteenth century the abbreviation of the holy name had become quite popular and was considered a talisman, similar in significance to a crucifix. IHS or YHS is based on an abbreviation of the word JHESUS in Greek. The cult of the Holy Name focused its attention on the figure of Christ and for my purposes in the novel, I associated their devotion with a group of pious Catholics resistant to reform.

On the matter of the printer's ink—I am basing its compounds on ether, which was discovered in 1275 by Raymundus Lullius, a Spanish alchemist. Known as "sweet vitriol," its paralyzing effects were noted by Paracelsus and his student, Valerius Cordus, in 1540. I have no evidence that ether was specifically used in compounding ink in the sixteenth century; however, its use as a solvent could have been possible.

Writing the Bianca Goddard Mysteries has been challenging in the sense that I am not an academic historian. Yet I write about life during the Tudors, arguably one of the most exhaustively researched periods in history with a multitude of devotees. I am acutely aware of my shortcomings, and I spend a great deal of time reading and researching the period. I do not record my references or provide a bibliography at the end of these mysteries, but I have shelves of reference books and notebooks filled with material from what I've learned.

My lack of training in history and the logistical hindrance of 3,000 miles of ocean and 500 years between myself and my subject matter, may result in misinterpretations, and for this I apologize. Generating an authentic "feel" and "atmosphere" of the time is chief among my goals for attempting these Tudor tales. I love the language, I enjoy learning about the politics and interplay of religion, and I never cease to be intrigued by the personalities of the time, whether real or made up. I so much prefer being transported to another time period that perhaps I presume that my readers wish this, too. Reading is the highest and most creative form of escapism—one must use her mind to imagine the landscape painted by an author's words.

I invite my readers to subscribe to my newsletter at **www.marylawrencebooks.com** for news of any forthcoming projects. They will be the first to know of any developments.

About the Author

Mary Lawrence lives in Maine and is the author of five Bianca Goddard Mysteries. Two of her novels— *The Alchemist's Daughter* and *The Alchemist of Lost Souls* were named by *Suspense Magazine* as best historical mysteries of 2015 and 2019 respectively. Her articles have appeared in several publications, including the national news blog *The Daily Beast*. Visit the author at MaryLawrenceBooks.com.

Printed in Great Britain
by Amazon